London Borough
of Hounslow

D0539088

The Beach House

The Beach House

JANE GREEN

MICHAEL JOSEPH
an imprint of
PENGUIN BOOKS

MICHAEL JOSEPH

Published by the Penguin Group
Penguin Books Ltd, 80 Strand, London WC2R 0RL, England
Penguin Group (USA) Inc., 375 Hudson Street, New York, New York 10014, USA
Penguin Group (Canada), 90 Eglinton Avenue East, Suite 700, Toronto, Ontario, Canada M4P 2Y3
(a division of Pearson Penguin Canada Inc.)
Penguin Ireland, 25 St Stephen's Green, Dublin 2, Ireland (a division of Penguin Books Ltd)
Penguin Group (Australia), 250 Camberwell Road,
Camberwell, Victoria 3124, Australia (a division of Pearson Australia Group Pty Ltd)
Penguin Books India Pvt Ltd, 11 Community Centre,
Panchsheel Park, New Delhi – 110 017, India
Penguin Group (NZ), 67 Apollo Drive, Rosedale, North Shore 0632, New Zealand
(a division of Pearson New Zealand Ltd)
Penguin Books (South Africa) (Pty) Ltd, 24 Sturdee Avenue,
Rosebank, Johannesburg 2196, South Africa

Penguin Books Ltd, Registered Offices: 80 Strand, London WC2R 0RL, England

www.penguin.com

First published 2008
2

Copyright © Jane Green, 2008

The moral right of the author has been asserted

Set in 13.5/16 pt Monotype Garamond
Typeset by Rowland Phototypesetting Ltd, Bury St Edmunds, Suffolk
Printed in Great Britain by Clays Ltd, St Ives plc

A CIP catalogue record for this book is available from the British Library

HARDBACK
ISBN: 978-0-718-14808-9

To Ian Warburg
For being my home

Chapter One

The bike crunches along the gravel path, weaving around the potholes that could present danger to someone who didn't know the road like the back of their hand.

The woman on the bike raises her head and looks at the sky, sniffs, smiles to herself. A foggy day in Nantucket, but she has lived here long enough to know this is merely a morning fog, and the bright early-June sunshine will burn it off by midday, leaving a beautiful afternoon.

Good. She is planning lunch on the deck today, is on her way into town via her neighbour's house, where she has spent the last hour or so cutting the large blue mophead hydrangeas and stuffing them into the basket on the front of the bike. She doesn't really know these neighbours – so strange to live in the same house you have lived in for forty-five years, a house in a town where once you knew everyone, until one day you wake up and realize you don't know people any more – but she has guessed from the drawn blinds and absence of cars they are not yet here, and they will not miss a couple of dozen hydrangea heads.

The gate to their rear garden was open, and she had heard around town they had brought in some super-swanky garden designer. She had to look. And the pool had been open, the water was so blue, so inviting, it was practically begging her to strip off and jump in, which of course she did, her body still slim and strong, her legs tan and muscled from the daily hours on the bike.

She dried off naturally, walking naked around the garden, popping strawberries and peas into her mouth in the kitchen garden, admiring the roses that were just starting, and climbing back into her clothes with a contented sigh when she was quite dry.

These are the reasons Nan has come to have a reputation for being slightly eccentric. A reputation she is well aware of, and a reputation she welcomes, for it affords her freedom, allows her to do the things she really wants to do, the things other people don't dare, and because she is thought of as eccentric, exceptions are always made.

It is, she thinks wryly, one of the beautiful things about growing old, so necessary when there is so much else that is painful. At sixty-five she still feels thirty, and, on occasion, twenty, but she has long ago left behind the insecurities she had at twenty and thirty, those niggling fears: that her beauty wasn't enough, not enough for the Powell family; that she had somehow managed to trick Everett Powell into marrying her; that once her looks started to fade, they would all realize she wasn't anyone, wasn't anything, and would then treat her as she had always expected when she first married into this illustrious family . . . as nothing.

Her looks had served her well. Continue to serve her well. She is tall, skinny and strong, her white hair is glossy and sleek, pulled back in a chignon, her cheekbones still high, her green eyes still twinkling with amusement under perfectly arched brows.

Nan's is a beauty that is rarely seen these days, a natural elegance and style that prevailed throughout the fifties, but has mostly disappeared today, although Nan doesn't see it, not any more.

Now when she looks in the mirror she sees the lines, her cheeks concave under her cheekbones, the skin so thin it sometimes seems that she can see her bones. She covers as many of the imperfections as she can with make-up, still feels that she cannot leave her house without full make-up, her trademark scarlet lipstick the first thing she puts on every morning, before her underwear even, before her bath.

But these days her make-up is sometimes patchy, her lipstick smudging over the lines in her lips, lines that they warned her about in the eighties, when her son tried to get her to stop smoking, holding up photographs in magazines of women with dead, leathery skin.

'I can't give up smoking,' she would say, frowning. 'I enjoy it too much, but I promise you, as soon as I stop enjoying it, I'll give it up.'

The day is yet to come.

Thirty years younger and she would never have dared trespass, swim naked in an empty swimming pool without permission. Thirty years younger and she would have cared too much what people thought, wouldn't have cut flowers or carefully dug up a few strawberry plants that would certainly not be missed, to replant them in her own garden.

But thirty years younger and perhaps, if she had dared and had been caught, she would have got away with it. She would have apologized, would have invited the couple back for a drink, and the husband would have flirted with her, would have taken the pitcher of rum punch out of her hand and insisted on pouring it for her as she bent her head down to light her cigarette, looking up at him through those astonishing green eyes, flicking her blonde hair ever so slightly and making him feel like the most important man in the room, hell, the only man in the room, the wife be damned.

Thirty years younger and the women might have ignored her, but not, as they do now, because they think she's the crazy woman in the big old house on the bluff, but because they were threatened, because they were terrified that she might actually have the power to take their men, ruin their lives. And they were right.

Not that she ever did.

Not back then.

Of course there have been a few affairs, but Nan was never out to steal a man from someone else, she just wanted some fun, and after Everett died, after years of being on her own, she came to realize that sometimes sex was, after all, just sex, and sometimes you just had to take it where you could find it.

*   *   *

The village of Siasconset, known to all simply as Sconset, is burning with a bright morning light by the time Nan arrives on her bike. She cycles past the Sconset café, round the corner past the Book Store that isn't a book store but sells liquor instead, and hops off at the general store to get some food.

All the way at the back there is still a refrigerator stuffed full of yoghurt, milk, eggs – the bare essentials of life – but the rest of the store is taken up with gourmet foods, sesame crackers, delicious sweetmeats; designer candles and the necessary wall of T-shirts, baseball caps and tote bags advertising that the tourists had been to Sconset for a vacation, were wealthy enough to afford to come to a place where billionaires play.

As always, she heads to the back, nodding at the tourists, waving hello to the woman behind the cash register.

She is a familiar sight in Sconset, her long linen skirts floating behind her as she cycles along on a rusty old Schwinn. It is not a bike you often see these days, with its huge oversized basket on the front, but it is the one that she and Everett bought when they spent their first summer here, back in 1962, when she was twenty, and he'd brought her home to Windermere to meet his parents.

Nan cycles slowly, one hand lightly balanced on the handlebar, the other wielding a cigarette. She waves at everyone she passes, greets them with a smile, stopping to chat if the whim takes her, or if she sees a neighbour busy in the garden.

Most wave back, but more and more often she is

noticing the change in the people around here, the people who don't wave back, who pretend they don't see the crazy blonde lady on the old bicycle, the people who are so bright and shiny, so clean and perfect as they walk down Main Street tapping on their iPhones, it almost hurts to look at them.

This wouldn't have happened had she been thirty years younger, she thinks from time to time, when yet another young, glamorous New York couple hesitate as she approaches them, weaving wildly on her bike as she attempts to light her cigarette without stopping. Thirty years ago he would have pulled a lighter out of his pocket and lit it for her, instead of turning when his wife prods him, sneering with distaste, as Nan's cigarette lights and the smoke wafts, as if planned, right under the woman's nose. She coughs dramatically, and Nan happily gives her the finger as she cycles off, while the woman gasps in horror and attempts to shield the eyes of the toddler who is with them.

What has happened to *people*, Nan thinks as she traverses the cobblestones. When did we become so *precious*? A family of six pass her, father, mother, then four little ones, like four little ducklings with sparkly aerodynamic helmets on. When did our children have to wear helmets, she thinks, turning her head to watch them wobble into the distance. When did we all become so scared?

She thinks of Michael, at seven, falling off the monkey bars and splitting his head open on the concrete ground. She didn't panic, it was just one of the

6

things that happened to everyone. She bundled him in the front of the car and drove him to Dr Grover's house where he was stitched up in the Grovers' kitchen as Mrs Grover served them lemonade and ginger snaps.

She never knew where Michael was when he was growing up. Someone had a boat on the marshes, and Michael and his friends once got stranded for the day. Nan only knew when they ran in the kitchen door, shrieking with excitement at what swiftly became their near-death adventure. Whatever adults were around smiled affectionately, one ear on the conversation, the other somewhere else, because life, in those days, revolved around the adults. Not around the children.

*

The first time Everett brought her to their summer house, Nan had no idea what she was letting herself in for. She had barely heard of Nantucket. Had vacationed only on the Jersey Shore, knowing little of what she later came to think of as 'old America' – the true Yankee families, the old-money families, whose ancestors had sailed over on the *Mayflower*, and who could trace their families back hundreds of years.

Her own parents had been English, had sailed to New York hoping for a better life than the one they left behind in Birmingham, and had moved to Ossining because of a distant cousin who lived there.

She had been this naive little girl, still known to all as Suzanne, who hadn't known what to expect when

Everett brought her home. There was no Googling to find out about the Powells, no one who could have told her the family was famous in Massachusetts for funding the majority of the renovation that has made Cape Cod what it is today, no one who could have explained the money she was marrying into, the privilege and history that came with the Powells.

She married Everett because she loved him, and as a wedding present his parents bought them an apartment in New York City. Nothing fancy, she would say years later, but it was utterly fancy, and for the first two years of their marriage Nan would wake every morning and think she had died and woken up in a Grace Kelly movie.

Nowhere did she feel this more than at Windermere. Built in the 1920s, just off Baxter Road in the village of Sconset, it stood high on a bluff, overlooking the Atlantic Ocean, its shingles grey and weary from being buffeted by the wind, but its lines graceful and elegant, the porches, in the old days, always abuzz with people.

Not a huge house, Windermere now sat on nine perfect acres. Originally a modest saltbox, over the years various careful additions had turned it into a stylish estate. The developers had started to circle, like vultures looking for their kill. The house would be torn down, Nan knew, if she ever let them get their hands on it, and it was a place that held too many important memories for her to let it go that easily.

It was the Powells' summer house – their idyllic

retreat from Memorial Day to Labour Day each year – a home filled with naked children, clambakes on the beach, and so much joy.

It was one of those naked children who caused her name change, that very first trip. 'It's Suzanne,' Everett kept saying to the little three-year-old – someone's daughter, or cousin, or something – who kept trying to drag her off to build another sandcastle. 'I want Nan to come,' the little girl kept saying, and Everett had laughed, so handsome then, his blue eyes crinkling in his tanned face. 'Nan,' he said, turning to Suzanne. 'Nan in Nantucket. I like it.' And since that time she had only ever been called Nan, had mostly forgotten her given name; she often found herself crossing out Nan when filling in forms that requested her full name, only realizing at the end that she hadn't written Suzanne.

When Nan thinks back to those early days at Windermere, she can almost hear the tinkling of drinks being poured and the musicians playing, she can almost see the fairy lights strung up around the house, the lanterns hanging from the trees, people laughing and drinking and dancing.

There were dinner parties that went on all night, Everett's parents – Lydia and Lionel – the first to lead their guests through the dunes for their notorious midnight swims, the shrieks from the guests as they hit the cold water audible almost in the centre of town.

Friends were always coming to stay, often not leaving for entire summers at a time, but Windermere was big enough, and the overspill could always stay in one of the four cottages on the far edges of the compound.

Two of the cottages were sold off after Lionel died and Lydia developed Alzheimer's. Lydia eventually went into a nursing home in Boston and Nan tried to visit her there as often as she could, sometimes bringing her son until it became too painful, towards the end, when Lydia wasn't even a shadow of her former self but a tiny, shrunken, white-haired old lady, whom Nan once walked straight past when she went to visit.

Everett had died by that time, or, as Nan put it for so many years, had gone. She had woken up one morning and the bed had been empty, which was not particularly unusual – he would often wake up and go for an early morning swim – but it wasn't until he failed to return that her heart quickened with a trace of anxiety.

She went down to the beach, and still she remembers that she knew, knew from the moment she turned over and saw his side of the bed empty, that there was something not quite right.

His T-shirt was roughly folded, weighted down by his father's watch. No note. Nothing. And the sea was particularly rough that day. Nan had stood and looked out over the waves, listening to the ocean crash around her as a tear rolled down her cheek. She wasn't looking for him, she knew he had gone.

She just didn't know why.

It turned out to be no coincidence that Everett's

grandfather had won Windermere in a poker match. Gambling, it transpired, skipped a generation and landed quite solidly on the shoulders of Everett.

Nan knew he loved his poker games, but had no idea they were anything other than fun, anything other than a reason to spend a night out with the boys, drink a few single malts and smoke a few cigars, or whatever it was they did.

But after he died, all those years ago, she received phone calls from the banks, then from various people to whom he clearly owed money, and, finally, from his accountant.

'It does not look good,' he had said.

Luckily, there were assets. The two remaining cottages on the edges of Windermere were sold, and then, a few years later, the New York City apartment. A big decision, but she had always loved Windermere, had loved the thought of making it a permanent home, and Michael was young enough that she thought he would benefit from a quieter life, a life that was simple, in a place they had always adored. It was in the late seventies, and she got so much money for the apartment she thought she would be fine forever.

'I leave it in your hands,' she had said to her stockbroker with a laugh, knowing that a pot that sizeable would be fine.

*

Nan doesn't have a stockbroker any more. Stockbrokers used to be revered, but she doesn't know anyone who calls themselves a stockbroker these days. These days she hears the summer people use phrases like M & A, bond derivatives and, perhaps more than anything, hedge funds. She still doesn't understand what a hedge fund is, knows only that the people who are building the biggest houses on the island, the husbands who fly in for the weekend in private jets and helicopters, joining wives, nannies and housekeepers, all seem to work in hedge funds.

She has her money in a hedge fund herself. Every month she receives a statement, but mostly she forgets to open it. Her mail has a tendency to pile up on a kitchen counter before being swept away into a cupboard somewhere, for Nan has no patience for the prosaic – bills bore her, and the only envelopes that are opened and responded to immediately are handwritten, and personal.

Today her financial advisor is coming for lunch, although Nan thinks of him less as a financial advisor and more as a friend. Not that he is much of either – she has not seen him in person for four years, and he doesn't advise her particularly, other than to have told her, all those years ago, that the hedge fund she subsequently invested in was a good one, started by one of the brightest traders at Goldman Sachs, and would be a wonderful place for her to put some money.

The phone is ringing when she walks in. She dumps the hydrangeas in the sink, and grabs the phone, running the water as she picks up.

'Hi, Mom.' It's Michael, ringing, as he so often does, on his way to work.

'Hi, my love. How are you?'

'Tired. It's hot and muggy and revolting in the city. I'm deeply jealous of you on the island – is it beautiful?'

'Not yet.' Nan smiles. 'But it will be. Why don't you come out? I miss you. It's too quiet here with just me rattling around.'

'What about Sarah? Do you still have Sarah?'

'She still comes once or twice a week to help me out,' Nan says, 'and I love having her around, but I miss my family, miss this house ringing with the sounds of people having fun. Remember when you used to come up here with all your friends for the summer? Remember how much fun it was? Why don't you come up with some people? Wouldn't they all kill for a vacation on Nantucket?'

Michael laughs. His mother never changes. 'They would undoubtedly kill for a vacation on Nantucket, if only they could take the time off work. And most of them are married now, with kids. It's different. They can't just sweep their families up and bring them out.'

'But why ever not?' Nan is genuinely perplexed. 'I adore children, this is the perfect place for children.'

'I know that, but it's just ... hard. People are busy, everyone's running all the time. But I would love to come. I'd love to see you. I can't make it up at the moment, the bosses are away for another week or so and I need to be here, but maybe I can come at the end of the summer.'

Nan turns off the tap and reaches for a cigarette.

'Oh Mom. You're not still smoking.'

Nan ignores him. 'How are things going with the girl . . . what's her name? Aisling?'

Michael smiles. 'Interesting. I like her. Still very early days but so far so good. She's fiery. Independent. You'd like her.'

'I'd love to meet her.' Nan is careful not to ask too much. 'Bring her.'

'Maybe I will. What are you up to today?'

'Making lunch. Andrew Moseley is coming.'

'Your financial advisor?'

'Exactly!'

'Is everything okay?'

'Why wouldn't it be?'

'It seems unusual for him to travel up to see you.'

Nan shrugs. 'I think, after four years, it's probably just due. Anyway, lovely to have some company. I'm making delicious salads straight from the garden, and Sarah has promised to drop off a lobster salad she made yesterday.'

'Sounds yummy.' Michael instantly pictures the table set on the deck, his mother's ballet slippers kicked off as she curls her legs under her after lunch, cradling a large tumbler of white wine in one hand, a ubiquitous cigarette in the other. 'Don't drink too much.'

Michael says goodbye with a sad smile, clicking his phone shut as he reaches his bike, which is chained to a lamp post outside his apartment on 94th and

Columbus. As he does so he is unaware of the admiring glance he's given from a tall blonde walking her dog.

Michael has always been unaware of his appeal, taken for granted his large green eyes, inherited from his mother, his easy smile, his all-American clean-cut looks.

At forty-two he looks much like the college football player he used to be, tanned and rangy, and utterly comfortable in his skin.

He undoes the lock and secures his helmet, slipping the phone into his backpack and weaving off down Columbus, making a mental note to phone Sarah, just to make sure that Mom is okay, to make sure that someone is looking out for her, that she isn't quite as alone as she sounds.

Chapter Two

'Tell me about how you met.' Dr Posner leans back in his chair and looks over at them, sitting at opposite ends of the sofa, the elegant brunette tucked awkwardly into the corner, twisting a strand of her shoulder-length bob nervously as she darts glances towards her husband, who sits still, staring at the floor.

The husband is slim, dark-haired, with coal-black eyes that occasionally rise to meet Dr Posner's, eyes filled with sadness and pain.

They are a handsome couple. She early to mid-thirties, he early forties, Dr Posner guesses. She wears printed capris, ballet slippers, a crocodile purse at her feet and a cashmere wrap bundled on her lap in case the air conditioning gets too strong. The husband is in jeans and a polo shirt; he is clean-cut, darkly good-looking with a light spring tan and a body that shows he goes to the gym at least four times a week.

They look as though neither of them has ever had a problem in their lives. Young, fit, beautiful, what could possibly be wrong? Although, of course, Dr Posner knows better.

Why else would they be here?

'Tell me why you fell in love,' Dr Posner says,

watching how the man shifts nervously. 'Tell me what brought you together.'

Bee looks over at Daniel, and as he meets her eye they both smile slightly, and Bee begins to talk.

'I was doing a house share in the Hamptons,' Bee says, her eyes misting a little at the memory. 'It was this house that had looked wonderful in the pictures, but once we got there it had basically been trashed by the people before us –'

'It was a wonderful pool, though,' Daniel interjects, and Bee nods with a smile.

'It was.'

'So, you were both in the house together?' Dr Posner asks.

'No.' Bee shakes her head. 'Daniel was staying a couple of houses away, but it wasn't a house share, he was with family friends.'

'I was horrified at the house shares.' Daniel grins properly, for the first time since walking in. 'All these people drinking and partying, everyone single, all looking around frantically to see if someone better had just walked through the door.'

'And you weren't?' Dr Posner looks at Daniel.

'No. That scene has never been my thing. My parents had these friends who had a house in Amagansett and they were away for the summer and said we could use it.'

'They knew they could trust Daniel.' Bee laughs. 'Anyone else would have trashed it in a day, but Daniel spent all day walking around with a vacuum in one hand and a broom in the other, scouring the floors for stray grains of sand.'

Daniel shrugs as he laughs, as if to say, she knows me so well.

'You're fastidious?' Dr Posner asks.

'He's a clean freak,' Bee says. 'He's the only man I know who makes the bed every morning and does all the laundry.'

Dr Posner smiles. 'He sounds like the kind of man most women dream about.'

Neither of them says anything, and there is a pause.

'Do you mind him being a clean freak?' Dr Posner asks eventually.

Bee laughs, but it's forced. 'Are you kidding? As you said, he's amazing. All my friends are jealous because he does all the washing-up, everything.'

'I can't help it,' Daniel shrugs. 'I get anxious if I'm surrounded by mess or dirt.'

'Let's go back to the beach house,' Dr Posner guides them. 'Tell me how the two of you actually met.'

'He was playing volleyball on the beach with some of the guys from the house. They were all pretty awful. You would think that out of ten guys in a house share at least one of them would have been nice, but even the ones who looked cute were just assholes. My friend Deborah and I decided to have a glass of wine at the beach, and then we noticed Daniel and his friend because, obviously, they were strangers, but also they were cute.'

As she continues talking, both of them begin to relax, their bodies sinking into the sofa, their voices growing more animated as they smile, interrupt one another, remember what life was like when it was simple, when there was nothing to worry about. When they weren't sitting at opposite ends of a leather sofa in a psychiatrist's office because neither of them is sure their marriage is going to make it.

'Daniel, did you notice Bee?'

'It was difficult not to.' Daniel grins. 'She was wearing a hot-pink bikini, and she kept smiling at me every time I looked at her.'

'So you were attracted to her?'

'I . . . yes. She was gorgeous. Of course.'

*

Had Daniel been attracted to Bee? Even now he doesn't know the answer to this. She was gorgeous, it was true. He remembers all the other men trying desperately to get Bee to notice them, but Bee didn't seem to have eyes for anyone other than Daniel.

He hadn't understood it. He wasn't looking for romance, had recently ended a four-year relationship with Nadine, whom he had loved, had been perfectly happy with, but she was the same age as him, thirty, and was desperate to marry him – or, at least, desperate to marry someone.

He loved her, but he hadn't wanted to marry her, hadn't wanted to make that sort of commitment, and eventually, after months of arguing, Nadine had issued the ultimatum that he had expected all along, and they had split up.

He knew Nadine hated him for it. She never believed he wouldn't come back. She thought that he would realize what he had only when it was gone, and would come crawling back on his knees, diamond ring in hand. But he hadn't. He couldn't. He felt safe in a relationship, but marriage was terrifying to him. He couldn't do it.

'It's because she's the wrong one,' his friends would say. 'When it's right, it's right.' But he had a nagging suspicion that, for him, that wasn't the case. That Nadine was possibly as right as it got, but that there was something wrong with *him*.

The holiday in Amagansett was supposed to have been a welcome break. He and Steve went there with cases of books, a leather-bound backgammon set and plans to play tennis every day.

He wasn't thinking about Nadine, or about anyone else. He was hoping to immerse himself in relaxation, and stay as far away from the burgeoning Hampton scene as he could.

But Bee had drawn him out, or perhaps she had drawn him in. Women like Bee didn't look at men like Daniel. Not that Daniel was unattractive, but he was ... understated. He was sensitive, quiet. He liked parties that were small and intimate, where you could connect with people, hear one another's thoughts, not parties with roaring music, meat markets where you couldn't hear one another think.

He and Bee should have been chalk and cheese, Bee loving loud parties, loud music, surrounding herself with friends; but she also loved conversation, was thoughtful and curious, with an energy and vivacity that he had never encountered, that made him feel, for perhaps the first time, truly alive.

Bee made everything fun. She was extrovert, glamorous, always laughing. Daniel suddenly understood how opposites could attract, and if someone like Bee could want someone like him, how could he refuse? What must it say about him that someone as great as Bee, someone that every man wanted, only wanted him? He must be better than he thought. And it was true: when he was with Bee, he felt like a king.

So Daniel was seduced into a relationship, and once he was there it felt safe – safer, certainly, than being single. Another four years went by during which time they fell into a predictable routine, living together at Bee's Upper East Side apartment, meeting friends for brunches and lunches and dinners, spending weekends in Central Park, or back in the Hamptons, until one night when Bee had been bitchy all evening.

'What's the matter with you?' he asked. 'Is your period coming?'

'God, that's what it is!' she said, jumping off the bed and going out into the hallway then into the tiny bathroom. 'I knew I'd been feeling off.'

But her period hadn't come, and when she checked her diary it seemed she had made a mistake with the timing. Either that, or her period was two weeks late.

A couple of months previously she had had a pregnancy scare, and she had bought a double pack of First Response. There was one left. Bee reached to the back of the medicine cabinet and pulled it out, calmly and quietly, knowing instantly, before the deep-pink line appeared, that she was pregnant.

She looked at herself in the mirror and a smile spread across her face. Bee hadn't even known she had wanted a baby just yet, and certainly hadn't consciously premeditated this as a means to trap Daniel. She had heard many times about the ultimatum Nadine had issued and wasn't about to make the same mistake. But although only in her mid-twenties, all around her Bee's friends were starting to have babies, her social life had become babyville, and she'd known that eventually she would want what her friends had – a big wedding and a honeymoon in the Bahamas, a baby and a house in Connecticut.

But at that moment Bee realized that she wanted the rest of her life now, and if it didn't happen in the order in which she had always dreamed, well so be it.

She came out of the bathroom clutching the stick behind her back, a secret smile on her face. 'What's the matter?' Daniel said, but he already knew, the fear was already in his eyes, disconcerting Bee only a little as she held the stick up for him to see.

Daniel started hyperventilating.

'It will be fine,' Bee said later, nestling in the crook of his arm in bed and ignoring his earlier reaction. Of course he was bound to react badly, she thought.

They'd never discussed children before, or certainly not in anything other than the abstract, and it was bound to take a little time to get used to.

But get used to it he would. Bee was, is, a woman accustomed to getting what she wants. Daniel has always said she is strong enough for both of them, and it is true. When Bee sets her sights on something it is rare for her not to get it, and she had set her sights on Daniel from the very first moment she laid eyes on him.

Stella was the flower girl at their wedding. At eighteen months old, she clutched at her mother's Vera Wang skirts and her father looked down adoringly as the minister pronounced them man and wife, acknowledging, with humour and a pointed look at Bee's pregnant stomach, that perhaps they had misunderstood the natural order of things.

Daniel hadn't expected to fall in love the way he had the moment Stella was placed in his arms in the delivery room. He looked down at her red, scrunched-up face, and he felt his heart almost literally explode.

And then along came Lizzie, and despite his fears that he could never love another child as much as he loved Stella, his heart expanded to fit them both.

Daniel still wakes up every morning excited about seeing his girls. He has been known to wake them up early, leaving Bee fast asleep, just so he can have some alone time with them before he goes to work, sitting at the kitchen table as they eat their cereal and asking them very seriously about their thoughts on school, friends, life.

It is his love for the girls that keeps him going, for together they are the light of his life, and if that life doesn't feel quite right, if he doesn't feel the way he thinks he ought to feel for Bee, it is comfortable, and easy, and what, after all, is the alternative?

When Lizzie was one, and Stella three, they moved out of the city into a pretty 1940s cottage in Weston, Connecticut. For a while Daniel commuted into the city, but his work was going well and after a year or so he started developing property in Norwalk, and soon they were able to move into a big new house they built themselves in Westport. They should have been happy. Bee certainly seemed to be happy; she had thrown herself into the children's school, the PTA and various organizations, and forever seemed to be seeing this one for lunch and that one for a meeting, arranging play dates and dinners, and organizing trunk shows in the spectacular great room in their new house.

While Bee was keeping busy, Daniel found that he couldn't stop running, and for a long time he thought that no one was noticing, thought that no one realized he wasn't happy.

Daniel honestly thought that if he filled up his life with distractions, he wouldn't have to face the truth. And the truth was that he adored his girls more than anything in the world, and he loved Bee.

But this marriage wasn't right.

*   *   *

Bee had been his best friend, but there was little left. He felt, more often than not, that they were two ships passing in the night, occasionally making contact, not because of passion but because of duty, because he didn't know how to say no, because there were only so many nights you could come home late and walk up the stairs with a heavy heart, praying she would be asleep.

He hadn't wanted to get married, but he had been persuaded to, and he had hoped that even though it wasn't what he wanted, perhaps if he ran fast enough, long enough, he would find that he had reached the end of the road and it had all turned out okay.

*

Couples' counselling. It was Bee's idea, and not the first time. They have, twice before, gone into therapy, both individually and jointly, and although Daniel has never been able to fully open up, and even though both times were short-lived, somehow they managed to recover something of their equilibrium and carry on with their marriage as if they were happy.

Bee started seeing a therapist soon after they met. She had baggage, she said, and it was so liberating, so useful to be able to have an hour to herself every week, to talk about anything she wanted, to be able to think clearly, speak clearly, process her thoughts and figure out the answers.

He was never sure what the questions were, but Bee seemed happier, and although Daniel had always thought therapy was for the seriously self-indulgent, he indulged her.

At first, Bee had merely talked about how wonderful she found it, but soon she started gently suggesting that perhaps Daniel should go and see someone, that even though he claimed not to believe in it, therapy would help him open up, help him realize his full potential.

'I don't want to realize my full potential,' Daniel had groaned, all those years ago. 'I'm perfectly happy as I am.'

Bee thought this wasn't possible. He was, she would say when they were arguing, the most closed person she had ever met. He never connected emotionally, she would say, it was like talking to someone through a steel wall. 'I can help you,' she insisted, and then she began to plead with Daniel to let her help him. And after a while he grew tired of saying no, so he agreed to see someone.

Not the same therapist as Bee, that would have felt almost incestuous, but another partner in the practice. He went a handful of times. Talked a little about his childhood, talked a little about his relationship with Bee, and started cancelling when his initial effort seemed to appease Bee, and she accepted that he'd made the effort and that was enough.

This time they have been seeing Dr Posner for four months. They ought to be getting better. The last time they tried couples' counselling it was three years previously, when they saw a man and a woman who had been recommended by a friend of Bee's, who had neglected to mention that they practised client-centred therapy, therefore didn't speak, merely reflected statements back to Bee and Daniel.

'He never supports me,' Bee would say. 'He's always busy doing something, he's always distracted and he never listens to me.'

There would be a long silence as they both looked hopefully at the husband and wife therapists, and eventually one of them would say, 'So you feel unsupported. Daniel is distracted and doesn't listen?'

'Yes.'

And the silence would continue until finally Bee, or Daniel, would get the giggles, and they would invariably leave the office shaking with laughter, which may not have been the desired effect, but certainly served to bring them close enough to quit the sessions after two months.

Dr Posner is different. They have a dialogue. He started by simply asking questions, but soon offered solutions, had a depth of knowledge that Daniel was surprised, and impressed, by.

Under other circumstances, he imagines he and Dr Posner would be friends. As it is, he feels as if he shows up every Wednesday morning in preparation for an attack. He meets Bee there, neither of them having talked about it in the morning at all, and squashes himself as far away from Bee as possible as she criticizes everything about him.

And the worst part is, she's right. He is distracted.

He is busy. He doesn't want to do things with her. He doesn't compliment her. He isn't kind, or loving, or affectionate, except when it comes to his daughters, where his heart knows no bounds.

Bee is right about everything, and so every Wednesday, when the assaults come, there is little he can say; he shrugs, giving an acknowledgement that she is right. If he had the courage, perhaps he could say that he is everything she says because – oh and this is so painful to think about, something he tries to push to the back of his head – because he doesn't love her. Loves her as the mother of his children, but doesn't love her in the way he had always expected to love his life partner.

He can't say that. Can't possibly cause this much pain. And a future without his daughters is not something he can contemplate. There are times, particularly in the middle of the night, when Daniel wakes up feeling as if he is suffocating. He knows sleep is not an option on these nights, and he goes upstairs to his office, breathing deeply to try to stay calm, grabbing a newspaper or book to try to take his mind off his fear.

So he sits in Dr Posner's office, in a studio over the garage, week after week, too frightened to face a reality that will change his life forever, withdrawing more and more, terrified that if he tells the truth he will never find his way back to the only life he has ever known.

Today Daniel isn't prepared. He is prepared for the usual attack, but is in no way prepared for Dr Posner's question.

'So how are things between you physically?' Dr Posner crosses his legs and looks from husband to wife nonchalantly, as if he is asking how was their morning, rather than a question about one of the most intimate areas of their lives.

Daniel can't look at Bee, he colours ever so slightly at the question and hears her snort, looks up to see her shaking her head derisively.

'Bee?' Dr Posner says questioningly, seeing he has more hope of getting information out of Bee.

'Do you mean sex?' Bee's voice is small, as Daniel continues to shrink into the other end of the leather sofa, his own legs crossed away from Bee, his arms folded protectively over his chest, his entire body language screaming that he would rather be anywhere other than here. 'I don't remember,' she says at last, looking over at Daniel. 'When was the last time, Daniel? Nine months ago? Ten? Longer? I've given up counting.'

'Daniel?' Daniel is mortified to be even discussing this, but at least he sees there is no expression in Dr Posner's eyes, no hint of judgement.

'It's true.' He shrugs, as if it doesn't matter.

'And why is it that you haven't had physical relations in nine or ten months?' He is asking Daniel, but Daniel can't find the words so Bee answers for him, and the pain in her voice is palpable.

'He will say he's too tired.' Her voice is almost a whisper. 'He will fall asleep while I'm in the bathroom brushing my teeth, and if I try to initiate he will brush me off or say he's too tired, or he has an important meeting in the morning and has to have an early night.'

'And who does initiate it?'

'Always me,' Bee says. 'It always has been, but in the beginning it wasn't a problem. I mean, I knew he didn't have a huge libido. It was one of the things I liked, that he wasn't constantly trying to grab me, that it wasn't all about sex – but to never want it? To never initiate it? It makes me feel ugly.' Her eyes start to well. 'I feel useless, and ugly, and incapable as a woman and as a wife. I feel rejected.'

There is a long silence, punctuated only by the soft sounds of Bee crying. Dr Posner pushes a box of tissues over to her and looks at Daniel, waiting, while Daniel looks at the floor.

'How do you feel about this?' Dr Posner asks eventually.

'Horrible,' Daniel says. But he can't say more. Can't say that he looks at his wife's body and feels a shiver of revulsion, that when they do make love he is only able to perform by closing his eyes and losing himself in a fantasy. How could he possibly say these words out loud? How could he possibly say this in front of Bee when he knows it would destroy her?

Chapter Three

The door to Jessica's bedroom, plastered with signs warning anyone over the age of thirteen to keep out, is open just a crack, and Daff fights her irritation as she glances over and sees Jessica's unmade bed, three cereal bowls on the bedside table, and crumpled clothes all over the floor.

Last week, Daff announced that if Jess refused to pick up her dirty clothes and bring them to the laundry room, Daff would no longer wash them. She didn't. For five days. And then she couldn't bear walking past the closed door knowing that more and more clothes were piling up, and eventually she had given in with an exasperated sigh and gathered up the clothes, sorting them out into darks and whites as she fought her anger and frustration, and wondered what had happened to the sweet little girl who adored her mother and listened to everything she was told.

Daff had had a difficult adolescence herself, and had joked that it would be payback with Jessica, but she didn't actually believe that, didn't believe that her sweet, adorable little girl, who thought her mother was God, would ever become the truculent teenager that Daff had been.

Nowadays it seems that Daff can do no right, Jessica

audibly snorting or grunting at her when Daff asks her how her day was, or pounding up the stairs, her grand finale a door slamming shut followed by muffled screams that can be heard from her pillow.

It wasn't always like this. When they'd been a family, when Jessica's father was around, Daff doesn't remember any conflict with Jessica. Jess would certainly never have dared speak to Daff the way she does now, would have been far too frightened of what her father would say when he walked in the front door and Daff told him what had happened.

*

It has been just over a year since Jessica's father left. A couple of months before that, Daff had come to realize that the colleague at work Richard had become such good friends with, was more than a friend. But when she'd told him what she knew, Richard had denied that anything physical had happened; he'd admitted to having feelings but said that she – Nancy, the other woman – had a husband, a family, that although he thought she was attractive, that didn't mean anything, and nothing would ever happen.

Daff had believed for a while because she had wanted to believe. Because the prospect of life on her own had been terrifying; surely the devil she knew was better than venturing out on her own.

She had found out about Richard and his colleague in the worst way possible. She had been running errands near Richard's office one day at lunchtime and had phoned him, wanting to surprise him. 'I can't leave,' he had said. 'We have a huge deal coming up and I'm swamped. I'm sorry, darling, but maybe tonight we can go out for dinner.'

So she hadn't bothered going to his office, but she had been in the neighbourhood and had walked past a restaurant, glancing in the window to check her newly blown-out hair, looking beyond her reflection to see her husband sitting in the corner with a woman, reaching out and stroking the woman's cheek, with a smile on his face that she had seen before. The smile he used to have when they first met, when he would reach out and stroke her cheek in an identical gesture, one that told her he loved her, would always take care of her.

Daff had frozen. She hadn't known whether to run in and scream at him, or her, demand to know what was going on, or whether to run away. She had, in the end, walked away. Very quickly. It wasn't until she reached the corner that she started hyperventilating. Not crying, Daff has never been the type to cry in public, but she was shaking like a leaf, and drove home as if in a coma, unable to believe what she had seen.

During the next few weeks Daff read everything she could about affairs. First about emotional affairs, the reasons why the friendships people form at work can be so dangerous, and then about emotional affairs tipping into real affairs. She knew then that if it hadn't already happened, it was only a matter of time.

You can heal, her latest book said. With therapy, counselling, honesty, you both can heal and can reach a place where you find happiness again. The trust takes longer, but it is possible to seal the cracks and, on occasion, to build a relationship that is even stronger than prior to the affair.

If that's the road down which you choose to go.

Richard, it was true, hadn't planned on having an affair. He had never thought of himself as the type to be unfaithful, he took his wedding vows seriously and, up until he met Nancy, had thought he was entirely happy.

There are those who say that affairs don't happen without reason, that there is always something wrong in the relationship for either spouse to start looking elsewhere, and there are others who say you are bound to be attracted to other people while you are married, but that you have a choice, and you weigh what you have to lose against what you may gain, and make your choice accordingly.

For Richard it was neither of those things. He married Daff because he loved her, he has never felt there was anything wrong with their relationship, and when it came to Nancy, when the unspoken attraction between them became so strong it was almost over-whelming, he felt there really was no other choice.

Daff has always been his friend, his lover, the first person he calls when anything goes wrong. Or right. Of course the passion had dulled somewhat, but they had been married for sixteen years so that was almost to be expected, and it certainly didn't mean he was looking elsewhere.

34

Nancy was unlike anyone he had ever met. Where Daff was naturally beautiful, at least in his eyes, Nancy was the most glamorous woman he had ever seen. Where Daff loved the simple life – being at home surrounded by friends, gardening, kicking her feet up on the porch with a cold beer at the end of the day – Nancy was sipping cocktails at trendy bars, high heels swinging off her feet, sophisticated, sexy, and seriously out of his league, or so he had thought.

Daff had dark blonde hair, streaked now with grey, that curled gently on her shoulders. It had been highlighted when they first met, but after Jess was born she hadn't bothered, nor did she use make-up much these days, spending most of the time in jeans and sweats, running around town getting on with the business of life.

Nancy, on the other hand, was immaculate. Not a hair out of place, never seen without perfect lipstick, she was beautiful, intimidating, and admired by everyone at the office from afar. When they were teamed together to work on a design project for a new restaurant in town, Richard was terrified, and immediately taken aback by Nancy's sweetness.

And more, by her interest in him. It became clear, very early on, that Nancy thought Richard was wonderful, hung on his every word, and Richard, after he got over his disbelief, was so flattered that a friendship became inevitable.

Email helped. At first the emails to one another were about their mutual project, but they quickly became more and more personal, fostering an intimacy that grew up so fast and so seamlessly that within weeks it felt as if she was his best friend, as if he couldn't possibly live without her.

And still, he wouldn't admit to it being any more than friendship. They would have lunch together every day, in the beginning always inviting colleagues to join, as chaperones, he realized later.

But they were both married, he would tell himself during those moments when he allowed himself to think it might be more. It would be insane to think that it was anything more than friendship. Insane to think that either of them would allow themselves to have an affair.

'I would never have an affair,' he announced one lunchtime after they had eaten and were sitting on a bench in the park, talking for what felt like hours.

'I . . .' Nancy stopped. She looked at him, looked at the ground and took a deep breath. 'I think that this could be dangerous,' she said eventually. Haltingly. She looked back up at him and he wanted to drown in her eyes. 'I think that it is very difficult for men and women to just be friends, and I needed to say it out loud so we . . . so we don't cross the line, so we're mindful.'

Richard grinned. 'I agree,' he said, and he did.

Another week went by. Then a confession. 'I'm sorry,' Nancy said, over an after-work drink in a bar, 'but I've never met anyone like you. I feel like you're my best friend in the world, which is ridiculous because we've only really got to know one another these last few weeks, but I can't imagine a life that you're not a part of.'

'I know.' Richard felt sixteen again. Omnipotent, ready to handle anything. 'I feel the same way.'

'I'm so confused,' Nancy said.

'I know.' Richard's voice echoed her sadness as he said again, 'I feel the same way.'

They became one another's obsession. Nancy, unhappy in her marriage, thought about nothing other than Richard, and Richard, happy enough in his, thought about nothing other than Nancy. The affair – truly an emotional affair at first – was really only ever just a matter of time.

And lust is a dangerous thing, particularly when your life is settled, when you have forgotten quite how heady, how all-consuming it can be. For lust is not just thrilling, it is addictive, and once you have a taste for it, it is very difficult to walk away.

The first kiss came in a Starbucks. After a lunch on a cold and rainy day, they had curled up on a sofa in Starbucks, and Nancy had covered their laps with her coat, had reached out underneath the coat and taken his hand, stroking his fingers, amazed at her boldness, amazed she had the nerve to make the first move.

Nancy never dreamed she would have an affair, and although she loves her husband, he is fifteen years older, and she feels increasingly that she has grown old before her time. Her sophisticated clothes, her glamorous make-up, are all part of the uniform that's required to fit in her husband's wealthy, older world.

Richard made her feel young again. He made her feel carefree. They were the same age, and she had forgotten what it was like to feel forty. Had forgotten what it was like to laugh.

Richard had leaned his head back on the sofa and closed his eyes. He had forgotten his body could tingle like that, had forgotten what it felt like to have every nerve on fire.

'What are you thinking?' he said eventually, opening his eyes and looking at her.

'I'm thinking that you should kiss me,' she said, fighting the impulse to run her fingers through his thick blond hair, wanting to place her lips softly on his eyelids, trace the muscles in his back with her hands.

'Kiss you?' he said, as if in a daze.

'Yes,' she whispered.

And he did.

They didn't leap into an affair. Not immediately. They met in clandestine hole-in-the-wall places, spending hours walking round parks, making out on benches for hours like teenagers. And that was exactly how they both felt: like teenagers. Falling in love for the first time.

Richard was so torn. He'd leave Nancy and go home to a woman and child he loved, a life he loved, and he couldn't understand why he wasn't happy, why it couldn't be enough. For when he was with Nancy he felt consumed with guilt, and when he was at home, all he could think about was Nancy.

Richard broke up with Nancy, determined to focus on his marriage, make it work, but he was so miserable, found life so unbearable without her, he went into her office after two weeks and told her he couldn't live without her, and the affair resumed.

Five days later he broke up with her again. He choked up as he explained that he had fallen in love with her, but he couldn't let the affair go on, he couldn't do this. He was sorry, but it was over, he had to end it.

But he couldn't stay away.

The first time they had sex, Richard couldn't perform. The second time they had sex he had got hold of some Viagra, and it was spectacular.

But it was only three weeks before Daff found out. He knew she was in the area, had thought it would be okay, but there were a lot of things that he thought would be okay – lust had, in general, clouded his reasoning so much that he spent much of his day in a fog.

It was a normal Thursday morning for Daff, a morning spent running errands, making phone calls, until she ran out to do some shopping and made that fateful call to Richard's office, then saw him in the restaurant with a woman.

'What did you do for lunch?' she asked him when he got home.

'Grabbed a sandwich at my desk,' he lied smoothly as he was flicking through his mail. 'How about you?'

'I saw you,' she whispered, hoping he wouldn't lie, hoping there would be a reasonable explanation.

'Saw me where?' His face was impassive, innocent.

'I saw you in a restaurant with a woman.'

'Oh, that!' He laughed. 'That was just Nancy. I joined her for a coffee. She wanted to talk about a project.'

'That wasn't a project,' Daff said. 'I saw how you touched her.'

'God, Daff, don't be so ridiculous. We chatted a bit about other stuff. She was upset about a row with her husband. What's the big deal?'

'What's the big deal? *What's the big deal?*' Daff was trying to keep her voice calm. 'The big deal is you don't stroke someone's face like that to comfort them. You don't look at someone the way I saw you look at . . . her . . . not unless there's something going on.'

'You're insane,' Richard said calmly. 'Look, what will make you believe me? I swear, you're the only woman I love. Jesus –' he switched tack, now raising his voice – 'how can you even think that? What kind of woman are you?'

'I'm your wife,' Daff said slowly. 'And I know you're having an affair.'

There was a long silence, and then, like a balloon deflating, Richard's energy disappeared and he admitted it.

He admitted that he had been friends with Nancy up until very recently, that he had realized she was attracted to him, and that the lunch when Daff saw them was the lunch when he was saying the friendship

40

finally had to end because it had become too dangerous.

'I don't believe you,' Daff said, feeling sick to her
stomach, unable to believe what she was hearing.

'I swear to you.' Richard took her in his arms.
'I know she's attracted to me, but that doesn't mean
I'm attracted to her, and even if I was I wouldn't do
anything about it. I love you. Really, I do.'

Daff didn't completely believe him, but she had no
proof. She allowed herself to be hugged, accepted his
apology, his insistence that he loved her, would never
do anything to hurt her or Jessica, and then, a few days
later, she set about finding proof.

It wasn't hard to collect the evidence, and Daff gave
herself two months to be sure. At the end of two
months, two months during which time Richard had
been attentive, loving, home on time and wanting to
make love almost nightly, Daff confronted him.

She did it quietly. Not wanting to make a scene, she
booked a table at a quiet Italian restaurant in town, a
place known for romantic dinners, for proposals and
celebrations, not for nights such as this.

'What's this?' Richard looked intrigued and happily
apprehensive as she slid a small white cardboard box
over to him. Daff hadn't said anything, and Richard's
heart started to beat a little bit faster.

The evidence came tumbling out. His mobile phone
records, receipts from hotels on days when he was supposed to be at work, itemized credit card bills showing

flowers bought, gifts paid for, none of them received by Daff.

And finally two notes that Daff found shoved to the back of his underwear drawer, almost snorting with derision as she unfolded them – his underwear drawer? Couldn't he have been more fucking imaginative, she had said when she phoned a friend to let her know.

One was sexy, the other soulful. This was no mere friendship, and as Richard unfolded the notes and realized what they were, there was nothing he could say.

When he found his words, later that night, Daff was stunned at what she heard.

'I didn't know it was possible,' he wept as he sat on the edge of their bed, 'to be in love with two women at the same time.' He looked pleadingly up at Daff, like a child seeking reassurance from his mother.

'I love you,' he cried. 'I don't know how this happened. I didn't plan this, Daff. I didn't want this, and I never wanted to hurt you.'

'You lied to me,' Daff said, unable to believe the pain she was in, unable to believe that she wanted to both hit and comfort him at the same time.

'I never meant to.' Richard put his head in his hands and groaned. 'It was a huge mistake. I'm so sorry.'

'You must be unhappy with me.' Daff started to cry herself. 'What did I do? What was it about me? About us?'

'Nothing. Oh God, nothing. You're amazing, there's nothing wrong with you. That's what I can't understand. How can I fall for her when I'm so happy with you, when I love you so much?'

'So which one of us do you want?' Daff asked, her voice suspiciously calm and reasonable, in part not to wake Jess, whose room was only down the hall.

'I don't know,' he wept, and something inside shifted for Daff, a little hardening of the piece of her heart that she had always thought would be reserved for Richard.

Richard moved out. Jessica wasn't aware of what was happening at first, only that Daddy needed to be closer to work, but then she was with him on weekends, and she would lie in bed at night, her heart pounding, knowing that her parents had separated, and believing herself to be somehow the cause.

If I am extra nice, she thought, then Daddy will come home and we will all live together again. If I do everything I'm told, I will not be punished like this.

She would pray to God as she cried quietly into her pillow, attempting to strike a deal with him, attempting anything in a bid to bring her family back together again.

Richard moved out, and Nancy didn't. What had seemed so tempting, so appealing, when Richard was safely ensconced in his marriage, suddenly became terrifying when he made himself so available.

'You can come and live with me,' he would say to Nancy over lunch, attempting a nonchalance he didn't feel. 'Or get an apartment nearby. Either way, just think, we can finally be together.'

Was it love or desperation? Nancy didn't know, but what she did know was that her own feelings were beginning to change. That suddenly, after weeks of planning a life together, she wasn't sure they had a future, couldn't see herself destroying her marriage to start again with Richard.

As the rose-tinted glasses fell from her eyes, she started to see him in a different light. The jokes he made, which in truth she had never found funny but had tried to ignore, seemed puerile and rather silly. His habit of gobbling up the bread basket in restaurants as soon as he sat down began to be deeply irritating instead of endearing. And mostly his desperation, his sheer *need* was the most difficult of all.

Her own husband, who had been cast as the devil during this, her first affair, now seemed to be exactly what she wanted. He was safety and security, he was friendship and trust. He was everything she knew she loved and wanted, and Richard, suddenly, was not.

'I can't do this,' Nancy said gently, a few weeks after Richard had moved out. 'I can't leave my husband.'

'What are you saying?' Richard's eyes widened in shock. He had blown his life apart for this woman and now she didn't want him?

Was she fucking kidding him?

Nancy didn't have answers. She just knew, categorically, that she couldn't do this. She had started tiptoeing around her husband, terrified that Richard's wife would contact him, let him know about the affair, find a way to ruin her marriage in revenge.

A surge of anger swept through Richard, and he stormed out, slamming the door of his car in a fury.

'I miss you,' he said to Daff that Friday when he came to the house to collect Jessica. 'I miss *us*.'

He expected Daff's eyes to soften, expected to see a chink in her armour, but there was none.

'You should have thought of that before you embarked on an affair,' Daff hissed quietly, careful not to let Jessica hear.

And despite the books she had read, despite knowing that an affair didn't have to end the marriage, suddenly, for Daff it was over. Not because of the affair, but because of the choice he had made. The affair she could have forgiven, in time. She understood that marriages weren't perfect, and that temptation exists, and that sometimes men – poor creatures – cannot help being driven by their libidos.

But she couldn't forgive him for leaving his wife and child for the object of his affair, especially when she knew that it wouldn't last. And she had known it wouldn't last, for she had seen Nancy, had found out about her, had parked outside her big colonial house and watched her pull up in her Range Rover, her husband arriving in his big 7 Series BMW shortly afterwards. She had known this was not someone who would leave this life for Richard.

They say revenge is a dish best served cold, but Daff

didn't want revenge, she was far too sad for that. She felt sadness for their marriage, for what she thought she had, and what she so quickly realized was merely an illusion; sad for Jessica, who thought she couldn't be heard crying at night, although Daff heard every whimper.

And she felt sad for Richard.

Daff had always thought of Richard as so powerful, so capable, so strong, but in one fell swoop she had lost all respect for him, and those times when he would turn up on her doorstep in tears – which seemed so like crocodile tears that it was all she could do not to slap him round the face to snap him out of it – she saw him as pathetic.

She saw him as a lost little boy, one who knew he had screwed up his life, torn it apart, and would try everything to get it back together again.

At times he would turn up with anger: if Daff had been more *this*, if she had wanted more of *that*, if she hadn't done *this*, said *that* . . .

Daff would just stare at him in disbelief, calling Jessica and walking away, leaving him with his false accusations on the doorstep.

He would phone later, always phoned later to apologize, to cry down the phone and tell her he couldn't live without her, but Daff, who had always castigated herself for being so black and white about everything in her life, knew that her feelings would never change.

*

The divorce was finalized three months ago. It could have got nasty, but Daff chose not to go down that road. They went to mediation and wrote their own agreement, Richard paying child support and a small amount of alimony. Not enough for Daff to survive on – something she had been frightened of since the beginning, when she had sat down and made a list of her options – but Richard, always the stronger of the two, refused to pay more, and at the time Daff didn't have the strength to fight and, naively, didn't realize quite how much she would need in order to live.

She'd known as soon as Richard left that she would need to get a job. Real estate was the most tempting and seemed the obvious choice for her. The market wasn't great, but Daff had always had a way with people, was liked by everyone; also the upside was so great, and the rewards so much larger than for any of the salaried jobs she was contemplating.

Within a few months of separating, she had her licence, and her first sale was a small cape in a neighbourhood close to her own.

She feels, in many ways, that she has the perfect job. She doesn't earn as much as she would like, but her hours are her own and she is able to be there for Jessica. She just wishes Jessica didn't so clearly want her to go away.

Jessica blames her mother for the marriage breaking up. She knows nothing of the affair – Richard and Daff agreed never to let her know – but Richard has made it quite clear to Jess that *he* would never have left his family, that living in a small apartment on the other side of town is not *his* choice, and so Jessica blames Daff, and her anger is so great, she can barely bring herself to look at her.

Chapter Four

'How was the lobster?' Sarah shouts through to the kitchen as she walks in, stopping to put the grocery bags of cleaning products away in the pantry.

'Delicious, as always. Oh I wish you had been here five minutes earlier. You would have met Andrew Moseley. Such a nice man.'

'So your lunch was fun?' Sarah walks into the kitchen.

Nan reaches over for a cigarette and takes her time lighting it, before shrugging. 'I'm not sure I would have called it fun. Lovely to have the company, but apparently the money thing is a disaster and he thinks I ought to sell the house.'

'What?' Sarah's mouth drops open in shock. 'Which house? *This* house?'

'There *are* no other houses any more.' Nan gives a rueful smile.

'But, Nan! That's terrible!' Sarah sinks down onto a chair opposite Nan at the kitchen table.

'Oh sweetie. Nothing is terrible.'

'But what do you mean, the money thing is a disaster?' Once upon a time, when Sarah first started here as a weekly cleaner, she would never have dared ask this of Nan. Nan seemed so grand, so imperious,

Sarah would scuttle around with her bucket of cleaning equipment, trying to keep out of her way.

That was almost fifteen years ago. Sarah was seventeen, trying to fund her studies, cleaning houses on the island for families she had known since she was a baby, families her own mother had worked for, her grandmother.

Now Sarah is part of the family. She still cleans for Nan, and cooks, and runs errands, but she is, effectively, Nan's daughter, the only difference being that her recompense is more clearly defined.

Sarah has always thought of Windermere as her second home – it is, after all, the place where she considers herself to have grown up, her twenties being a difficult, unstable time, the only stability seeming to come from Nan.

And now Nan is talking about selling the house? Sarah couldn't live without this house, without Nan, and the two are intermingled in her mind – there could not be one without the other – and the prospect of losing them is terrifying.

Sarah may now have a husband and a home of her own, but Windermere is the place where she came to understand what 'home' meant: that anyone can live in a house, but homes are created with patience, time and love. And Windermere has always felt more of a home to her than anywhere else. More, even, than the home she is now starting to build with her husband.

'You know me and money.' Nan smiles. 'Andrew started talking about hedge funds and high risk and large returns, and it seems the hedge fund had put all their money with something they shouldn't have, and the market dropped hundreds of points the other day, whatever that means, and it seems we've all lost everything.'

'But, Nan!' Sarah is shocked. 'What are you going to do?'

'When you get to my age, you tend not to worry about these things happening. It's only money, after all.'

'So you have more?'

'Well ... not really. But I imagine it's highly unlikely I'll sell the house. We'll all have to put our thinking caps on and come up with something.'

'Have you told Michael?'

'Not yet. I'll call him later.' She stubs the cigarette out roughly in the crystal ashtray that is now yellow and cloudy with age, and she looks Sarah firmly in the eye.

'I'm not going to sell this house, though,' she says. 'Hell will freeze over before I sell this house.' And Sarah leans back in her chair with a sigh of relief.

*

'Do you really think it's that simple? We go away for a weekend and it makes everything okay?' Daniel looks doubtfully at Dr Posner, who raises his eyebrows.

'No,' Dr Posner says. 'I don't think anything is that simple, but I certainly don't think it can do harm. I think it may be a good opportunity for you and Bee to reconnect, to remember what you both saw in one another before you got caught up in being parents, in the frantic pace of life with children.'

'That's what I've been trying to tell him,' Bee says. 'And it was a wonderful opportunity. Hardly anyone else was bidding on the weekend in Nantucket, it includes flights, and it's only for a couple of days. It cost almost nothing,' she concludes defiantly.

'I think you did a good thing,' Dr Posner says, validating Bee. 'I think you should both go and enjoy it.'

The weekend away was one of the silent-auction prizes at the breast cancer charity gala they had been to a few weeks before. It was one of the galas that all their friends went to, all of them working themselves up into a tizzy of excitement at the items on offer in the auction, the biggest prize being a week at Atlantis in the Bahamas, leaving the field free for Bee to swoop in and claim Nantucket.

She hadn't even particularly wanted to go, even though she had a vague recollection of her dad talking about Nantucket, saying what a magical place it was, but she wanted to bid on *something*, and there were only two other names and it had been so cheap. Perhaps a weekend away was what they needed, although of late it had seemed they would need nothing short of a miracle to bring them back together again.

For while they lived as husband and wife, they were feeling, increasingly to Bee, like room-mates, and room-mates who were drifting further and further apart. Daniel was still perfectly nice, pleasant, but it was as if someone had reached in and switched off the light. Any warmth, any intimacy that they had once had, had disappeared, leaving Bee with the peculiar feeling that it had all been an illusion.

*

Jordana dusts a fine coat of translucent powder across her nose and tucks her hair back into her chignon before slipping into the workroom.

'I'm just checking to see how that necklace is coming along for Mrs Branfield,' she says, as Michael looks up from his workbench and smiles at her.

'I finished it yesterday,' he says. 'Hang on.' And he walks over to the safe, quickly turns the combination and pulls out a velvet box.

'Oh Michael!' Jordana gasps as she looks at the diamond flower, the pear-shaped diamonds, as the petals, set prettily around an emerald, with delicate marquise-cut emeralds as the leaves. 'She'll love it.'

'I hope so,' Michael says. 'It may make coming to terms with the divorce a bit easier.'

Lesley Branfield was the former wife of the very successful owner of a large make-up company. She had never managed to have children during their seven-year marriage (her first, his fourth), and had consequently considered herself somewhat screwed during their divorce (wives one, two and three had ended up with smallish alimony but huge child support).

She had, however, been left with their Upper East Side apartment, a cottage on Shelter Island, and all the furnishings, clothes and jewellery, which is where Michael came in.

Her husband, while wealthy, was too cheap to pay retail. If Lesley Branfield fell in love with a ring, or a pair of earrings, or a beautiful necklace at Cartier or Tiffany, they would borrow it (you'd be surprised at what the jewellery stores do for their wealthiest, well-known customers), photograph it, and take the photo into the back room at Jordana & Jackson, where Michael could create an exact replica for a fraction of the price.

The rich may like the best of the best, but they still love a bargain.

And since the divorce Lesley Branfield had decided that rather than do an Ellen Barkin and sell everything, she would simply remodel, thereby eradicating any painful memories that may have come with the original jewellery.

'I'll phone her and tell her it's ready,' Jordana says. 'She'll be so happy. Oh Michael, you've done a really beautiful job. Thank you.'

'It's a pleasure.' Michael smiles, turning to get back to work.

'So how's everything going with your new girlfriend?'

He shrugs. 'It's okay.'

'Just okay?' Jordana laughs. 'That doesn't sound so good. What's going on?'

In different circumstances it might perhaps be odd

for the boss to be talking to her employee about his love life, but since they opened the second store in Manhasset Jackson has been spending more and more time there, and Jordana has found herself turning more and more to Michael for help with the store.

Of course there are others – the two sales assistants who work in the store – but she would never really talk to them, would never ask their advice; and there is something calming about Michael, something that makes her want to open up and confide in him, and she has found herself forming an unlikely friendship with him. For the first time in years she has found herself looking forward to getting in to work.

Not that she doesn't like her job – she and Jackson decided, even before they got married, that they would create a line of high-end, affordable jewellery stores, which is exactly what they are beginning to do – but the Manhasset store had been Jackson's baby from the outset, and she had felt, left on her own in the Madison Avenue store, that life had become a bit dull.

Which is why she is so enjoying this friendship with Michael. Sometimes they have lunch together, a sandwich in the staff room usually, occasionally walking over to the park if the weather is nice enough. It is just lovely to have someone to talk to again. To have a friend at work.

'No, better than okay,' Michael says. 'I really like her, it's just . . .'

'Not the one?' Jordana smiles.

'Oh God,' he groans. 'I feel like every time I meet

girls who are really great it's just a matter of time before I start to find problems with them, and then after a while I start to think that maybe it's not them, maybe the problem is with me, and that I'm the one who needs to work through it, and so I stay in these relationships but I can't commit and then they start accusing me of being a commitaphobe and all I want to do is run as far away from them as possible.'

Jordana starts to laugh. 'Do you think perhaps that's a sign that you are a commitaphobe?'

'Which bit?' Michael grins. 'The running away from them as far as possible bit?'

'Well, yes.'

'Hmm. You think?'

'What do you think?'

'Me? I think I'd love nothing more than to find a wonderful woman, a true partner in every sense of the word, who I could spend the rest of my life with. I just don't think I've found her yet.'

'And this . . . Aisling?'

Michael nods.

'Aisling couldn't be the one?'

Michael sighs. 'She's doing that changing thing.'

'What changing thing?'

'You know. That thing where on the first few dates they act as if everything you do is wonderful. They adore the fact that you ride a bicycle because it's so ecologically sound, and they love that you're a jeweller because it means you're creative and soulful, and they think it's wonderful that you have a rent-controlled pre-war on the Upper West Side because they say they've always dreamed of a rent-controlled pre-war on the Upper West Side.'

'So far so good.' Jordana shrugs.

'And then dating becomes more serious, and then they ask very casually whether you've ever considered a Vespa, and it would really make a huge amount of sense because not only is it cool but then the two of us could travel together. And then they start wandering around your apartment looking meaningfully at the walls and floor, and they tell you that the apartment would be really amazing if the floors were sanded and stained, and it costs almost nothing, apparently, to have your bathroom re-tiled and your bathtub re-enamelled, and Smith & Noble do great custom blinds that are really not that expensive . . .'

Jordana starts to laugh again.

'And then one night when you've had a really great dinner and you're starting to think that perhaps you can overlook the warning signs – even though the warning signs always lead to the same place and frankly your instincts about the warning signs are never wrong – they look you in the eye and ask if you'd ever want your own jewellery store. Or they'll ask you where you see yourself in five years' time and you see nothing but disappointment in their eyes when you tell them that ideally you'd love to be settled down with the right woman, living in the same apartment, working for the same company.'

Jordana puts a hand over her heart and breathes an

exaggerated sigh of relief. 'Phew. You're not leaving us any time soon?'

'Not planning on it. And that's the problem. They can't believe, can't accept, that I'm happy with my life exactly as it is. All these girls want to help me discover my inner mogul, convinced that somewhere I have this hidden, untapped, fathomless well of ambition that only they can help me access, and none of them want to accept me as I am.'

'So has that happened with Aisling?'

'Yes. Things were going great, and then she asked the five-year question, and said she couldn't understand how I could not ask for a partnership in this business, or want to set up on my own. "You could make so much more money," she kept saying, and I kept trying to explain that I wasn't motivated by money. And then, inevitably, she asked how I could support a family and I explained that I didn't have a family to support – and of course she wants a family, so suddenly I seem like horrible husband material.' Michael sighs, shaking his head.

'That's tough,' Jordana says. 'She sounds like she probably isn't the one for you. I do think that your goals have to be the same or, at least, have to be in tune with one another for it to work, and if she's motivated by money, or at least by a husband with money, then that's not right for you. Thankfully,' she says and laughs, 'Jackson and I were both equally motivated by money.'

Michael laughs too. 'That's what I like about you,' he says. 'You don't mind admitting it.'

'Listen, as I always say, I came from nothing and I grew up wanting everything, and knowing that I would find a way to get it. I loved sparkly things as a little girl, and worked damned hard at that gemmology course before I went to work for a jeweller. I just don't understand these girls who expect their husband to provide everything for them.'

'Me neither,' Michael says. 'Why is it those are the ones I keep finding?'

'You must be looking in the wrong places.' Jordana smiles. 'Right. I'm back up to the floor. I'll phone Lesley Branfield and let her know. I'm sure she'll want to thank you herself. Are you around the rest of the day?'

'I'm going nowhere,' Michael says. 'At least, according to Aisling.' And they both laugh as Jordana closes the door of the workshop behind her.

Chapter Five

'Isn't this nice?' Bee reaches over at LaGuardia and strokes Daniel's arm, and he smiles at her, wondering if perhaps his sense of being lost is an overreaction, for he does love Bee, does love so many aspects of his life.

'What do you think the girls are doing?' Daniel says, and Bee laughs.

'Are we going to spend the entire time talking about the girls?'

'Isn't it crazy? Our first trip in years without them, and I miss them so much.'

'Stella was very upset, but they'll be fine. My dad will spoil them rotten.' Bee smiles. 'He was so excited to have them, and it turns out he really does know Nantucket well. He's given me a list of places we have to visit.'

She glances down at Daniel's suitcase. 'Why is it I can come away with nothing, and you seem to have packed your entire wardrobe?' she says, attempting a laugh which doesn't quite conceal the irritation behind the comment.

'Because I haven't been to Nantucket before and I have no idea quite what to wear. I've got "preppy" covered with polo shirts and pink and green, and "old

Yankee" with seersucker and flip-flops. I just wasn't sure and I hate getting things wrong.'

'I've got three T-shirts, a black jersey dress in case we go out and two pairs of shorts,' Bee says. 'I could have packed in a backpack. I'm the girl, I'm supposed to be the one who brings the trunk for the weekend, not you.'

Daniel shrugs and tries to laugh at himself. 'You know I'm an old woman,' he says eventually.

'Yes, you are.' Bee looks at him with affection in her eyes. 'That's one of the reasons why I love you.'

'I know,' he says, and he knows he ought to say 'I love you too' – the words are on the tip of his tongue, and he tries to say them, he looks at her knowing she's waiting to hear those words – but instead he finds himself rubbing her knee affectionately before standing up. 'I'm going to get a newspaper,' he says abruptly. 'Shall I get you a *People*?' And he turns and walks towards Hudson News before it gets any more difficult.

Daniel has never been able to say 'I love you' with ease. He wasn't brought up like that, he often tells Bee, although that isn't quite true. His father was cold and distant, but his mother had always showered him with love, and he had always and easily told her he loved her.

Bee was also an only child, and the apple of her parents' eye. Both of them told her that she was the most precious child in the world, and that no one could possibly love a child more than they loved her, and she believed them. She grew up in a world of safety, security and outward expressions of love, and believed her parents to have a perfect marriage until her mother left her father after she went to college.

'I am tired of the secrets,' her mother once said, and Bee had asked what she meant, but her mother had just shaken her head wearily and said she didn't want to talk about it, and Bee hadn't wanted to push. She had hoped, for years afterwards, that they would get back together, even though she was an adult, even though it shouldn't have made any difference to her, but despite the divorce being amicable, friendly even, her mother always said it was an impossible situation.

Bee had tried to talk to her father about it but he hadn't said much. Not that this was unusual; her father was often quiet, pensive, lost in another world, except when he was playing with Bee, when he was fully engaged, wholly attentive and brimming over with love for her.

Bee had always assumed that when she got married, her husband would treat her in much the same way as her father had, and she doesn't understand, has never understood, why she has ended up in a marriage with a man who seems incapable of truly loving.

But Bee is not ready to give up. Not yet. Her force of will is so strong she is convinced she can change things, and convinced she will turn Daniel into the man she knows he really is, the man she knows he can be.

*

Jessica settles back into her car seat and watches her father, who looks over at her from time to time and smiles, reaching out to squeeze her knee as he drives.

She loves him so much it sometimes hurts. He is, without question, the best daddy of all time, and even though she didn't appreciate him so much when he and Mom lived together, since he's been gone she feels she has truly come to understand him, and as her attachment to him has grown, so has her dislike of her mother.

It started as ambivalence. Even when her parents were still together her mother was starting to annoy her. Constantly nagging Jessica to tidy her room, or do her homework, or change her clothes, her hair. And then she forced her dad to leave, thereby ruining her life. What was ambivalence has turned very rapidly to hate.

Sure, there are times when they get on. Sometimes her mom will take her for a manicure, which is always fun – then they're kind of like girlfriends, although it only lasts for a short time and then her mom always ends up trying too hard and Jessica wants to scream at her.

Jessica knows her dad would never leave her, and the only reason he left is because of her mom. And how does she know this? Why, her dad told her, of course. He said, quite clearly, that he would never have left Jessica, that he loved her more than anything and that this wasn't his choice to live in a small apartment in a different, less expensive neighbourhood. He'd give anything, he said, to move back into their home, to be a family again, but it was her mother who had told him to leave, who was driving this.

Jessica wasn't particularly surprised to hear that. She knew her father loved her too much to leave, knew it had to be something to do with her mother.

'I hate you!' she screamed at her mother soon after her dad left, daring to say those words out loud for the first time. 'You've ruined my life and I hate you!' She ran up to her room, expecting her mother to come racing up the stairs after her to punish her, or shout at her, or something. But there was silence.

Jessica sobbed loudly into her pillow, then stopped after a while because no one was coming up to see if she was okay. She tiptoed to her door, cracked it open very gently, and heard her mother crying quietly downstairs.

Good. She felt a glimmer of remorse, quickly covered up by a smug sense of satisfaction. Her mother deserved to feel the pain that Jessica felt every second of every day since her mother had thrown her father out. There was nothing that he could have done that would have justified that, and so Jessica continues to blame her mother, trying to figure out how she can get to live with her dad full-time.

'Can we go to Four Brothers?' Jessica asks, the amusement arcade having become one of her favourite places. When they had been living together, she had rarely been allowed to go there, only as a special treat once in a while, and once there her parents had never paid her that much attention. Like every other place they had gone to when they were a whole family, they had gone with other people, friends, so the grown-ups could hang out together and the kids could go off and do their own thing.

Jessica doesn't ever remember her dad playing arcade games with her, for example. Doesn't remember her parents sitting at the diner and talking to her as if she were an equal. She remembers them going out a lot at night while she stayed home with a babysitter, remembers them going away for weekends while she went to her grandma's.

Now her dad does everything with her. Jessica is not old enough to understand about guilt, but she is old enough to reap the benefits, and old enough to know how to manipulate so she always gets what she wants.

'Daddy?' she will say breathlessly as they stand outside Kool Klothes, the coolest store in town that her parents always said was horribly overpriced and ridiculously trendy. 'Who shops in there?' her mother used to say, glancing disdainfully through the window at the sequinned tiny T-shirts and low-slung studded denim skirts.

'Can I?' And she has learned that as long as she shows enough excitement and a wide-eyed gratitude, as if to say she can't believe how lucky she is, he will buy her whatever she wants.

A curious mix of adult and little girl, at thirteen she has curves, breasts, a budding interest in boys, but the divorce has brought about a regression, and she now attaches herself to her father like a limpet, curling herself around him when he stands, sitting on his lap and leaning into him, sucking her thumb while he sits on the sofa to watch television.

She has developed a new routine when she is with her father. She reaches out her arms to him at bedtime and he lifts her up and carries her upstairs to bed, lying down behind her and stroking her back until she falls asleep. I am so lucky, she thinks, as she lies there – the only time in her life she feels absolutely safe and secure. I love my dad and he loves me, and no one can take that away from me.

'So? Can we?'

'Can we what?' Richard seems distracted.

'*Dad!*' she whines, rolling her eyes. 'I just asked you if we could go to Four Brothers.'

'Maybe later, sweetheart,' he says. 'I thought we could go to Belucci's for lunch today.'

Jessica's face falls. 'Why Belucci's?' she says. 'We always go to the diner.'

'I know, sweetheart.' He smiles at her indulgently. 'But today I want you to meet a friend of mine, and I thought we could go somewhere nice, somewhere special.'

Jessica's heart skips and she narrows her eyes. 'What kind of friend?'

'Her name is Carrie and she's really nice.'

Jessica feels as if she can't breathe, but she tries to make her voice sound normal. 'Is she your girlfriend?'

'No, darling.' Richard laughs. 'She's just a new friend

of mine who I'm hanging out with and I thought you'd like her.'

'You swear she's not a girlfriend?'

'Jessica! I would tell you if she was my girlfriend.'

'So how do you know her?'

'I met her through friends, and I promise you, you'll like her.'

'Why?' Jessica starts to pout. 'I don't want to meet her. I don't care if she's nice, this is supposed to be Daddy–daughter time, not Daddy–daughter–and new friend time. I don't want to meet her. I want to go to Four Brothers.' Her voice starts to pitch higher and Richard looks at her, unsure for a moment of what to do, what to say, then he decides to be firm.

'Sweetheart, we have a plan to meet my friend, and then afterwards maybe we'll go to Four Brothers. We'll still have Daddy–daughter time, I promise.'

'No, Daddy!' Her voice becomes a scream. 'I don't want anyone else to join us. That's not fair, Daddy! You're ruining our time together! I hardly ever see you any more and when we do we get to do our special things together and it's not fair that there's someone else joining us. That's not fair, Daddy, and I'm not going!' Tears are now streaming down her face as she thumps her fists on her knees in a fairly accurate interpretation of a three-year-old's tantrum.

Richard is horrified. This is the first time he has changed their plans since the divorce, and really, what's the big deal? He's been seeing Carrie for a few weeks now, and she's great. He knows Jessica will love her, because everyone loves her. It's the first time he has thought that he might be able to see a future with one of the many women he has dated since his initial separation from Daff just over a year ago, and he had this vision of the three of them having a wonderful lunch, Jessica charming Carrie with her cuteness and the funny impersonations she always does for him, and Carrie charming Jessica with her warmth and humour.

'Jessica, stop this!' He pulls the car over to the side of the road as Jessica dissolves into full-blown sobbing. 'We're going and that's the end of it. I suggest you pull yourself together right now.'

'I hate you!' she starts shrieking through her sobs. 'I hate you and I'm glad you don't live with us any more!'

And Richard shakes his head, utterly helpless. He has no idea what to do.

*

Nan strides up the dirt driveway, narrowly avoiding a small bulldozer that's shifting a pile of earth from one side to the other.

'Good morning,' she calls out to the men standing around, most of whom just smile in return, until she calls out jauntily, '*Buenos dias.*'

'*Buenos dias, señora!*' they say in return, parting to let her through. They are not sure who she is, but surely she belongs here, perhaps she is someone who is interested in buying this house? Perhaps a realtor coming to inspect the property? It is, after all, nearly finished.

Nan steps gingerly along the plank leading up to the front entrance — the stone steps are not quite ready — and then pushes the front door open, striding through the enormous living room to the French doors at the back.

'Good God,' she says to herself, turning and looking up at the twelve-foot-high coffered ceiling, the sweeping staircase, the elaborately panelled walls. 'Who in the hell needs a house like this in Nantucket?'

She takes her time. Walks down the corridor to the kitchen, gasps at the size of the kitchen, the Viking eight-burner stove, the Sub-Zero fridge and the marble countertops.

'But where's the pantry?' she mutters, opening doors and walking around. 'How do you have a kitchen this size and no pantry? Where are you supposed to put the food?' She directs these questions to a Guatemalan plumber who's lying on the floor tightening something under the sink. He doesn't understand but smiles widely and nods.

'Ridiculous,' she says, continuing her journey. Up the stairs to the bedrooms — the master bedroom having walk-in closets that are each larger than her bedroom in her house — and then downstairs to the basement.

A fully equipped gym, a steam room that easily accommodates ten, a massage room fitted out with professional massage table. A pool room and bar, and then through to a twelve-seat movie theatre, complete with leather reclining seats and a full-sized old-fashioned popcorn machine in the foyer.

'Hello? Can I help you?' A large man walks into the movie theatre as Nan is trying out one of the reclining seats.

'I don't know,' Nan says. 'Can you? Do you know how to make these go all the way back?'

'I do,' he says. 'You push on the arms.'

Nan pushes on the arms and goes flying backwards until she's lying prostrate. She starts to giggle. 'Oh well done.' She thanks him. 'I think I may have to have a nap. It's terribly comfortable. You ought to try it.'

'I have,' he says. 'I'm Mark Stephenson. I'm the developer. And you are?'

'Oh how horribly rude of me!' Nan struggles to sit up but finds she can't quite manage it so extends a hand instead. 'I'm Nan Powell. Neighbour.'

The man's eyes light up. 'You're Nan Powell? You have that wonderful house on the bluff?'

'I do indeed,' Nan says. 'And I have a question for you. Who exactly is buying houses like this on Nantucket? Who needs a massage room, a games room and a movie theatre?'

Mark Stephenson chuckles as he settles into the recliner next to Nan. 'You'd be surprised,' he says. 'Nantucket isn't what it used to be.'

'Tell me about it, my dear.' Nan shakes her head. 'I've been here for over forty years, and my late husband's family even longer. But do you really expect to sell this?'

'I do.' He nods.

'And what's the price?' Nan says.

'Why? Are you interested?'

Nan laughs. She likes this man.

'It's twelve and a half.'

'Twelve and a half?' Nan is confused. 'Twelve and a half *what*?'

'Twelve and a half million.'

'*What?*'

Mark Stephenson repeats himself.

'But that's *ridiculous*! That's a fortune. Why would anyone pay twelve and a half million dollars for a house? And especially a house that doesn't even have a pantry.'

'Ah, well, the type of people who will be buying this house probably won't cook very much. They're more likely to be eating out.'

'Not the type of people I want to have as my neighbours, I shouldn't think.'

'I love your house.' Mark Stephenson decides to change the subject. 'I got lost one day and drove up the driveway, and I have to tell you, you have one of the most special properties I've seen. Tell me, how many acres do you have?'

'Well, we used to have eighteen, but after we sold off the cottages it went down to nine. It is lovely, though, isn't it? I must say, even without a massage room or a movie theatre it does still somehow work for me.'

The developer throws his head back and laughs. 'It's the sort of house I could see myself in,' he says. 'It's a true family house. One that has clearly seen generations of people and ought to have children growing up in it.

Lord knows I know how my own children would love that sort of space.'

'Oh you have children?'

'Three boys.' He makes a face and Nan laughs.

'And where are you?'

'We're in Shimmo,' he says. 'Great for town, but I've always loved Sconset. We come out here with the kids and they just cycle around the centre of the village for hours.'

'So why don't you move into your house?' Nan asks.

'I wish I could!' Mark laughs. 'I can't afford it. Anyway, I'm building what the market demands, not what I would necessarily choose for myself. I far prefer older houses.'

'Oh me too,' Nan says. 'You'd doubtless love Windermere. Say, I'd really like to show you the inside of the house sometime. Why don't you come and join me for a drink one evening?'

'I would love to, Mrs Powell,' he says, stretching over with a business card that appears to have materialized from nowhere.

'Oh call me Nan,' she says with a laugh, a girlish giggle. 'Everyone else does.'

*

Jessica sits at the table and stares at her plate.

'So what grade are you in?' Carrie leans over and tries to engage Jessica.

'Seventh,' Jessica mutters, not looking up from her food.

'Oh I remember seventh grade,' Carrie says, and Richard shoots her an encouraging yet sympathetic look from across the table. 'I had a terrible time in seventh grade. Lots of bullying and there was a dreadful girl called Rona Fieldstone who made my life a misery.' There's a pause. 'Is it still tough in seventh grade or do you like it?'

Another long silence as Jessica tries to ignore Carrie, her whole being clouded in misery.

'Jessica!' Richard says. 'Carrie is talking to you.'

Jessica shrugs, and Carrie looks at Richard helplessly.

'How are those pancakes?' Carrie tries again. 'I love the smiley face,' although this was a lie. She doesn't quite understand why a thirteen-year-old is ordering the chocolate-chip smiley-face pancakes from the children's menu, nor does she understand why she holds her father's hand throughout the entire meal, only letting go when Richard laughingly points out that he won't be able to eat the French toast without his right hand.

The day before, when Jessica had refused to go to Belucci's for lunch, Richard had watched her tantrum in the car, and honestly didn't know what to do about it. Where was his lovely, happy, smiling daughter? Who was this evil, screaming being who couldn't be consoled?

'Fine!' he'd eventually snapped, grabbing his mobile phone and stepping out of the car, slamming the door behind him.

'I'm so sorry,' he'd said to Carrie, hating that he

was disappointing her. 'We're going to have to try to reschedule. Jess is just melting down. I can't do this to the poor kid. I'll call you later.'

He'd finished the phone call and turned to see Jessica smiling brightly as she sat there, her window wide open as he said goodbye.

'I love you, Daddy,' she'd said, as he got back in the car. 'I just didn't want to have our alone time spoiled.' She'd held his hand all the way to Four Brothers, and the only thing he could feel was relief that the tantrum was over, that she was back to his lovely, happy daughter again.

Today he hasn't given her a choice. He takes her to the diner for breakfast, as he always does, and they sit in the booth they always do, but when Carrie joins them, sliding in opposite them and telling Jessica how thrilled she is to meet her, how many lovely things she's heard about her, Jessica disappears – the Jessica he has been enjoying all morning is replaced by the same truculent horror as yesterday.

Richard watches this behaviour, aghast. He is embarrassed that his daughter is being so rude, mortified that she refuses to answer a single question, helpless as he watches Carrie struggle to make conversation, only to be rebuffed again and again. But what can he do? He can't force his child to be polite, and he so wants to show her off – he wants her to show Carrie that she really is his funny, creative, sweet little girl. He wants Carrie to understand why he loves her so much.

Carrie gives up and turns to Richard. 'So how was your meeting on –'

'Daddy?' Jessica interrupts, finally looking up at Richard. 'Ellie got into trouble at school on Friday. She was caught writing a note to Lauren and Miss Brookman found it and read it to the whole school.'

'Really? That sounds embarrassing. Sweetheart, Carrie was talking. I'm sorry, Carrie, what were you saying?'

'I was just asking you about the meeting on Friday.'

'Oh I can't believe I forgot to tell you about –'

'Daddy! I don't like these pancakes. They taste weird. Here. Taste one.'

Richard leans forward and tastes her pancakes. 'They're fine, Jess. Delicious. Sorry, Carrie. So we were pitching –'

'They're gross.' Jessica spits her food onto the table.

'Jessica!' Richard reprimands her sharply. 'Pick that up right away. That's disgusting.'

'It's not disgusting.' Jessica's voice starts to rise. 'What's disgusting is you surprising me with your friend. This weekend is supposed to be about you and me. Why is she here? Why is she ruining everything?'

Carrie stands up. 'I should go,' she says gently.

'No,' Richard says firmly, 'I want you to stay.' And Jessica dissolves into a mass of heaving sobs.

Chapter Six

Daniel sits on the bench outside the Hub while Bee stocks up on newspapers, shells for the girls and funny books about Nantucket. The road is absolutely quiet, although everyone they met yesterday said they wouldn't believe how busy it would be next month once the season had truly got underway; that you would barely be able to move for tourists wandering up and down the cobbled streets; that the traffic would be terrible, old beaten-up Land Cruisers owned by the islanders replaced by Range Rovers and Escalades too big, too flash for the down-to-earth island.

On the other side of the road a dog barks from the cabin of a pick-up truck while his owner has scrambled eggs and bacon in the garden of the Even Keel, and locals wander up and down, shouting good morning as they bump into one another while buying the local paper.

It is lovely here, and Daniel is surprised at how relaxed he feels, how easy it is to be here with Bee, how, for the first time in months, he doesn't feel tangled up in knots.

They are staying at the Summer House, in a tiny little cottage covered in tangled roses that makes Daniel think of a fairy tale, the enchanted house in the middle of the magical forest.

But it isn't in a forest. It's in Sconset, across the road from the ocean where they sat last night, listening to the waves crash and talking about – what else? – how much they miss the girls.

They drove home after dinner in town and Daniel felt the familiar fear as he climbed into bed. How could they possibly not make love on a weekend away? He braced himself as he listened to Bee in the shower.

She came out in pretty, white, broderie anglaise pyjamas, and climbed into bed next to him, immediately opening up her book, and he began to relax. Perhaps she wasn't expecting anything after all.

But then, when they'd turned out the lights, just as he was drifting into sleep, Bee started tenderly stroking his thigh, and he lay with his eyes closed for a while, feeling her fingers circle him gently. He was so relaxed, and it felt really quite good, and so when she snuggled into him he nuzzled her back, and they ended up kissing, then one thing led to another … and when they had finished Bee lay her head on his chest and smiled.

She knew this weekend was exactly what they needed.

*

Daff parks her BMW in the driveway and taps her way up the garden path to the front door, her file in one hand, mobile phone in the other.

'Daff!' The front door is flung open and a short blonde woman with a small child attached to her right leg extends her arms to give Daff a hug.

'You look wonderful!' Daff says, and it is true. She has not seen this woman, Karen, since she sold her this house – one of her first big sales – and now she is returning to value it as Karen is unexpectedly pregnant with her third child, and they need something bigger.

'And who's this?' Daff crouches down to say hello to the small person. 'Oh my goodness!' She looks up at Karen. 'I haven't seen Jack since he was a baby. Look how big you are!'

She has careful notes about all her clients, their children's names, ages, where they are in school, their hobbies, interests, where they go on vacation. She has developed a reputation, in a very short time, for being one of the nicest realtors to deal with – always honest, a hard worker, known as being someone who can close a deal and, more importantly, someone everyone likes being around. Most of her clients go on to become friends, and Karen is one of the few that Daff doesn't see regularly, only because Karen is so busy with her children, her PTA work and her charities.

'I can't believe what you've done!' Daff says, following Karen into the kitchen. 'It's beautiful.'

'I can't wait to show you. The addition is wonderful and I love this house more than anything, but it's still not going to be big enough when the baby comes.'

They have coffee then do the tour, Daff exclaiming over the new master bedroom suite, the walk-in closets, the beautiful sun room with floor-to-ceiling French doors, which used to be a rickety and rather dirty screened-in porch.

The cherry kitchen, always dark and depressing, has been replaced with white wooden cabinets, black iron hardware and white marble countertops. The whole house has been beautifully decorated, and Daff pauses as she walks up the stairs, the wall being covered with family photographs.

'I love what you've done here.' Daff smiles as she looks at the family pictures, remembering how she once had a picture wall of happy family snaps – until the marriage split-up, when she had to take down all the photos of Richard. And knowing that it would pain Jess immeasurably to see just the pictures of her father removed, she proceeded to take down all of them, putting up a large mirror instead, and placing the photos carefully in a box in the garage.

'Where's this?' She points to a picture of the family sitting on a deck at twilight, the ocean behind them. 'It's beautiful.'

'That's Nantucket. We go there every summer. Isn't it wonderful?'

'I've never been, but this looks truly gorgeous. Do you have a house there?'

Karen laughs. 'Years and years ago my parents were looking to buy, and back then, for a couple of hundred thousand, you could have bought something wonderful on the ocean, but they decided it was too expensive. Now we're all kicking ourselves because no one can afford it any more, but we rent there every summer.'

'The same house?'

'Never. Some years we've had wonderful houses, and others we've had horrors, but the island is still wonderful and when you're outside all the time it doesn't make much difference.'

'I'd love to go,' Daff says. 'Nantucket is one of those places people always tell me I would love.'

'Oh but it's true,' Karen says. 'You really would.'

'Maybe I'll take Jess there sometime,' Daff says. 'Although right now I'm public enemy number one. I'm lucky if she even comes to the diner with me, never mind Nantucket.'

'I think there's something magical about the island.' Karen smiles gently. 'Amazing things happen there. It's where I met my husband, for starters.'

'Well, the very last thing I need is another husband.' Daff laughs. 'Perhaps I won't be going there after all.'

*

Carrie pours herself a glass of wine as she gets dinner ready, still feeling jarred by the events of the weekend. She has always considered herself someone who loves children. She has nieces and nephews, and is adored by them, and although she has no children of her own, she has always assumed that if the man she would eventually end up with had children, it would be nothing but a blessing.

And Richard might very well be that one. At thirty-seven Carrie has had her fair share of suitors, but none of them has ever been right, has ever been the man she feels she ought to settle down with. A successful journalist, she is forever meeting people, forever going out on dates, but it wasn't until she met Richard that she started to think she might be happy settling down, could see herself with someone for the rest of her life.

So early to say that, she chides herself, when those fantasies creep in, but she has never been one of those girls who spend their life looking for Mr Right, and she has assumed that it is quite possible she will never get married, which is absolutely fine.

And yet after two months she realizes she adores Richard. And it is more than just adoring him; she knows that they make a good team. The fact that he's already been married is also a good thing, in her book. He has told her all about his affair with Nancy, and although infidelity is not something she is remotely comfortable with, Richard has been honest about the reasons why it happened, honest about his regret and remorse, and honest about why he had allowed himself to fall in love with someone else when he was married.

'It doesn't make it right,' he explained to her, 'but I understand now that as wonderful as Daff was, is, she and I were not the right match, and I feel as if Nancy was the catalyst to make me understand that.'

Carrie likes that he only has good things to say about Daff. She doesn't feel threatened by Daff in the slightest, nor concerned by his closeness to his daughter. She had been so looking forward to meeting her.

Had imagined them becoming close friends – shopping together, cooking together, an instant family.

Nothing had prepared her for Jess, for the pain she is so obviously in, for the attachment to her father and the jealousy that came with it. Her anger, her hurt, was so incredibly jarring to Carrie that after Richard dropped her home, after that miserable hour at the diner, Carrie seriously started to question whether they had a future after all.

Richard came straight over after he dropped Jessica off, and they talked. He talked about his guilt, his horror at seeing her behave like that, his need to give Jessica what she needed, his desire to be present for her, to be a proper father, not to be like one of those fathers who just disappear after the divorce.

And Carrie felt her heart melt. This was, after all, one of the reasons that she was falling in love with him. Because he wasn't the type to run away, because he was good, because he wanted to look after his daughter.

'She just needs time,' he said eventually. 'Think about it. She's been used to her mother and I being together, then her whole world fell apart when we divorced, and this is the first time I've introduced her to someone else. You have to understand how difficult this must be for her.'

'I do understand,' Carrie said. 'I do. It's just . . . it was just so upsetting to me, and understanding it doesn't prevent me from feeling hurt. And shocked.'

'I know,' Richard murmured, standing up and

putting his arms around her, pulling her close. 'I know how shocking it was. Trust me, I was shocked too. I've never seen her behave like that. I'm going to talk to her, but I need you to be your kind, loving self. Okay?' And he pulled back and looked into her eyes.

Oh shit, Carrie thought to herself. This journey may well be hell, but I'm in too deep and there's no going back. Not now. Not now that I love this man.

*

'These may be the best banana oatmeal pancakes I've ever had in my life,' Daniel says, looking down with horror at his expanding stomach as the waitress refills his coffee cup in the Sconset Café.

'Why is it we always eat so much more on vacation?' Bee laughs, reaching over the table to squeeze Daniel's hand, so happy they finally made love, so happy that she feels at last, after such a long time, that she has a shot at getting her husband back.

They pay the bill, then walk outside, stopping at the tiny realtor next to the café while Bee puts her sunglasses on and squints at a small iron table in the courtyard, stacked high with papers weighted down with large stones.

'Oh look!' she says. 'They leave their listings on the table! Isn't that clever?'

'What, you mean if we happen to have a few extra million lying around and decided, on a whim, to buy a cottage?'

'But we have to look,' Bee says, taking his hand and

pulling him through the gate. 'Come on, you know you want to.'

Twenty minutes later they are sitting inside, with the realtor, looking at pages of rentals on the island.

'Can we go and see it?' Bee turns breathlessly to Daniel. 'Doesn't it look perfect for us?'

And looking at the little cottage on the shores of Lake Quidnet, Daniel has to admit it does look like a gorgeous proposition, and hell, it's not buying, it's just a summer rental, and if Bee and the girls were here for a few weeks he could fly back and forth, and maybe a little bit of space would do them some good.

'Okay,' he says. 'But you know if we took a summer rental I couldn't spend the whole holiday out here.'

'I know, I know, but the girls would love it here and you could come every weekend, couldn't you?'

'I'm sure I could,' Daniel says.

'Will you phone and see if we could come now?' Bee asks, and the realtor picks up the phone.

Chapter Seven

Aisling had given Michael a huge hug when they split up, and although he felt empty for a little while once she had gone, he knows from many, many past experiences that they will probably remain friends, at least until she moves on to a new boyfriend, after which time she will disappear out of his life, reappearing if and when she splits up with the next one.

They may or may not then end up sleeping together again, but it will be understood by both of them that it is merely physical, and there will be no chance of either of them falling for the other, and the cycle will continue.

At forty-two Michael has to admit he rather likes his life. His closest friends have been friends for years, and although most of them are now married with kids, and he doesn't get to see them nearly as often as he would like, when they do get together it is always life-affirming, and he counts himself lucky to be surrounded by good people.

He likes his job, is lucky to have his apartment, and enjoys Manhattan far more than he ever expected to. True, he misses being able to get out of the city every weekend in the summer – his salary can't quite manage the Hamptons – and when he talks to his mother he misses Nantucket hugely, but all in all he has to say his life is a good one.

None of his friends can understand how or why he is still single, and people are forever trying to fix him up on dates, but although there are times when he thinks it would be nice to have a significant other, he has never felt as though he has missed something.

After all, his father died when he was only six, and he was raised by a single mother who may have had numerous flings but never had a serious relationship that he was aware of. How could Michael possibly know what he is missing when he has never had it, nor borne witness to it, in the first place?

'Are you all right, darling?' Nan can tell, within the first few seconds, that something is up.

'I'm fine,' Michael says and sighs. 'Aisling and I are over.'

'Oh love. Already?'

'Well, she clearly wasn't the One.'

'Don't worry, Mikey,' she says, reverting to his childhood nickname. 'One of these days you will find someone who is perfect for you and all the pieces will fall into place. You'll see.'

Michael smiles. 'I'm not worried, Mom,' he says. 'I just feel, you know, a little sad. Just the constant disappointment of realizing that the person you are getting to know is not the person you hope they'll be.'

'And that's fine,' Nan says. 'It's all part of life's rich experience. Why don't you come and see me? Spend a few days on the island? That would make you feel better.'

'Maybe I will,' Michael says non-committally. 'Work is tough right now, but let me see if I can get some time off.'

'Tough? How can it be tough? It's approaching summer, aren't all those rich clients of yours off on vacation? This must be your quietest time, surely?'

'Unfortunately there's never a quiet time here, but I will try, Mom. Promise.'

'What are you doing tonight?' Jordana comes into the workroom, her eyes sparkling.

'Why?'

'That new jewellery store on Sixty-fourth is opening and they're having a party. I thought we could go and check out the competition.'

'You want me to go with you?' Michael is surprised. Despite working together all these years, despite numerous occasions when they have socialized together, it has rarely been just the two of them, and there has been an energy of late, a charge in the atmosphere, a tension that is not entirely comfortable.

'Would you? Jackson's staying in Long Island tonight and I don't want to go by myself. Plus it would be helpful to have my jeweller there in case there's anything interesting our clients might like. I need your expert eye.'

'Oh it's my expert eye you're interested in now, is it?' Michael raises an eyebrow, then looks quickly back at the loop in his hand. He didn't mean it to come out like that, like a flirtatious question. Good Lord, no. He doesn't know where to look.

Jordana steps back in surprise, then smiles at his embarrassment. How unexpected. Michael flirting with her. How ... sweet.

'That and your company,' she says gently, and he looks up with relief.

'What time?'

'It's six o'clock. Shall we go as soon as we shut up shop?'

'Sure thing.'

And as she walks back upstairs he can't help but wonder why it is that this suddenly feels like a date.

'Here.' Michael comes back from chasing a waiter through the crush, holding two glasses of pink champagne high above his head.

'Cheers!' Jordana grins at him then looks around. 'There are an awful lot of people here.'

'Only because of the free food and drink.' Michael smiles.

'So what do you think of their stuff?'

Michael shrugs. 'A little ordinary, although I like the insect collection.'

'You do? I always find insects a little creepy.'

'Depends what they are. The diamond tarantula isn't quite my thing.'

'I'm glad to hear it.' Jordana smiles.

'But I love the ladybird and the emerald dragonfly.'

'Could you do something like that?'

'Of course, but actually I'd love to do fish.'

'Fish?'

'Yes, fish.' Michael grins. 'I grew up on Nantucket, remember? I spent my childhood out on our little Boston Whaler catching fish.'

'I know you've probably already told me this a million times over the years, but tell me again how you ended up a jeweller? It sounds like you would have been happier being a fisherman.' She has known Michael so long, but realizes she has never paid him much attention before. All of a sudden, she is seeing him in a different light, is interested in what he has to say.

'I've been asking myself that question for years. My mom had wonderful jewellery she inherited from my grandmother, and I was always fascinated by the stones.'

'So . . . fish. Do you think it would sell?'

'I don't know, but I'd love to make something and see what people think.'

'You know, I think that's a really interesting idea. Let me talk to Jackson and see what he thinks, but I like it. I see how it could work.' Jordana drains the rest of her glass as Michael watches in surprise, then grabs another couple of glasses from a passing waiter. 'Oh don't be so stuffy,' she says. 'We're here so we may as well enjoy ourselves.'

Michael watches her, catches her eye for just a few seconds too long, and quickly looks away. He isn't planning on doing anything. Jordana is his boss. And she's married. Even if he were into married women, which he isn't, she wouldn't be his type. So why is there suddenly a frisson between them? These glances that go on a split second too long. Secret smiles into her glass. Her giggling and leaning into him.

Michael likes her. Has always liked her. Just not in that way, and how could he possibly entertain these thoughts, how could he possibly even think about ... that ... with his boss? Michael shifts guiltily and tries to focus on something else, moves away when she leans in the next time and places a hand on his arm. He tries to act as if their relationship is the same as it has always been: friendly, professional, cool.

But she's lonely, and he's lonely, and there are just the two of them, or at least that's how it feels, and there's so much champagne, and they're laughing at the silliest things, and he walks her back to her apartment a few hours later and she asks him to see her upstairs in the elevator, and he becomes acutely aware, standing in the elevator, of every breath, every muscle, every fibre in her being, and when the doors open they turn to one another and, truly without knowing how it happens, Michael finds himself kissing her.

*

Michael wakes up, disoriented. The sheets feel too soft to be his, the room is too dark, and turning his head, feeling the dull ache of a hangover, he sees a mass of dark blonde hair on the other side of the king-sized bed.

It takes him a few seconds, and then he sits up with a start. Fuck. Jordana. She is still asleep, and he reaches over quietly and picks up his watch. Almost 6 a.m. He could sneak out of here, get out before she wakes up, go home and have a shower, wash the guilt and unease away.

What was he thinking? He pads out of bed and into a bathroom, closing the door softly so he can pee in private. Oh shit. Jordana. His boss. A married woman. Married to his other boss. Not good news. Not good at all.

So what was he thinking? He wasn't. He had had too much to drink and although he'd always thought Jordana was attractive and pleasant, and hell, okay, a little sexy, he'd never thought of anything else.

But Michael had always been an expert at rescuing women. If there was a call for a knight in shining armour, Michael would be the one knocking at the door. If there was a woman in distress, Michael would leap in to make it all better. His heart was too big, his mother always said, but he liked that he was able to help, to make a difference. Which was probably how he'd ended up in this mess. Jordana had seemed so tough when he had started working for them all those years ago, but recently he'd seen another side to her, he'd seen her as lonely, as sad, and it had resonated with him.

He tiptoes back into the bedroom and goes flying over a high-heeled shoe, kicked off in abandon last night as they collapsed onto the bed, frantically pulling off one another's clothes. 'Shit.'

As he lands with a thump on the floor, Jordana sits straight up in bed.

'Ja— Oh.' She was about to say her husband's name, catching herself just in time as she sees Michael. 'Hi.'

'Hi.' Michael stands awkwardly, not sure what to do, wishing he hadn't fallen into such a deep drunken sleep, wishing he had had the foresight to get out of here long before Jordana woke up.

'How are you?' she says. 'Did you sleep?'

'I slept like a log. You?'

'Me too. The champagne, I imagine. Are you ... okay?'

'Let me get dressed,' Michael says, vulnerable suddenly in his nakedness. 'Let's get some coffee and we'll talk.'

Inside the café Michael orders two cappuccinos and, as an afterthought, a couple of almond croissants. He leans against the counter while he waits, and turns to see Jordana sitting at the table. It still feels surreal. He hasn't a clue what to say to her. He knows this can't be repeated, that there are many sins you are never to commit, and sleeping with the boss is the primary one.

Not to mention that Jackson would kill him. And he likes Jackson, has always liked Jackson. What the hell is he doing?

'We can't ...' They both start speaking at the same time, and laugh awkwardly.

'This is wrong,' Michael says finally. Gently.

'I know.' Jordana's smile is rueful. 'Wonderful. But wrong.'

'Have you ever . . . ?'

'Done this before?'

Michael nods and Jordana shakes her head. 'I can't believe I've done it now. I'm not the type to be unfaithful.'

'Do you think it counts if it was just a mistake, one night that will never be repeated?'

'I'm hoping it doesn't.' Jordana sighs, and takes a bite of her croissant. 'You're so lovely, Michael. I'm sorry this is so awkward, but thank you for making me feel so special last night.'

'You're lovely too,' Michael says, and he stretches across the table, takes her hand and squeezes it, looking her in the eye. 'I know things are difficult with Jackson now, but, even though I'm not the answer, you'll find your way through it. I know you will.'

'I know,' Jordana says. 'I'm not sure how, but I'm sure you're right.'

Jordana knocks on the door of the workroom and comes in with a smile. 'Mrs Silverstein just came in. She said she didn't have time to see you today but she'll pop in tomorrow to thank you personally. She adores the ring, said to tell you you're a genius.'

'The lady obviously has impeccable taste.' Michael grins at Jordana, relieved that there is no tension from last night, that they truly are able to be grown-up about this, to put it behind them and carry on as if nothing ever happened. 'What do you think of this?' Michael beckons her over and Jordana looks down to see that he is already working on a sketch of a fish pendant.

'I love it,' she says, delighted, tracing the outline of the fish. 'I love the gills in – what are they, yellow diamonds?'

'I thought yellow sapphires. I want these to be fun, a mix of diamond and semi-precious, but something that might appeal to a younger audience.'

'It's beautiful,' Jordana murmurs, and Michael turns his head to smile at her and finds himself looking at the curve of her breast through her unbuttoned shirt, and he feels a rush of blood to his head, and the world stops, yet again, and this time, when Jordana leans down and kisses him, it feels like the most natural thing in the world.

'I'm sorry,' he gasps, feeling as though he is swimming up for air.

'I'm sorry too,' she says, stepping back and adjusting her shirt, running her fingers through her hair and wiping off the smudges of lipstick around her mouth.

'Oh fuck,' he groans, wanting nothing more than to sweep everything off the worktable, throw her on it and drive himself inside her.

'This isn't a one-night stand, is it?' Jordana says slowly, and Michael sinks his head in his hands before looking up at her.

'What are you doing tonight?'

'I was going to Manhasset,' she says. 'But I can get out of it.' There's a long pause. 'If you want me to.'

Michael looks at her, helpless. 'Yes,' he says finally. 'I want you to.'

For someone who has always been a terrible liar, Jordana is finding it surprisingly natural to lie to her husband about where she is and who she is with. She is discovering that if she tells him some of the truth, she will not flush and look away, and he will not question her.

Under different circumstances, she would never have an affair, but this doesn't feel like an affair. For starters, this is someone she knows, someone who has always, until very recently, felt like a brother to her. Twenty years, she has known Michael. In the beginning, she will admit to having had a huge crush on him. Jackson even used to tease her about it, but he was never really threatened, never worried that Jordana would actually do anything, and Michael, despite how attractive women found him, never posed a real threat, was too nice a guy, too clever to ever have an affair with the boss.

And because Jordana is not the type to have an affair, to weave a tissue of lies to prevent her husband suspecting anything, because she is not the type to do all of the things she suddenly finds herself doing, she starts to think that perhaps this is different.

Perhaps this is not just an affair. Perhaps Michael – as unlikely as she ever would have found this up until a few days ago – perhaps Michael is The One, perhaps she made a terrible twenty-year mistake with Jackson, and God has made this happen because Michael is the one who listens to her, who understands her.

Michael is the one she is supposed to be with.

*

Dr Posner leans back in his chair and steeples his fingers together, peering over the top at Daniel, who is shifting uncomfortably in the corner of the sofa, and he waits.

The seconds become minutes, and still Daniel doesn't say anything.

'Daniel?' Dr Posner starts, gently. 'You wanted to see me alone?'

Daniel nods, looking miserable.

'Is there something you want to talk to me about?'

He nods again, his eyes flickering up to meet Dr Posner's before he looks away.

'I think . . .' Daniel starts, his voice almost a whisper before he stops and sighs. 'There's something I haven't ever been able to talk about . . .'

Dr Posner waits.

'Oh God.' Daniel's voice is a moan, his pain and confusion evident, and Dr Posner knows what Daniel is about to say, has suspected it from the first.

Daniel closes his eyes, unable to look at Dr Posner, his guilt and shame too much to say the words while looking someone in the eye.

And his voice, when it emerges, is broken and hoarse.

'I think I might be gay.'

*

It is something Daniel has always known. His big secret. The one he has spent his life running from. He has spent his life trying to pretend that it is not the case, that he can be what he thinks of as 'normal', that he can be the son, the husband, the father that everyone expects him to be.

He has known since he was a boy, even before his teenage years, those years when he pretended to be interested in girls even though alone, at night, the fantasies that aroused him most always featured boys and, more specifically, his best friend at school.

He would lie there, trying to push the fantasies aside, terrified of being different, terrified of anyone finding out, trying to convince himself that he was interested in girls, that as long as he had a girlfriend, stayed around women, he would be like all the other boys, he would be normal.

And he loved women. Surely that must mean something, he would tell himself. He had always been much more comfortable with women so surely he must be straight, like everyone else, even if he never developed a fascination with breasts the way the other boys did, even if the girls he dated were, well, boyish.

Then, at college, he remembers trying to date a girl who didn't seem to know they were dating. The night he first attempted to kiss her she had pulled back in surprise.

'But I thought you were gay,' she said, and he had recoiled in horror.

'Why?' he demanded. 'Why would you think that?'

'I just assumed,' she said, and she never gave him the reasons.

He built himself up. If he looked masculine, macho, there would be no doubt, for he assumed she had thought he was gay because he was skinny.

He made sure he always had girlfriends. Lovers. Women around him all the time. Long-term relationships. Being with a woman meant he didn't have to think about it, didn't have to think about the hard bodies that he felt so drawn to in the gym, the men who occasionally gave him searching looks, the men he tried to ignore.

Until Steve.

Friends for years, they had gone to Amagansett the summer he met Bee, and the night before they met Bee, he and Steve had got drunk together, and, despite thinking about every detail, every second of that night for years, despite thinking of it still, he is not sure how it happened, but he and Steve ended up sleeping together.

What he remembers most about that night is how every bone and every fibre of his body felt as if it was on fire. *This* is what I've been missing, he remembers thinking. *This* is what it feels like to be turned on. *This* is what I've been waiting for my entire life.

And it didn't feel unnatural, or strange, or wrong. It felt like he had come home. It felt like the most wonderful, thrilling, incredible night of his life.

In the morning they could barely look at each other, and when they did Daniel found himself announcing he wasn't gay, and Steve agreed. They said it wouldn't happen again.

Daniel noticed Bee later that day. A woman. Safety. Bee meant not having to travel down a path Daniel wasn't ready to travel down. Bee meant security. She meant not having to think about his night with Steve, what it really meant, not having to shock his parents, tell his friends, live a life that Daniel didn't want.

Because he didn't want to be gay, and he thought if he didn't want to enough, then he wouldn't be.

For years it was easy to keep running. At night he would replay that one night with Steve, and the temptation to find it again was sometimes overwhelming. On an overnight trip in Boston to inspect a building the company was thinking of buying, he walked past a gay bar with a few men standing outside, eyeing him up and down, giving him that look that he doesn't know, but he knows . . . oh how he knows.

In many ways it would be so easy to go inside, he thought, to be led into a back room, to have a nameless, faceless encounter that might put some of these fantasies to rest, might allow him to put it behind him. No one would know, no one would be hurt. But he's married now, he has his beautiful girls, and if he started down that path there is a part of him that knows there would be no going back.

Secrets become harder to keep the older you get. The things you think you can suppress, those idiosyncrasies and fantasies you hope no one will ever discover, become harder and harder to hide as the years advance.

Partly it is maturity – the fear of discovery grows smaller, less significant, for you learn that none of us is perfect, that human nature is flawed, that life twists and turns in all sorts of unexpected ways and it is okay to end up in a different place to where you expected.

In Daniel's case the secret is like a tumour, growing larger and firmer deep inside him, refusing to go away by itself, refusing to lie dormant, metastasizing last month when he got a phone call from Steve. Steve, whom he hasn't seen since his wedding day. Steve, whom he has tried very hard to forget.

'I'm in your neck of the woods.' Steve's voice was so familiar, but different. 'It's been so long but I thought I'd look you up.'

'It has been years.' Daniel laughed. 'How great to hear from you. How've you been?'

'Life's been good,' Steve said. 'So how about it? Drinks? Dinner? I'd love to see Bee and I hear you've got two beautiful girls.'

Steve came for dinner. Bee made loin of pork stuffed with apricots and prosciutto, and Steve brought two bottles of Pinot Noir.

As soon as he walked in, Daniel knew. Steve hadn't run with fear from the life that had been calling him for years, Steve hadn't pretended to be someone he wasn't. Steve had struggled with it, and then had given in.

'These are our dogs –' he passed photos around as they sat at the table, the girls having gone off to bed –

'Mimi and Bobo.' Small Westies sat on the doorstep of a beautiful colonial house. 'And this is Richard.' An older, bearded man, smiling on the deck of a boat. 'My partner,' he added, although he didn't need to.

'Not husband?' Bee rescued Daniel from his crippling awkwardness, his heart pounding fast, colour rising to his cheeks.

'Not legal in our state, sadly,' Steve said. 'But one day we will. We've been together almost ten years. The love of my life.' And he looked up and caught Daniel's eye, and this time Daniel felt shame for a different reason. He felt shame for not being brave enough to do what Steve had done, and envy – oh God, so much envy for Steve having the life that all of a sudden Daniel realized he had always wanted.

They went out after dinner for a drink at the bar at Tavern on Main. Daniel recalled seeing *Brokeback Mountain*, looking longingly at the characters played by Jake Gyllenhaal and Heath Ledger embracing furiously at their reunion, and he parked the car on Main Street hoping that that might happen for him, that Steve would grab him and take him into an alley.

Brokeback Mountain. He had seen it with Bee, then seen it by himself. Six times. He had sought out gay films, gay literature, programmes on television with a gay bent, glazing over at the love scenes, trying to reassure himself that he was turned on just because it was sex, not because it involved two men.

Perhaps he was bisexual, he had started to think, but then he would lie in bed at home and watch Bee, so feminine and womanly, her breasts so full, her secrets and wetness so utterly repellent to him that he almost shuddered at the thought of her.

'I am lucky,' Steve said, nursing a beer as they sat at a quiet corner table. 'Lucky because you changed my life, you made me see that I wasn't being honest, and I couldn't carry on living a lie. I have meant to thank you many, many times, but it has been so many years, and I guess life just got in the way. So how are you? How has life been for you?'

With hindsight it would have been so easy for Daniel to open the floodgates, to let it all come pouring out, and who better to talk to than Steve? But he found he couldn't, couldn't admit that he was living the very lie Steve was talking about, had lived it for years, had almost, *almost* accepted it, until Steve had phoned out of the blue, had turned up to show him what his life could have been had he been brave enough to embrace his true self.

'I'm great,' he lied that night. 'Couldn't be better. I adore my girls, and seem to be living the American Dream.'

Steve stared at him hard, and they left after that beer.

'You take care,' Steve said. 'Look after yourself.'

And although Daniel hadn't confessed, it was seeing Steve again, seeing how comfortable he was in his skin, that made it impossible for him to suppress those feelings any more.

*

He loves Bee, but can't love her in the way she needs. He has always known that, but has thought that what they have is enough. He has assumed that if he stays, and he is going to stay, has no choice but to stay, they would make it work. And then there are the girls. He doesn't want to be anything other than a full-time, present father. He is terrified of what might happen should they get divorced, terrified that Bee might turn into one of those crazy women who poison their children against the father.

How can he possibly tell her why he is leaving? How can he get those words out, tell her that he is gay? Yet sitting here in Dr Posner's office, saying those words out loud to someone else, it is as if a cloud has lifted, a cloud that has been sitting on him his whole life, and he knows now, without a doubt, that there is no going back.

Daniel has never felt he had any other choice, but suddenly, since seeing Steve, he has realized that there might be another option after all. That simply accepting the truth, which had always seemed so terrifying, so utterly overwhelming to him, may be all he has to do if he ever wants to know what it is to be Steve.

What it is to be happy.

Chapter Eight

'Nan, do you know you have messages?' Sarah hauls the large paper bags in and puts them on the kitchen table, then she starts to unpack the groceries.

'Oh I know, darling.' Nan picks up a pile of coupons from the grocery store, walks over to the answering machine and lays the coupons on top of the blinking red light. 'It's terribly annoying seeing that thing flashing all day. I keep putting papers on top of it and someone –' she shoots a look at Sarah – 'keeps taking them off.'

'Well, I'm sorry,' Sarah says, and laughs, 'but generally red blinking lights mean there are messages, which means someone's trying to get hold of you. Don't you want to listen? What if it's important?'

'It's Andrew Moseley.' Nan sighs. 'He wants to talk to me about money, and while I think he's absolutely charming, I really don't want to talk to him.'

Sarah stops unpacking and watches Nan light a cigarette, worry in her eyes.

'What are you going to do?' she asks gently. 'I know things are tough. Will you have to . . .'

Nan looks up sharply. 'Sell Windermere? Absolutely not. I don't need much so I was thinking perhaps I ought to sell some of the furniture, some of the things in the house that I really don't need.'

Sarah looks dubious.

'Some of this stuff is wonderful, the antiques dealers would have a field day. And think of all those tourists and people spending twelve and a half million dollars on houses – don't you think they need furniture? And this isn't that reproduction stuff you find at the furniture stores, this is the real McCoy – people will pay a fortune for this.' Nan gets animated as she gestures around at an antique Welsh dresser, the oak kitchen table.

'Right,' Sarah says, trying to sound upbeat, and not wanting to point out that almost every piece of furniture in the house has coffee-cup rings, cigarette burns, is in a condition that no antiques dealer would be the slightest bit interested in.

'And then there's my mother-in-law's jewellery collection. She collected paste earrings for years, and I have them all in boxes in the attic.'

'Okay.' Sarah recalls opening the boxes once upon a time and seeing what she thought was a load of junk. But she's not a jewellery expert, and who knows what people will pay. 'So you think this would be enough?'

'For the time being,' Nan says, enthusiastic now, excited at the prospect of a project. 'And once it's over we can figure out what to do next. Who knows, maybe I'll get a job.'

'Folding T-shirts at Murray's Toggery?' Sarah grins.

'You never know.' Nan winks. 'Stranger things have happened. Why don't we start pricing some of the furniture? Let's see what we can actually get rid of.'

* * *

By the end of the afternoon, Sarah's clipboard is filled with scribbles and notes, rough sketches of the furniture Nan has deemed suitable for selling.

'Are you *sure* you don't need your bed?' Sarah asks, somewhat dubiously.

'I'll keep the mattress,' Nan says firmly. 'But the damn thing's too high for me anyway and I've never liked how ornate it is. That was Everett's choice, not mine.'

'And the chest of drawers?'

'No. I feel like it's time to spring-clean. Clear out all the cobwebs, start afresh. I feel lighter already just thinking about it. So tell me, my dear, how much does all this come to?'

Sarah looks down at her clipboard, and clears her throat. 'Well, if everything is worth what you think it's worth, we should make around two hundred and fifty thousand from this sale.' She wants to laugh, the figure should be laughable, except it isn't funny. It's just completely and utterly mad.

Nan has spent the afternoon pulling figures out of thin air. 'This is beautiful,' she'd gesture at some ugly little stool. 'People pay a fortune for these on eBay so let's price this at five thousand dollars.'

Five thousand dollars! She'd be lucky if anyone paid five, Sarah thought.

'Are you *quite* sure you want to get rid of all your things?' Sarah asks again.

'I'm quite sure I need the money. And it will be fun! You and I can advertise it this week, and just imagine, we'll fill the house with billionaires snapping up our furniture. Honestly, Sarah, I know you're worried, but this is good stuff, and they won't find anything like this anywhere else.'

Sarah casts a glance over at the fraying tapestry chair in the corner that has one broken leg and is falling apart. Nan priced it at six thousand dollars. And then there are the clothes. Moth-eaten dresses from the sixties, and fur coats that have developed alopecia while reclining in a hot attic over the years – bald spots all over them, but Nan believes there is a thriving market for vintage clothes, and as she said to Sarah, modelling a particularly skimpy fox-fur jacket, 'What woman doesn't feel beautiful in a real fur?'

Well, she thinks, Nan's certainly right about them not finding anything at this price anywhere else.

She takes a deep breath and follows Nan downstairs to draft the wording for the ad, wishing that Nan hadn't cloistered herself away quite so much, for why else would she be pricing things so ridiculously? If she had any idea how the real world worked, she wouldn't dream of asking what she's asking, and good reproductions of most of this furniture can be found at every Pottery Barn in the country.

WONDERFUL ESTATE SALE IN FAMOUS SCONSET HOME!

Once-in-a-lifetime opportunity! Beautiful antiques – beds, hutches, dining table – Chippendale-era, stunning collection 1920s jewellery, vintage clothes and genuine fur coats!

Everything must go!

Open House, Saturday 30 June, 9 a.m.–5 p.m., Sunday 1 July, 10 a.m.–4 p.m.

No early birds please!

Nan has made a special effort for the sale. Resplendent in one of her vintage dresses, her hair is pulled back in a chignon, her lipstick is perfect, and she truly does look like the lady of the manor.

Sarah, on the other hand, is exhausted. She doesn't want Nan to be humiliated, but she can't see any other outcome. She has spent the last few days cleaning furiously, attempting to patch up the furniture to make it presentable, trying to justify the absurdly large price tags Nan has insisted on placing on everything.

Nan has set up a folding table by the front door. At the back of the hallway is a large chestnut table ($25,000) on which are two enormous glass decanters filled with lemonade, a platter of chocolate chip cookies in front to entice the buyers.

The first people arrive at 8.45, and Nan flings open the front door and invites them in.

'We just bought a home in town,' says the wife, enthusiastically entering the hallway. 'And we're desperate for furniture. We've found fabulous pieces in estate sales at home in Boston, so we can't wait to see what you've got.'

'Oh how wonderful.' Nan welcomes them in, and proceeds to walk them around the house, not seeing how their faces fall as they see the condition of the furniture, nor their shock at the prices.

'I think she's crazy,' Sarah hears the wife whisper to the husband at one point when Nan, playing gracious hostess, excuses herself to personally welcome some more people who have turned up.

The house fills up, and Nan notices something curious: there are several men on their own, clearly disinterested in the sale, but interested in the house. More than once she finds someone on the widow's walk, gazing out to the ocean, or walking around the garden, winding their way through the long grass to the beach.

'Developers,' she says to Sarah and sniffs, watching one man get out a notebook and scribble something.

'You're right,' a voice says, and she turns to see Mark Stephenson, builder of the twelve-and-a-half-million-dollar house, standing in the doorway.

'Mr Stephenson,' she says, genuine warmth in her voice as she extends a hand.

'Mrs Powell,' he says, stepping over the threshold and bending down to kiss her cheek.

'Nan,' she corrects.

'Nan. Of course. I saw you were having an estate sale and couldn't resist. I'm still waiting for my invitation for drinks, you know.'

'I can offer you lemonade.' Nan gestures to the table with raised eyebrows and a smile, and Sarah watches with fascination, for while Nan is twenty years older than this man, she is clearly flirting, and Sarah suddenly sees how stunning, how irresistible, she must have been.

'I'll take it,' he says, taking her arm as they cross the room. 'And you are a clever woman. I know most of these men.' He nods hello and waves at someone walking upstairs. 'They *are* all developers and they're all checking out your house.'

'I'm not selling it, you know. Everything inside the house. Not the house.'

'You wouldn't want to sell it to any of them anyway,' Mark said. 'Even if you were interested they'd tear it down in a heartbeat and have four McMansions up before you could blink.'

'I take it you wouldn't do that sort of thing?' Nan looks at him with a smile. 'You're, what? A developer with a heart?'

'I'm an artist who fell into developing,' Mark says. 'I'd love a house like this but not to tear down. I'd love to live in a house like this.'

'An artist?' Nan gazes at him coolly. 'I knew there was more to you than met the eye. What sort of an artist?'

'I paint,' he says. 'I went to Parson many moons ago, but couldn't make a living out of it and fell into my father's business of real estate. I hate saying I'm not like all the others, but it's true, and I think it's one of the reasons why people like working with me. I'm not a shark. I live in Nantucket because I love how strict the planning and zoning regulations are, I love that the houses have to be shingle, and although I have built ridiculous houses, it's to cater to the changing market, not because I would ever want to live in a house like that. Basically,' he adds, shrugging, 'I have always believed there is more to life than money. I think that's what makes me different.'

'I'm glad you're here.' Nan leads him up the stairs to show off her house. 'You can protect me from the rest of those sharks. Now let me show you some of my furs – imagine how thrilled your wife would be with a beautiful vintage fox.' And he follows her into the master bedroom.

'Three hundred dollars? *Three hundred dollars?* Good Lord.' Nan sinks down in the chair with dismay and Sarah looks defeated. 'Don't these people have any taste? Don't they know good furniture when they see it?'

'What do you want me to do?' Sarah asks. 'Shall I take the price tags off?'

'Oh Lord, I don't know,' Nan says. 'I need to go and lie down. I'm exhausted. Let's just leave things as they are for now. Let me have a nap and let's talk later.'

At two o'clock in the morning Sarah's phone rings. She snaps on the light and grabs the phone, immediately worried, for phone calls in the middle of the night can only mean an emergency.

But this is no emergency. This is Nan, unable to sleep with excitement.

'I've got it!' she says. 'I'm going to open up my house!'

'What?' Sarah's voice is croaky.

'I'm going to rent out rooms! My furniture may not have sold but everyone loved the house, so we're going to turn it into a summer boarding house! I have five bedrooms I could rent out, and that's the solution! It may not make me a fortune but it will certainly bring in enough to live on. I'm so excited I can't sleep. Come over in the morning and we'll start planning it, but, oh Sarah, just imagine it – Windermere filled with people again. I don't know why I didn't think of this years ago!' And with a peal of laughter she disappears, leaving Sarah to roll over and go back to sleep.

*

Daff props her full-length mirror against the wall in her dressing room at just the right angle to take off around ten pounds from her reflection, and smiles in approval. She is smart but casual in dark jeans, ballet flats, a white shirt and a tan belt. The jeans are new – her closet is stuffed full of clothes that no longer fit her, fifteen pounds miraculously melting away during the divorce.

She is now a size six – she has never been a size six in her life, was always a comfortable ten – and although for a while she felt skinny and gorgeous, now she has decided she will be perfect if only she loses another ten pounds, hence the propping-up of the mirror to make her appear even skinnier.

Tonight she has a date. Her first in a while. And she is excited. She is going into the city to meet him at the Oyster Bar in Grand Central. She has seen his photo and he is handsome and sounds fun, and Lord only knows she could do with a bit of fun.

For a few months after they separated, Daff had cried herself to sleep at night with loneliness and exhaustion.

As a young single girl, right before she and Richard got together, she had been more than capable, she had thrived. She could do anything herself, from dealing with the IRS when there were problems with her tax returns, to driving to Home Depot and having them cut timber to size so she could build her own bookshelves.

Nothing had been too difficult for Daff before she was married, and yet when she was first single again, post-separation, she found she was overwhelmed by everything. She had got so used to the rhythm of being married – she looked after the house, Richard looked after the money – and when she had to do everything herself she found she had forgotten how to do it, couldn't face it.

Bills would come in and mount up in piles in the kitchen, Daff forgetting to pay on time, or not getting round to ordering new chequebooks. Her mobile phone was forever getting cut off, her gas running out, not because she didn't have the money to pay, but because she was so disorganized, so overwhelmed, that she spent her life in a constant state of inertia.

When Richard was still at home they shared tasks, and if ever anything got too difficult, or she didn't want to deal with people, Richard would step in and take over. Theirs may not have been a perfect marriage –

since the day he moved out she had begun to view their marriage in a very different light – but they had found a way of making it work.

While she was married Daff would have told you they had a great marriage, but she knows that Richard would not have looked for someone else, would not have been able to fall in love with another woman, if that had been the case. Partly she thinks they got married too young – neither of them had had enough time to sow their wild oats – and partly they had become complacent. They took one another for granted, and she can admit now that she missed affection. Intimacy. Sharing things.

She and Richard had never had the sort of relationship where they would kiss, or cuddle, or hold hands. It felt, she can see this now, more like a business relationship that worked, even sex becoming a trans-action.

What had happened to the loving, excitable, affectionate girl Daff had always been? She told herself, while she was married, that this was a real relation-ship, this was what grown-ups did, this was how she was supposed to behave, and it was only afterwards that it began to occur to her that she had simply been with the wrong man. A man she liked enormously, but a man who wasn't her true partner in any way.

Dating. The very word filled her with dread. She didn't think she would ever be ready for dating, but almost as soon as she was single, people started wanting to fix her up. Good Lord, she thought, who are all these single men supposed to be in my town, where everyone seems to be married?

Some of the married couples she and Richard had known were still friends, but many of them were not. She had always assumed, while married, that newly divorced women were a threat, which is why they always complained that they had been abandoned by their still-married friends, but now she understands that she is a threat for different reasons: if her own marriage, her marriage which appeared to be so perfect, could come apart so easily, what did it say about theirs?

The dissolution of her marriage seemed discomfiting for many, raising uncomfortable questions about their own relationships that they weren't ready to ask, so when she stopped being invited to events she would always have been invited to with Richard, she accepted it.

During those early months she had often felt lost, hadn't wanted to go anywhere, see anyone. She remembers a newly single divorcee at work saying the hidden blessing of divorce was she got to have every other weekend off from the kids, and one night a week to go out and have fun.

Fun? What does that *mean?* Daff didn't know. She would go to bed and sleep away her depression – sleeping pills prescribed by her concerned doctor knocking her out until midday.

The weekends when Jess was away were the hardest. Not easy when Jess was there, with Jess already blaming

Daff, but when she was with her father, Daff had no idea what to do with herself. She would drive over to friends' houses, the lone single woman, and the husbands tried to act as if it were normal that Daff would be there without Richard, without Jess, while their own children – many of whom had grown up with Jess, were friends with her – played in swimming pools and followed their parents' advice not to ask Daff about Jess.

She spent the entire weekend in bed a few times. Watching television, gossip shows, home-decorating shows, the food network, over and over, drifting in and out of sleep, unable to answer the phone or the doorbell.

She doesn't know when she started to feel normal again, but at some point she did, and finalizing the divorce gave her closure, enabled her to truly move on. She had heard of some people throwing 'divorce showers', celebrating when the decree nisi came through, but she felt a deep sadness on the day of her divorce, sitting in the courtroom with Richard, both of them having shared so much, having created a life, a child, both of them now feeling like strangers.

The train rumbles along the tracks as Daff buries herself in her book. She loves this journey, has started coming into the city once every couple of weeks, to see a play, go to a museum, visit friends. All the things she used to love doing before she got married, before she got buried in suburban life – being home to get Jess off the bus, PTA meetings, school plays.

Through the tunnel and into Grand Central, Daff thinks of Sam's last email to her, and smiles. She is new to this world of computer dating and is only just starting to dip a tentative toe back into the pool of potential partners. She joined match.com last month, and Sam was the first person to 'wink' at her.

They have been corresponding now for three weeks. He is in his early fifties, a little older than she would normally have gone for – Richard and she are both the same age, forty-one – but he is fit, and handsome, and funny, at least in his emails.

She is first to arrive. She looks expectantly at the men standing round the bar, hoping to recognize him, hoping he will recognize her, but there is no spark of recognition in anyone's eyes, and she takes a seat, ordering a vodka and tonic to sip until he shows up.

She feels someone looking at her and turns, catching the eye of a nice-looking man in a suit. He smiles at her and she gets up. 'Sam?' she says. He doesn't look anything like the photo, she thinks, but nice.

'No. Sorry.' He shrugs with a smile, and she sees he has a female companion.

'Oh God,' she groans quietly as she sits back down, wanting the ground to open and swallow her up.

'Daff?' He is late. Daff looks up from where she has been buried in her book the last twenty minutes, and frowns.

'Yes?' *Do I know this man?*

'Hello!' Delight is written all over his face.

'I'm sorry,' she says, confused but polite. 'Do we know each other?'

'I'm Sam!' he says, pulling out a stool and perching next to her.

But you can't be, she wants to shout. Sam is fifty-one, and handsome, and tall. You are eighty-five and look not unlike my grandfather.

'Well, you *are* gorgeous.' Sam leers at her. 'You never know what to expect when you meet these women. Let me tell you, some of those pictures they post up look like supermodels, and then you meet them and they're dogs.'

Are you kidding? Daff wants to say this, but doesn't. Instead she thinks she might burst into tears.

Sam orders a vodka martini then looks her up and down, running his tongue over his lips as he grins at her, not noticing her suppressing a shudder of horror. 'We're going to have a good time tonight,' he says lasciviously, pressing a knee against hers. 'I'm a *very* energetic man.'

'I'm sorry.' She jumps up. If he had been a sweet old man she might have humoured him, but this? This is a horror that no woman should have to put up with. 'I'm actually not feeling well. I have to go.' She fumbles around in her purse and throws a twenty on the counter. 'Here,' she says. 'I'll get the drinks.' Sam looks down at the guilt money and sneers.

'You're all the same,' he starts, and without hearing whatever else he says, Daff turns and runs out.

One day I will laugh at this, she tells herself on the train going home. But right now, all she wants to do is cry.

Chapter Nine

Michael raises his hand and stands up, squeezing past Jordana to give Leo a huge bear hug, then turning to Wendy and wrapping her in his arms.

He may not see them that often, but they are among his oldest and dearest friends, and whenever they make it in to New York from their home in Woodstock he always makes sure he finds time for them.

Tonight he had plans with Jordana, but when Leo phoned and said, laughing, they were in town with no kids, Michael cancelled his plans and arranged to meet them for dinner.

Jordana is thrilled. Meeting Michael's friends – not the ones who pop into the shop from time to time, but his real friends, his old friends whose opinions he values – must mean this relationship is as important to him as it is to her.

For Jordana never expected to fall in love at the ripe old age of thirty-nine. Not to mention that she's married, and up until a few weeks ago had assumed she would stay married, to Jackson, for the rest of her life.

Michael doesn't know what this is, this ... relationship he's having with Jordana, but he does know he feels more alive than he has in years. He who has always been the passive one in relationships, who has always been chased rather than the chaser, has suddenly found himself falling head over heels for Jordana.

But love? He isn't sure. It feels too all-consuming to be love, too dangerous, too addictive, for that is exactly what she feels like – his addiction. He is living on adrenaline, the thrill of seeing her, the illicit meetings, the astonishingly fantastic, passionate sex.

He may love her, he certainly sees through the image she presents to everyone else – the glossy blonde high-lights, the tan make-up, the huge diamond studs and high heels – to the vulnerable little girl hiding behind the armour. He loves her best, and she is at her most beautiful, when she has just stepped out of the shower, her hair twisted into a ponytail, her skin naked and clean. She looks real, he tells her then, and too beautiful to cover herself up with make-up.

He would love to see her in jeans and a T-shirt, and not the jeans and T-shirts that she and her friends in Long Island wear: tight boot-legged jeans over high-heeled boots, enamel and gold chains snaking round their necks, huge gold buckles on their cowboy belts. He wants to see her in old faded Levi's, riding boots, a soft white shirt, with no make-up and no jewellery.

For, despite his obsession with her, whenever Jordana starts talking about a future together – and she is spending more and more time talking about a future together – Michael starts to worry. Not because she is pushing too far too fast – he seems to be travelling at exactly the same breakneck speed – but because, however hard he tries, he doesn't see how they could fit into one another's lives, not when she is so concerned with status, money, keeping up with the Joneses.

The way she lives is just so very different from the way he lives. He has no desire to step into her world, and although she says she is fed up with the materialism in hers, he doesn't think it would be that easy for her to leave it all behind. He doesn't think she really wants to.

Jordana lives in a 9,000-square-foot colonial McMansion in Great Neck, with an apartment on the Upper East Side. She drives a Mercedes SL (silver, convertible), shops at the best shops in Manhasset (Chanel, Hermès) where they all know her on a first-name basis, and lunches with her girlfriends at Bergdorf's at least once a week.

She has her hair coloured every four weeks at John Frieda, and had been going to Sally Hershberger for cuts long before Sally Hershberger was, well, Sally Hershberger.

She wears full jewellery every day, 8-carat diamond studs being low key for her, and casually slips on an armful of diamond tennis bracelets every morning.

Jordana and Jackson vacation at the Four Seasons in Palm Beach every Christmas, where they go with a group of their best friends, and the women sit round the pool in Juicy Couture and Tory Burch resort wear, flicking through glossy magazines as the men talk sports and business, rarely looking up from their BlackBerries.

Jordana has never wanted anything more out of life. Certainly she never thought she wanted a man who lives in a small, shabby pre-war on the Upper West Side, who rides a bike to work, who hasn't bought an item of new clothing in years – the T-shirts he throws on when he's not at work all have holes in them and fraying edges, they are faded and torn from years of washing.

But, to Jordana, there is something so fresh about him, so different from Jackson. Jackson, who, like her, grew up with nothing, is constantly insecure about how he will be judged, and he needs the McMansion, the Mercedes, the money, to prove to everyone that he is as good as they are, that he belongs in the club.

Michael doesn't seem to want to belong in any club, and he is unlike anyone Jordana has ever met. He is a man who seems utterly comfortable in his skin, who doesn't feel the need to prove himself to anyone, and when she is with him she feels a security that is new.

Like all women, Jordana is something of a chameleon, able to adapt to whoever her man wants her to be. When Jackson announced, all those years ago, that he liked blondes, she went straight out and had a full head of golden highlights. Now that Michael has admitted his penchant for the natural look, Jordana has started wearing less make-up, flatter shoes, trying to be the perfect woman for him.

But even with less make-up, flatter shoes, Jordana is still quite unlike anyone Michael has been involved with in the past, and as Leo and Wendy sit down at the table to have dinner with their old friend and his new squeeze, shaking hands with Jordana and saying how nice it is to meet her, they exchange a furtive look of quiet alarm.

*

Carrie had thought that winning Jess over would be easy, but what she is beginning to understand is that you don't win your stepchildren, or your pseudo-stepchildren, or your boyfriend's children, over once. You win them over every day. Sometimes every hour. And sometimes every minute.

There is a part of her that understands Jess. She may not have been the product of a divorce, but she had been an unhappy child, had gone through the pre-pubescent awkwardness, had longed to be thin and pretty when all around her were discovering boys and she was always left at home.

But she finds Jess's tantrums so jarring. Her parents were not confrontational – unhappiness was expressed through silence, moods, depression, not through shouting and crying, and Carrie is helpless in the face of Jess weeping and wailing, shrieking, as she does, that Carrie has ruined her life, that she hates her.

Carrie tries to ignore it, and there are times, particularly when Richard isn't around and it is just her and Jess, when Jess is gorgeous – sweet and chatty and clever – and Carrie relaxes, lets down her guard, thinks that they are finally friends, that it will all be fine.

Until Richard reappears and Jess shoves Carrie out

the way, climbs onto her father's lap, throws a tantrum to get his attention, and Carrie feels, once again, superfluous.

*

'So what do you think?' Michael and Leo are walking behind the two girls, who are attempting to bond, post-dinner, over window-shopping down Madison Avenue, even though Wendy, a yoga instructor and doula, couldn't be less interested in looking at designer shoes for several hundred dollars.

Leo sighs, then stops and looks at Michael. 'Do you want me to be honest with you?'

Michael's heart plummets. Whatever it is Leo's going to say, it's not going to be what he wants to hear, but he isn't surprised. 'Of course. You always are.'

'I think you're playing with fire. Not only because she's your boss, and she's married, which, as far as I'm concerned, is nothing short of sheer insanity, but because she's not for you.'

'You barely know her,' Michael says miserably. 'I get what you're saying about her being married and the work and stuff, those are all the issues I'm struggling with myself, but she's not who you think.'

'Look, she's great. I'm sure she's a great girl, and for someone else she's perfect. But not you,' Leo says. 'I believe that *she* believes it when she says she doesn't want the lifestyle any more, she doesn't want the jewellery and the designer clothes. I believe *she* believes it when she says she would be happy living in a farm in the country with you. But I don't believe that's true. I believe you're both having an extraordinary relationship that is incredibly intense and electric, and unsustainable. One or other of you is going to wake up very soon and realize this is not real.'

'What if we don't?'

'I don't know.' Leo shakes his head. 'But, Michael, look at her.' They watch Jordana pointing out a floor-length leather coat, trimmed with mink.

'I love that one,' they hear her say. 'I'll have to come in tomorrow.'

Leo turns to Michael and raises an eyebrow. 'You really think a girl like that is right for a guy like you?'

'I don't know,' Michael says. 'I still think she's not what she appears. There's more to her than meets the eye.'

'I don't doubt it for a second,' Leo says. 'But you asked me to be honest, and I have been. I just hope that neither of you gets hurt, that's all. It's a dangerous game you're playing. Just be careful.'

'I will,' Michael says, and when they reach the corner, all four say their goodbyes, and Michael and Jordana jump into the first yellow cab they see.

'They hate me,' Jordana says, as she settles into the back seat of the cab, on their way back to her apartment.

'They don't hate you,' Michael says, wondering how honest he should be.

'So what did Leo say?' She wants his friends' approval so badly, but she knows she didn't get it. How could she have got their approval, when she had nothing in common with them, nothing to talk about, little to contribute when the conversation moved to politics and Buddhism.

'He said he thought we came from very different worlds,' Michael says carefully.

'And? What does that mean?'

'I think he struggled with seeing us together.' Michael sighs. 'I struggle with that myself.'

'We can be together. It's not about meshing your world and my world,' Jordana says urgently. 'It's about creating a new world for the two of us, and that's something we can do. Something we *will* do.' She smiles and snuggles into his shoulder. 'Just you and me,' she says. 'Living somewhere else. Somewhere where we can start afresh.'

Jordana is convinced this is more than an affair and she is spending more and more time talking of the future, of the world they will create together. She is insistent that this must be more because that seems to be the only way she can justify it. If this were just an affair she would not be doing it . . . but this? Michael? This is true love. This is about soulmates.

Little does she realize that everyone who has an affair tries to justify it in the same way.

*

Today Richard is playing in a tennis match. He collected Jess last night and brought her back to the house. When Carrie came out of the kitchen where she had been cooking macaroni cheese – Jess's favourite – and said hello, Jess just looked at her, then shot her father an evil glare and ran upstairs to her bedroom without saying anything.

'Should I go up?' Carrie asked Richard, standing awkwardly in the hallway listening to the bedroom door slam as Jess threw herself on the bed, wailing like a four-year-old.

'No,' Richard said. 'Let's just leave her. She has to learn. You are part of my life now, and she's going to have to get used to you being here.'

After a while, as the wailing grew louder, he looked worriedly up the stairs. 'Jesus,' he said quietly. 'I don't know what to do about this. I think I should go up.'

'Don't.' Carrie lay a hand on his arm. 'I think she does this for your attention. You go up and she gets exactly what she wants. Leave her. Let her calm down by herself.'

'What if she can't?'

'She's thirteen years old,' Carrie said with a smile. 'Of course she can.' But she wasn't sure.

When no one went upstairs to check on her, Jess came stomping downstairs, collapsing on the sofa with her arms crossed, shooting evil squinty looks at Carrie, who tried to ignore her. Despite feeling almost crippled with anxiety, with wanting Richard to step in to stop this behaviour, she acted as if everything were normal, and Richard eventually took Jess outside to talk to her.

Carrie couldn't make out all the words, but weeping

and wailing soon gave way to normal conversation, and when they both came back in Richard looked exhausted, but relieved.

'I'm sorry,' Jess said, coming back in, looking at Carrie with such sad eyes that Carrie flung her arms around her and gave her a huge hug.

'It's okay,' Carrie said, stepping back to look in Jess's eyes. 'I understand. How about tomorrow, while Dad's playing tennis, you and I go shopping?'

'Really?' Jess's eyes opened wide with delight. Money was always tight at home now, and Mom never took her shopping any more, she was too busy working or she didn't have the money, and she never wanted to take Jess to the stores Jess wanted to shop at anyway, she wanted Jess to still dress like a little girl.

'I thought maybe we could go to Kool Klothes, or Claire's. Have a girls' day. What do you think?'

'I'd love to,' Jess said, so happy and so light that Carrie found it impossible to reconcile this delightful child with the screaming monster of a few minutes ago.

Maybe this is the beginning of a new leaf, she thought. Maybe a girls' day is just what they need.

'I can't help it, you know,' Jess says to Carrie as they sit in the coffee shop, Jess with a large hot chocolate with marshmallows and whipped cream, *and* a chocolate-glazed doughnut (her mother would *never* let her eat this much at the coffee shop – if she was with her mother she might get a bottle of vitamin water and a bagel, so this is much more fun). 'I hate it when I scream like that but it feels like a volcano exploding inside me and like I haven't got any choice but to let it out.'

'I understand.' Tears well up in Carrie's eyes. She feels so grateful that this child is confiding in her, and she is moved by the pain and confusion she sees in Jess, the pain and confusion she remembers so well from her own adolescence. 'I do. I think this must be incredibly hard for you.'

'And my mom doesn't understand any of it,' Jess says bitterly, taking a bite of her doughnut. 'She just shouts and screams and I hate living with her.'

Carrie smiles. 'I was a bit like that with my mom at your age. Not the shouting and screaming, we didn't shout in my house, but I didn't like my mom for a long time either. Although as I got older I realized she was just doing the best she could.'

Bond, she is thinking. Bond, but don't drop Daff in it, for Daff deserves nothing but support from Carrie, and how hard it must be to be a single mother of an angry teenage daughter.

'Are you and Dad going to get married?' Jess asks suddenly, catching Carrie off guard.

'I ... don't know. Maybe. I think it's probably too early to be talking marriage, but we're spending a lot of time together and I think right now we're quite happy and don't want to change anything.'

'But you're kind of living together, aren't you?'

'Well ... I'm spending a lot of time at your dad's place.'

'You've got stuff there now.' Jess looks straight at

Carrie, who feels her shoulders tense, preparing herself for an onslaught. 'First you just had a toothbrush but now you have clothes there. Have you moved in?'

Carrie laughs nervously. 'No, I still have my own apartment.'

Jess gazes at her coolly. 'I was thinking that I might move in with Daddy,' she says, waiting for Carrie's reaction. 'He misses me a lot and I'm his daughter. No one can look after him better than me.'

'I'm sure that's true,' Carrie says, in a falsely bright tone. 'But I'm sure Mommy would be upset.'

'Upset?' Jess snorts with derision. 'She'd be thrilled. I think she's going to talk to him about it.'

Carrie keeps smiling, but her stomach is turning. I can just about cope with this every other weekend and one night during the week, she thinks. How would I possibly cope if this were all the time?

'Can we go to Kool Klothes now?' Jess says, standing up with a bright smile. 'I can't wait to show you this blue top I saw in there last week. It's just like the one you have with the sequinned flowers. We could be twins!' And linking her arm through Carrie's, they walk out, Carrie floored once again by her mercurial behaviour.

'Hi, darling.' Daff opens the front door and Jess pushes past her and marches upstairs with carrier bags full of clothes. 'What do you have there?'

Jess ignores her and Daff turns to Richard, helpless. 'Is she in a mood?'

'No,' he says, marvelling again at how he and Daff

131

can stand here and have these polite conversations as if they were strangers who barely know one another, as if he hasn't seen her shave her bikini line in the bath, sit on the toilet for half an hour with a magazine, as if he doesn't know what she looks like just at the moment of orgasm.

'Has she been okay this weekend?'

'She was great. A little rocky when she arrived, but I think these transitions are always hard. We went shopping.' He doesn't mention Carrie, not yet. He doesn't want to rub Daff's nose in it, for he knows from Jess that Daff has no one, and he suspects she would not be ready to hear about Carrie yet.

Richard doesn't know that Jess, in one of her rare moments of treating Daff like a human being, has told her all about Carrie. In one breath she will say she hates Carrie, hates her for stealing her father, that she never gets Daddy–daughter time any more, and in the next she will say that Carrie took her for a manicure, or did something fun with her, or talk proudly about something that Carrie has done.

Her conflict is clear, and Daff is careful not to show her pain at hearing about Richard's girlfriend. It is also clear that this girlfriend is different. Daff Googled her and found a picture of her from the local paper. She looks normal. Pretty. Nice. She looks like the sort of woman Daff could see Richard with.

Although she asked for this divorce, although she was the one who asked Richard to leave, she didn't expect him to find happiness so quickly. From all accounts it won't be long before they are living together. When Jess talks about her, Daff listens and murmurs validation of whatever it is Jess is saying. 'She's so annoying,' Jess will say, and Daff will say, 'I understand it must be annoying for you at times.'

'She's taken my daddy away from me,' Jess will cry, during those times when she's overwhelmed and tearful. 'I know it's hard,' Daff will murmur, rubbing her back. 'But no one can take your daddy away, he loves you more than anything and nothing's ever going to change that.'

'So where was he at the baseball game last week?' Jess looks up at her mother. 'Where was he at the school concert? If he loved me so much why wasn't he there?'

'He has work,' Daff says, but she wonders the same thing.

How is it she is the one doing everything – she washes Jess's clothes, makes sure her homework is done on time, packs her snacks, shows up for all the school events, the plays, the class performances, the baseball games, the ballet workshops, liaises with her friends' parents, never misses a single beat – yet she is the one Jess hates most of the time?

Why is it her father, who may spend time with her every other weekend but doesn't do any of the day-to-day stuff that moves Jess through her life, doesn't appear at any of the events because he's too busy working, wouldn't know Jess's teacher if she sidled up to him at a singles bar . . . why is it he can do no wrong?

This is when she resents him. She is working so hard, doing so much, while Richard does so little, and still Jess has him on a pedestal.

Daff sighs and goes into the kitchen. Once upon a time she would have knocked on Jess's door to see if there was anything she needed, but Blue October is already pounding from her room, so Daff opens the fridge and pours herself a glass of wine.

Chapter Ten

Daniel is surviving on a mixture of fear and adrenaline. He has promised Dr Posner he will explore this further, not rock the boat just yet, wait until he and Bee are with Dr Posner to tell her, if, in fact, that is the route he chooses, but now that his secret is finally out, now that he has told someone, he wants to stop living this lie immediately, wants to be able to be who he really is.

Every night when he parks his Land Rover next to Bee's Mercedes wagon in the garage, walks in the mudroom door of their beautiful centre-hall colonial, puts his briefcase down, walks through into their huge kitchen where the girls are curled up on the sofa at one end, watching *Hannah Montana* on the HDTV flat screen that sits above the stone fireplace, he feels his heart pound, and he doesn't know how much longer he can pretend.

He is not sleeping at night. He lies awake for hours, sometimes looking at Bee, wondering how he can tell her, what words he will use, so scared of the pain he will cause her. He loves her. He just doesn't love her the way he needs to love her. But she is his partner and the thought of hurting her, causing her pain, is almost unbearable.

Bee is so strong, but he can see this destroying her.

And what about her friends? The close circle of friends Bee has found while he is at work, the people they hang out with at barbecues in the summer, meet in town for riotous dinners at Zest. Not that any of the men are necessarily his type – Daniel has always felt more comfortable with the wives – but he has tried to fit in, has done a pretty good job, he thinks, even making sure he knows the latest sports news before they get together so he can pretend to be interested.

And everyone is interested in property, so they all find common ground. Most of the husbands work in finance, but all of them want to invest in real estate, build houses, do what Daniel is doing, and they all know everything about the real estate in the town, spending Sundays going to Open Houses and inspecting layouts and finishes, scouring the local paper and memorizing the property transfers by heart. Real estate, Daniel has decided, is porn for married people.

'How about that house on Old Hill Road?' one will say. 'Can you believe it's on for five million?'

'Well, the one on Hillspoint sold for six,' someone will chip in.

'But that has water views,' another will add.

'Only if you're standing on tiptoe on the roof,' Daniel will say, and they all laugh.

'You know the developer bought that for three? What do you think that cost, Daniel? Three-fifty a foot?'

'Maybe four,' Daniel will say with a shrug. 'The finishes are good.'

How will he face these people, these men who drink

beer, love sports, drive Escalades and Wrangler Jeeps? How will he ever be able to show his face in this town again once they find out he's gay?

And they will find out. In a small town such as this, dramas don't happen too often, and when they do, everyone wants to know everything. He knows of several divorces already, husbands leaving wives for the babysitters or secretaries, but this? A husband or wife leaving because they've come out of the closet? He doesn't know anyone in Westport who has gone through this.

He can't run away, can't move to another area, start afresh. He can't stray from his girls, because, whatever happens, he is determined to be in their lives almost as much as he is now.

Those nights he lies awake in bed, he fantasizes about his perfect life. He sees himself in a condo, maybe in one of those cool loft-like developments in South Norwalk. Or in a small house by the beach, maybe on Mill Cove, although there are no cars allowed on the tiny island and it must be a nightmare to get groceries up there in winter when it's snowing.

But imagine how the girls would love a house on the beach! Imagine waking up, throwing open the doors in your living room and stepping out onto sand! Imagine turning over in bed and seeing the person you love, being able to reach out and stroke his arm, smiling to yourself as he sleeps, tracing the outline of his hard, smooth chest.

These are the fantasies Daniel has suppressed his

whole life. The fantasies that have been chasing him for years, trying to sneak their way in, only ever able to hit a home run when he is asleep, when his subconscious welcomes them, when he wakes up unbearably turned on, having dreamed he was with a man. Always with a man. Just a dream, he would tell himself, guilt and shame hitting at the same time as the memory of the dream. Doesn't mean anything.

Except now he knows it does.

They are off to Nantucket in two weeks. The house they looked at when they were there for the weekend was just as lovely as it appeared in the pictures: a grey shingled cottage overlooking both Lake Quidnet and the bay, and Bee was so excited, the realtor so enthusiastic, Daniel found, despite the dread, he couldn't say no.

There *was* something magical about Nantucket, Bee's father was right, and while Daniel was there, strolling through the village with Bee, he had started to relax, to think that perhaps things would be okay, perhaps they would find a way through the mess that had become their marriage, for they were still friends. Best friends.

And now it is done. The cheque for the holiday – a small fortune, but worth it, Bee had said – was sent last week, the contracts had been signed, and a series of emails between the landlords and Bee were still flying back and forth.

Try to do your shopping off-island, they had recommended – far cheaper! They sent instructions as to how to get the Oversand permits if they were driving a car that could go on the beach. Bring your own beach towels, they reminded her.

Getting out of it isn't an option, but how can he go to Nantucket for what he knows Bee is hoping will reinvigorate the romance in their life, given what he has finally been able to admit to himself?

Just last night Bee put down the magazine she was reading in bed and turned to him with a smile.

'I feel really good about this summer,' she said, putting out a hand and taking his, squeezing it with affection. 'I think it's a new start for us. Thank you for taking this house, for doing something that I know you weren't sure about, but that I truly believe will make us happy.'

Daniel nodded mutely, swallowing the lump of fear in his throat.

'Wasn't it wonderful, being in Nantucket that weekend?' Bee snuggled into him and as a reflex Daniel put his arm around her. Feeling nothing.

'Mmm,' he said, non-committally.

'I do love you, you know,' she said, looking up at him.

'I love you too,' he said, and this was easier, because it was true.

''Night.' She pecked him on the lips, rolled over, and reached out to switch off her bedside light.

Daniel felt relief wash over him.

''Night,' he said, and went back to his book.

*   *   *

No one sleeps together any more, Bee told herself, when she was forced to think about it. On the days when she and her friends got together for coffee, or lunch, or had play dates with the kids, if ever the subject of sex came up, all of them would laugh and say, 'Sex? Who has time for sex? Who even wants to have sex any more?'

They would joke that they were running out of excuses to give their husbands, that the headache excuse was far too old and boring, and that they were constantly having to come up with new ones.

'My husband thinks my period lasts two weeks of every month,' Jenny had said recently with a grin and they had all roared with laughter.

'After I had my second baby I told my husband my gynaecologist had advised me not to have sex for a year,' said someone else. 'And he believed me!'

Maybe she wouldn't want sex, Bee thought, if Daniel wanted it all the time. Maybe the only reason she misses it so much, misses the intimacy, the warmth, the closeness, is because he refuses. Isn't it human nature to always want what we cannot have?

No one is having sex, she tells herself when nagging doubts, horrible thoughts that she refuses to permit, try to make their way into her head. We have young children, we are exhausted, all we want to do when we climb into bed is sleep.

And she tries very hard not to think about the fact that it is Daniel's refusal, not hers. The one time she

140

contributed to one of those joking conversations, she realized it wasn't normal.

'I know!' she'd added. 'Daniel does this thing where he'll stay in the shower until he thinks I'm asleep so he doesn't have to have sex with me!' And she'd looked around for laughter, and seen only sympathy and slight embarrassment.

She didn't bring it up again.

*

'I think you have to spend some to make some,' Sarah tells Nan, standing over the large cardboard box and cutting it open to reveal packages of crisp white sheets. 'And it really wasn't expensive,' she adds. 'All things considered. And you didn't have enough sheets for the bedrooms you want to rent, so we had to do it. Oh – they had a special on towels too, so I ordered four sets of white towels.'

'You think of everything,' Nan says with a smile, ripping open the packaging and cooing over the softness of the towels. 'And while Andrew Moseley would probably have a heart attack, I couldn't agree more. We can't have our tenants sleeping on anything other than the best.'

'Speaking of tenants, I think we're nearly ready to post our ad.'

'Oh I'm so pleased!' Nan claps her hands together. 'I can cycle into town later and post the ad on the message board.'

Sarah pauses. 'We should put it online too,' she says. 'On Craigslist and some of the other online boards. Those are the best ways these days.'

'I think you're absolutely right,' Nan says. 'Come upstairs and see what I did to the blue room this morning.'

Both Nan and Sarah have spent every day transforming the house. Old faded rugs have been rolled up and put in the shed, and Sarah has sanded and waxed the wooden floors of the bedrooms, as her brother Max re-grouted tiles in the bathrooms, painted walls bright white and cornflower blue.

They have shopped together online, Nan going over to Sarah's house to access her computer, marvelling at what can be found, stunned that you just point and click, and two days later magnificent things arrive on your doorstep.

They have labelled each bedroom by colour. The blue room has, naturally, blue walls, pretty blue and white toile curtain panels, with matching bedspread, valance and pillow, and a jug of fresh hydrangeas on the old washstand. A blue and white checked quilt that Sarah had lying around is thrown haphazardly over the little loveseat in the bay window.

The green room is white, with a green and white vine design on the fabric of the panels and bed. A bowl of viburnum stands on the chest of drawers that had been stained and burnt, but Nan had reluctantly agreed to paint it and it is now a muted and pretty antique white.

There is a red room, a white room and a patriotic room – the stars and stripes of the flag echoed in both the bedspreads and a flag that Sarah found, framed, at a tag sale. But the biggest changes are in the rest of the house.

White canvas slipcovers have been thrown over the sofas and armchairs in the living room, blue and white pillows piled on top, giving the room a freshness and a lightness it hasn't seen in years.

The coffee rings on the tables, the burn marks, have been covered with stacks of books. Beautiful vases Sarah has found are filled with fresh flowers. All the fusty, dusty rugs have been replaced with simple sea-grass rugs, cut and bound from offcuts going cheap at a carpet store on the Cape that was going out of business.

The dining table has been sanded down, stained and waxed, and Max re-grouted the subway tile in the kitchen so all is gleaming and white.

'It will be a bed and breakfast,' Nan announces as she pulls the mask off her face, switching the electric sander off just as she finishes the last corner of the kitchen table.

'Don't you have to talk to Planning and Zoning about that?' Sarah looks up from where she is sealing the counters, worried.

'Probably, but I won't. It won't be official, but how could I possibly have people living in the bedrooms and not give them breakfast at least? I won't advertise as such, and I know we've put coffee machines in each of their bedrooms, but, my dear, I'd feel guilty if

I didn't feed them. And just imagine what fun it will be, all my tenants sitting round the kitchen table. It will be like old times.'

'I don't know that everyone will necessarily want breakfast,' Sarah says. 'You may not even want them sitting round the table. You may not like them.'

'Ha! True!' barks Nan with a grin. 'But I'm usually pretty good at sizing people up and I won't let anyone in that I don't like.'

'But if we advertise online, you won't be able to meet them. You'll just have to take them in good faith.'

'I can tell on the phone,' Nan says. 'Did I ever tell you about George?'

'George?' Sarah shakes her head.

Nan sighs and sits down, lighting up a cigarette with a dreamy smile. 'George was the first man I fell in love with after Everett died.'

'He was? How come you never mentioned him!' Sarah sits down opposite, wishing she still smoked.

'Sometimes I think it's easier not to think about the what ifs,' Nan says sadly. 'What if I had agreed to move to London with him, leave Windermere? What if I had known he would meet someone else a few months later and marry her?' She sighs.

'But I met him on the phone,' she continues. 'He was an old school friend of Everett's, from Middlesex, and he phoned to pay his respects when he was summering on the island one year. Well, I knew from the minute he said hello that I would fall in love with this man, and do you know, he came up to the house for a drink that night, and I did! I swear, I took one look and fell head over heels in love.'

'And?'

Nan smiles at the memory. 'And we spent a blissful summer together. I was in such a fog after Everett died, and didn't think I would ever find anyone, wasn't looking to find anyone, and then lovely George came into my life, and even though it wasn't forever, it made me see that I could be happy again, that Everett's death wasn't the end of the world by any stretch. Although by that time I was still struggling to get out of the mess Everett left me in.'

'I don't understand.' Sarah shakes her head. 'If you were happy together why didn't it last?'

'George was my bridge from grief to living again. I think I knew that it was this perfect bubble that wouldn't continue, and then he got a job in London. Goodness, it sounded so glamorous, but Michael was so little and I didn't want to uproot him or disrupt his life any further, and we promised we'd stay in touch.' Nan stubs out her cigarette before continuing.

'I did think he'd come back for me, though,' she says wistfully. 'And then I received an invitation to his wedding. Millicent Booth Eden was her name. I sent a lovely crystal decanter, although it may have smashed by the time it crossed the Atlantic, and then we lost touch.'

'Haven't you ever thought of finding him again?' Sarah says excitedly. 'You could probably Google him. You can find anyone. I spend hours Googling people

I went to school with, old boyfriends, anyone I can think of.'

'Maybe you could,' Nan says with a smile, snapping back into the present. 'George Forbes. From Boston originally, last heard of in London.'

'God, wouldn't it be lovely if we found him and he was – I don't know, divorced or widowed or something, and he came back and you fell in love and lived happily ever after.'

Nan smiles widely. 'My sweet Sarah, don't you know that I'm going to live happily ever after anyway?'

Later that afternoon Nan cycles into town, a sheaf of papers tucked into her basket. They have photocopied pictures of the house, pictures of the rooms, the magnificent view from each of the windows.

Rooms to rent for summer in beautiful old Sconset home with water views and direct access to beach. Own bed and bath. Breakfast available on request. Unique opportunity!

She parks her bike on Main Street and pins one of her adverts to the board, standing for a while to read about what's going on in town. Yoga at the children's beach, she notices, thinking that perhaps she ought to do something to stretch these old bones.

'Nan?' She turns to see Patricia Griffin, another old-timer, rounding the corner and pausing when she spies Nan.

'Hello, Pat.' She smiles. 'How are you? How's Buckley?'

'Oh you know,' Patricia says. 'Life goes on as usual. What's this I hear about you having furniture sales?'

'Just an idea,' Nan says. 'Out with the old and in with the new.'

'I heard the developers were circling like vultures.' Patricia laughs.

'They were a bit. Not that I'm selling.'

'Good. It would be a shame to see your house torn down. Did you hear what happened to the Oldinghams?'

'Up at Madaket? No, what happened?'

'Their neighbour persuaded them to sell him their house, offered them a price they couldn't say no to, apparently, but he vowed he was going to preserve it, he said he wanted an extra house for his children to stay in and he was going to create a compound.'

'And did he?'

'The minute they closed, the bulldozers were in tearing the house down. Three huge mansions are going up now.'

'And what about the Oldinghams?'

'Gone back to the Cape, but isn't it awful?'

'Well, they won't be getting their hands on my house if I have anything to do with it.'

Patricia smiles, then catches sight of the board. 'What's this? You're renting rooms?'

'I am.' Nan stands proud. 'It's too quiet for me these days. I thought what fun to fill the house with people, and I need something to keep me busy.'

'What a good idea,' Patricia says. 'Lovely to see you,

Nan. We ought to get together. Maybe you'll finally come and join the gardening club.' And with that she hurries off home to inform her husband that it's true, Nan Powell is clearly having financial trouble after all.

Chapter Eleven

This afternoon, Daniel does something he has secretly, guiltily, wanted to do for years. His meeting was cancelled, and he walked out of the office, his cheeks burning, as if his colleagues could look through his eyes and see into his soul, see where he was really going.

He has known about the Maple Bar for years. It's a gay café and bar in New Haven. He has always been drawn to it, as he has to so many gay cafés and bars, but has never dared do anything other than drive by, looking wistfully at the blacked-out windows.

He has memorized the address, terrified of even having a gay bar appear on his Google history. He hadn't used the word gay. Had just put in maple and New Haven, then adding tree after the address came up, figuring he could come up with some story about researching maple trees in the unlikely event this would ever be discovered.

He has done this before, on his computer at home. He has become an expert in wiping out his cache, his history, his cookies, but still has a lingering fear that somehow someone would be able to see that occasionally, when the temptation has grown too great, he has stumbled upon gay sites, has looked at pictures, read stories with desire burning in his eyes.

He puts the address in his GPS, and drives on auto-pilot, not sure of what he will do once he gets there, sure only that he has to go, has to see whether this is real, whether he truly does want this thing that he is about to blow his life up for.

The bar is dark, and quiet. A few men sit or stand by the bar, a handful of others are grouped around a pool table. Music plays, and Daniel walks to the bar, sits down to stop his legs shaking, and immerses himself in the bar menu to avoid making eye contact.

'Hi there.' He looks up into the face of a friendly barman. 'Hot out there today, huh?'

Daniel smiles. 'I've been in an air-conditioned car all afternoon so it hasn't been so bad.'

'What can I get you?'

'I'll have a Sam Adams.'

'Coming right up.'

He takes a sip and turns three-quarters on his stool, noticing that in the shadows of the room there is more activity. A couple stand against the wall, making out roughly, before walking through a doorway at the back.

Daniel watches, can't tear his eyes away, his heart pounding with fear. And excitement.

'Wanna play?' A young, dark-haired man catches his eye and offers a pool cue, and Daniel shrugs.

'I'm not much of a pool player,' he says.

'Me neither,' says the man with a grin, sitting down on the stool next to Daniel. 'I'm Mike.'

'Daniel.' They shake hands, and Mike orders a drink.

He isn't fey, or feminine, or butch. He doesn't have leather chaps, or pierced ears, or a limp handshake. He is a regular guy, jeans and a T-shirt, a friendly smile, short back and sides. He looks exactly like every other guy Daniel knows, and finally he starts to relax.

'So ...' Daniel says awkwardly. 'Are you ... a regular?'

'You mean, do I come here often?' Mike laughs. 'I guess. I live near and, let's face it, there aren't exactly dozens of gay bars around here. I haven't seen you before. Are you here on business?'

'Not exactly. I've known about this place for years but I've never ... I just haven't got around to checking it out.'

Mike takes a swig of his beer then smiles. 'Married, right?'

Daniel looks down guiltily at his finger. He thought he had taken the ring off. He had.

'I can always tell,' Mike says. 'You have the look. Married, with kids I'd say, and very unfamiliar with this.'

'You're good,' Daniel says eventually with a shrug. 'That's exactly right.'

'We get a lot of marrieds in here,' Mike says. 'Usually this is their secret life, the wives have no idea that they're into men, but I don't think that's the case with you.'

'My wife has no idea I'm ... into men.' The words sound so unfamiliar tripping off his tongue.

'But you look tortured. You want to tell her, right?'

'What are you?' Daniel is amazed. 'A psychiatrist or a mind reader?'

'I can be anything you want me to be,' Mike says with a raised eyebrow, and Daniel suddenly realizes that he is flirting with him, and that this might not be as safe as he had assumed.

As Daniel leaves the bar, his mind is lost in thought. Once he'd understood that the flirting was harmless fun, he opened up to Mike, made a second confession, and each time he tells his story, says the words 'I'm gay', it feels more and more natural, more and more right.

'Wanna go into the back room?' Mike had said, after they had been talking for an hour, and Daniel had hesitated. He had wanted to, more than anything in the world, but he couldn't. He couldn't be unfaithful to Bee, couldn't do this to her, nor to himself. It was bad enough that he was unfaithful in his mind. The physical act would be too overwhelming for him right now.

It had taken every ounce of strength he had to say no.

Even now, as he walks to his car, he is tempted, over and over, to turn around, walk back in, allow Mike to take his hand and lead him into the back room.

He makes it to the car, and makes it to the highway, and even though he fights the urge to turn around at every single exit, he finally manages to make it home.

It just doesn't feel like home any more.

*   *   *

Lizzie and Stella are staying at a friend's house, and Bee, who never has a night away from the girls, is setting the table in the dining room for dinner.

She wants tonight to be special, a precursor to their trip, and because she's a disastrous cook herself she stopped at Garelick & Herbs earlier and picked up stuffed chicken breasts, wild rice, various salads – all Daniel's favourites.

The iPod is plugged in, the music is romantic, and although Bee feels a little self-conscious – the two of them will be slightly lost at their eighteenth-century French refectory table in their formal red dining room – eating in the kitchen as they always do means they'll sit without talking much, Daniel may start reading the papers halfway through, and the meal will be over in ten minutes.

Bee wants to relax tonight. No children ... No excuse ... She wants to light candles, sip wine and talk to her husband. Really talk to him. She wants to reconnect with him, like they did in Nantucket. She wants it to be romantic. She wants him to remember why they're together, why they got married. What it means to be in love, for whatever else is going on, she is quite sure he loves her, he just needs help to show it.

'So do you think we ought to book something before we go? I was looking through this magazine and we could charter a boat, go out for a picnic.'

'Sure,' Daniel says, forcing down another mouthful

of chicken, his throat having closed up because he doesn't know how he's going to do this.

'Daniel, for God's sake,' Bee says with a sigh, placing her knife and fork down with a clatter. 'Could you show a bit of enthusiasm? You agreed to take this house in Nantucket and now you don't seem to want to go, which, quite frankly, is ruining it for me.'

'It's not that I'm not enthusiastic.' Daniel lays his own knife and fork down and closes his eyes for a few seconds. He opens them to see Bee looking at him quizzically.

'What is it?' she asks, her voice almost a whisper. 'There's something wrong, isn't there? Is it ... me? Is this it? You want to leave?'

She has never asked him that before. Perhaps she has been too scared of the answer, and Daniel, up until very recently, had never thought that this would be the way it happens.

As he looks up and finally meets her eyes, he sees she wants him to say, 'No, no. Don't be silly. Of course not.'

But he can't. Not now. This is it, he realizes. His window of opportunity, which feels frightening, and unreal, but if he doesn't take it now, he doesn't know how he can carry on living such a huge lie, a lie that seems to be growing bigger and bigger with every passing hour.

Daniel struggles to form the words. This isn't how he wanted it to happen. He had made a commitment to Dr Posner to have some more private sessions with him, to work out how to tell Bee, but he has to do it now, and as he tries to speak, Bee's hand flies to her chest.

'Oh my God,' she whispers. 'You are. I think I'm going to be sick.' She jumps up, running to the bathroom where she retches into the toilet bowl.

'Bee, I'm so sorry.' Daniel runs after her and helps her up, standing helpless in the doorway as she rinses her mouth out.

'Just tell me,' she says. 'Tell me why. Things are going well. I thought we were making progress, that's the point of this vacation, for God's sake. Oh God,' she groans. 'The vacation. What am I supposed to do?'

'I'm just not happy,' Daniel says. 'I can't keep pretending that things are fine when they're not.'

'What do you want me to do?' Bee says quietly. 'Whatever you need, I'll do. I'm sorry I put pressure on you about sex. I'm sorry. I won't do that again. What do you need? Whatever you need I can do it, I swear. Daniel, I love you, I'll do anything to make this work.' Desperation shines in her eyes as she pleads, convinced she will find a way.

'There's nothing you can do,' Daniel says sadly. 'I swear, this is nothing to do with you. This is just about me, about figuring out what I want.'

'So figure it out. You don't have to leave to figure it out. Stay. I'll help you, or give you the space. You can sleep in the spare room if you want, but don't go. Please don't go. What about the girls? What about me?' And the last ounce of strength seems to leave her as Bee collapses to the floor in sobs, Daniel wanting nothing more than to put his arms around her and make it better, but he can't.

Nor can he tell her the truth. That already he feels relief. That he feels more pain than he could have imagined, hurting Bee, leaving the girls, but that the cloud that has weighed upon his shoulders his entire life, the cloud that has only grown darker and heavier throughout his marriage, has finally dispersed.

He can't tell her this marriage is over, nor can he tell her the reasons why. Not yet. There is only so much pain you can cause one person in one go, he realizes, and it's not necessary for her to know – there will be time for that later.

Perhaps other people find it easier to sever the ties with a clean cut, but Daniel can't do that. The concept of needing space feels right. It feels like something Bee could live with, something that isn't going to end her world.

It gives her false hope, he knows, but he would rather do this gently, kindly, figure out how to drop the bomb when she is stronger, a little more used to dealing with life on her own.

'I love you, Bee,' Daniel says. 'I'm so sorry but I can't stay here any more.'

'Where will you go?'

'I'll stay at the Inn tonight. I'll figure it out. I'll phone you tomorrow, maybe I can see the girls after school. Right now I have to go upstairs and pack.'

And he reaches down, but Bee pushes him away

when he tries to console her, so he leaves her on the floor, with tears streaming down her face, and goes to throw a few of his belongings into a bag before heading out through the door.

Chapter Twelve

It's not often these days that Michael has a night to himself, he realizes. Most of his time has been taken up with Jordana, and the nights he isn't with Jordana he's usually with friends – drinks, a quiet dinner in a neighbourhood restaurant: the typical New York life.

Tonight Jordana went back to Long Island – she and Jackson had a benefit of some kind, but Michael didn't ask much. He tries not to think about Jackson, about how he would feel, about what kind of a person he must be, sleeping with Jackson's wife. It's the only way he can do it.

She has been his drug, his obsession, but slowly he is starting to feel as if he's awakening from a dream. Slowly he's starting to wonder what the hell he's been doing.

Just two weeks ago he thought she was possibly the most gorgeous woman he had ever seen. He had always found her attractive, but once they got involved he thought she was beautiful, more than beautiful. Mesmerizing.

And now, overnight, he has started to notice that she has bad posture, her shoulders slumping forward when she walks. Her voice is high-pitched and nasal, which he used to find cute, and now finds ever so slightly irritating. He found it endearing, initially, that she was trying to change to please him, swapping her heels for flats, her hairspray for hairclips to pull her hair back into the natural ponytail he loves, but now he finds it odd that a woman would have so little sense of self-worth she would change herself entirely to suit whichever man she was with.

The rose-tinted spectacles, it seems, are falling away from his eyes, and suddenly he realizes he doesn't know how to get out. He's been in this job for twenty years — it is more than his job, it is his life, his family, and although from time to time he has thought of leaving and going somewhere else, he never thought it would be because of a situation like this.

And Jordana, who can sense him pulling away, seems to be keener still, more desperate, more in love than ever before.

He needed tonight, a night off, a night to himself, more than he could have dreamed. A night of freedom, interrupted only by the numerous text messages flying in from Jordana.

v. boring here. Miss you LOTS! J xxx

where r u? want to phone! Love u!

Can u call me?

Tried to call. No answer. Am worried ... xxxx

He pocketed his phone in the bar and left his jacket draped over the back of the chair, trying to ignore the buzzing.

'Looks like someone's trying to get hold of you, mate,' said the English man sitting next to him, gesturing at his vibrating jacket pocket with a grin.

Michael raised his eyebrows and shrugged. 'I'm trying to go AWOL tonight.'

'Ah, the missus giving you a hard time?'

'Sort of. Not the missus. The mistress.' He snorted at his own joke.

The English guy gave a knowing grin and a wink. 'Big girl trouble, then. Husband found out?'

'Oh God,' groaned Michael. 'I damn well hope not.'

'Friend of yours, is he?'

'You could say that.' Michael ordered another beer, and one for his new friend. 'He's my boss.'

'Wife of the boss? That takes brass balls, mate.' He shook his head. 'We've got an expression at home: don't dump on your own doorstep.'

'Yes, well,' Michael said. 'I wish I'd heard that a few weeks ago.'

'Cheers.' The man lifted his glass. 'Here's to secrets and lies.'

Secrets and lies? Michael knew that this wasn't who he wanted to be, wasn't how he ever wanted to live.

'No,' he said, pausing. 'Here's to fresh starts and new beginnings.' And he drank the rest of the bottle down in one.

*   *   *

He is asleep when he hears the ringing. Over and over. At first he hears it in his dream, and swimming up to consciousness he understands it isn't in his dream, it's real. He reaches for the phone only to hear the dialling tone, at which point he realizes it isn't the phone, it's the doorbell.

He glances at the clock as he stumbles through the darkness to the buzzer. 2.37 a.m. Who in the hell is ringing his doorbell at 2.37 a.m.?

'Yup?' His voice is fuzzy with sleep.

'Michael? It's me. Jordana.'

'Jordana? It's 2.37 in the morning. What are you doing here?'

'Michael, will you just buzz me in?' she says. 'It's dangerous out here.'

Moments later she appears at Michael's front door.

'I've left him,' she announces, rolling a large Louis Vuitton suitcase into his tiny apartment.

'What?' Michael is almost speechless, but manages to splutter out this one word.

'I've done it,' she says, looking up at Michael, tears in her eyes, but whether they are of sadness or happiness he's not altogether sure.

'What do you mean, you've left him?' Michael feels as if the wind has been knocked out of him; he has no idea what to say.

'We had a huge row tonight,' Jordana says, wheeling her case into the bedroom as if she belongs there. 'I'm not proud of myself but I told him he didn't make me happy and that our marriage was over.'

161

'He doesn't . . .' Michael feels sick. He looks up at Jordana, incredulous at what she has done – and Jesus, if she's done this, who's to say she hasn't told him everything. 'He doesn't know about . . . us?'

'No!' Jordana laughs. 'Are you nuts? He'd *kill* me. God, he'd probably kill you too. There's no way I was going to tell him about you although he asked me if there was someone else.'

'What did you say?' Michael is still struggling to wake up from what is feeling increasingly like the worst nightmare he has ever had.

'I said why do men always assume there's someone else, why couldn't it just be that I'm unhappy and I don't want him any more?'

'Oh God, Jordana,' Michael says. 'I just . . . I didn't expect you to do this. We could have talked about this, you could have prepared me. Where are you going to go?' He looks up just in time to see her face fall.

'What do you mean? I thought I could stay here. With you. Jesus, Michael. I thought you'd be pleased.'

'I . . .' He sighs. 'I'm just shocked, Jordana. Of course you can stay here. Tonight. But you can't stay here after tonight. If Jackson found out it would kill him.'

'Jackson's not going to find out.'

'It's not a chance I'm willing to take.'

'Fine,' Jordana says. 'I'll get a hotel round the corner or something so we can sneak back and forth. Hey! Sounds kind of romantic!'

She walks over to where Michael is sitting on the bed and stands in front of him with a seductive smile on her face, a smile that Michael used to find so sexy, but now finds downright terrifying.

'Tell me you're pleased,' she coos, reaching down with her small, cool fingers, stroking him gently in just the way he likes. 'Tell me you're happy to see me.' She pouts like a little girl. 'I thought Mikey was going to be happy to have his girl all to himself.'

'I am happy,' Michael lies as Jordana pushes him back on the bed and climbs on top of him, and then he stops thinking about anything at all.

*

'I feel so nervous,' Nan says with a laugh, pulling off the gardening gloves and sitting down on the bench in the potager, taking a packet of cigarettes from the trug at her feet. Sarah has finally managed to rid the house of the smell of smoke and is refusing to let Nan smoke anywhere other than outside.

'Why?' Sarah looks up from where she is helping Nan plant out the rest of the garden, a handful of seeds in her hand.

'I know it's ridiculous – how could he not love Windermere? But I feel like I'm being interviewed, and what if he doesn't like us?'

'You said you liked him on the phone, so that's a good start, isn't it?'

'That's true. He sounds terribly sweet. Unhappy but sensitive. A good first tenant, I should think.'

'Do you know anything about him?'

'He said his wife and children were spending their

holiday up on Quidnet, and he wanted something small and inexpensive on the island so he could be close.'

'He wants it for the rest of the summer? That's a good start.'

'He said he'd be back and forth a bit, but he'd love a room for the whole of August, and obviously he'll pay for everything in advance.'

'So when does he get here?'

'Around three. Oh I do so hope he likes us.' Nan stubs out her cigarette with her foot and pulls her gardening gloves back on. 'Now, where do you suppose is the best place for me to stake these tomatoes? They're so overgrown, I wish I'd cut them back earlier.'

If it is possible to gain a new lease of life after three weeks of scrubbing, painting, plastering, hammering, staining and sewing, then a new lease of life is exactly what Nan has got.

She has had no time to swim in neighbours' pools, although the summer crowd is now firmly ensconced and Nan knows better than to risk getting caught, and she has had little time to cycle around town on her bike.

Other women might be exhausted at her age, having worked the way she has worked to get the house in shape, but Nan feels alive again. She knew as soon as Daniel phoned that he would be perfect for the house, and hopes the house is perfect for him.

For the first time in years, Nan feels like giving parties again. She is well aware of her reputation as something of a recluse, for even though she is out and about in town all the time, it is rare for people to come up to the house, and the truth is she hasn't felt like entertaining these past few years.

But now, walking around her house that is so fresh and clean it feels almost new, cycling up her driveway that she and Sarah tackled with gallons of Roundup so the crushed white clam shells are no longer hidden by the copious weeds, she wants to show it off.

She wants Windermere to be the house she remembers of old.

'Sarah!' she shouts, gazing at the big old maple tree in the garden. 'Do you think it's possible to get fairy lights this time of year?'

Sarah puts her trowel down and walks over to where Nan is standing. 'I think anything is possible in the age of the computer. Why? What are you thinking?'

'I'm remembering the parties we used to have. Lydia, my mother-in-law, used to string little white fairy lights through the branches of this maple tree. We'd hang lanterns overhead and it was like dancing under a thousand moons.'

Sarah starts laughing. 'Good heavens, Nan. Are you planning a party already?'

'I don't know,' Nan says. 'But I was remembering how beautiful it used to be. I'd like to see it look like that again. I'd like to see this place come alive.'

*

Michael looks up wearily as the door to his workshop opens. It used to be that he was left on his own in here for days at a time. He loved the solitude, loved the silence. Creating jewellery was like a meditation for him – he didn't have to think, he just felt his mind settle into a peace that enabled him to tap into his deepest creative well.

These last few weeks Jordana has changed that. She is in and out all day long, and while he welcomed the activity in the beginning – it was exciting, invigorating, energizing – now he longs for the peace and quiet of old.

But it's not Jordana. It's Jackson, and as soon as he sees Jackson, Michael feels a terrible guilt.

He has managed to avoid him – easy since Jackson has been spending so much time on Long Island – and on the rare occasions Jackson did come into the city Michael found it easy to act, easy to be easy, to simulate the same friendly banter they have had for years.

How can he do that today? How can he do that knowing that Jordana left Jackson last night, and came to his apartment and spent the night? How can he pretend, when he is fucking his wife, and in doing so seems to have fucked up Jackson's life?

Jackson looks terrible. He walks in like an old man, bags under red-rimmed eyes, exhausted, having aged ten years overnight.

'Are you okay?' Michael says, not knowing what else to say.

'Not really.' Jackson pulls up a stool and sits down with a deep sigh. 'Jordana left me.'

'What?' Michael feigns shock, but with it comes

genuine upset. He never meant for this to happen, never meant to hurt anyone, least of all Jackson, who has been nothing but kind to him all these years. Jackson to whom he owes everything. 'Jackson, that's terrible. I'm so sorry.'

'I just can't believe it.' Jackson shakes his head. 'She said she was unhappy, I wasn't giving her what she needed. Michael, I've given that woman everything!'

'I know.' Michael shifts uncomfortably in his seat, feeling sick, and sorry, and scared, wishing there were some way to turn the clock back, wishing he hadn't been quite so impulsive, wishing he wasn't the cause of all this pain.

'What more could anyone want? And I love her. I love that woman. She means everything to me.' And with horror Michael watches as Jackson starts to cry.

*

'Jess! Breakfast!' Daff calls up the stairs, then goes back to the kitchen, sliding fried eggs onto pancakes.

Daff had always wanted to be the kind of mother who made breakfast for her child every day. She wanted to be the sort of woman who made her own granola, who watched *Martha Stewart* and proceeded to copy some, if not all, of the crafts, who had a beautiful little vegetable plot out back where tomatoes climbed over wire obelisks and clematis tumbled over a white picket fence.

Daff knows women like this. There are hundreds of mothers in school who do precisely this, who have immaculate crafts cupboards at home, who bring in beautiful doll's houses for show and tell that they've just thrown together using shoeboxes and leftover scraps of wallpaper.

Daff has been feeling inadequate around these women since kindergarten. Hell, even before that – since pre-school. They are the mothers who fight to be room mother, who organize coffee mornings with home-baked scones and fresh lemonade, who float around school hallways with beatific smiles on their faces, never getting stressed, never getting overwhelmed, and never – God forbid – shouting at their children.

Sometimes Daff wonders if Jess would treat her better, be nicer, if Daff were a better mother. If she made macaroni cheese from scratch instead of using Kraft's best. If she and not Mrs Entenmann made the chocolate-chip cookies she brought in for the school fair. If she, in short, were like those other mothers – Supermother, she thinks wryly.

Supermother does not have a daughter who sneers every time she tries to talk to her. Supermother does not have piles of papers and bills taking up almost all the counter space in her kitchen, and Supermother does not give her daughter Cheerios for breakfast, day after day after day after day.

So today Daff is going to be Supermother. It's Saturday, her weekend with Jess, and she is determined to have a good weekend. She is taking Jess up to see their friends, Barb and Gary, who have a beautiful old horse farm in Roxbury, Connecticut.

They have four kids, and when they were all young, when Barb and Gary were neighbours, Jess and the oldest girl were best friends. They haven't got together in a while, and Jess has always loved horse riding, so it will be, she hopes, a lovely surprise to take Jess up there for the weekend.

The weekends are a struggle now that she is a single mother. She feels a need to be present for Jess in a way she never used to, to think of wonderful things for her and Jess to do, to keep Jess happy, whereas when she was married she and Richard would just do whatever needed to be done on weekends – running errands, seeing friends, gardening – and Jess would just slot herself in.

But nothing seems to be keeping Jess happy these days. At least this weekend will be fun, and Jess is always better when she's around other kids her own age.

'Jess!' Daff goes back to the stairs and calls again, finally walking upstairs and knocking on the bedroom door in exasperation. 'Breakfast is on the table,' she says, trying to keep the irritation out of her voice, for that is not how she wants to start this weekend. 'I've been calling you.'

Silence.

Daff tentatively pushes open the door, and there is no Jess.

'Jess?' A question. She checks the bathroom.

Nothing. Her own bathroom, for Jess has now decided that what's hers is hers and what's Daff's is also hers – Daff's hairbrushes, conditioner, bubble bath and make-up all go missing on a regular basis – but Jess is not upstairs.

'Jess?' Daff's voice is louder now as she shouts downstairs. She's not in the family room, the living room, the library. She is nowhere to be found.

Daff finds herself tearing round the house shouting Jess's name, panic rising in her throat when the phone rings. She picks it up, breathless, feeling the tears start to come.

'It's Richard. Jess is here. I think you'd better come over.'

*

Daniel hasn't been anywhere by himself, for anything other than work, for a very long time. It is a very odd feeling, to be sitting on this ferry, surrounded by families going on vacation, going on vacation himself but without his family.

He had wanted to travel there together, wanted still to spend as much time as possible with the girls, but Bee had disagreed.

'You left,' she'd hissed, anger finally starting to take the place of devastation. 'You don't get to pretend you're still part of this family.'

'But I am,' he'd said, hurt and dismayed. 'I'm their father. That's never going to change. I'm always going to be part of their family.'

'Yes, but you're no longer part of mine,' Bee had said, putting down the phone.

Some days were better than others. Some days were fine, some found Bee in tears, some found her pleading and others, particularly these last few days, found her in a fury.

Then the vacation was upon them, and Daniel refused to let Bee take the girls for a whole month to Nantucket. He insisted on being there too, wanted to come with them, to pretend for the sake of the girls, but Bee refused.

'If you want to be on the island at the same time I can't stop you,' she'd said, adding reluctantly, 'and the girls would be pleased. But don't expect me to pretend that everything is fine between us. This isn't my choice. This isn't ever what I would have chosen.'

He had Googled rentals, wanting something cheap, easy. Something that he could leave, to come back to Westport for work, travelling back to Massachusetts on weekends.

Cheap and easy doesn't come cheap, or easy, on Nantucket. He didn't need much. A whole house seemed extravagant. He assumed there would be a condo, but there was nothing that was suitable, and nothing in his price range. Not that he had ever had to think about money before, but he had no idea what he would be paying in child support, in alimony, and now was not the time for extravagance.

He had found a room in an old house. It looked

clean. Nice views. The landlady said she adored children, there'd be more than enough room if the girls
wanted to come and have a sleepover.

As soon as she'd said that, his decision was made.

Chapter Thirteen

Daff hasn't been in Richard's house before, and she can't help but be curious. She follows him through to the kitchen, noticing the furniture he took from their shared house, and the new things he has bought – the rugs, the flat-screen plasma, the bookshelves.

It is neat and tidy, far tidier than Daff's house. Richard spent their marriage berating Daff for her scattiness, and she is astonished at quite how ordered he is. There is not a paper out of place, nor a pile on any of the kitchen counters. But nor are there any of the things that, for Daff, make a house a home. The photographs, the invitations stuck to the fridge, the cookery books stacked haphazardly on the shelves. The little objects she has collected over the years, the shells, the interesting boxes.

I couldn't live like this, she thinks, sitting down at the kitchen table – Pottery Barn, she recognizes it from the catalogue – and looking round expectantly.

'Where is she?' Daff says. 'I was so worried. I can't believe she left the house and came to you. How did she even get here?'

'She walked,' Richard says seriously.

'She walked? But it's miles.'

'She left at three in the morning.'

'What?' Daff sits up straight, shocked. 'Three in the morning? At thirteen? Oh my God! Anything could have happened to her.'

'I know. That's what I said.'

'I can't believe it. That's punishable. She's going to have a curfew from now on.'

'I agree,' Richard says quietly, 'but there's a bigger problem.'

'What?' Daff is suddenly fearful.

'She doesn't want to go home.'

'What do you mean, she doesn't want to go home?'

'She's got this thing about living with me, and she's refusing to go home.'

'She can't refuse to go home. I mean, she can, but she's thirteen. She doesn't get to do what she wants. She has to come home.'

'That's what I wanted to talk to you about. I know you and she are struggling, and although it won't be permanent, I thought maybe the best thing right now might be to have her here for a while.'

'What do you mean, a while?'

'I don't know, and I'm sure it's just a phase, but she is adamant and I can't see the harm in trying.'

'But I'm her mother,' Daff says frantically. 'She has to be with me.'

'Daff, this isn't a reflection on you,' Richard says gently. 'My sister hated my mother when she was a teenager, and look at them now, they're the best of friends and you'd never know the hell they went through all those years ago. Jess reminds me of my sister, and maybe this is just something girls sometimes go through. I think if the two of you had some space from one another, it might help.'

'I don't know what to say,' Daff says quietly, and, hating herself for it, she is torn. There is part of her that is desperate to cling on to her daughter. There is nothing like the mother–daughter relationship. How can Richard tell Jess about boys, and make-up, and periods, and all the things she is going to have to deal with any second now? And there is another part of her that longs for peace and quiet, that longs to live in a house where she doesn't feel like she's walking on eggshells every minute of the day her daughter is home, waiting for the next eruption, crying quietly in her bedroom at the end of the day, wondering when she will ever get her daughter back.

'She loves you.' Richard's expression softens when he sees Daff's eyes fill with tears. 'She's just filled with hormones and she doesn't know what to do with all her emotions.'

'I know.' Daff swallows. 'I was the same. But, Richard, you work. How can you be there for her? Who will be home when she gets off the bus? How could you possibly take care of her?'

'I have Carrie too,' Richard says. He didn't want to have this conversation, not yet, but she has to know.

'Carrie. Your girlfriend?'

'Yes. She just moved in with me. She's a writer and she works at home. She's here all the time.'

'She doesn't mind taking on Jess?'

'They get on. Not always, and God knows it isn't easy, but Carrie seems to know what she's in for, and she's supportive of anything that might make life easier for all of us.'

'Do I get to meet her?'

'I think you should. I thought maybe you and Carrie could have a coffee. It might be easier for the two of you to get to know one another without me there.'

'Okay,' Daff says. 'You have to let me digest all of this, Richard.' She sighs. 'This is huge. I just don't know.'

'I understand,' he says, standing up. But Daff looks suddenly so lost, he finds himself holding his arms out, and without thinking she steps into them and allows herself to be hugged.

'I'm so sorry,' he whispers, shocked at how familiar she feels, realizing that although he has moved on with Carrie, he will never fully move on, and not just because they have a daughter together. And he is sorry. He may have found happiness, but the fallout from his infidelity is so much bigger – it is so painful to see Jess so unhappy, and Daff so lost – that he still sometimes wonders what the hell he was thinking.

'I know,' Daff says, tears falling down her cheeks. 'Can I go and see Jess?'

Jess is sitting on her bed, cross-legged, listening to her iPod. She takes the earplugs out of her ears as soon as she sees Daff and, for once, looks contrite.

'Oh Jess.' Daff sinks down and takes her in her arms, and Jess allows herself to be rocked like a baby.

'I'm so sorry, Mom,' she says. 'I didn't think about the things that could happen. I just wanted to see Dad.'

'I know. But please don't ever do that again.'

'Did Dad talk to you?'

'About living here?'

'Yes.'

'You want to?'

'It's not that I don't want to live with you,' Jess says, looking like the five-year-old she once was. 'It's just that I miss Dad so much. I want to live here for a bit.'

'I said I'd think about it,' Daff says, blinking back the tears as she looks around the room. 'Hey, I love this room. Who painted that mural?' She points to a mural of *Hairspray*.

'Carrie did,' Jess says sheepishly. 'She knows that's my favourite movie so she painted the mural as a surprise.'

'Wow! She's really good.'

'She helped me decorate the room too.' Jess points out the futon, the pillows, the bookshelves. 'We went to Ikea to get the stuff and it was so cool. I didn't want to tell you –' she looks awkwardly at her mom – 'I mean, I didn't know what to tell you. About Carrie and stuff.'

'It's okay,' Daff says. 'I'm happy that Dad has a girlfriend. Do you like her?'

Jess shrugs. 'Sometimes. I mean, I like her when it's just her and me, but I don't see why she has to be

Dad's girlfriend. I don't think he needs a girlfriend, but maybe they can just be friends after a while, and that would be much better.'

'I understand that,' Daff says. 'It must be very hard to share your dad.'

'Yeah. Now that they're living together she's always around and there's no special time for just him and me. That's why I want to be here, to live here, I mean, because that way I'll get tons more ordinary time with him.'

'You think so?'

'Oh yeah. He already said. So can I, Mom? Can I come and live here? I'll still see you all the time, but can I be here? Did you think about it yet?'

'Not yet.' Daff smiles, rubbing her daughter's back and thinking how lovely it is that they are even able to have a conversation. It has been months since Jess talked to her about anything without a sneer, and for her to reveal how she feels about Carrie is huge. Maybe this isn't such a bad idea after all. Maybe they could try it out over the summer, see how it goes.

But then that leaves Daff. On her own. What on earth is Daff supposed to do all by herself?

The answer comes to her as she drives home. She is thinking about work, what she has listed, what she can do to market her properties, when she remembers the pictures she was looking at in that house. Nantucket.

Why not go to Nantucket? This is the first time in

thirteen years she doesn't have to think about someone else. She could have an adventure. Go somewhere new. Meet new people.

And making a mental note to Google Nantucket and find out about rentals, Daff finds herself smiling all the way home.

*

Michael walks in the apartment to the smell of melting butter and garlic. It smells wonderful, smells like he has made a mistake and walked into someone else's apartment, or the restaurant on the corner.

'Hello?' He pokes his head tentatively into the kitchen, for he thought Jordana was leaving today, was going off to stay with friends, a hotel, *something*, and he's not sure he can bear the guilt now that Jackson has chosen him as an unwilling confidant.

Jordana looks up from where she is sautéing onions and garlic, in the corner of the tiny kitchen, pleasure in her eyes.

'I thought I'd cook you dinner,' she says. 'To say thank you for taking me in last night.'

'I didn't think you'd be here,' he says. 'I thought you were going to a hotel.'

'I am,' she says, her face falling at Michael's lack of pleasure. She thought he'd be thrilled – what man, what self-respecting bachelor wouldn't be thrilled to have a beautiful woman cook him dinner?

What Michael so clearly needs, above all else, is a woman to look after him. She hasn't just shopped and cooked – and her cooking days in Great Neck were long gone – she has dusted the apartment. She needs Michael to realize how wonderful she is, how good his life could be with the two of them together, for she senses his distance, and this is the only way she knows to get him back, to make herself indispensable, to make his life better with her than without.

That and a spectacular blow job.

'I'm booked into the St Regis,' she says, laying down her spoon and turning off the gas as she rubs her hand slowly on the front of his jeans, and Michael, despite himself, groans.

'Want me to stay or go?' She sinks slowly down to her knees and unzips him, knowing the effect she has on him, knowing she is all-powerful where this is concerned.

'Stay,' he gasps, and with a satisfied smile on her face she takes him in her mouth.

Michael lays down the knife and fork and sighs. He's trying to eat the pasta. He knows it's probably delicious – it smells delicious, looks delicious and if he were able to taste anything at all, it would undeniably taste just as good, but he can't.

He has forced one mouthful down, but he can't do this. Can't play happy families when he knows, suddenly and without any shadow of a doubt, that he and Jordana are not meant to be together.

It is as if he has just awakened from a trance, the shock of Jackson's pain, the shock of all their lives being turned upside down, enough to force him back to reality, a reality that Jordana has no part of.

'What's the matter?' Jordana is happy. She has him where she wants him, has been besotted with him since the first kiss, and has only been able to leave Jackson, to blow up her life, because she has barely thought about Jackson since that very first day when her fantasies became a reality.

This is what she has been waiting for these weeks, but this is not the way it is supposed to happen.

In her fantasies Michael is as adoring as he has always been, only more so, his gratitude immeasurable for her having had the courage to leave her husband. He welcomes her with open arms and tears in his eyes, telling her how much he loves her, how they will start afresh.

She would even have children for Michael, and Jordana never wanted children in her life. But imagine little Michaels, the product of their love for one another! She has even thought about coming off the pill, because, let's face it, she isn't getting any younger.

And Jackson? Jackson would deal with it. He'd have to. And at some point he'd find someone else, and then perhaps they'd all be, if not friends, then at least on friendly terms. Jordana certainly bears him no animosity, she doesn't want to hurt him in the slightest, but Michael is her *soulmate*. How can she miss an opportunity like this? How can she spend the rest of her life knowing she was with the wrong man? Jackson may take a while, but ultimately he would realize that

Jordana was not his soulmate, would realize that she had done the right thing.

Her heart beats faster as she watches Michael struggle to chew. He does not look the way she thought he would look. He looks like a man carrying a weight on his shoulders. He looks like a man who is about to say something she knows she doesn't want to hear, and she doesn't want this to happen, wants to turn the clock back to a few weeks ago when everything was perfect. She feels a wave of nausea as Michael opens his mouth to speak.

'I can't do this, Jordana,' he says softly.

'Can't do what?' She is almost choking.

'I saw Jackson today.' Michael looks up and meets her eyes. 'He's in so much pain. I feel horrible. I don't know that I can do this to him.'

'I know,' she croons, thinking that if it is only his concern at hurting Jackson, she can deal with that, knows her way round that. 'Of course it will be painful in the beginning, but I swear that in time he'll see how wrong we are for one another.'

'Maybe,' Michael says. 'Maybe you and he are wrong for one another, but I still ... I can't ...'

'Can't what?'

'I can't be with you,' he says eventually, his voice soft.

Jordana sighs. 'Okay. Fine. We'll take a break until things settle down. I understand you feel horrible about this, and maybe it's a good thing, maybe it's too risky to keep seeing one another, so I can wait.' She stretches across the table and takes his hand. 'We're worth waiting for,' she says earnestly.

There is a long pause and then Michael shakes his head. 'Jordana, I think you're amazing. I think you're beautiful, and clever, and funny, and talented . . .'

'Oh my God,' she groans, her eyes widening in disbelief. 'I know there's a but coming.'

'In another life you would be everything I would look for in a woman, but we come from such different worlds. It isn't just that you're married, and I work for you, and I like your husband. That's bad enough, but there's more. You've always talked about not meshing your world and mine, creating one that both of us can live in, but I don't see it. I don't see how we do that.'

'We can,' Jordana insists. 'I'd love to live a simple life with you. I don't need all this stuff. I'd give it all up for you.'

'But I don't want you to,' Michael says. 'You wouldn't be true to yourself.'

'I've got many different sides.' Jordana's desperation is becoming evident in her voice as she tries to reason with him, tries to refute all his arguments. 'You just know one limited side, and you think that's all there is but that's not true.'

'I don't think you're limited, but . . .' He sighs. This is so difficult. In such a short time they have become so incredibly close, but he knows, finally he knows, there is no way they belong together, and this has to end now. How does he tell her without destroying her?

'Jackson loves you,' he says, trying to convince her.

'And you may have your hard times but who doesn't? You've been together for years, and I don't think you should throw it away for me. I think the two of you belong together. I think you owe him a second chance. Maybe this was what was needed, a catalyst to bring the two of you closer.'

'You have to be fucking joking!' Jordana's voice is hard as she sits back in her chair and looks at him with disbelief. 'I've blown up my life for you and now you're telling me to go back to my husband because you don't want me? I don't fucking believe this.'

'It's not that I don't want you.' Michael feels pathetic in the face of her anger. 'It's just that I don't see us together, and I don't want to be responsible for this.'

'You're a fucking coward,' she stands up and hisses. 'You just loved screwing the boss until it became serious. I can't believe I fell for this. I can't believe I fell for you. Jesus Christ.' She runs her fingers through her hair as she looks around the apartment frantically. 'I've been so fucking stupid.'

'Please don't leave like this.' Michael stands helplessly in the doorway as Jordana throws the last of her things back in her suitcase, refusing to look at him, refusing to say anything. 'Can we talk about this?'

But she doesn't say a word to him. Zips her bag shut as tightly as her lips, then shoves past him and slams the elevator button, turning her back as he shuts the door of the apartment gently, not sure how he feels. Upset. Sad. Relieved.

*   *   *

The phone rings at 3.02 a.m.

'It's me.' Jordana's voice is husky down the phone. She has been crying, the rage of a few hours ago having worked itself out of her system by the time she reached her hotel room.

'Yes?' Michael is cautious.

'I'm sorry,' she says, and this time she breaks into sobs. 'I love you. I really do. More than I've ever loved anyone, and I know we belong together. I know we can make this work. Please don't do this to me, Michael. Please give me a second chance, give us a second chance.'

'It's late,' Michael says eventually. 'It's been an exhausting day. Why don't we both go to sleep and talk again tomorrow morning? Everything will be clearer in daylight.'

'Okay,' she says. 'And I do love you.'

Michael puts the phone down and goes over to his computer. He opens a blank document in Word and starts to type.

*

Jackson sits in his office and tears open the envelope after looking at the return address on the top left-hand corner. Why would Michael, his jeweller, be writing to him? He unfolds the piece of paper and starts to read, shaking his head in disbelief, then he lays his head in his hands.

'Oh Christ,' he says, raising his eyes to the ceiling, his voice loud. 'Why me? What the fuck am I supposed to do?' And with that he picks up the phone and calls Jordana.

'I know you don't want to talk to me,' he says into her voicemail. 'But I want to talk to you. Come to the shop at three o'clock today.'

'What's the matter?' Jordana knew from the tone of his voice that morning that something was wrong, and she is shaking as she walks into his office.

'Well, quite apart from the fact that my wife left me two days ago, this morning I received this.'

He slides the paper over the desk to Jordana, and as she sees Michael's name at the bottom, she instantly feels sick.

'What is it?' she whispers, but she knows.

'Read it,' he says coldly, and she does, finishing it and looking up at Jackson in confusion.

'He's left?'

'Can you believe it? Twenty fucking years I've looked after him and now he's gone. No notice. Nothing. What the fuck am I supposed to do?'

And Jordana bursts into tears.

Chapter Fourteen

Michael sits on a bench in Hyannisport harbour and watches the high-speed ferry take off, crammed with excited holidaymakers, before making his way to the old-fashioned freight ferry that takes twice as long, but is the way he always travelled back and forth as a kid. It wouldn't feel right to travel any other way.

Already, he feels a wave of excitement at being home, the smells, the sights, and mostly the comfort of being back where he belongs, for the last month or so has unsettled him, and he needs to be back on terra firma for some much-needed stability.

He feels terrible about running away, leaving both Jackson and Jordana in the lurch, but he couldn't think of another way. Jordana's behaviour was scaring him, he could easily imagine her telling Jackson, or refusing to take no for an answer, and he knew that the longer he stayed around her, around the situation, the more dangerous it would be.

Michael has never been a coward, but the need to be away from New York, to be back home where he belongs, was overwhelming, and he truly felt he didn't have a choice.

He sent an email out to all his friends to see if anyone wanted to sublet his apartment, and someone had immediately emailed back – they had a friend of a friend visiting from London who would take it for six months, cash payment, no questions asked.

He hauls his backpack up and walks over to the ferry, smiling to himself as he sees a couple of cars lining up, boats attached to trailers behind them, their rear bumpers plastered with Oversand Vehicle Permit stickers from years gone by, each year a different colour, each year proclaiming their right to drive on the beaches.

It brings back many memories. Someone, every year, usually a non-islander, gets stuck on the beach, their wheels spinning madly on the sand. And when he sees cars with the stickers in Manhattan – shiny black Range Rovers – the stickers proclaiming their owner's exclusivity, their ability to vacation on what has become a millionaire's paradise, it still makes Michael laugh. He has always thought the stickers belong on old Land Cruisers, vintage jeeps, beaten-up pick-up trucks, not the hedge-fund manager's version of the same.

It is chilly on deck, but he wants to see the first glimpse of the island. Wants to step off and walk past the people lining up at the Juice Bar for ice cream, past the store on the corner that's been there forever with the ACK hats and Nantucket T-shirts, up Main Street to see what has changed since the last time he was here.

'Mike?'

He looks up and smiles. 'Jeff?'

'Hey, man!' They give each other a hug. 'I thought it

was you! Haven't seen you for years. What are you up to? Heard you were a big-time jeweller in New York City.'

Michael smiles. 'Not quite. But I did work for a big-time jeweller, although God knows you wouldn't know it from my salary.'

'Amen.' Jeff smiles.

'And how about you? I heard you were married with kids.'

'Yup. Married Emily, have two boys and a girl.'

'You're still fishing?'

'Every day. Took over my dad's business in town a few years ago.'

'Boat repairs?'

'Yup. The old man still works there but I run it now.'

'So how's business?'

'Crazy. All these millionaires with huge boats who haven't got a clue.'

'So you're charging them a fortune?'

Jeff grins. 'They can afford it. Anyway, you have to charge a fortune. Living on the island nowadays costs a fortune.'

'That's what I hear.'

'So how long are you back for?'

'I don't know.' Michael shrugs. 'Mom's getting on in years and the house might be getting too much for her. I need to stay for a while.'

'Well, if you need a job at the boatyard you give me a call.'

The edge of Coatue comes into sight and Jeff and

Michael stand up and lean on the railing, Michael unaware that a smile is playing on his lips, for there is no place like home. Never has been. He just hadn't remembered that until now.

'It's still beautiful,' he says with a sigh.

'Yeah. It's changed, but it's still my favourite place in the world.'

'I'm not sure I realized it until now, but I think it may be mine too.'

'Bet you didn't miss the traffic?' Sarah asks as they turn the corner into a wall of cars.

'Wow? What happened?' Michael cranes his head to see what's causing it. 'Looks like Manhattan.'

'I know. You should try parking.'

'No, thanks. Not today. How is Mom, then, Sarah? Really. I talk to her and she sounds great, but this whole boarding-house thing sounds nuts. Do you think the house is getting too much for her?'

Sarah lays a hand on Michael's arm. 'I know you're worried, but she's actually amazing. Your mom has more energy than anyone I've ever met, and renting out these rooms seems to have given her a whole new lease of life. Anyone else would have been exhausted at the prospect of getting the house ready, but she was extraordinary – she just never stops. And,' she continues, 'the first tenant arrived and she adores him.'

'You're sure he's not an axe murderer?'

'A property developer. Although that may be the same thing?' Sarah snorts at her joke.

'A property developer? And she let him in the house? I thought she hates those developers – every time I talk to her she tells me how they're circling to get their hands on the house.'

'Yes, but this one's not local. He's from Connecticut and doesn't seem to be a threat. Poor guy just separated from his wife, and she and the kids are in a house out on Quidnet and he wanted to be close for the summer.'

'Anyone else?'

'There's a woman coming in a few days. Daff something or other.'

'Do we know anything about her?'

'You know your mom – I think she got her life story in the first five minutes. Single mother, daughter staying with the dad for the summer, has always wanted to come to Nantucket.'

'Maybe she and the other guy will get together.' Michael laughs. 'Wouldn't that be something? A little romance over at Windermere. God knows it's been years since that house has seen anything romantic.'

'Well, how about you, Mr Powell? Speaking of romance, any special ladies in your life?'

Michael shivers. 'Not something I want to talk about. Let's just say I'm taking a break from romance for a while. A few years, perhaps.'

'Shame. Sam's got a couple of nice women working at the store, if you change your mind.'

Michael laughs. 'I'll let you know. How is Sam?'

'Busy as ever. But life's good. We're happy. Lucky.'

'That's great to hear. Thank you again, Sarah. For

taking such good care of Mom. Honestly, I don't know what we'd do without you.'

'I don't know what I'd do without her,' she says softly. 'She's more like family than my own family.' And as Sarah looks over at Michael with a smile, the traffic finally starts to move.

Nan's laughter peals through the house as Michael walks through the front door.

'Hello? Mom?'

'Darling!' Nan comes barrelling down the hallway, apron on, wooden spoon in hand, looking exactly as he remembers her.

It is only now he realizes that he has a morbid fear of seeing her and not recognizing her, expecting her to be stooped, or slow, getting older.

But she looks exactly as she has always looked. Her hair pulled back in a chic chignon, her lips a dark red, her figure as slim as ever and, most importantly, she looks happy.

'Oh Michael!' She flings her arms around him, squeezing him tight, then steps back to look at him, a smile of delight spreading over her face as she cups his chin. 'You look handsome but sad,' she says, gazing into his eyes. 'You need to be home, I think. Oh how I've missed you!' And she links her arm with his and leads him down the hallway and into the kitchen.

'Oh. Hi.' There is a man standing at the island, dicing onions very small and wiping away tears with a piece of paper towel.

'I'm sorry.' The man blinks. 'These damn onions.'

'I thought my mother had said something to upset you.' Michael laughs and shakes his hand. 'I'm Michael.'

'I know. Your mom's been telling me all about you. I'm Daniel.'

'Nice to meet you, Daniel. And forgive my asking, but aren't you the new tenant?'

'I am.'

'Why are you in the kitchen dicing onions? Aren't you supposed to be down at the beach, or at the whaling museum or something? Relaxing and being a tourist. Not cooking.'

Daniel laughs. 'Believe it or not, I love cooking. Nan needed some help and frankly she's been keeping me entertained with wonderful stories all morning.'

'Don't believe a word she says.' Michael grins as Nan looks at him fondly.

'It's lovely to have you home,' she says. 'Isn't my son gorgeous?' She turns to Daniel with a smile as Daniel flushes a deep, dark red and turns away to wash his hands.

Oh my, she thinks. Perhaps I have misread the situation somewhat. And deep in thought she leads Michael out to the porch to sit down and catch up properly.

*

Lizzie and Stella jump out of the car and run up the driveway as Daniel opens the front door. His heart lifts as he bends down for them to jump into his arms.

'Daddy!' they both cry, covering his face with kisses, one girl in each arm, their little arms linked tightly around his neck.

'Oh girls,' he says, his smile so wide his face is almost hurting. 'It's so good to see you.'

He looks up to where Bee is standing awkwardly in front of the car.

'I'll pick them up at five,' she says, coldly.

'Can we make it six?' he says. 'I'd love them to have dinner here. Please, Bee. I haven't seen them for a week.'

She pauses then nods. 'Fine. I'll see you at six.' And barely looking at him she gets into the car.

Nan watches from the window, her heart aching at the pain she sees. There is something so familiar about Bee's pain, the loss, the anger. Something so heart-wrenching about seeing it played out on her doorstep, Daniel's joy at having his daughters back, the pain of a marriage ending in divorce.

Daniel had told her they were separated, and when Nan asked if there was a chance they would get back together, a chance this separation was temporary, an opportunity for them to sort out their differences, he had shaken his head adamantly.

'It's over,' he had said.

'And does your wife know that?'

He had closed his eyes to block out the pain. 'We haven't said those words, but I think she knows.'

'Do you know what you are looking for?'

'I'm getting there,' he had said with a small smile.

'But right now I'm not looking for anything. I'm just looking to spend as much time with the girls as I possibly can.'

Nan watches as Daniel leads the girls round to the garden, to play in the old rowboat that sits at the bottom. It must be very hard, she thinks – realizing that his situation is not as simple as she first thought, not after she glimpsed the way he looked at Michael – it must be very hard to lead a life in which you are not being true to yourself.

Understandable, to take the easy route, to do what is expected of you, to follow conventions, although Nan has never done anything for anyone other than herself.

Not that she is selfish, but she has always lived true to herself, hence her reputation as an eccentric. That poor Daniel needs to be honest with himself, she thinks. As long as he lives in denial he'll struggle, and as she wanders into the kitchen she suddenly has what she thinks is a wonderful idea.

The garden centre is quiet, the pots of hydrangeas lined up in the front wilting in the heat. Nan parks her bike at the side and walks up the alleyway, admiring the picturesque herb garden they have planted as inspiration, stopping to pet an old ginger cat rolling on his back in a patch of warm sunlight on the path.

'Nan?'

'Jack! Lovely to see you.'

'And you, Nan. What an unexpected surprise. How's your vegetable garden this year?'

'Wonderful. That fence we put up worked wonders. No deer at all. Sarah and I have been gorging ourselves on lettuces, peas, cukes and tomatoes. But they're nearly over.'

'I've still got masses of tomatoes here. Like tiny bunches of grapes and as sweet as candy. You ought to take a couple. What can I help you with today?'

'I was thinking about putting in a flower garden. Nothing too grand – a couple of beds with an arbour and a bench, just in front of the meadow. I was wondering if you might send one of your lovely men to help.'

'Of course, Nan. I could send James over tomorrow.'

'James? Do I know James?'

'No, he's new. But he's good.'

'What about that nice Matt? He's always very helpful when I come in. Any chance of having Matt over? I'm sure James is very good, but I know Matt, I think I'd be more comfortable with him.'

'Absolutely,' Jack says. 'He's out working on a job in Tom Nevers until the end of the week, but I can send him over on Monday. How does that sound?'

'Monday? Perfect!' And with a jaunty wave Nan climbs back on her bike, and smiles as she starts the journey home.

'Lemonade, anyone?' Nan carries the tray outside and the girls leap up and down. 'It's home-made,' she says, pouring a glass for Daniel as well, and handing the girls a doughnut each, having stopped at the Downyflake on the way back.

'You're spoiling us,' Daniel says with a smile.

'Quite right too,' she says. 'It's lovely having little ones around to spoil. Lizzie? Stella?' The girls gather round Nan, crumbs around their mouths; they are still a little intimidated by her, but curious.

'Do you know what a widow's walk is?'

They shake their heads.

'It's a deck on the roof, and in the old days the wives would go out at night and stand on the deck to try to see their husbands coming back from sea. You have to climb a ladder to get up there. Would you like to go and see?'

'Yes! Yes!' They jump up and down with excitement as Nan leads them inside.

She turns just as they walk in. 'Oh Daniel? I hope you don't mind but I've got someone coming to help dig a couple of flower beds on Monday. Michael's busy so I was hoping, if it's not too much trouble, you could give a hand.'

'Of course,' Daniel says. 'I'd be happy to.'

The gravel crunches as Bee pulls up. She shuts the door softly then walks up the path.

'You must be Bee,' Nan says, coming to the door. 'I'm Nan. And Daniel's just on his way back from the beach. He took the girls for a picnic. Please come in.'

'It's okay,' Bee says. 'I'll wait in the car.'

'Absolutely not.' Nan ushers her in. 'I won't hear of

it. Come and sit with me in the kitchen. I could do with the company.'

Bee, realizing that no is not an option, follows her down there.

As soon as they reach the kitchen, the door bursts open and the girls come in.

'Mommy!' they squeal and rush over to kiss Bee, who refuses to look at Daniel.

'Bee and I were just getting to know one another,' Nan says warmly. 'I was hoping she'd stay for a glass of wine. Bee?'

'I can't,' Bee says, tense again now that Daniel is here. 'I have to get the girls to bed. But thank you.'

'Daddy,' Lizzie winds herself around Daniel's legs as her eyes fill with tears, 'I don't want to go. I want to stay with Daddy.'

'Come on, Lizzie.' Bee kneels down. 'You'll see Daddy again very soon.'

'But I want to stay.' Lizzie starts to sob and Stella joins in.

Bee peels Lizzie away and carries her to the car, while Daniel carries Stella. Nan watches a terse conversation – she can't hear, but it doesn't look good – and then, when the girls are safely buckled in, Bee drives off, and Daniel comes back into the house, heading straight up the stairs to his room.

'Daniel?' Nan stands at the foot of the stairs, quietly.

He turns.

'Can I do anything for you?'

'No,' he says. 'I just didn't expect . . . I didn't think it would be this painful.'

'Because it was your decision?'

He nods.

'It's always painful,' she says. 'But better you live a life that is true to yourself.'

He looks at her curiously. 'What do you mean?'

'Just that we all deserve to be happy, and it is easy to make a wrong choice. If Bee is not the person for you, then you shouldn't stay out of a sense of duty.'

'Was your choice right?'

'My husband?' Nan is surprised. It is not often anyone asks her about Everett these days. 'He was right. For me. But perhaps I was not right for him. He committed suicide, you know. Drowned himself. He had a gambling problem, and I, of course, as is so often the case, had no idea. I didn't realize, until it was too late, how many demons he had. For a long time I blamed myself, thinking I could have done something different, picked up on the signs, been better somehow, could have stopped him gambling, but after a few years I came to terms with it.' Nan pauses for a moment, but Daniel doesn't interrupt her thoughts.

'But if I can impart some wisdom, a little of which I seem to have learned at my ripe old age, I do think,' she says gently, 'that nothing in this world happens without a reason. That we are all exactly where we are supposed to be, and that the pieces of the puzzle have a tendency to come together when you least expect it.'

'What do you mean?'

'Oh goodness. Am I talking in riddles again?' Nan laughs. 'I just mean that you ought to relax and trust that it will all be okay in the end.'

'I hope you're right.' Daniel sighs wearily as he turns to go on up to his room.

Chapter Fifteen

'Isn't this wonderful?' Richard beams across the table at Jess and Carrie, the soft candlelight in Mario's casting a flattering golden glow over everyone. 'My two favourite girls together, all of us having dinner as a family.'

Carrie catches sight of Jess rolling her eyes, but she reaches out and takes Richard's hand, relieved that finally there is calm in the house, bracing herself for the next outburst.

She realizes now that she hadn't been the slightest bit prepared for Jess moving in. She had still carried a fantasy of them all living happily ever after, believing that a large part of Jess's behaviour was down to adolescence, and living with a mother who didn't seem able to stop her appalling behaviour.

'No child of mine would ever behave like that,' she'd told one of her editors at lunch just the other day. 'I can't believe the mother puts up with it. I would never allow it.'

'Why do you think she does?' the editor had asked.

'I think she's probably too frightened of the tantrums. Everyone is.'

'Even Richard?'

'Especially Richard,' Carrie had groaned. 'Jess has

everyone wrapped around her little finger. She knows exactly when to scream, and for how long, to get her own way.'

'How old is she again?'

'I know ...' Carrie had sighed in exasperation. 'Thirteen. Going on thirty.'

Earlier today, before dinner, they had all gone to the farmers' market. Richard and Carrie were holding hands, when Carrie was shoved roughly out of the way by Jess, who inserted herself between them, grabbing her father's hand and squeezing herself up against him.

Carrie stepped aside, and Richard disengaged himself.

'Why, Daddy?' Jess started to whine. 'I want to hold your hand.'

'I was walking with Carrie,' he said. 'You just shoved her out of the way. Here, you go on my other side.'

'No, Daddy!' The whine got louder. 'I want to walk on this side. Why does she have to come anyway?' Jess turned and shot an evil look at Carrie, who pretended not to see.

'Jess, come on. Be nice.'

'Why?' Jess pouted. 'Why do I have to be nice?' And suddenly she started to scream. 'I hate her,' she shouted, standing in the middle of the street and stamping her foot while people stopped and stared. 'I hate her. Why does she have to live with us? She ruins everything.'

Carrie watched, feeling sick. Sick with anxiety, with frustration. She watched Richard take Jess aside to talk to her, Jess collapsing in sobs as Richard put his arms around her to soothe her. Twenty minutes later he walked Jess over to Carrie to apologize, but Carrie had seen Jess get exactly what she wanted: her father's undivided attention for twenty minutes, while Carrie was left standing on the sidelines.

The editor had paused to order another glass of wine before looking back at Carrie. 'If the mother isn't setting boundaries, and Richard isn't, do you think you can?'

Carrie had shrugged. 'I don't think it's my place. I don't want to act like a parent, that's not my job. And anyway, I think she'd hate me even more.'

'Does she hate you?'

'I don't think so, not really. I think if it weren't for the fact that her father and I were living together, we'd get on like a house on fire.'

'You like her?'

'I love her. And her pain reminds me of when I was young. When she's nice I adore her, and when she starts with the tantrums I just think she's the most awful child I've ever met.'

'You sound like you've really got your hands full,' the editor had said.

'I have. But –' Carrie had smiled – 'I love him. And this is a young girl in a lot of pain. It will sort itself out. It has to.'

'I'd love a story on it,' the editor had said. 'Being an unofficial stepmother.'

'Not yet,' Carrie had replied. 'Or perhaps under a pseudonym.' And they'd both laughed.

Carrie thinks about that lunch, thinks about how complicated this relationship is, when Jess sidles up to her after they get home from Mario's, and offers to help her dry the mugs in the sink.

'Can I watch *Gossip Girl* tonight? Please?' she says. Carrie sees Richard smile out of the corner of her eye, and she looks at Jess in surprise. This is the first time Jess has asked permission of Carrie for anything, treating Carrie like a parent.

'What time is it?'

'Nine. Please, Carrie? Can we watch it together? I really want you to see it and I promise I'll go to bed straight after.'

'Promise?'

'Does that mean it's a yes?' Carrie nods and Jess leaps up with joy and flings her arms around Carrie. 'Thank you! Thank you! Thank you! You're the best!' And as Carrie reaches down to hug her in return she finds her eyes have filled with tears. Perhaps this is the breakthrough she has been waiting for.

*

Daff puts down the phone and sighs. Jess always sounds so distant when she phones. She remembers a colleague of hers, a divorced mother, saying she never phoned her kids when they were at their dad's, always waited for them to call her, because she would usually be interrupting them and they weren't in the mood to talk to her and she would end up feeling unsatisfied and upset.

Daff knows that it is better to wait for Jess to call her, but she is so frightened Jess won't call her, so frightened she is losing her daughter, that she can't resist calling, even when Jess clearly doesn't want to talk to her.

Her phone rings again and she snatches it up, hoping it's Jess calling back, wanting to chat.

'Daff? It's Laura. How are you?'

'I'm great, Laura, how are you?'

'Good. I'm just ringing to see if I should pick you up.'

There's a silence as Daff's mind starts working furiously. 'I feel completely stupid,' she says eventually, 'but pick me up for what?'

'Oh Daff!' Laura starts to laugh. 'You said you'd come to PJ's tonight, remember? It's singles night? I'm going with the girls.'

Daff groans inwardly. She had said she'd come, but that was weeks ago, and at the time it had seemed an abstract concept. The last thing she wants to do tonight is get dressed up and go out with a friend from work. She is looking forward to a hot bath, climbing into bed in some oversized pyjamas, and spending the night watching back-to-back *Law & Order*s.

'I . . . was that tonight? Oh Laura, I didn't realize it was tonight . . .'

'What are you doing? You can't make an excuse.'

'I'm just exhausted,' Daff tries lamely. 'I'm planning on an early night.'

'No way,' Laura says. 'I'm not letting you off the hook that easily. We're meeting there at seven and you have to come.'

'I really don't think . . .'

'Daff, when was the last time you went out and had some fun? I've been divorced much longer than you, and I remember those early days of getting into bed and watching television, but you can't do that forever. I know you can't use Jess as an excuse, and I promise you we'll have a good time. If you hate it you can leave, but you have to at least try it.'

An hour later Daff walks into PJ's, squeezing through the throngs of people, looking around for Laura and trying not to look desperate.

What the hell am I doing here, she thinks, hoping there is no one she knows sitting in the restaurant who might peer down and see her, obviously single, definitely not searching – but they aren't to know that.

The women who surround her are dressed up to the nines – little black dresses, halter-necked sundresses in bright colours, tan skin exposed, tottering in super-high platform shoes. Everyone is made up, dressed up, the men in slacks and polo shirts, everyone looking around to see who is there, who has just arrived, who might be worth talking to.

Oh God, Daff thinks, not seeing Laura. Can this get any worse?

PJ's has always been a thriving restaurant, but for years the large deck overlooking the water had been underused.

Occasionally they hosted weddings on the deck, and they had a few plastic tables and chairs, but it wasn't until new owners took over and transformed it into a bar that PJ's became a serious destination.

They started singles nights on Thursdays and Sundays, live bands on Saturdays, and quickly found that people came from miles away to cram onto the deck, drink frozen margaritas, flirt with the cute barmen they employed every summer. If there is such a thing as a professional singles scene, then PJ's is the epicentre, the place where singles, divorcees and even the secretly married come looking for adventure, come to find love.

Perhaps not love. There is something too mercenary about the people here, they look jaded, look like they're too busy searching to ever actually find – the thrill is all about the chase, the flirtation, the conquest, rather than finding a happy ever after.

'Hello!' Daff is leaning on the bar waiting for the barman to notice her, figuring that at least if she has a drink in hand it will give her something to do while she waits for Laura to arrive. She looks down to see a short man with a large smile grinning lasciviously at her.

'Hello,' she says, turning back to the barman, willing him to come over, to notice her, to get her a drink so she can get away from this man.

'I haven't seen you here before,' he says. 'I'm Adam.'

'Hi.' She doesn't want to tell him her name, but nor

does she want to appear rude. 'I'm Daff,' she says even-tually, hoping that if she sounds unfriendly he might go away.

'So is this your first time?'

'Um, yes.'

'Divorced?'

'Yes.'

'Me too. Can I get you a drink?'

'I don't know. Can you?' Daff is now exasperated. 'I've been standing here for about fifteen minutes and the barmen haven't even noticed me.'

'Hey! Nick!' Adam cups his hands around his mouth and hollers. 'Get over here and get the lady a drink!' The barman looks over and grins at him, and seconds later Daff is sipping a strawberry daiquiri.

'Thanks,' she says with a smile. 'That was very kind of you.'

'I suffer from knight in shining armour syndrome,' he says. 'How about trying to find a table so we can sit down and get to know one another?'

'That's ... well ... I'm meeting friends and I think I should probably stay by the bar.'

'Okey-dokey. Fine by me. So tell me all about yourself, Daff. Why is a beautiful woman like yourself coming to a place like PJ's on a Thursday night?'

Damn good question, Daff thinks. Why indeed?

An hour later Daff stands up, ready to go. Adam, while not her type in the slightest, has been her saviour, for Laura has not appeared, and Daff is ready to kill her, but at least she has not had to stand around looking desperate, and has been able to have a perfectly fine conversation with Adam.

'Leaving so soon?' Adam says, when Daff finally says she really has to get home.

'I need to get back for the babysitter,' she lies. 'But thank you again.'

'Let me walk you to your car.' Adam jumps off his bar stool and takes her arm. Daff stiffens. This was not what she had in mind, but her car is close, and soon she will be rid of him, safely back at home.

'Can I call you?' Adam says, as Daff presses the button to unlock the doors.

'You know, you've been very sweet,' Daff says, 'but I'm really not ready to date anyone just yet.'

'Who said anything about dating?' Adam grins. 'I was just hoping for a kiss goodnight.'

Daff looks at him in horror.

'I'm kidding,' he says, and she forces a laugh.

'Seriously, though,' he persists, 'I'd really like your number. I'm not looking to date anyone either, but perhaps you and I could make one another happy in different ways.' He raises a confident eyebrow at her.

'What do you mean?'

'Well, don't you get lonely going to bed by yourself every night? I find friends with benefits to be the easiest solution. You and I both stand to win. No commitment, just passion.' He growls on the last word and moves closer, putting an arm around Daff's waist.

'Oh Jesus,' Daff groans, shoving him away and

getting in the car, gunning the engine without waiting to see what he's saying, although she glances in her rear-view mirror as she drives off and he's shouting something.

'That was the worst night of my life,' she says out loud as she drives home. 'Not only am I going to kill Laura, I'm never ever going to a singles night anywhere for as long as I live.'

It's not even as though Daff wants a relationship. What she wants, right now, is to find herself again. When she was married, she knew who she was. Perhaps she wasn't entirely true to herself – she always felt, married to Richard, she was playing a role, being the dutiful wife, the loving mother, to the extent that she stopped thinking about what it was that would make her happy – but now that she's no longer married she realizes she doesn't have a clear definition of who she is.

Living in this small suburban town where everyone is married, everyone is defined by their role in the community, their involvement in school, she doesn't have a role any more.

Slowly, she realizes, her social life has dropped off. The couples they were friends with are no longer her friends. *Friendly*, yes, but she is no longer invited to dinner parties and get-togethers on her own, unless there is a single man someone wants to introduce her to, but they are few and far between.

She runs into those women sometimes at the grocery store, their trolleys piled high with industrial packs of Bounty, giant plastic bottles of Tide, three quarts of fat-free organic milk, and she feels self-conscious about her own shopping, particularly now that Jess is no longer at home – a couple of yoghurts, sliced ham from the deli, a small packet of organic granola and half a pint of milk.

'We must get together,' the women will say, eyeing her small hand-held basket with pity as they pretend to be embarrassed at all their provisions. 'Groceries,' they'll say with a sigh. 'Isn't this a pain?'

Soon after the divorce she had read in the local paper about a women's support group. She had gone, not because she particularly wanted support, but because she was lonely, was still trying to adjust to not having a husband to cook for, to having to do everything herself, and was hoping to meet some other women who had shared her experience, perhaps find friends, women she could get together with and have dinner, a coffee perhaps.

But she had found it frightening and toxic. A room full of bitter, angry women, all of whom seemed to have a worse story about the awful ex-husbands in their lives, from abuse, to laziness, to infidelity. Daff left the room each time in a deep depression.

'What about your husband?' someone would invariably ask as they lined up by the coffee machine in the break, and Daff, who could have regaled them with stories of Richard's affair, chose instead to shrug and say it was just one of those things that didn't work out, and they quickly lost interest.

What she needs now, she realizes, is a fresh start. A change of scene. She is booked on the ferry to Nantucket in three days, and she needs this rest more than she has ever needed anything. She needs to get away from home, needs to lie on beaches with stacks of good books, hell, maybe even start painting again. She needs to remember who she was before she became a wife, a mother and, most recently, a divorcee.

She needs to decide who she's going to be next.

Chapter Sixteen

'Oh good.' Nan peers out of the kitchen window as she does the washing-up. 'That nice man from the garden centre's here. Daniel, would you mind just running out and telling him I'm in the kitchen? I'll be out in a minute.'

Nan watches as Daniel walks outside and introduces himself to Matt, pointing inside then nodding and climbing up into the back of the truck to help get the tools.

How could they not like each other, she thinks. Matt, short but perfectly formed, his arms a deep rich tan from working outside in the sun, with longish brown hair and a ready smile, is nothing short of adorable, and a perfect foil for the more brooding Daniel.

What a lovely couple they would make, she thinks, smiling to herself, wiping her hands on a towel. Not that she's trying to push anyone into anything, but that poor Daniel is so sad, and so obviously confused. Amazing that his wife doesn't seem to know, but this must be so hard for Daniel. He looks like he could use, at the very least, a friend.

They work hard, Daniel and Matt, side by side. Nan watches from the window like a mother hen, emerging from time to time to check their progress, bringing them cold lemonade, then calling them for lunch.

'I set the table under the pergola,' Nan says. 'You two need a break and I have to dash off to the A & P with Michael.' And with a jaunty wave, she's gone, a smile on her face.

She would love to stay, but knows they will be more comfortable alone.

Matt walks in front, grinning as he sees the table. Daniel, following behind, looks away as Matt pulls off the gardening gloves and tucks them absent-mindedly into the back pocket of his jeans, then looks back at the smooth curve of Matt's backside in rough, faded Levi's, blushing as Matt turns and catches his gaze.

Two linen placemats are laid out, a white bowl of salad greens from the garden, toasted pine nuts and feta, beautifully cut roast beef sandwiches, and a basket of what smells suspiciously like freshly baked bread.

'Damn!' Matt slaps his thigh. 'She forgot the candles!'

'What?' Daniel looks at him in confusion.

'Well, doesn't this feel like we're being set up on a date?' He grins again, not entirely unhappy about the situation, as Daniel's eyes widen.

'We are? But ... Nan doesn't know ... ?' Daniel's voice trails off.

'Doesn't know what? That I'm gay? Oh Daniel, everyone on the island who knows me knows I'm gay. I think it's sweet. She thinks we'd make a nice couple.' He raises an eyebrow at Daniel, who flushes and looks away, not knowing what on earth to say, unused to flirting with a man, and particularly with a man so unexpectedly cute.

'Oh shit.' Matt's face falls. 'Don't tell me you're straight. Oh my God! I'm so embarrassed.'

'No, no,' Daniel lays a hand on his arm as Matt sinks his head in his hands. 'I am gay –' and even as he says those words he feels relief flood through him – 'it's just that . . . I'm newly gay.'

'You just came out?'

'Well, not officially. I don't understand how Nan knew?'

'Because you thought you were as straight as they come? Oh honey . . .' Matt throws his head back and laughs. 'I hate to disappoint you but we can always tell.'

'Nan too?'

Matt shrugs. 'Nan? Of course. Shall we sit down? This food looks delicious and, bless her, she's even left cold beers in the cooler for us. I think we should treat this as the date it's supposed to be.'

Daniel sits, gratefully taking a swig of the beer Matt hands to him. 'I was married until about a minute ago.'

'Married? *Married?* To a *woman?*'

Daniel nods.

'No wonder you're so jumpy. This really must be new for you. Were you faithful or were there men on the side?'

'God, no!' Daniel says. 'I've got two daughters. I'd never be unfaithful.'

'But you've always known you were gay?'

Daniel nods.

'Me too.' Matt dishes out the salad as he talks. 'I guess I was lucky. My dad left us when I was four, and my mom always had tons of gay friends. It seemed completely natural to be gay and, honestly, I don't ever remember having a conversation about it, or ever officially coming out. It just evolved, and was never uncomfortable, or an issue. I've met so many married men over the years. Actually –' he looks coy for a second – 'I've had affairs with one or two, but I've known so many men who are married and who can't see another way. Most of them stay married their entire lives and the wives never know.'

Daniel nods. 'That's how it was for me. I've always known, but I didn't want to know, didn't want it to be true. I thought that being married to a woman would somehow keep me safe.' He snorts. 'Isn't that ridiculous?'

'No. I think a lot of men feel that way.'

'But I thought I could do it, and then something happened. A guy I was once . . . well, we had a fling years ago, before I was married. I hadn't seen him for years then he got back in touch, and he came out years ago – and I saw what my life could have been, could still be, and realized I couldn't live a lie any longer. I just couldn't do it.'

'I think that's incredibly brave,' Matt says. 'I can't imagine what it would be like, having to tell all the people in your life: Jeez, sorry, but I made a mistake; after all these years of you thinking I was straight, guess what?'

'Oh God,' Daniel groans. 'I'm trying not to think about it.'

'What was your wife's reaction?' Matt is curious now. 'Is she okay?'

Daniel looks down at the table. 'I haven't told her yet,' he says slowly.

'Are you going to?'

'Of course!' He looks up. 'I just don't know when. Or how. I feel like I've caused her enough pain. She thought everything in the marriage was great. Well, almost everything . . .'

'As in, you never wanted to sleep with her?'

Daniel shrugs with a resigned smile.

'Got it. You know, though,' Matt says, 'I know people who have told their wives, and it's almost made it easier, because it stops being about them, they stop being able to blame themselves. I think when relation-ships end we spend so much time thinking about the "if onlys": if only I'd been more understanding, or less understanding. If only I'd been nicer, or worked less, or any number of things. Okay, I'm rambling now, but the point is that the *what if*s can wreak even more havoc on a situation that's already difficult. If your wife knew the truth, she'd know she couldn't have competed, she couldn't have done anything differently to make you stay. It may be that it makes it much easier for both of you.'

Daniel nods slowly. 'I'd never thought of it like that. I guess I'd just thought of trying to avoid causing her more pain.'

'I'm not saying she's going to throw her arms around you and thank you, then want to be your best friend, although, frankly, stranger things have happened.' He gazes intently at Daniel. 'You might want to think about telling her the truth.'

'Wow.' Daniel shakes his head in surprise, a smile on his lips. 'I can't actually believe I'm talking about it now, so freely, like this.'

'Feels good, doesn't it?' Matt raises his beer.

'It does. It really, really does. Cheers.' And they both tuck in to the food.

Nan stays away for as long as she can, going straight back out to the garden when she finally gets home.

Daniel's almost finished digging one bed, Matt turning the soil on the other one, and Daniel is laughing at something Matt has been saying. Oh goody, Nan thinks, they like one another.

'How are my beds?'

Matt looks up. 'Almost done. And thank you, Nan. Lunch was delicious.'

'Entirely unexpected but wonderful,' echoes Daniel. 'Thank you.'

'You two look like you're getting on.' Nan can't help herself.

'It's remarkable,' Matt says. 'In the four hours since we met we've fallen head over heels in love and we'll be moving in together next week.'

Nan almost keels over in shocked delight. 'Really?'

'No!' Matt shakes his head as Daniel grins and looks

away. 'Not *really*. But now at least we see you did have an ulterior motive.'

'Was it that obvious?'

Matt shrugs. 'It was the flowers on the table that did it. We were wondering where the candles were.'

'I did think about candles,' Nan says, seriously. 'I just thought it was a bit unnecessary, given that it's a hot summer's day.'

'We were joking,' Daniel says, thinking how strange it is to say 'we', when referring to anyone other than Bee.

'Oh boys,' Nan says. 'Stop being so wicked. Let me show you how I want these beds planted out.' She takes Matt's arm and walks him up to the house to show him the pictures she's cut out of a garden magazine.

'Did you mind?' Later, long after Matt has gone, Nan comes outside and sits next to Daniel, sinking into one of the old, scratched-up Adirondack chairs overlooking the bay. 'Was it horribly presumptuous of me?'

'A little, but I don't mind. Can I ask you, though – how did you know?'

'Oh darling. An old bird like me? I've learned to listen to my intuition these days. I didn't when I was younger, you know, and every time I ignored it, it got me into trouble. Now I find that the little voice is almost always right, and there was nothing in particular, just a feeling.'

'Okay.'

'Were you worried you were suddenly behaving like a screaming queen without realizing it?' Nan laughs.

'I was a bit.' Daniel grins sheepishly, and she shakes her head.

'Not a bit of it. But now do tell me about Matt. Isn't he lovely? The two of you seemed to get on.'

'We did. He's a good guy. Helped me see things another way.'

'Good.' She nods, loving being the mother hen again, loving having people to look after. 'Oh my gosh,' she says, looking at her watch. 'The new tenant will be here any minute and I was hoping to make dinner for all of us, a sort of getting-to-know-you night.'

'Can I help?'

'You most certainly can. I'm making the chowder; you can do the crab cakes. Let's get a move on and see if we can all sit down for eight.'

*

Daff puts her bags down and goes over to the window, sinking down and curling her feet up under her, looking out of the window with delight, a sigh of satisfaction escaping her. She has seen views like this many times over the years – sunlight glinting off water, boats bobbing gently in the ocean – but she has been too busy to enjoy them.

She has been too busy to do a lot of things she enjoyed, she has started to realize, things that once upon a time, before she became a wife and mother, fed her soul.

Painting, for one. She hasn't painted for years, but right before she packed, when she was sorting out her office, she found a tiny travel watercolour kit. She put it in her case, and bought a small pad of watercolour paper to go with it.

She used to listen to music all the time before she was married. She would turn it up loud when she was alone in her apartment at night, and dance, sometimes for hours. She remembers calling it the soundtrack to her life: Neil Young when she was a teenager, Joni Mitchell and Cat Stevens when she went away to school.

Why is it that the soundtrack to her life stopped on the day she got married?

She has started listening to music again. Pouring herself a glass of wine and soaking in a hot bubble bath, Jack Johnson crooning softly as she tips her head forward to take a sip, revelling in having to be nowhere else, having to do nothing for anyone else, for the rest of the night.

But she misses Jess. Oh how she misses Jess. Not the Jess of late, the truculent, angry, hostile teenager, but her lovely little girl, her sunny, warm, clever Jess, a Jess she knows is still hiding somewhere deep inside.

Better though, for now, that Jess is with her dad. Perhaps they both need this break from one another. Daff doesn't see this move as permanent, and has a strong suspicion that Jess will be on the phone soon, begging to come home. And perhaps then they will find their feet again, will be able to be mother and daughter again, friends and allies instead of enemies. She met up with Carrie and liked her, understanding that someone like Carrie might be good for Jess, and this is just a trial after all, it doesn't have to last long, just long enough for her to regain her equilibrium.

Nantucket is a well-deserved break, a time during which both Daff and Jess will be able to heal. She has her oils in her bag, a burner, and a CD of meditations that she hasn't listened to for at least ten years, maybe longer.

This is a place to be reborn, she thinks, curling up tighter and hugging her knees. It feels as if a weight has been lifted, as if she can start again, and what a special, magical house to have found.

Everything does happen for a reason after all, she thinks.

*

'Should we go into the living room?' Nan keeps asking, topping up everyone's wine glass. 'Sarah cleaned in there especially. I really think we ought to be sitting in there.'

'Mom, relax.' Michael smiles at her, taking the bottle out of her somewhat unsteady hand and pouring the wine himself. 'Everyone's happy in the kitchen, and it's lovely in here. We'll use the living room another time.'

She smiles at him. 'You're right.' And she lowers her voice to a whisper. 'So what do you think of the new tenant?'

Michael looks over at Daff, who is standing next to Daniel at the stove as he fries the crab cakes, asking him quiet questions about his cooking.

'She seems nice,' he says. 'But sad.'

'I think so too.' Nan nods. 'Terribly nice and probably on a journey to happiness herself.'

'What's her story? Do you know?'

'Divorced. Single mother. Daughter staying with the father and girlfriend, and I think this is the first time she's had for herself in years. I rather think she's slightly lost, doesn't know what to do with herself. Perhaps you'll take her and show her the island tomorrow? I think she'd love it.'

'Mom?' Michael says warningly, shaking his head with a groan. 'Please tell me you're not matchmaking again?'

'Whatever do you mean?' Nan is shocked.

'I love you, Mom, and I know you. You always used to try to set me up with everyone.'

'I did not!' She is mock appalled.

'What are you two talking about?' Daniel finishes off frying the crab cakes and he and Daff wander over.

'Michael's accusing me of matchmaking him with everyone,' Nan says indignantly.

'She did!' Michael laughs. 'Whenever she found any single women on the island, she automatically told them about her son and I'd come home and find strangers waiting for me on the porch.'

'Some of them were lovely,' Nan says. 'You dated one or two.'

'One or two out of one or two hundred. That's not exactly a good track record.'

'Sounds like you were interviewing for the position,' Daff says, turning to Nan and laughing.

'I was but we never did find the right candidate, did we?' She arches an eyebrow and revolves her head slowly to give Michael a mock glare.

'Speak for yourself,' Michael says, as his mobile phone begins to ring, again, from the corner of the kitchen.

'Darling,' Nan says crossly, 'that thing's been ringing all afternoon. Can't you turn it off?'

'I'm sorry, Mom. I thought I had.' He goes over to the phone and picks it up to look at the number flashing on the screen. Jordana. Again. The sixth time she's called in the last two hours. There are a string of messages, but he stopped listening after the first two. Her first was full of tears, her second full of rage.

There is nothing he can say to make it better, to make it different, and he cannot help but feel an overwhelming relief that he got out when he did. Hopefully, if he just lies low and stays unavailable, she will realize that there is no going back, will finally be able to move on.

He presses the button to turn the phone off, this time checking that it is actually off, and drops the phone in a drawer. He hates mobile phones anyway, and certainly doesn't need one now. A disastrous love affair that has led to no job, no social plans to make – why on earth does he need to look at this constant reminder of the way he has fucked up his life?

He closes the drawer softly and goes over to his mother. 'Shall we sit down?' he whispers in her ear. 'I'm starving.'

*   *   *

'This is bizarre,' Daff says, helping Nan clear the dishes. 'I feel incredibly comfortable here. It feels like I'm having dinner with people I've known for years.'

'It's Windermere,' Michael says. 'Seriously. It's the house. It was always like this when I was growing up. I'd forgotten how it does that to people.'

'He's right,' Nan adds. 'This house brings people together.'

'So much so I've barely seen the island,' Daniel says. 'I've been here a week and I've hardly left this house, other than when I'm with the girls.'

'Is there stuff for them to do here?'

'Are you kidding? Tons! Fishing, boating, ice creams. It doesn't get better than this. And I've been taking them to crafts at the whaling museum most afternoons. They love it. Your daughter should come out. I think this is a great place for kids.'

'She's not really a kid any more,' Daff says. 'She's thirteen. She'd probably think crafts at a museum "like, ohmyGod, suck".' Daff does an accurate impersonation of a surly teenager and Nan smiles.

'A tough age,' Nan says. 'Michael was relatively easy but I had lots of friends with daughters who turned into horrors as teenagers. They came back, though. All of them grew up to be best friends with their mothers.'

'I hope so,' Daff says, and the sadness in her eyes as she looks away is undeniable.

'Michael, why don't you show Daff some of the island tomorrow?' Nan suggests, breaking the discomfort, and Daff starts to laugh.

'This isn't one of your famous fix-ups, is it? Because if it is, you need to work on your subtlety.'

'Subtlety's never been one of Mom's strong points.' Michael grins. 'But don't worry, I'm strictly unavailable.'

'You are?' Nan turns to him in horror. 'Is there something you should be telling me?'

'Just that after this last relationship, I'm taking a break. Seriously. No more dating for me for a year. I need to get my life back in order before I even think about sharing it with anyone else.'

'Hear, hear!' Daff raises her glass in a salute. 'I agree. My forays into the dating world have also been disastrous. Right now I just need to find myself again.'

Daniel clears his throat. 'I'm not quite sure how to tell you this, but I need to get it out of the way. I . . .' He stops, unsure why he is telling them when he hasn't even told his wife, but this feels easier, confessing to people who don't know him as a husband and father, as a family man, confessing to people who know him simply as Daniel, who won't judge him in the same way. 'The reason my marriage broke up,' he continues, 'is that I'm gay.'

There's an awkward silence.

'Congratulations?' Michael says, and Daff laughs.

'Oh God, I'm sorry,' she apologizes quickly. 'I just don't know what to say. I mean, I assumed you were.'

'That's terrible!' Daniel says. 'Everyone keeps assuming I'm gay now that I'm no longer with my wife. How is it that no one ever thought I was gay while I was married and now everyone does?'

Nan lays a hand on his arm. 'I suspect it won't be as much of a surprise to other people as you might think, and that's not a bad thing. Think of all the things you have to look forward to, a life in which you no longer have to keep secrets.'

'It's the one thing I try to keep thinking of,' Daniel says. 'The one thing that keeps me going. That, and my daughters. Obviously.'

'Will we meet them?' Daff says.

'Absolutely. They'll be here tomorrow. Bee's dropping them off at four.'

'Bee?'

'My ex. And she doesn't know yet so don't say anything. Please.' He sighs deeply. 'I know it's wrong, telling you before I tell her, but I'm so scared of telling her, and every time I say those words out loud it becomes a little less scary.'

'We understand,' Nan says gently, and looking around at each of them, Daniel feels a huge sense of relief, for he can see that it's true.

'Tell me about the girls,' Daff says, changing the subject, sensing it becoming difficult for him. 'Jess was so adorable when she was little, I miss it still.'

Daniel's face lights up as he tells her all about Lizzie and Stella.

Chapter Seventeen

Daff and Daniel start laughing as Michael struggles to manoeuvre the bicycles out of the shed.

'What?' Michael looks up at Daff, as Daniel shakes his head in disbelief.

'You're not serious?' Daniel chuckles.

'About what?' Michael is bemused.

Daff chimes in. 'We're riding those?'

Michael looks down at the bikes. 'What's wrong with them? Admittedly they're a bit dusty but I'll wash them up and oil them and they'll be as good as new.'

'How old *are* they?' Daniel asks.

Michael grins. 'I think they were one of my mum's wedding presents.'

'They look it.' Daniel gingerly takes one and wheels it around the courtyard. 'Actually, they look older. If you took those onto the *Antiques Roadshow* you'd probably find they're worth a fortune.'

'Oh come on.' Michael looks down at the bikes. 'They're not that bad.'

'Of course they're not,' Daniel says. 'They're gorgeous. I'm just not used to seeing people ride bikes like that.'

'But they're classic bikes. They're beautiful.'

'You're right. They are, but I live in a town where

everything has to be new, and shiny, and the best. If you're going to ride a bike it has to be a top of the range mountain bike, and no more than two years old.'

'Well, where I come from we love the old classics. Give me a beaten-up old jeep, or a classic Schwinn any day.'

'I agree.' Daff smiles. 'But Daniel's right. We live in an age when we're expected to wear our wealth on our sleeves, when money is God and the more you have the more you're expected to display it. You can't believe some of the houses being built in my town.'

'Oh I can,' Daniel says. 'Let me guess – seven thousand square feet is now the norm?'

'Yup.' She laughs. 'And that's slightly on the small side. Then there are all the things you have to have with it: his and her closets, each the size of a bedroom, sweeping staircase and marble floor in the centre hall . . .'

'Range Rover in the garage?' Michael contributes.

'Or the Hummer for the wife,' Daff offers. 'But I'll tell you my favourite. The local paper did an article about a house that went up on the water a couple of years ago. It was done by some big-name architect, and decorated by one of the big New York designers, and it was . . . wait for it . . . twenty thousand square feet.'

'Who in the hell needs twenty thousand square feet?' Michael gasps. 'I mean, seriously? What for? What does anyone *need* with that? Do they have an army of children?'

'No, young couple in their late thirties – he'd evidently made a killing from hedge funds – and they had two small children. And here's my favourite part: throughout this article they kept being quoted saying things like they were very unpretentious, and they wanted the house to be cosy and informal. They said they were very down to earth and wanted it to be inviting and reflective of who they were.' Daff cracks up laughing, along with Daniel, while Michael shakes his head in astonishment.

'How do you make twenty thousand square feet cosy?' he asks, genuinely perplexed.

'You don't.' Daniel shrugs. 'And trust me, everyone I've ever met who lives in one of those houses will tell you the same thing: they're very down to earth and not pretentious in the slightest, and they're ever so slightly embarrassed they ended up with such a big house.'

Daff sighs. 'Give me an antique any day.'

'Me too,' Michael says. 'As far as I'm concerned the old houses in town right here on Nantucket are sheer perfection.'

'I love those!' Daff says. 'Didn't we drive past them on the way out here the other day? I'd love to see them again properly. Can we do a tour?'

'Of course,' Michael replies. 'Just give me a chance to get the bikes cleaned off. Daniel, are you going to come?'

'I don't think so,' Daniel says. 'But thanks. I feel like I've abandoned work a bit, so I'm going to look for somewhere with wifi in town and get some work out of the way.'

'You're sure?'

'I'm sure. The girls are with me this weekend and I need to get all this stuff done before they arrive so I can just truly focus on them.'

'You sound like a wonderful father,' Daff says, her eyes suddenly sad as she thinks about Jess.

'I have wonderful children,' he says, and bidding them goodbye he turns to go inside.

*

Nan lies in bed, surrounded by magazines. It's not often she does this, relax in bed and let the house get on without her, but for the first time in months she feels safe enough to do it, safe enough mostly because Michael is back, because the house finally feels alive again.

The wheels of the house, deep in the underbelly, are creaking and groaning but turning again, pushing a life force, an energy, through the house that is gathering a momentum of its own.

What a relief that it is not solely down to Nan to breathe life into Windermere; what a relief to know that Windermere has awoken, will continue, possibly even without Nan.

For Nan is tired these days. Unsurprising perhaps, given how much she has had to do, especially now that Sarah has gone to the Cape with her husband's family until the end of the summer. Nan hadn't realized, before now, quite how much she takes Sarah for granted, nor quite how much Sarah does for her.

And she misses her, wishes that after all her work in transforming the house, Sarah were here to join in the fun of being with these wonderful people. And she also wishes Sarah were here to insist on sending Nan upstairs, protesting all the time, when Sarah can see that she's exhausted.

Nan is careful not to show anyone how tired she is, doesn't want anyone to worry about her, but this morning, after breakfast, after she made pancakes, scrambled eggs and bacon for everyone, she walked back upstairs and saw that she had forgotten to make the bed, and it looked so warm, so inviting and cosy, that all at once she felt exhausted, so she kicked off her shoes and sank back into bed, falling quickly into a deep sleep.

She didn't even hear Michael poke his head round the door, smiling at her as he walked over and tucked the covers around her, much as you would do to a child.

Nan awakened feeling a little better, but still not quite herself. Probably coming down with something. She had, after all, been around those adorable little girls – Stella and Lizzie – and weren't children just like little mobile Petri dishes of germs? Wouldn't it be just her luck to have picked up some kind of ghastly summer flu that was sweeping the elementary schools of Massachusetts?

'Can I get you anything?' Daniel knocks on the door and comes in.

'No thank you, Daniel,' she says, with a smile that is

trying to be as luminous as always. Ten minutes later Daniel reappears with a cup of tea.

'You are a love,' she says. 'Now where is Michael? Have you seen him?' She pats her bed, inviting Daniel to perch on the edge.

'He and Daff have taken out those ancient bikes to go exploring.'

'Oh good,' Nan says. 'I hope they have fun. I have a sense that there could be a romance between them. Is that awful of me to say? You mustn't say anything.'

'I won't.' Daniel smiles. 'And I feel the same thing. Michael invited me along but I graciously declined. I thought that the two of them ought to be alone some-how.'

'Good for you,' Nan says. 'So what are you up to today?'

'I do have to work. I'm off into town. Are you sure I can't get you anything else? Do you need me to call a doctor or anything?'

'Good heavens, no! I'm not truly sick, just feeling a little under the weather. I'm fine. I don't believe in doctors anyway. I only ever believed in Dr Grover, who used to patch up all the local kids when they tore them-selves up. But not for us adults. Quite unnecessary, I think.'

'You're sure?'

'Quite sure.' And with a smile she waves him out of the room.

*

'Are you certain you're okay?' Michael keeps stopping on his bike, way ahead of Daff, waiting for her to catch up, which she does eventually, puffing away like a lunatic.

'Absolutely,' she says, forcing a smile and trying not to show quite how out of shape she is. 'It looks a damn sight more fun than it is, though,' she says wryly, and Michael laughs.

'When did you say you last exercised?'

'I didn't.' She puts on a fake scowl. 'In between working, being a single mother, running my life and that of a truculent teenager, I haven't quite been able to fit in those good old Pilates classes.'

'Let's take a break,' Michael says, climbing off his bike and sinking down onto the grass. 'We can sit for a while. So ... your life sounds busy. Is your ex involved?'

'With me or my daughter?' She raises an eyebrow.

'Your daughter's with him now, isn't she? So that's a given.'

'True. I have to say, I think we get on fine. I thought at the time that I would never get over the pain, but I came to see that there was a reason he looked outside the marriage, that if it had been as good and as perfect as I thought, he would never have looked elsewhere.'

'I'm sorry,' Michael says. 'I didn't realize.'

'That's okay. I didn't tell you. But yes, I am that clichéd woman who discovers her husband is having an affair.'

'And you didn't want to give him a second chance?'

Michael cannot help himself, he is thinking of Jordana, of what would happen if Jackson found out.

'I always thought I would. I mean, in those conversations where you imagine the worst and you wonder how you'd react, I think I always thought that I might be able to forgive an affair, that infidelity doesn't have to be the ultimate destroyer of a marriage, but Richard couldn't choose, and that's what I couldn't forgive.' She sighs. 'That's enough about me. What's your story?'

'Me? I don't have a story.' Michael grins.

'Forty . . . what? Three? Four?'

'Close. Two.'

'Ever been married?'

'Nope.'

'*There*'s a story right there.'

'Maybe, but it isn't nearly as exciting as it sounds. I think I just chose badly. I had a couple of long-term relationships with women who were great in many ways, but who weren't great for me. I never found peace in a relationship, and now I thank my lucky stars I didn't end up marrying them because it wouldn't have ended well.' He pauses. 'And then there was my latest unfortunate incident.'

'Oh yes?'

'I hate even admitting it, particularly when your husband had an affair, and I'm not proud of it at all . . .'

'You had an affair with a married woman?'

Michael nods, and when he looks up he sees Daff's eyes are gentle. Despite what has happened to her, he is not being judged.

'Was that the crazy ringing of the phone last night?' She raises a knowing eyebrow.

'Oh God. Is it that obvious?'

Daff smiles. 'I've been there before. I figured it was something to do with a woman. So, what now?'

'It's over. Completely.'

'For both of you?'

'That's the problem. For me, absolutely. But she wants to carry on. She has this crazy idea that I'm her soulmate. And I adore this woman, truly I do. She's someone I've known for years; but as I've come to know her better I've realized there's no way we belong together, and I had to leave.'

'Aha! So that's the reason you fled back home to Nantucket.'

'Pretty much. What are you fleeing from?'

'Not fleeing from,' Daff muses, standing up and stretching. 'Looking for, I think. Looking for who I am.'

'Before you became a wife and mother?'

Daff looks at him in surprise. 'Exactly! How did you know?'

'I don't know.' Michael stands up with her and climbs back on his bike. 'It just seemed to make sense.'

Michael shows Daff all the places a first-timer to Nantucket should see, and then some of the places that aren't so necessary, but that are important to him. He takes her to the Sankaty lighthouse, scene of his first kiss, the jeweller's where he used to work on Saturdays, where he discovered he loved his craft, and out to Coatue, where he and his friends used to have wild drinking parties late at night on the beach.

They stop at the Club Car for lunch, and later the Juice Bar for ice creams, walking back outside to find a group of boys from the bike shop next door standing around their bicycles.

'Are these yours?' says one.

'Yup.'

'Man, I haven't seen bikes like this in years. My dad grew up on one like this. This is a *serious* bike.'

'I know. It's been around for a long, long time.'

'Can I take it to the end of the road?'

'Sure.' Michael watches as the kid cycles off, and Daff turns to him in amazement.

'What?' Michael looks at her.

'He could steal it,' she whispers uncertainly.

'He's not going to steal it. He'll be back in a minute.'

'I can't believe you trusted him with your bike. What if he doesn't come back?'

'He will. But if he doesn't we'll hitchhike home.'

Daff gasps. 'Hitchhike? Are you crazy?'

Michael starts to laugh. 'I'd be crazy if I was proposing hitchhiking on, say, the Bruckner Expressway, or on Third Avenue, but this is Nantucket. Anyway, I'm joking. We won't have to hitchhike. He'll be back any second.'

Fifteen minutes later Daff stands back and raises an eyebrow at Michael.

'Who's going to be hitchhiking now?' she says.

Michael shakes his head. 'Damn. I can't believe that. I really thought he was a good kid.'

'You're not as savvy as you seem, Mr-I-live-in-New-York-City.' Daff laughs.

'Oh no?' Michael grins as the kid screeches up next to them.

'I got carried away.' He climbs off the bike and hands it to Michael, who gives Daff an 'I told you so' look. 'That is one *sweet* bike. I almost took off with it,' he adds. Michael returns his smile, and pointedly ignores Daff, who is trying not to laugh.

'You're obviously a lucky man,' she says, as they wheel the bikes round the corner.

Michael looks at her in disbelief. 'Hardly,' he says wryly. 'I used to think life tended to play out the way you expect it to. If you expect the best in people, generally they'll give you the best, and if you expect the worst, then that's what you'll get.' He sighs. 'I'm not so sure any more.'

'You should be sure. I think that sounds very wise,' Daff says. 'And very true. I think a lot of the time I operate out of fear, but your way sounds much better.'

'Fear of what?'

'Of everything. Of not having enough money, of Jess not wanting to come back, of not getting enough work, of losing my home.'

'Sounds like a scary place to live.'

'It's not as bad as it sounds. It's not like I think about these things every day, nor that the fear is so bad it's

238

ever crippling, but I'm aware of things being hard, and mostly I think I'm aware of the buck stopping with me. If I don't get enough work, then I don't have enough money, and if I don't have enough money, then I could lose my house, and there isn't anyone else I can turn to for help.' Daff laughs nervously. 'Oh God! Will you listen to me? I sound like a neurotic wreck. Listen, I love my life, I'm just aware that I have a huge responsibility, and sometimes that feels a little overwhelming. That's all.'

'I get it,' Michael says. 'I feel much the same way most of the time. Let's go and sit down on that bench.' And as they walk over to it, he places his hand on the small of her back, an unconscious gesture, a kindness, but Daff is immediately aware of the warmth of his hand on her back, and is stunned that a feeling of absolute safety washes over her as she allows herself to be guided to the bench.

*

Daniel is standing at the island in the kitchen when they get back, chopping carrots.

'What are you doing?' Daff asks, sitting at the kitchen table. 'Where's Nan?'

'She's not feeling well,' Daniel says, then turns to Michael. 'I'm making her some chicken soup but I'm wondering whether we should call a doctor.'

'She was fine this morning,' Michael says, bewildered. 'What's the matter with her?'

'She says she's fine, but she looks grey and seems

exhausted. She's probably coming down with some flu-type thing.'

'I'll go up and see her,' Michael says, heading for the door.

'I hope she'll be okay,' Daff says.

Michael turns round just as he walks through the doorway. 'Oh she'll be fine. She's as strong as an ox. Just you wait and see.'

Sure enough, two hours later Nan comes downstairs ready to start cooking dinner, looking absolutely fine.

'How are you feeling?' Daff rushes over, but Nan waves her away.

'I'm as right as rain,' she says firmly. 'I just needed a lazy day in bed. But something smells delicious, did someone make dinner?'

Daniel shrugs. 'Me, I'm afraid. I didn't want to disturb you so I just thought I'd go ahead and do it. Do you mind?'

'Mind? I'm thrilled!' Nan walks over to the dresser and pulls out a packet of cigarettes and an elegant gold lighter from the drawer. 'I'm just going out to the porch for a ciggie. I'd love a drink, Michael, darling. Could you mix us up some Martinis? Daff? Daniel? Coming?'

They follow her out and Michael looks at her with concern. Until fairly recently he had assumed his mother would go on forever, that there would never come a time when he looks at her and has to worry, but tonight, for the first time, he actually *sees* her frailty, rather than worrying about it in the abstract, and as they walk across the deck he takes her arm, and she looks at him happily.

'I love you, Mom,' he mouths, and she smiles at him before sinking into a chair, taking a cigarette out of the pack and putting it to her lips for Daniel to light.

Chapter Eighteen

Richard and Carrie are downstairs eating dinner. Jess is supposed to be sitting with them but she's in her room, angry.

Her dad had said that he would take her to the amusement arcade today, and now, all of a sudden, he and Carrie have to build bookshelves and they have to go to Home Depot, so he doesn't have time to take her. Maybe they'll go tomorrow, he said.

This happens all the time. All the things they did before Carrie came along, he doesn't have time for any more. Sometimes he pawns her off on Carrie, and yes, it's fun, going to the nail salon with Carrie, or going out for lunch, going shopping to one of the cute teen stores in town, but it's not the same as being with her father.

This isn't what she expected when she ran away from her mom's and insisted on living with her dad. She thought it would be just like it was before Carrie came along – time with him, just the two of them, having fun. Sure, she knew things were different now, she couldn't pretend that Carrie didn't exist, but she still thought he'd make her the priority, and now it seems that Carrie is the priority.

Sometimes she just feels so angry – like she explained it to Carrie – it's as though a volcano is going to explode inside her. She had to come upstairs, because otherwise she might have just stood on the kitchen table and screamed, and screamed, and screamed.

She knows she says terrible things when she's angry, and she's trying to contain herself, trying to stay in her room, but it's not much better in here except she's just less likely to say something awful to her dad.

Taking a deep breath, Jess crawls over to the other side of the bed and reaches into her bedside drawer, pulling out the stuffed animals and the make-up. She doesn't wear make-up, not usually, but this is so sparkly, and so inviting, why not? Maybe she should start. She has just lined the animals up on the pillow and opened the box of glittering eyeshadows, when she hears footsteps coming up the stairs.

Quickly she sweeps everything into the drawer and slams it firmly shut, crossing her arms and pouting as Richard knocks gently on the door.

Jess had been standing in Target with her friend Kayleigh when the urge came over her. She wasn't even sure why she did it – she had twenty dollars in her pocket that Carrie had given her when she'd begged for money, but there were huge lines at checkout, the lipgloss had been cheap, and who would ever miss it or care, she thought, as she slipped it up her sleeve.

'I've had enough,' she said quickly to Kayleigh, her heart pounding, her voice breathless and high with anxiety. 'Let's go.'

'I thought you wanted to see the bedroom stuff,' Kayleigh said.

'Not today. We'll come back tomorrow,' Jess said, and walked out, not looking at anyone, guilt preventing her from catching anyone's eye until she was safely in Kayleigh's mom's car, when the burst of adrenaline made her high and giggly.

'What's the matter with you?' Kayleigh kept asking. 'You're crazy!' They had both giggled uncontrollably.

That had been a few days ago. Since then Jess has stolen more make-up, toiletries, a variety of Webkinz and some Polly Pocket toys. She doesn't know why she is doing it, nor why she is drawn to those things – she doesn't wear make-up or use toiletries, and she has long outgrown Webkinz and Polly Pockets – but she can't help it and certainly can't explain it.

Each time she leaves the store, something safely hidden under her sweatshirt, each time she manages to get home without getting caught, she feels happy in a way she hasn't felt in months, not since before the divorce.

Every time she is in her room she gets her stuff out and looks at it. She opens the boxes and sets out her wares in lines, colour-coded, moving them around in different arrangements, but she doesn't use anything, doesn't take the tags off the toys, doesn't scrape off the stickers. She just likes to see what she's got, although the buzz is short-lived. The first time, when it was just a lipgloss, she felt high all night, happy and giddy with excitement. Every time she opened the drawer and saw the shiny pink tube, she felt good again.

Already, after only a few days, the excitement isn't as great, but still more than she usually gets in her boring old life. Maybe she should try somewhere else. Maybe next time she should go to Kool Klothes.

*

'So what do you want to talk to me about?' Bee is nervous, running her fingers around the top of her coffee cup in the Sconset Café. 'I thought you wanted our lawyers to handle everything.' She can't keep the bitterness out of her voice, nor the fear.

Daniel takes a deep breath and tries to speak, but nothing comes out.

'What is it, Daniel?' Bee looks at him closely. 'Whatever it is, just tell me.'

Daniel shakes his head then looks at her. 'Bee, I haven't been completely honest with you.'

Horror floods into her eyes as a thought comes into her head. 'You were having an affair,' she whispers, her breath catching in her throat. Not a question, a statement.

'No.' He shakes his head. 'I would never do that to you. I swear to you, Bee, I've never been unfaithful to you.'

Her relief is palpable. 'So what is it? What could be so terrible that you can't tell me?'

'I don't know how to tell you.' His face is white, his

breath short and shallow. 'This is something I've known for a long time, but something I didn't want to face. I thought I could just deny it, but I can't do that any more . . .'

'You're gay.' Bee spits the words out, a reflex, she doesn't think about what she's saying and expects Daniel to rebuff her, to laugh or tell her she's being ridiculous, but she also knows, as soon as the words are out, that they are true, and when Daniel looks down, unable to meet her eye, it's confirmed.

'Oh Jesus!' Bee shakes her head and laughs bitterly as she looks up at the ceiling. 'I can't believe this is happening to me.'

Daniel doesn't know what to say. 'I'm so sorry,' is the only thing he can manage.

'*You're* sorry?' She attempts a laugh again, still bitter, mirthless. '*I'm* sorry. I'm sorry I didn't listen to all my friends before we got married. Everyone told me they thought you were gay and I told them they were ridiculous, you were just sensitive, in touch with your feminine side. I can't believe how stupid I was.'

'You weren't stupid. I didn't even know myself.' Daniel doesn't know what to say. He had expected many things, but not this bitter derision, not this anger.

'Oh my God!' Bee says again. 'No wonder! No wonder you never wanted to sleep with me. I thought it was *me*, that you didn't fancy *me*, that I was somehow deficient, not sexy enough, not thin enough, not curvy enough, whatever . . . It *was* me, but not in the way I thought.'

Daniel shrugs uncomfortably and looks away.

'You *swear* you never slept with anyone else?' she says suddenly. 'You swear on your life?'

'I swear.'

'I mean – God, the health risks. You swear . . .' She pauses, then says something she never thought she'd hear herself say. 'You swear on the children's lives?'

'I do.' Daniel is shocked, but at least he is able to answer truthfully. 'I swear on the children's lives I have never been unfaithful. Bee, honestly, this is new to me too. You don't have anything to worry about.'

'I did have AIDS tests when I was pregnant,' Bee spits, 'so at least I know we're all fine.'

'Jesus, Bee.' Daniel shakes his head in disbelief. 'Is that all you have to say? That you're relieved you haven't got AIDS?'

'I don't know, Daniel. What do you want me to say? That I'm thrilled? That now I know it wasn't me and there is nothing I could have done to save our marriage? Do you want me to welcome you into my life as my new gay best friend? Should we hang out together and gossip, perhaps? Or maybe you want to come into my closet and tell me which clothes I should keep and which I should chuck. Come to think of it, you always were pretty good at that.'

'Jesus, Bee. Do you have to be so goddamned bitchy?'

'You know what, Daniel?' Tears start to fall as Bee stands up abruptly from the table. 'Yes. Yes, I fucking do. My husband of nearly six years has just announced that our entire marriage was a sham, that everything I ever believed to be true was a lie – and you don't think it's okay to be bitchy? I don't even know what to say to you.' Bee shakes her head and holds up her hand to stop Daniel saying anything in return. 'I can't, Daniel. I can't talk to you any more. Not tonight.'

And with that, she's gone, and Daniel sits there with his cold coffee for over an hour, unable to think. Unable to move.

*

'Are you okay?' Daff's sitting on the porch, sketching, as Daniel walks down the driveway. 'You look terrible.'

'I've been better,' he says and sighs.

'What is it?' Daff puts her notebook down and gestures for Daniel to sit.

'I just told Bee.'

Daff's eyes widen. 'You mean, you just *told* her?' Daniel nods. 'Oh God,' she says, wanting to put her arms around him to hug him but not quite sure if that would be appropriate, given that this is someone she barely knows. 'How did she take it?'

Daniel snorts. 'Let's just say not well.'

'I'm sorry.'

'Me too. I suppose I had this romantic vision of her accepting it and appreciating my honesty, and of us being able to walk away from this as friends.'

'That could still happen,' Daff says gently. 'It will just take some time for all of it to sink in, I imagine. And she's bound to be upset in the beginning. This is something you've presumably lived with, on some level, for years, but it's got to be an enormous shock to her.'

'It wasn't that she was upset that was so difficult. It was her anger.' Daniel sighs again. 'I just didn't expect the force of her anger.'

'It must have been so hard.'

He nods. 'Hey, thanks for listening.' Daniel turns to Daff and this time she just opens her arms and gives him a hug, and he holds her gratefully before letting go.

*

'Nan? There's something wrong with the bedroom window in my room.' Daff coughs discreetly as a wave of smoke from Nan's cigarette wafts gently up her nose. 'I can't open it.'

'Michael will take a look,' Nan says. 'He went into town a little while ago, but he said he'd be back before lunch. I'll send him up as soon as he gets in. Have you any sort of breeze in there? Windermere gets stifling so quickly without the windows open.'

'A little. I opened the bathroom window, but it's not great. Still, better than air conditioning any day.'

'I quite agree.' Nan smiles before breaking into a coughing fit.

Daff shifts uncomfortably. 'Nan, I know it's none of my business but do you think the smoking might be making you ill?'

'Why, because of this cough? I've had this for years!' Nan says. 'The cigarettes have nothing to do with it, and even if they did I'm an old dog and utterly unwilling to learn new tricks.'

'I worry about you,' Daff says. 'I just don't think they're good for you.'

'Of course they're not good for you.' Nan chuckles. 'Nothing that's fun ever is, and I'd rather live a happy shorter life than a dull long one.'

'Why do I doubt that anything in your life has ever been dull?' Daff grins.

'It was all terribly exciting when I was young,' Nan says, and smiles. 'Lately it did get a bit dull, although now I feel more alive than I have done in years.'

'Well, that's good to hear,' Daff says. 'Daniel's chicken soup clearly did the trick.'

'Oh look,' Nan says. 'Here comes Michael. Michael, darling? Daff's window's sticking. Can you go up with her and take a look?'

It shouldn't feel intimate, standing in her bedroom with the landlord's son, but Daff unexpectedly feels slightly awkward. If this were in her home, or in a kitchen, she could offer him a coffee, do something with her hands, but standing here, next to the bed, she is suddenly very aware of her proximity to Michael, and suddenly aware of his masculinity, something she really hasn't noticed before.

As he leans up to examine the window jamb, his T-shirt – a faded old Nantucket red T-shirt, fraying at the edges – rises up and exposes his stomach. Daff shouldn't look, doesn't know why she is looking, and she is embarrassed to feel a flush rising on her face. She only looked for a second, but enough to see an expanse of flat, tanned stomach, the line of muscle, faint hair disappearing into the waistband of his shorts.

'I see what the problem is.' Michael cranes his neck and Daff notices the breadth of his shoulders, his strong hands helping him to balance as he looks up. 'We need some oil and we'll be fine. It's just sticking a bit.' He looks down at Daff and smiles, and she blushes, turning quickly to hide it.

'I'll go and ask Nan,' she says, hurrying out through the door, pausing only when she is safely outside the bedroom.

Good God, she thinks, leaning against the wall. I know this feeling. I remember this feeling from another lifetime, one I haven't even thought about in years. This feeling, this heart-quickening, surging, faint-making feeling is lust!

She giggles to herself. She hasn't thought about a man, any man other than Richard, for years. And Richard was her husband, the feelings he elicited in her were entirely different from the feelings she is feeling right at this very second.

She had lusted after Richard in the beginning, but after Jess was born desire had all but disappeared, coming back in odd spurts at awkward times.

Sometimes she would walk upstairs thinking she was looking forward to making love, and then she'd have a hot bath, as she did every night, and she'd climb into her long white flannel nightgown, as she did every night, then slip between the cool sheets with her book, and by the time Richard had finished watching television, or reading the paper, or doing whatever he was doing, and came to bed, reaching for her, the only thing she ever wanted to do was sleep.

Not that she didn't enjoy it once they had started, but she was never the instigator, never the one who leaned over and started stroking his thigh, or snuggled up to him, reaching down to rub his stomach, reaching lower, and lower.

She was someone, she decided at some point during her marriage, who didn't have a high libido. She had forgotten about the times when she was single, the flings she had, the relationships where the excitement, the thrill, the sheer lust were enough to drive her crazy.

She had forgotten what it felt like to look at another person and feel a flash of heat, imagine what it would be like to caress their stomach, bury your nose into their neck just to smell them, feel their strong hands around your waist, lifting you up, turning you over.

She had forgotten.

Now she remembers.

Chapter Nineteen

Bee swings up to the front door in a crunch of gravel, and gets out of the car, her face frantic with worry.

'What is it?' Nan is on her knees pulling weeds out of the gravel. 'Are the girls okay?'

'Yes.' Bee's voice is breathless. 'It's my dad. I need to see Daniel. Is he here?'

'I'll go and get him.' Nan gets up quickly and lays a hand on Bee's arm as she passes her, a quick reassuring squeeze. Whatever is wrong, Nan knows that it will pass. One of the other joys of getting older, she has realized: you become more accepting, of both the good and the bad.

Daniel had said it hadn't gone well when he had told Bee the truth, and however much she likes Daniel, and she does, she feels for Bee, knows what it is like to suddenly be a single mother, to have the rug pulled out from under your feet when you think that everything in your life is perfect.

And there is more than that. There is something about Bee that touches her heart. She doesn't know what it is, and this is a woman she has barely spoken to, but there is something about her eyes, the sadness, that is so familiar to Nan it is almost painful.

'What is it?' Daniel comes rushing out, his reluctance

forgotten once Nan told him there was something wrong. He hasn't seen Bee in two days, but was planning on having the girls the next day, and was already dreading seeing her, dreading the force of her anger, her bitterness and fury.

'My dad,' Bee says, and finally she allows herself to crumple, and Daniel steps forward and takes her in his arms, resting his chin on her head as he has always done, rubbing her back in a gesture at once so familiar and now so alien. He doesn't know if he is supposed to be doing this, but he doesn't know what else to do, and this is Bee. His wife of six years, the mother of his children. A woman he loves. A woman he may always love, just not in the way she has always wanted.

'What is it?' Daniel says when her tears have subsided and she seems to realize where she is, pulling abruptly away and wiping her wet cheeks.

'He's had a fall. The hospital called this morning. He's drifting in and out of consciousness.'

'Oh God.' Daniel's eyes widen. 'Is he going to be okay?'

'They don't know. I have to go, though. The girls are playing with the next-door neighbours at the house and I don't want them to hear there's anything wrong with Poppa, but there's a flight to LaGuardia this afternoon. Can you take the girls?'

'Of course.' Daniel doesn't hesitate. 'Is there anything else I can do?'

Bee shakes her head. 'I'll phone when I get there. I'll drop the girls back here in about an hour.'

'Fine. And Bee, I'm sorry. I'm sure he'll be okay.'

Bee doesn't say anything. She turns and walks back to her car, and Daniel wants to reach out to her, make it better, but there's nothing he can do.

Bee is shaking so hard she has to pull over at the side of the dirt track from Nan's house. She buries her head in her hands and lets the proper crying start. 'Why me?' she screams out to the silence of the empty road. 'Why is this happening to *me*?'

For Bee is not used to not being in control of her life. Bee is, has always been, the golden girl. Good things happen to Bee, not things like this. Not her husband leaving her and announcing he is gay. Not her father falling and there being no one other than Bee who could possibly look after him.

And her father is not old, for God's sake. It's not like he's a frail old man who is destined to be ill. He may be seventy, but he is the healthiest, fittest seventy-year-old she has ever seen, looks years younger, everyone has always said so.

As the only child of divorced parents, Bee has always known, has always assumed, that at some point the roles would be reversed and she would have to look after her parents. Not her mother so much – her mother remarried ten years ago and Fred adores her, and even if he were to go first, her mother would be okay. But her father has never found anyone since he divorced Bee's mother. He has seemed to withdraw more and more the older he has become, and Bee has had to step into a parental role, phoning him every day, making sure he is okay, inviting him to their house for all the holidays, even, on occasion, trying to introduce him to nice women she has met.

But this she isn't ready for. Not yet. He isn't supposed to have falls, or serious illnesses, or anything serious for years. He's her father, for heaven's sake. He's the one who's supposed to be looking after her, particularly now, when her entire life is falling apart.

Why is this happening to her now?

Bee screams and howls, the wind carrying her anguish away, and when the rage has finally dissipated she breathes slowly and deeply, then turns the engine back on. 'I can do this,' she tells herself, driving down the road past all the new construction, the builders looking at her curiously, her eyes clearly red and raw from crying. 'I can do this,' she says, and by the time she turns onto the main road, she knows she can.

*

Lizzie and Stella are already at home at Windermere. Nan comes out, barely able to contain her excitement at having the two little girls to stay, and takes them both by the hand.

'I've got trunks full of wonderful dressing-up clothes,' she tells them, leaning down so she is on their level. 'Sparkly gowns and velvet capes.'

'Do you have fairy dresses?' Lizzie asks.

'Most definitely,' Nan assures her. 'And somewhere I should even have genuine fairy tiaras. Did you know that a few little girls who have stayed here have even seen real fairies in the garden?'

'No!' Lizzie's eyes widen as she looks at Nan. 'Real ones? What do they look like?'

'Oh they're quite beautiful,' Nan says. 'But they only come if you build houses for them.'

'Houses? What kind of houses? How do you build a fairy house?'

'You have to use only natural things, like shells from the beach, and twigs, and grass to tie things together. You have to make them a roof so they don't get wet, and a bed to sleep on, and then they'll come back. I haven't had fairies in this garden for a while, but no one has built them a house.'

'Can we build them a house?' Stella asks.

'Well, I suppose we could,' Nan says, and the girls leap up and down with joy.

Michael watches Nan from the doorway with a smile. It is astonishing, really, how she has come to life, surrounded by people. Of course when he was a child here, Windermere was always filled with people, with laughter, with life. But after his father died everything seemed to shut down, and he never would have thought it possible for the house to recapture some of the glamour of days gone by.

The window frames are still rotting in places, numerous shingles are missing on the roof, there is clearly an extraordinary amount of work needed to restore Windermere to its former glory, but the house feels again like the house he grew up in, like a house that contains both history and happiness.

Michael was concerned when he first heard Nan was opening up her house to strangers, concerned when she told him about their financial situation, not that he was surprised.

He is apprehensive about telling her his true thoughts, that he thinks she should sell. He loves Windermere, would hate to leave it, but while renting rooms out for a summer may bring her a sense of security, there's no way it's going to save the house.

While the house does look better than it has done in years, the improvements are so clearly superficial. A coat of paint may temporarily hide the wood rotting away underneath, but it won't hide it for very long. You can seal the cracks in the windows, oil the hinges, patch things up for a while, but here on Nantucket he's not sure the house will survive another winter.

The money isn't in the house, Michael knows that, but in the land, and the small amount of research he has done leads him to believe the right developer will pay a fortune for their land.

If it were up to him, he would sell today. Install Nan in a gorgeous cottage, one that is newly built, that needs little money for maintenance, can still give her a garden, an ocean view. He loves this house but he is not sentimental about it, not in the way that Nan is, which is why he hasn't talked to her about it, not properly.

She will not leave. Perhaps at some point, perhaps when she realizes there is no other way ... Until that time, until she realizes that a few hundred dollars a week will go almost nowhere, Michael will let her believe that everything will be fine, will let her hold on to her fantasy a while longer.

Look at how happy she is now, with the little girls looking adoringly up at her as she leads them inside to find the sparkly, glittery clothes in the dressing-up trunks she had been saving for ... what? Granddaughters?

Michael sighs. Life isn't running the course he had expected it to. He thought he was perfectly happy, safe, secure in his job, in his life in New York City, and now here he is, back home, on a hiatus from his life.

Look at the others living here at Windermere. Daff, who thought her marriage was fine until her husband had an affair, who loves her daughter but doesn't have her daughter. Daniel, who has spent his entire life living a lie.

His mother may be living in something of a fantasy world, but at least she is happy. At least she knows what she needs to be happy: her house, her family, being surrounded by people she enjoys.

It is time, he thinks, that he figures out exactly what *he* needs to be happy, and exactly where he ought to be going next. Lost in thought, he turns and goes inside to get a pen and piece of paper from the kitchen, and opening the phone book he starts to jot down the addresses of all the jewellery stores on the island.

It's time to take the next step.

*

Bee lays her head against the back seat of the town car and closes her eyes. She is exhausted in a way she didn't know possible, emotionally drained, like a rag doll that has lost all its stuffing.

After all the pain, the anger, the anguish and fear of the last few weeks, all that is left is numbness. She closes her eyes and fantasizes about sleep. About going to bed for weeks, cocooning herself in a soft, dark, warm bed, not waking up at all until things are back to normal. But even she doesn't know what normal is any more. It's not as if she can fantasize about Daniel coming home, not now. There isn't any hope left at all, just a desire to close her eyes and sleep and sleep, and sleep.

Bee knocks gently on the hospital door then pushes it open when she doesn't hear anything.

Her dad is lying in bed, eyes closed, tubes running into his arms. He looks utterly familiar and so different at the same time, the same father she has always known and loved, but old, lying here so frail and weak, helpless as a child.

'Dad?' She chokes back a tear and leans over him, almost jumping as he opens his eyes.

'Bee!' He smiles, and raises his arms, and she lies on his chest, squeezing him tightly.

'Ouch!' he says. 'Not too tight.'

'Sorry, Dad.' She wipes her eyes. 'Oh Dad, I was so worried. I thought you were unconscious.'

'I was, but then I was just sleeping. I'm glad you're here, Beezy.'

Bee is relieved that, up close, he still smells like Dad, still smells like home, and in the safety of the crook of his neck she feels the tears well up again. For a moment she fights the desire to curl up in the safety of his embrace, like a little girl whose daddy can rescue her from everything.

She blinks back the tears and forces a smile. 'Thanks for dragging me away from the beach.'

'I figured you'd have forgotten about me,' he says. 'Throwing myself down the stairs was the only way I could think of to get you to remember your old dad.'

Bee grins, her first genuine smile in what feels like weeks.

'Well, I'm here now. Happy?'

'Better now that I'm seeing you,' he says, his eyes softening.

'What happened?' she asks. 'Do you remember?'

'No idea,' he says. 'I don't remember a thing, but the pain is excruciating.'

'Do they think you need a hip replacement?'

'I'm having another X-ray this afternoon. I've been completely out of it. Maybe you can sit down with the doctors and find out.'

'Of course,' Bee says. 'That's what I'm here for.'

*   *   *

'It's me.' Bee paces in the waiting room as she calls Daniel's mobile phone. She never knows what to say these days. When they were together she never had to introduce herself, and now saying, 'It's Bee,' sounds too formal, ridiculous when just a few weeks ago no introduction was necessary.

'I know,' Daniel says. 'How's your dad?'

'He's going to be okay,' she says. 'We're waiting for the results of an X-ray, but the worst-case scenario is a hip replacement and then recuperation, but given that he fell down a flight of stairs, it could have been so much worse.'

'Thank God,' Daniel says, and he is relieved. He likes Evan, has always considered himself lucky to have in-laws he got on with, considered part of his family. One of the hardest things about separating from Bee is, he now realizes, separating from her family, knowing that they will never look at him in the same light again, will never again welcome him into their arms as the son they always wanted but never had.

'So how long do you think you'll have to stay?'

'I have no idea.' Bee sighs. 'Hopefully, we'll know more tomorrow. How are the girls?'

'They're wonderful.' Daniel smiles, looking over at Lizzie and Stella, who are standing on stools, cutting out pastry shapes for jam tarts, with Nan.

'Nan is having a field day having them here,' he says, aiming for a normal conversation, knowing that talking about their children is the only way they are currently able to pretend that everything is okay, to have a conversation that doesn't end in a shouting match, with accusations hurled.

'We spent the afternoon foraging at the beach for clam shells and sticks to make fairy houses.'

Bee laughs, despite herself. 'Fairy houses? It sounds like you're running a day camp.'

'It feels like it. Nan's got activities lined up for every hour, it seems. They're in heaven.'

'Can I talk to them?'

'Of course. Hang on. Girls!' Bee smiles as she hears Daniel call out to them. 'Mommy's on the phone.'

Bee waits, expecting to hear 'Mommy!' but instead she hears Stella saying, 'I'm busy. I can't talk now.'

'Lizzie –' Daniel's whisper is audible – 'talk to Mommy.'

'I can't,' Lizzie says loudly. 'I'm cooking.'

'Come on,' Daniel says firmly, and a second later a distracted Lizzie is on the phone.

'Hello?' Bee, so excited at the thought of talking to her children, now feels hurt, and empty.

'Hello?'

'Hi, darling! It's Mommy!'

'Hi, Mommy.'

'Are you having fun? What are you doing?'

'We're cooking.'

'What are you cooking?'

'I don't know. Nan, what are we cooking?'

'Jam tarts,' Bee hears Nan say.

'Hello? Lizzie? Are you there?'

'Bee?' It's Daniel again. 'I'm sorry, but they're distracted. Can we call you back?'

'Don't worry,' Bee says. 'I'll try again in the morning.' And putting down the phone, she quietly goes back to see her father, trying not to think about the pain of her children not missing her as much as she's missing them.

*

'Ooh look,' Nan opens the envelope, admiring the handwriting first, then proffers the invitation around the kitchen like a rare gift.

'What is it?' Michael looks up from the kitchen table where he's making notes.

'An invitation! Jack at the garden centre's having a party. On Saturday night, at home, and it says bring houseguests. I think that means all of you.'

'A party?' Daff says. 'What kind of party? I've brought nothing party-ish. Unless you can wear shorts and a T-shirt.'

'You can borrow something of mine,' Nan says. 'We're about the same size.'

'Thank you,' Daff says. 'Although maybe I could buy something in town. It would be nice to treat myself. God knows it feels like I haven't got dressed up in years.'

'Years?' Daniel laughs. 'You've only been here a few days!'

'I know, and I've been living in ratty old clothes the

entire time. You wouldn't recognize me if you ran into me at home.'

Michael looks up with a smile. 'Why? Do you turn into a pumpkin on the New York border?'

Daff laughs. 'No, but I'm a bit more glam than this.'

'How much more glam?' Michael thinks of Jordana, immediately picturing Daff caked in make-up, glittering jewels in her ears, high-heeled boots on her feet, and he shakes his head. The picture doesn't feel right at all.

'Just more respectable. You know, make-up for work and stuff. Smooth glossy hair instead of this curly mess,' she says, gesturing at her curls falling out of a loose ponytail.

'I like you like this,' Michael says. 'I'm sure you look great the other way, but I think most women look better more natural. I never understand why women plaster themselves with make-up and stuff to hide who they really are. I've always preferred the natural look.'

'I'll bear that in mind,' Daff says, not meaning for it to come out nearly as flirtatiously as it does, and she quickly turns away, a flush rising, as Daniel raises an eyebrow with a smile, and Michael, embarrassed, suddenly thinks of something he has to do outside.

Chapter Twenty

The days are lazily blending into one another, each day sunnier than the last, each person in the house finally feeling relaxed and at peace.

They have all established something of a routine.

Daniel is woken up at the crack of dawn each day by a small person's face centimetres from his own. 'Daddy? Are you awake?' Loud stage whispers from Stella that never fail to bring a smile to his face as he climbs out of bed and goes downstairs to make them breakfast.

Nan is always downstairs first. She had grand plans of being the hostess with the mostest, but she is tired these days and grateful that Daniel is so good in the kitchen, so at home. Breakfast has now become Daniel's responsibility, and Nan plays with the girls as he whips up pancakes, or waffles, or French toast.

Michael is usually next, stumbling into the kitchen half asleep, his hair mussed up, the old, faded T-shirt that he slept in crumpled, a pair of cargo pants and flip-flops on as he yawns his way to the coffee machine, barely able to speak until that first cup of coffee.

Daff comes down last, breezing in clad in shorts and a T-shirt, wide awake and terminally happy.

They have taken to eating outside on the terrace, the

girls and Nan setting the table every morning, thick glasses filled with cornflowers and hydrangeas taking pride of place in the middle of the old scrubbed table.

After breakfast, Michael has been taking off to run errands, or helping Nan fix something around the house, for there is always something that needs to be done.

He wishes there was a way to keep Windermere but, as romantic as he is, he is also a realist. He sat up with Daniel one night to discuss it, the two of them nursing large single malts as they sat at the kitchen table while the rest of the house slept.

'It's a wonderful house.' Daniel looked around the kitchen as he sipped his whisky. 'They don't make houses like this any more, but it hasn't been maintained, and it needs renovating.'

'What do you think?' Michael leaned forward. 'A couple of hundred grand?'

Daniel was shocked. 'No! I think half a million would be more like it,' he said. 'If not more. Everything needs doing. It's a gut job, and I'm not sure it's worth it. Obviously, it's worth it to you, and I hate saying you have to tear down something so wonderful ...' He sighs. 'I'm not sure what the alternative is.'

'Really? A gut job? You don't think we could get away with fixing what needs to be done for far less?'

'I wish I could say yes, but it needs new bathrooms, new wiring, new plumbing. The shingles need replacing, it needs a new roof, the windows are all rotting. And that's just looking at it now. With these old houses the minute you start working on them, the more you find out what's wrong.'

Michael is aghast. 'How do I tell my mom?'

'You don't.' Daniel shrugged. 'Not until you absolutely have to. I've been checking out the real estate here and the good news is that this is worth millions.'

'I know.' Michael sighed. 'But where would she go?'

'With that money? You could build her something small and gorgeous, build something for yourself, I imagine, and still have enough left over so that neither of you would have to worry ever again.'

'But money isn't everything. Mom's never been motivated by money, and I think she'd be heartbroken at the prospect of leaving.'

'I understand.' Daniel nodded. 'But it may not come to that. If my recent experience has taught me anything, it's that things have a habit of working out in life the way they are supposed to, if you are able to just relax and trust in the workings of the universe.'

Michael grinned. 'Funny,' he said. 'I believe much the same thing. It's very New Age of us, apparently.'

Daniel grinned back. 'Well, it seems I really am a new man after all.'

*

'The window's stuck in my room again.' Daff wanders into the garden to find Nan, on her hands and knees, weeding the tomatoes. 'Any ideas?'

'I'll send Michael up to have a look,' Nan says. 'He should be back from town any minute.'

268

'Thanks.' Daff smiles. 'I'm having a lazy morning in bed reading and waiting for the fog to clear.'

'It will be gone by lunchtime, then it'll be a perfect day for the beach. Are you around for lunch?'

'Oh don't worry about me,' Daff says. 'I may go to the village and grab something.'

Nan shrugs. 'Fine. Oh listen. That's Michael's bike on the gravel. Let's go and ask him about that damned window.'

A few minutes later Daff perches on the bed as Michael starts to work and, again, she has that feeling she had just the other day. Lust.

Until the other day, when this first happened, she might have said that she fully expected never to feel this way again, that perhaps it wasn't possible, once you hit your forties, to feel this, that it was just for kids, for younger people in search of a thrill.

But no. It is quite clear that this is lust, and Daff is stunned. She has been aware that she likes Michael, that she feels safe with him. She likes the way he places his hand in the small of her back to guide her into a room. She likes that he looks after his mother, that he seems to want to look after her too. She wakes up in the morning and smiles at the thought of seeing him stumble around the kitchen to refill his coffee cup; she thinks he looks like a cute little boy with his hair mussed up and his eyes filled with sleep.

'Ah-ha! I've got it.' Michael groans as he reaches up. 'It's this bit that's sticking. Can you pass me that box knife?'

Daff goes to the toolbox and passes him the knife, feeling another shiver as her fingers accidentally brush his.

Oh for God's sake, she tells herself, embarrassed. You're a grown woman. Stop behaving like a teenager. But still, she has to fight the urge to glance at herself in the mirror on the other side of the room, checking that she looks okay.

'All done,' Michael says, and for a second they just stand there, looking at each other, the air suddenly charged as Daff fumbles for something to say.

'Are you going to the party?' Michael asks softly, and Daff nods. The party Jack from the garden centre has invited them to is this evening. Daff is surprised to realize she is excited about tonight in a way she hasn't been excited for ages.

Michael reaches out and slowly tucks a strand of hair behind Daff's ear.

'Wear your hair down,' he says. 'You look beautiful.' Then, turning, he walks out of the room, leaving Daff to sink down on the bed with a hand on her fluttering heart.

*

Jess scuffs round Wal-Mart, looking like any other young teenager, not meeting anyone's eyes, covertly checking for security guards.

She doesn't call it *stealing.* Jess would *never* steal, and anyway, this isn't from a person, it's from a huge conglomerate, therefore it doesn't count. In the couple of weeks since she started, she has amassed a startling amount of goods. Both drawers in her bedside table are stuffed full, and she has taken to locking her bedroom door just in case her dad or Carrie should walk in and question her.

She lines up her wares in silence, feeling, in an odd way, safe when she is surrounded by this stuff that is hers and only hers, for only she knows about it.

Occasionally, as she looks at it all, she feels a pang of guilt, but she shoves it away by remembering the exhilaration, the burst of adrenaline and excitement when she first gets out of the store, the pockets of her coat containing some small thing, the fact that she got away with it making her dizzy with power.

Today she has decided to do things differently. Today is her first time at Wal-Mart, and why not get something for her? Something she actually wants, something she might want to buy?

She moves past the tables piled high with sparkly T-shirts, and stops, unfolding one, attempting to look nonchalant, look like every other girl as she slowly slides one from the bottom of the pile into her tote bag.

She leaves the T-shirts, shaking her head as if she has changed her mind, and moves on, to a table with hats. Again, the same motion, pretending to be focused on one thing as she covertly slips another item of clothing in the bag, looking around afterwards to check no one has seen.

'I'm done,' she says when she's walked over to her friend Alexandra, who's browsing in the CD section.

'Wait. Which should I get? Beyoncé or Fergie?'

Jessica shrugs. 'Fergie, I guess. Don't you have an iPod shuffle, though?'

'I did, but I lost it and my parents refuse to get me another one. Have you got one?'

'Not a shuffle.' Jessica shakes her head. 'I just remembered there was something else I wanted to look at. Wait here!' And she runs off towards the electronic section of the store.

*

Daff is not a woman who lives for shopping, but today she has an image in her mind of who she wants to be tonight, so she heads into town determined to find the dress she has created for herself in her imagination.

She has spent the morning daydreaming about the party tonight. She sees herself standing, a glass of champagne in hand, her lightly waved hair floating on her shoulders, in a gauzy, shimmery summer dress while Michael stands next to her, laughing at something she says before slowly leaning down and kissing her.

'You're the most beautiful woman I've ever seen in my life,' he says, in her mind, and she snorts out loud and berates herself for suddenly regressing to her teenage years.

Nevertheless, she is filled with anticipation as she strolls up Main Street, turning into Water Street where she seems to remember a number of small boutiques. The first two are shockingly expensive, and there is nothing there for her, but as soon as she walks into the next she knows she has found it.

A floaty chiffon dress in turquoise and sea-green, it sets off her tan beautifully. The owner brings out delicate tan-leather sandals, flat and plain, apart from a tiny enamel and gold turtle on each side.

'You look exquisite,' says the woman in the shop, and Daff almost hugs her, for it is true, she looks quite beautiful. Quite unlike herself. Her eyes are sparkling, her skin is glowing, and she feels excited, as if she is on the brink of something wonderful, as if there is a world of possibilities out there, all of which are waiting for her to just come and grab them.

Back home, Daff spends a long time getting ready. Nan lets her soak in the large claw-footed tub in her own bathroom, and Daff sits at the dressing table, rolling her hair in fuzzy Velcro curlers so it falls in exactly the waves she had imagined.

Just a touch of make-up, some bronzer to bring out her tan, mascara to emphasize her eyes, a slick of clear lipgloss, and it's true: tonight Daff is no longer a dowdy housewife, frazzled working mother and divorcee. Tonight Daff is a temptress. Beautiful. Exotic. Able to get anything she wants.

'Wow!' Daniel whistles as Daff walks out of her room.

'You look like a princess,' Stella gasps.

'Thank you.' Daff twirls. 'You like?'

'You look stunning,' Daniel says. 'Could this be for anyone special?' He winks and Daff blushes.

'I just wanted to wear something other than shorts and a T-shirt.'

'Well, if you did want to impress anyone, that would be the dress for it.'

Stella and Lizzie continue looking at Daff in awe as she takes their hands and follows Daniel down the stairs. Just as they reach the bottom the doorbell rings.

'Shall we?'

'I'll go.' Daniel opens the door to see a small, skinny blonde on the doorstep. She is dressed head to toe in black, black Prada sandals on her feet and giant diamond studs in her ears.

'Hi,' she says, clearly nervous. 'Is Michael here?'

'Yes.' Daniel opens the door wider and gestures for her to come in, sneaking a raised eyebrow at Daff. 'Who shall I say is here for him?'

'I'm Jordana,' she says, and Daff, standing there in all her finery, suddenly feels like bursting into tears.

*

Jessica has never felt quite this high. There is a buzzing in her ears, and although she is aware that Alexandra is talking to her, she can't hear anything she says. She tries to stay focused on the door, waiting for the mad rush that will sweep her up and carry her home; and they almost make it, they're almost there, when Jess feels a heavy hand on her shoulder.

She turns, fear in her eyes and her breath catching

in her throat, to look into the eyes of a huge security guard.

'Miss?' he says. 'Will you please come with me?'

'What?' Jess tries to shrug him off, puts on a half-hearted act of teenage defiance. 'What have I done?'

'If you could just come with me.' He doesn't let go of her arm, and Alexandra stands there, wide-eyed with terror, as he starts to lead Jess off.

'It's all a mistake,' Jess says frantically to Alexandra, terrified of what will be said among her friends if they find out. 'Call my dad.' And with that she is gone.

*

'There's someone here to see you,' Daniel says softly to Michael. 'She's in the hall, waiting. It's Jordana.'

'Oh ha ha.' Michael snorts. 'Very funny.'

'He's not joking,' Daff says, and one look at the sorrow in her eyes and Michael knows Daniel is serious.

'Oh shit,' he whispers, the colour draining from his face. 'What is she doing here?'

'I don't know,' Daniel says. 'But you can't just leave her in the hall. I told her you'd be right there.'

'Oh man,' Michael groans, knowing that his evening is now ruined, knowing that whatever she has come for, it cannot be good. 'Okay. Let me go and see her. Daff, can you take my mom to the party? I'll be there just as soon as I can.'

Daff nods.

'I'm on babysitting duty tonight,' Daniel says. 'But I can take the girls out if you need some private time?'

'No, no. It's fine. This won't take long.' He sighs long and hard, running his fingers through his hair. 'Let me go and see what she wants.'

Chapter Twenty-one

Jordana sits down gratefully in the living room; she didn't think her legs would be strong enough to support her. She is so nervous she almost stopped the car on the way over here, to throw up.

She wasn't going to come here, wasn't planning to come, but she missed Michael so much, knew that if she could only see him, if he could only see *her*, he would realize how much they had together, how much he was throwing away.

Jordana had been, after all, the most beautiful and popular girl in her town. She was the cheerleader that all the boys wanted to go out with, she was the one who had her pick, was surrounded by the popular girls and the cutest boys.

People didn't walk away from Jordana. Jordana walked away from *people*, and rejection was not something she took lightly, was not something, in fact, she had had much experience of at all.

'I've missed you,' she says, looking into Michael's face for a sign of some of the warmth, the love she is convinced is still there, but his face, for the time being, is cold.

'It's been a few weeks,' Michael says. 'It feels longer. How is everything? How's work?'

'It's ... okay.' She shrugs. 'Not the same. I found a temporary jeweller to come in and help out. I'm in the city and Jackson's in Manhasset pretty much permanently.'

'Are you back together?'

'No. He wants to try couples' counselling, but I'm certain it's over.'

Michael looks up and meets her eyes. 'Does he know?'

'About us?' Even saying the word 'us' makes her feel better. 'No.' She shakes her head. 'He has no idea.'

'Okay.' Michael sighs, and they sit in awkward silence for a while before he finally asks, 'Jordana? Why are you here?'

She takes a deep breath, then stands up and comes over to where he is sitting on the other sofa, sinking down next to him and taking his hands. She has planned this for weeks, knows exactly what she will say, and she gazes into his eyes as she finally gets the opportunity to deliver her well-rehearsed speech for real.

'Michael, I'm here because I love you. Because what we have is special. Because I've never known anyone like you before in my life, and because I know, I absolutely know, that we belong together. I also know that you're a good man, that you have so much guilt because you think of me as a married woman, and you care about Jackson, but my marriage to Jackson was over long before you and I started, and it would have ended anyway.'

'But, Jordana –'

'Wait, let me finish.' She puts up a hand to silence Michael before continuing. 'I know that you don't believe me when I tell you that I am ready to start again, ready to give it all up, and I have realized that you're scared I'm doing all this for you, that it's too much of a responsibility for you to take all that on, but I would have reached this point anyway. One of the things I loved about being with you is that we didn't need expensive restaurants and fast cars and flashy jewellery to be happy. When I am with you I feel completely myself, I don't have to prove anything to anyone. That's how I want to live my life from now on: a simple life with none of the trappings, which have never brought me what I really wanted. Happiness.'

Michael looks at the studs glittering in her ears, the eternity ring of emerald-cut diamonds, one carat each, now resting on the fourth finger of her left hand, and decides not to comment.

'What I've missed with Jackson is a partnership, and that's what I feel with you. You are the most wonderful man I've ever known, and you make me feel safe in a way I've never felt before. I came here because I can't throw this away, it's too important, and I know that if we do we'll never find it again in anyone else.'

She lapses into silence, looking expectantly at Michael, who can't meet her eyes. He is still shocked that she is here, shocked further at how dramatic her words are.

Michael is not someone who finds it easy to express

himself, but if he could, he would be tempted to tell her that she's probably seen one too many romantic movies, and ask if she is completely out of her mind.

'Well?' she says eventually, attempting a smile. 'Do you have anything to say?'

'Um, Jordana ...' He meets her eyes and sighs, unprepared, not knowing how to say it. 'I think you're an amazing woman. I think you're strong, and beautiful, and incredibly brave for coming here and saying what you just said. Our relationship has been extraordinary, both our friendship over the last twenty years and, obviously, more recent events.' When he pauses, she smiles indulgently at him. He shakes his head. There's no getting round it. He just has to be firm.

'But,' he says, watching as her face visibly twitches, 'however wonderful a woman I think you are, and I do, I don't think we do belong together. Not because of guilt over Jackson, but because I honestly can't see a future for us.' He stops, sighing. 'I wish I could tell you something else, but it would be a lie, and it would be wrong for me to lead you on in any way.'

'Just because you can't see a future for us right now, doesn't mean there isn't one,' Jordana says quickly. 'Of course it's hard for you to visualize – after all, our worlds are so different, but if we tried, we could see. I'm not saying we have to jump into anything permanent, but we could just take things slowly, see how we go. I could prove to you that I'm right.' She attempts a smile.

'I can't,' Michael whispers, shaking his head. 'I'm sorry, Jordana, but I can't.'

'But why not? I don't understand, why not?'

'Because I'm not in love with you,' Michael says finally, his voice still a whisper. 'Because this isn't right. This isn't what I want.'

'But how do you know what you want? How can you know if you haven't had it?' She is clutching at straws, and they both know it.

'Jordana, you shouldn't have come all this way. I'm sorry. I'm so sorry.'

'Please, Michael.' She feels herself close to tears, is almost embarrassed at her behaviour but her feelings for him are so strong that she can't just leave, can't let him throw this away without a fight. 'Just give us a chance. Please. I promise you won't regret it.'

'I can't, Jordana. You should go.'

'There's something else,' she says, standing up.

Michael looks at her wearily, and there is fire in her eyes.

'I'm pregnant.'

*

'Dad?' Bee holds his hand and strokes it gently, having sat for a while watching her father snore softly. When she first saw him in hospital she was stunned at how old he looked, but she is getting more used to it now.

He opens his eyes, squinting at the light, then slowly focuses on her.

'Bee?' He smiles and Bee leans forward, hugging him.

'Hi, Dad. How are you feeling today?'

'Not too bad. There's still some pain, and the doctor says I need lots of rest. But I'm so glad I didn't need the hip replacement. Not this time.'

'Thank God,' she whispers. 'Can you fly?'

'I left my wings at home.' He smiles again. 'Why?'

'I want you to come back to Nantucket with me, so I can look after you.'

'Ah. Nantucket. Is it still the most magical place on earth?'

Bee smiles and nods. 'How long is it since you've been?'

'Many years.' Evan's eyes close for a moment. 'A lifetime or two.'

'So how about it, Dad? You'd love our house. And it means I could look after you properly.'

'Maybe,' Evan says, wincing. 'Let me think about it.'

'What's to think about?' Bee says firmly. 'Who else is going to look after you?'

'I could get a nurse,' Evan says.

'That's ridiculous, when you have me. The girls will love having you there, and I promise I'll give you a quiet time.'

'How are those darling girls?' Evan smiles at the thought of them.

'They're great. They're enjoying some special time with Daniel.'

'What about Daniel? Are you two going to be able to patch things up, do you think? For the sake of the girls?'

She laughs bitterly. 'I'd say the chances of us getting

back together are slim to none. It's a long story, Dad. One I'll save for when you're feeling stronger. God knows I don't want to give you a heart attack.'

'Why not? At least I'm in the right place for it. What's the story? Did he come out of the closet at last?'

Bee turns white. 'What? How did you know?'

'Oh Beezy. I'm so sorry. I didn't know. I just always had a feeling. How are you? Are you okay?'

'Oh Dad,' she says. She takes a deep breath and looks out of the window, trying to compose herself. Bee is trying so hard to be strong for her dad, to be the one to look after him, to be the grown-up, and she doesn't mean to, but she bursts into tears.

'Ssssh.' Her dad puts his arms around her and wishes it wasn't so painful, seeing someone you love hurt as much as this. 'It's okay, Beezy. Ssssh. Daddy's here.'

And finally, in her father's arms, at a hospital bedside in Stamford, Connecticut, she feels, for the first time in a long while, that someone is looking after her.

*

Daff wants to enjoy herself, to lose herself in the party, but every time someone new walks into the garden she looks up expectantly, hoping it will be Michael. It never is.

She was standing with Nan for a time, left to get a glass of punch, came back to find Nan being swept onto the dance floor by Jack. She smiles as she watches her, thinking what a lovely party it is, the lanterns glimmering among the trees, pretty people wandering up and down the lawns, and thinking how much better it would be if Michael were here.

'Hello.'

She turns to see a man smiling at her, extending a hand. 'I'm Mark.'

'I'm Daff.'

'Daff short for Daphne?'

'It should be. That's what everyone thinks, but it's Delphine. My mother was French, and when I was young my little brother couldn't pronounce it and he called me Daff. It stuck.'

'It's cute. So how do you know Jack?'

'I don't. I'm here with a friend.'

'I saw you with Nan earlier.'

'Yes. Actually, she's my landlady.'

'Ah-ha, you're one of the tenants I heard about.'

'Oh? You know Nan, then?'

'Not really. We've met. She came to look at one of the houses I built and I'm desperate to get my hands on Windermere.'

'You're a developer?'

'I am and Nan's sitting on one of the best properties on the island. Has she talked to you at all about selling?'

Daff turns and looks at Mark. He is smiling and he seems pleasant, but there is something in his eyes that is steely, something that she instantly doesn't trust, and she knows that the less she says, the less information she gives him, the better.

'I'm just a tenant.' Daff laughs lightly, turning away. 'Why would she talk to me about anything like that?'

'It's worth an awful lot of money, you know,' Mark says. 'The prices here are extortionate.'

'I've heard.'

'So what about you?' Mark changes the subject. 'What do you do when you're not being a tenant in Nantucket?'

'I'm actually a realtor,' she says with a laugh. 'In Westchester.'

'Ah. So we're both on the same team, then.' He grins. 'Are you here with your husband and kids?'

'No.' Daff shakes her head, wondering when she will get used to these presumptions, when she will be able to tell people she is divorced without feeling like a failure somehow. 'I'm ... divorced. My daughter's with her father at the moment.'

'So did you get into real estate after your divorce?'

'After the separation. Yes.'

'It's a tough business right now. Nantucket's different. It's an island so the prices will always hold, but I know the rest of the country is really suffering. How are things where you are?'

'Not great.' Daff is trying to think of a way to get away. She knows she should be polite, but this is not a comfortable conversation for her: he wants to know too much and it feels like he has an agenda. But she doesn't know how to extricate herself.

'There should be some new activity in the fall,' she says, looking over to the drinks table, about to excuse herself. 'You know how it is, summer's always hard.'

'Well,' Mark leans closer, 'between you and me, if

Nan were to agree to sell to me this summer, I'd make sure there was something in it for you.' He winks. 'Just business. I know you understand. We could do a deal privately, no agent, and I'd give you a percentage. Here –' he slips a card into her hand and she gazes at it numbly – 'give me a call and we can talk some numbers. Between you and me,' he says again, looking at her intently.

'Mark Stephenson!' Nan appears, her elegant red crêpe gown swishing around her ankles.

'Nan Powell! You look as beautiful as ever.' He kisses Nan on each cheek as Daff shudders. 'Would you do me the honour of allowing me to have this dance?'

'Seeing as you asked so nicely, how can I possibly resist?' Nan giggles, and the two of them walk across the lawn, leaving Daff standing there looking at the card pressed into her palm.

A percentage. Of what? What could the house be worth? Millions, she knows, but how many? Six million? Seven? ... And what kind of percentage? Her mind quickly tumbles some numbers around. Three per cent, say, of six million would be one hundred and eighty thousand dollars. That's a fortune. She wouldn't have to worry for ages.

Oh *God*! *What* is she thinking? She couldn't possibly do that to Nan, couldn't possibly get involved in anything so shady, so underhand and so, well, sleazy. She is tempted to rip the card up, feeling dirty just having had a conversation with that man, but she pushes it into her purse and covers it up with tissues, pretending that if she can't see it, it isn't there and will just go away.

*

Michael is sitting on the porch, glass of whisky in hand; he's lost count of how many he has had. Daniel came to see him earlier, asked if he was okay, but Michael couldn't speak, didn't know what to say.

In some ways he feels like he's been waiting for this moment all these years. He has spent his life astounded that none of his girlfriends, his lovers, his past conquests has ever become pregnant, and now finally it is as if this was always supposed to be – his past has caught up with him at last.

He feels numb. Shocked. Scared. Once the words were out, he looked at Jordana in fear, feeling his chest tighten up, his breath coming out in short, sharp bursts as he struggled to breathe, hoped that somehow he had misheard, that he was about to wake up from this nightmare.

Jordana had left, had stormed out in a whirlwind of tears and drama, announcing that she was staying at the Wauwinet, that she was having this baby, that if she had to do it alone, she would, and that she was stunned by his reaction, his inability to speak, let alone breathe.

A baby. With Jordana of all people. Every time he thinks about it he feels like he wants to crawl under a blanket and never come out. How can his life have spun so wildly out of control? How can he be responsible for another human being when he seems to have messed up his own life so badly?

He can't think of anything worse than having their lives entwined, because of a shared child, until the end of their days.

It is almost as if, he reflects grimly, he was having an out-of-body experience. After just seeing her tonight, her highlighted, over-made-up, desperate, obsessive, sparkly self, he kept thinking, what the hell was I *thinking*? What the *hell* was I thinking? A friend, yes. But a partner for the rest of my life? Hell, no.

If only he had ignored that chemistry, kept Jordana as the distant friend she had always been, gone out with her that night, that first night, and headed home to the Upper West Side. Alone.

And Jordana, how will she cope with this? With an illegitimate child by a man who doesn't feel the slightest bit equipped to cope with it himself, a man who just can't be there in the way Jordana wants, can't be the husband or partner she needs.

Tonight he didn't see her as vulnerable, as being in need of a knight in shining armour, someone to rescue her and make it all better. Tonight he saw her as damaged. Insecure.

And perhaps just a little bit crazy.

'Michael? Is that you?'

He looks up, seeing Daff standing in the darkness, so beautiful in that dress, so fresh, and clean, and different from Jordana, and as he looks up, unsure what to say, he realizes that his shoulders are shaking, and that tears are streaming down his face.

'Sssh.' She glides over, puts her arms around him, strokes his back, kissing the top of his head and soothing him as she would a child. 'It's okay,' she whispers, rubbing wide circles on his back as he leans into her and cries. 'It's okay.'

Slowly the tears subside, and he is still in her arms, and she has stopped rubbing his back, and it's not quite so comfortable. He pulls her down gently so she is on his lap, never taking his arms from her, nor hers from him, then he is kissing her, and oh my Lord, this is not what he should be doing when he has just discovered he is going to be a father, but this is Daff, this feels like a safety net in the most awful storm he has ever known. And more than that, as he kisses Daff and feels her arms wrapped around him, he feels, finally, *right*.

'What's that?' Minutes later, a buzzing.

'Oh God.' Daff jumps up guiltily, embarrassed, and reaches into her handbag for her mobile phone. 'Who would be calling me this late?' She looks at the number and her heart stops. It's Richard's number. There is something wrong. Jess. She flips the phone open as terror flutters across her chest.

Jess sobbing down the phone. Like a little girl.

'Jess? What is it? Jess? What's the matter?' Fear is making her shout, desperate to know that Jess is okay.

'I miss you, Mommy,' Jess says, gulping for air through the tears. 'I need you, Mommy.'

Daff immediately goes into mother mode. 'I miss you too, Jess. I love you. But tell me what's wrong. What's the matter? What's happened?'

'Daddy's going to call you,' she says, the sobs starting again. 'But I want to come and live with you. I hate it here. I don't want to be here any more.'

'Jess?' Daff's voice is firm, even though her heart is not. 'What's going on? Let me talk to your father.'

Chapter Twenty-two

Windermere is absolutely still at night, quiet and at peace, yet listen a little more carefully and you will hear the sounds of tossing and turning, of people struggling with dilemmas, of an inner turmoil that is anything but peaceful.

Michael is still numb with fear. A baby. Jordana is pregnant with his baby, just as he's met a woman with whom he feels, for perhaps the first time, a real connection. There is no way in the world he can see this ending well.

He has never had strong feelings about abortion, has never had to think about it, other than knowing various women who have had one, has always felt that it is a woman's right to choose.

But what about the man? Where is his choice? Michael can't think straight, can't think of anything worse than bringing a baby into the world under these circumstances. He has never thought of himself as a father in anything other than the abstract, but a parent with *Jordana*? He would laugh if it wasn't so unthinkable as to be almost painful.

Terminate, he wants to shout. Get rid of it. But this is not his body, he cannot say anything, and now he is terrified he will pay for his mistake for the rest of his life.

Tomorrow he will go and see her. Talk to her about it. See if he can convince her. See if he can prove to Jordana that this won't be good for anyone, that this isn't, cannot possibly be, the right thing to do.

For Michael is ill-equipped to be a father, his own father having died when he was only six. He has no concept of what a father is, of the joy that comes from seeing your child, a life you created, being brought into the world.

And he has never thought of himself as having responsibility for another life. A responsibility so huge the mere idea of it is utterly overwhelming to him. He has always taken care of his girlfriends, his mother, but that's different. However childlike some of them have acted in their time, they are still adults, capable of taking care of themselves.

Michael was never prepared for this; never prepared for having to suddenly grow up.

On the other side of the house, Daff sits in the window seat, staring out at the blackness, the odd blinking light from one of the boats bobbing on the water. She sips slowly from a cup of sweet, warm tea, trying to soothe her jangled nerves, hoping it will send her back to sleep.

There is so much to think about. Jess, her darling Jess, shoplifting. How can her little girl have been caught shoplifting? It doesn't seem to make any sense, but Richard was perfectly clear. It wasn't a mistake, he and Carrie went to pick her up and he was shown the contents of her bag.

*

Even when he was shown the evidence, Richard wanted to believe that there was an alternative explanation, but there wasn't, and Jess's initial denial swiftly turned to hysteria as she became a little girl, hoping that Daddy would make it all better, would make all the bad stuff go away.

They wouldn't press charges, they said, after Richard had explained their situation, said she was struggling with her parents being newly divorced. Given that it was, as far as they were concerned, her first offence, next time she would not get off so lightly, they said sternly, showing them out of the store.

Jess ran straight up to her room, slamming the door, after Richard told her the consequences of her behaviour. He was taking her computer away, and she would be grounded for a month.

'I hate you,' she screamed at him from behind the door. 'I hate it here! I wish I'd never been born!'

Carrie and Richard sat at the kitchen table discussing what to do in low voices.

'Do you think maybe she should see someone?' Carrie offered tentatively, sure that this would help, but unsure how Richard would feel about it.

'See someone? Like who? A shrink?'

'Maybe not a shrink, but a therapist perhaps. Some-one she could feel safe with, someone she could talk to.'

Richard sighed. 'I just think it's ridiculous. Sending a thirteen-year-old girl to a therapist. I know this shop-lifting thing is bad, but Jess is not a bad kid, she's just a kid going through a rough time. Carrie, you were a thirteen-year-old girl, and you said it wasn't easy for you either. Surely you know how this is.'

'I do know,' Carrie said. 'But I didn't steal. And I never ever would have dared speak to my parents the way she speaks to you.'

'Well, times are different now. And she doesn't do it often, and she doesn't mean it.'

'Richard, whenever she doesn't get her own way she screams that she hates you, or hates me, that we've ruined her life, not to mention other unspeakable things, and you let her.'

'I'd rather she were able to express herself,' Richard said quietly.

'But it's not appropriate,' Carrie said. 'I'm not saying she's not allowed to feel those things – she should be able to feel everything – but it's not appropriate to vomit those feelings out whenever she finds them overwhelming.'

'I disagree,' Richard said. 'I think it's far better to let them out than to suppress them. I was never allowed to be angry, never allowed to be anything other than happy and pleasant when I was a child, and for years I struggled with this repressed anger. I never want Jess to go through that.'

'Why not? In case the repressed anger leads to something terrible like . . . shoplifting?'

'That's not fair.' Richard was stern.

'Maybe not, but I see a child here who is struggling and who will do anything for attention, including shoplifting. Don't you see that's what this is about?'

'She gets attention. I give her tons of attention.'

'I know, but she always wants more. It's never enough, and this stealing is a cry for help. Richard, we wouldn't be responsible if we didn't get her some help.'

There was a long silence as Richard tried to digest what she was saying, for some of it made sense. He adored his daughter, loved her more than anything in the world, but it was true that sometimes he didn't understand her. He tried so hard to listen to her, to validate her, to allow her to be herself without judging her – all the things that he never had when he was a child – and yet she still seemed to be in such pain, and at moments like this he felt like a terrible parent, utterly helpless.

'I'll think about it,' he said finally, looking up and meeting Carrie's eyes.

'Thank you,' she said, and she reached across the table and squeezed his hand.

Sometimes it's enough, she realized, just to be heard.

Jess was crouched outside the kitchen door, listening to every word. She hated Carrie at that moment, hated her father, wished she could turn the clock back to when her mother and father were married and every-thing made sense.

She quietly went back upstairs into the master

bedroom and called her mother, and, as she dialled, the tears started to fall. Living here wasn't what she'd expected, not now that Carrie had ruined it, and for the first time in a long while she wanted to be away from her father.

If he and Carrie were going to reject her, she was going to reject them first.

'Mommy?' Her tears were genuine when she heard her mother's voice. 'I want to be with you.'

Richard agreed to send Jessica to Nantucket. Perhaps it would do her good, he thought; get her away from the bad influences here. Jessica must have been influenced by a friend to steal, would never have thought of this herself, despite what Carrie thinks.

And a girl needs her mother, he had realized. He had thought this might be an ideal opportunity for Jess and Carrie to bond, and even though there were times when they seemed to get on amazingly, when Jess truly wanted to be with Carrie, ultimately she wasn't her mother and never would be. Richard was almost grateful that Jessica asked to leave. He felt like he'd been on an emotional roller coaster ever since Jess had moved in. He needed a break, needed to think about something other than his troubled teenage daughter for a change. Let Daff deal with it for now.

*

Daff is ready for Jess, but worried about what's going on in her daughter's life. She has missed her, of course, but hasn't pined for her in the way that other women she knows talk about pining for their children on the rare occasions they have some time off.

It is a fallacy, she thinks, that all mothers ache for their children when they are not with them. It is guilt that makes them say that, a fear that they are not good enough mothers if they are not thinking about their children twenty-four hours a day.

Daff thinks about Jess. Often. But she has also loved being seen as a woman, as an individual, as something other than a *mother*. She has loved that she has got to know new people, created a world out here in Nantucket where she is someone other than a dowdy suburban housewife and mom.

This evening she was a temptress, for God's sake! Remember that kiss! She shivers, wishing it had led to more, but the spell was broken with Jess's phone call. Even though she stayed, once she had finished talking to Richard, and asked Michael what was the matter, wanting to check he was okay, her mind was focused on Jess, and they had decided to call it a night, to talk about it another time.

There was also Mark Stephenson to think about and his strange offer. She didn't want to consider it, knew it was underhand, deceitful; she could never do that to Nan, or Michael. But it was such a lot of money – it would set her up for life, would afford her a freedom she has only been able to dream about since her divorce.

For working in real estate these days is hard. And

getting harder. It isn't like the good old days when everything was overpriced and running out through the door, bidding wars were commonplace, realtors making a fortune.

Almost every middle-aged woman she knows in town who decided to go back to work after raising her children is a realtor. Every week it seems yet another one has joined the fray, got her licence, turned up at one of the hundreds of open houses, each one of which now offers bigger and better lunches in a bid to attract the realtors.

There is so much inventory. The builders who thought the boom was going to last forever are still building the huge new houses, only now the houses are sitting for months, sometimes years, their prices dropping dramatically until the builders either go into foreclosure, or sell them at a loss.

It is getting harder and harder to survive as a realtor in her town. Even the people who are supposed to be the best – Marie Hathaway and her team, four stunning blondes who regularly take the back page of the local paper and are known for having the highest-end houses in town – aren't doing so well. Once she has paid all her marketing expenses – those full-page ads and monthly flyers may be good for exposure but don't come cheap – *and* paid her team, Daff has heard that what's left in the pot isn't nearly as much as Marie leads everyone to believe.

When Daff and Richard were married, she never worried about money. She did the odd job here and there – she was a professional organizer for a while, painted Christmas cards and had house sales – and what little money she earned was bonus money, a little extra to enable her to buy a cute pair of boots she saw, stay in a better class of hotel when they went away, buy Jess the latest pair of Uggs that she absolutely had to have because everyone in her class had them.

If she had a quiet period while she was married, it was just a quiet period. It didn't hold the weight it holds now. For while Richard pays both alimony and child support, she has been left with the mortgage and the bills, and the little that Richard pays isn't nearly enough to assuage her fears about her future.

Her dream is to have enough money to put some away every month, build up a nest egg so she knows she can relax, knows that she will always be okay.

She dreads being in a position where she may have to sell her house. This is the house Jess was born in, and where else would she go? To some extent she understands Nan, why she won't leave Windermere, and yet it is worth millions. Nan may worry on a day-to-day basis, but she has a choice, and selling this house would make her a very wealthy woman.

Not to mention what it would do to Daff. Millions for Nan, and maybe a couple of hundred thousand for Daff, enough to set up the nest egg, enough to feel that she could breathe.

What if she talked to Nan, showed her perhaps just a different way of looking at things? Daff couldn't, obviously, make Nan do something she doesn't want to do, but she could perhaps steer Nan in a different direction, and would it really be so terrible to make Nan a wealthy woman?

She wouldn't have to deal with draughty windows and disappearing shingles any more. She could have a beautiful cottage on the beach, with more than enough money so she would never have to worry about anything ever again.

Daff continues to sip her tea, trying to convince herself that persuading Nan to sell the house would not be so awful after all.

*

Nan wakes up, cold and shivery. She pads out of bed and goes to the closet, dropping her wet nightgown in a puddle around her feet and pulling on a fresh, dry gown, instantly feeling warm.

She pushes the covers back on the other side of the bed, the side she still thinks of as Everett's side, and as she climbs in her dream suddenly comes back to her.

How strange, she realizes. She had dreamed of Everett. When he died, she had dreamed of him often at first, the dreams so vivid, so real, she remained convinced he was somehow watching her from above, able to visit her only when she was asleep, to reassure her that both of them would be okay.

She hasn't dreamed of him in years, but now she remembers the dream she had of him tonight. She had been visiting the Nantucket Lightship, curious to see it since it had been turned into, first, a luxury home, and now a luxury hotel.

In truth, Nan has read magazine articles about the lightship, has seen how beautifully it has been deco-rated, the wood panelling, the understated elegance of the formal living and dining rooms, but in her dream it was garish, with loud colours, nothing matching, bright oranges and greens, colours designed to agitate.

She wound her way through the bedrooms in her dream, knowing she was about to find something, just not sure what it would be, when she came across a smiling man, lying on a top bunk.

'Hello, Everett,' she said, feeling at once calm, safe, and not the slightest bit surprised to see him, even though this Everett looked nothing like her Everett. Despite that, she knew it was him.

'Hello, Nan,' he said, and he threw back the covers, inviting her to join him in the bunk, except it wasn't lascivious, it wasn't sexual, it was inviting her home, and she climbed in, surprised only that the sheets were not warm and dry, but grateful to have found Everett again. And then she woke up, in a cold sweat.

Now she finds she cannot go back to sleep. The dream has unsettled her and Jordana's appearance has unsettled her, not because she knows anything about Jordana, but because she saw Michael out on the terrace, and senses that something big has happened, that changes are afoot and they are not necessarily good.

Isn't it ironic, she thinks, just when you think your

life is smooth and everything is exactly as you want it, a spanner is thrown in the works and everything changes again. Bee will be back with her father soon, those delicious little girls will be leaving, and in their place Daff's daughter will be here.

And this Jordana, who is so clearly in love with Michael, is so clearly wrong for him. What is she doing here, and why is she here just as Daff and Michael seem to be getting so close?

It feels as if an ill wind has suddenly started to blow through the house. Try as she might, Nan can't still herself enough to go back to sleep.

She lies in bed, thinking, until the sky starts to lighten outside her window, then she gets up, makes herself some tea, and walks down to the beach, breathing in the salty air and, finally, down here, starting to feel a sense of peace.

Chapter Twenty-three

Daniel checks his piece of paper to make sure he has the number right, then pulls up into the narrow driveway next to the house. There are people here already – his is the third car there, and as he approaches the front door he can see into the living room where people are congregating, glasses of champagne in hand.

'Daniel! You made it!' Matt opens the door and ushers him in. 'I'm so pleased you're here. Come and meet everyone.' Daniel walks awkwardly into the living room, suddenly feeling apprehensive for there are only men in here, and, unlike when he went to the Maple Bar, this is the first time Daniel has ever been in an environment where everyone, including himself, is openly gay.

'I'm sorry I didn't make it to Jack's party,' Daniel says. 'I heard it was good.'

'I'm sorry you didn't make it too. It was fine. For me it was more about chatting up clients and making sure I stayed sober and didn't say anything to upset anyone,' Matt says. 'Champagne?'

'I'd love some.'

'Daniel, this is Keith.' A small man with trendy glasses smiles warmly and shakes Daniel's hand.

'You must be new to the island,' he says.

'Relatively. I'm just here for part of the summer. I'm renting a room out in Sconset.'

'He's in Nan Powell's place.' Matt places a hand on Daniel's back as he talks, and Daniel is surprised at how natural it feels, how nice. 'Remember?'

'Oh God!' Keith's eyes light up. 'You have to meet my partner, Stephen. He's been in love with that house for years.'

'Which house?' A much older man, with twinkling eyes and almost laughably preppy in pink chinos, a green polo and a blue cashmere cable sweater over his shoulders, strolls over.

'Nan Powell's,' Keith says. 'Daniel's renting there for a few weeks.' He turns back to Daniel. 'Stephen's an architect and every time he's been interviewed he says that the Powell house is the one he'd most like to get his hands on.'

'It's a wonderful house,' Daniel says. 'Is all your architecture residential?'

'Stephen specializes in authentic historic renovations,' Keith says, his chest visibly puffing up with pride. 'Although he's done some commercial work in town.'

'And Keith, as you see, specializes in being Stephen's partner, spokesman and chief PR,' Matt explains, and the others laugh.

'Sorry, sorry.' Keith and Stephen exchange a look filled with fondness as Keith laughingly apologizes. 'I'm just so proud of him. I'm going off to get a refill. Anyone else?' They shake their heads.

'Have you been inside the house?' Daniel asks. 'Do you know Nan?'

'No and no,' Stephen says. 'I've heard she's a character.'

Matt interjects. 'She is, but in the best possible way. I don't think she's nearly as eccentric as people believe. I think she's cultivated this persona so she can get away with things.'

'I agree entirely.' Daniel nods. 'She's actually frighteningly normal.'

'Frightening being the operative word?'

'No.' Daniel laughs. 'You should come over sometime and meet her. She adores visitors. Come and see the house.'

'I really would love that,' Stephen says, before Matt steers Daniel over to meet the rest of the people in the room.

'I apologize for Keith,' Matt whispers, as they walk. 'They've been together forever and Keith still treats Stephen like a child sometimes, even though Keith's twenty years younger.'

'How long have they been together?'

'I think this year is their eighteenth anniversary.'

This year would have been his sixth anniversary with Bee. How odd to think that he could have been Keith, could have been happily with someone for all those years, not having to pretend to be someone, or something, he is not.

*

305

Michael walks through the Wauwinet, smiling at the understated elegance, the quietness and luxury that he remembers from when he was a child.

He walks through to the porch at the rear, seeing Jordana immediately, trying not to stare at the people sitting around having drinks, people he recognizes from the papers, celebrities, politicians, business moguls, all of them in shorts and T-shirts, all of them looking like regular Joes.

He approaches Jordana nervously, apprehensive about what he has to say, uncertain of how he can convince her that having a baby won't be a good idea.

She is sitting facing the ocean, shaded by a large straw hat and huge Gucci wrap-around sunglasses. She is in a sparkly white beaded sarong, an embroidered gold Buddha on the back offset with gold sequins, and flat, strappy sandals. She would look perfect in the Hamptons, but here in Nantucket, where everyone else is in cycling shorts after long bike rides, baseball caps, faded T-shirts and not a scrap of make-up, she looks like a fish out of water.

Again he wonders what on earth he was thinking, those moments when he allowed himself to believe, to truly believe, that he and Jordana might have a future together. His whole affair was so completely out of character, it was almost as if he were playing a role in a movie – nothing about it was real.

And how unfair, he thinks, fear settling onto his chest as he approaches her table, that the consequences are this real.

Jordana looks up, sees him, and takes her sunglasses off. Her eyes are red, puffy. It is clear she has been crying for many hours. For a second Michael feels a twinge of irritation – her sunglasses came off so quickly, was she trying to make him feel guilty at hurting her so badly, trying to manipulate him in some way?

'How are you?' He doesn't know what else to say as he sits down and orders a coffee from the waiter, who appears obscenely cheerful given the circumstances.

Jordana shrugs. 'I've been better.'

'How many weeks are you?'

'I don't know exactly. I missed my last period, so probably seven, maybe eight.'

'What does your doctor say?'

'I haven't been to the doctor yet.'

His heart jumps. 'So maybe you're not pregnant? Maybe this is all a mistake.'

Jordana looks at him witheringly. 'I've missed my period, my breasts are enormous and I'm throwing up every day. What do you think that is? A phase?'

'It could be anything.' Michael grabs on to false hopes, desperate for things to be different.

'No.' She shakes her head. 'I'm pregnant. I know.'

'But how do you know?'

'Because I'm a woman and I just know.'

'And you're definitely keeping it?'

'What do you mean?' Jordana's voice is cold.

'I mean, have you thought, seriously, about what this means? Jordana, of course I'll do the right thing. I can't make you give the baby up or get rid of the baby, but you and I aren't going to be together, this isn't going to be the cement that holds our relationship together. I'm so sorry for everything, for splitting you and Jackson up, for . . . for everything.'

For getting involved with you is what he was about to say, but he held back.

'I am so sorry that this is happening,' he continues, 'and if you go ahead and have this baby, of course I will do the right thing for the baby. I would be involved in the child's life, I wouldn't just walk away and have nothing to do with it, but you and I are not going to be together, and Jordana, have you thought, have you really thought about what it's like to be a single mother?'

'I know plenty of single mothers,' Jordana says archly. 'I know exactly what's involved.' But her voice is shaky.

Michael ploughs on, certain she's not convinced, certain he can change her mind. 'I know women who spent their entire lives wanting to be mothers, who found themselves pregnant, without partners, and went ahead,' he urges. 'My friend Suzy got pregnant after a short fling, had always wanted a baby and now has an eight-year-old daughter, and hasn't been out in eight years. And when the little one was a baby, Suzy was exhausted all the time. There was no one to relieve the burden, no one to support her when she was at the end of her tether, couldn't cope. And you know what Suzy says now? She says that although she wouldn't change anything, although she loves her daughter more than anything, if she could have done things differently she would have done. She won't say her daughter is a mistake, but she does say the circumstances were a mistake, and that she has had no life for eight years.' Michael pauses, letting the words speak for themselves.

'Is that what you want, Jordana? Is that really what you want? Because this isn't about a cute baby in designer clothing, who you can treat as an accessory. This is hard work. Exhausting. Much, much harder as a single parent.'

'Don't patronize me,' Jordana says bitterly, when Michael has quite finished. 'I know exactly what I'm doing, and however hard it might be, I am not going to have an abortion. I couldn't live with myself knowing I had destroyed the life of our baby, and I'm disgusted you would even seriously suggest that to me.'

'I'm sorry. I didn't mean to patronize you. I just think these are the worst circumstances in which to bring a baby into the world. This isn't an unexpected gift, this is just wrong.'

'So is that it?' Jordana stands up, pushing her chair back so hard it almost falls over.

Michael sighs again. 'I don't know what else to say,' he says quietly.

'How about goodbye?' And she storms off inside, leaving Michael to walk miserably to his car.

*

The dinner has been served, and quiet conversations are occurring around the table, replacing the raucous laughter that erupted throughout the meal.

309

Roasted leg of lamb stuffed with figs and feta, Israeli couscous, a sumptuous raspberry pavlova for dessert. Never has Daniel eaten so well, nor felt so comfortable.

This is what he has been missing, he realizes; *this* is what he was looking for during those years of driving past gay bars, yearning. Ironically, *this* is why he was so reluctant to leave Bee all those years – because he didn't know there was anything else out there, didn't know it could be like this.

Three couples, all men, two of them married, and he and Matt. None of them having to prove anything, or hide anything, or feel anything other than completely relaxed in their skin.

Daniel looks around the table until his eyes finally come to rest on Matt, who is smiling at him.

'What?' Daniel cannot help a smile in return.

'It's nice, isn't it?'

'What?'

'Being out of the closet. Being with others like you.'

Daniel nods, swallowing a lump in his throat as Matt reaches over and gives his arm a reassuring squeeze.

'It feels like I'm home,' he says finally, tears in his eyes. 'I just never thought it would feel this normal.'

'I know,' Matt says. 'But it is normal. Just not the normal you were used to. Speaking of which, how are things with you and your wife now?'

'Soon-to-be-ex wife,' Daniel corrects. 'Not great. She didn't take it well, obviously, but there seems to be a détente for now. I'm trying very hard to remind her constantly that whatever we feel about each other, it isn't about us, it's about the girls.'

'And by that I suppose you don't mean us?' Matt gestures around the table and Daniel laughs.

'No. These girls are much shorter and they're related to me.'

*

'You're such a big girl. I can't believe you're flying all by yourself.' Richard had wiped tears from his eyes as he stood hugging Jess goodbye at security.

Jess had squeezed him tightly, not wanting to leave, not wanting anything to change, but Carrie had sat at the computer with her yesterday, and they'd looked at pictures of Nantucket, read about the beaches, the museums, the boat trips, and she couldn't help but feel a shiver of excitement at going somewhere new.

'Tons of celebrities go to Nantucket,' Carrie had said, and they'd looked up a list on the computer. Jess had gone to bed and dreamed of being discovered by someone famous; maybe Tom Hanks would spot her and decide she'd be perfect to play his daughter in his next movie.

In the departure lounge, she had looked up and she had actually seen someone famous! For a minute she thought it was someone she knew, a friend of her dad's, but then she realized it was the actor who played the dad in her favourite sitcom. It was Walter Driscoll. She watched as everyone gradually became aware of his presence, a dull murmur that went around the room as people pointed and whispered, eventually coming over to bashfully ask for an autograph or a photograph.

She was desperate for an autograph, had never been this close to a celebrity before, but she was embarrassed, didn't know what to say. She sat there, pretending to be buried in *Harry Potter*, pretending not to be interested in Walter Driscoll.

'Is anyone sitting here?' His familiar baritone was directly in front of her, and Jess looked up and immediately blushed as she shook her head.

'I see you're enjoying it.' He gestured to her book with a smile. 'I finished it a couple of weeks ago and loved it. I bet you were at the bookstore at midnight for that.' He raised an eyebrow and Jess smiled and nodded.

'Thought so. Don't tell anyone –' he leaned towards her – 'but I was too.'

'I . . . I really like your show,' Jess ventured, deciding that he may be a celebrity, but he was also a real person and, more than that, he seemed normal. Nice.

'You do?' He seemed genuinely delighted. 'Who's your favourite character?'

As Jess chatted away, charmed by Walter Driscoll, she forgot she was supposed to be scared of flying for the first time on her own, forgot she was supposed to be missing her dad, and by the time she and Walter made their way onto the plane, Walter was regaling her with stories of what he got up to as a teenager on Nantucket, and she couldn't wait to get there, to drive on the sand as he did, to go out lobstering and picnic on Coatue.

'Excuse me?' The woman sitting next to her on the plane leaned forward. 'I have to ask: that man you were talking to in the departure lounge ... was that Walter Driscoll?'

'Yes.' Jess nodded, proud to have been the one whom he chose to befriend.

'I told you,' she said, turning to an older man with a smile. 'My dad said it wasn't, but he's only seen his show once. Is he nice?'

'Really nice,' Jess said. 'He gave me his address in Nantucket and said my mom and I should go and see him.'

'Wow. You must have made a good impression.'

'Well, I told him I want to be an actress when I grow up.'

'That's a very good thing to be.' The woman nodded. 'I've got two girls, but they're much younger than you, and right now they both want to be fairy princesses.'

Jess smiles. 'I used to want to be a fairy princess too when I was younger.'

'I'm Bee,' says Bee. 'It's nice to meet you.'

Jess gets off the plane, and walks over to the gate with Bee and Evan. She says goodbye to Walter Driscoll – his wife is picking him up at the airport – and scans the crowd of people there, desperately looking for her mom.

There she is. Looking so familiar, so like Mom. Jess

breaks into a run, and seconds later she is wrapped in her mother's arms as both of them start to cry.

'I've missed you, baby.' Daff squeezes her tightly, not realizing until this very second how much that is true.

'I've missed you too, Mommy,' Jess sobs, sounding so like a little girl, so like the sweet little girl she used to be, that Daff never wants to let her go.

'There he is.' Bee sees Daniel, standing next to a woman who, oh what a small world this is, is obviously that sweet girl Jessica's mother. Jess and her mother are now wrapped around one another, and Daniel is watching them, a smile in his eyes. How ridiculous, she thinks, that in different circumstances she might have thought he and this woman were involved.

Bee walks over to Daniel, holding her father's arm, standing back as Evan and Daniel shake hands.

Daniel looks straight in his eyes. 'I'm glad you're okay.'

'Thank you, son,' Evan says, before looking around at the airport. 'Good God. Look at this place! It's huge.'

'Huge?' Daniel laughs. 'It's not huge. It's tiny.'

'No, it used to be tiny,' Evan says. 'The last time I was here was many years ago, and this really was tiny. Goodness. It makes me feel old.'

'Old but healthy,' Bee says, taking his arm, unhappy that she still has to rely on Daniel for so much, but knowing that it was easy for him to meet them at the airport, to pick up the girls on the way to their house.

'Thank God,' Evan says, and they walk over to the car.

*

Nan is standing on a step ladder painting the front door a bright purple, Lizzie and Stella, both with their own paintbrushes, are crouching at her feet and working on the bottom of the door, as the car pulls into the driveway.

'What is she *doing*?' Bee says.

'I have no idea.' Daniel grins, opening the door. 'Nan? What are you doing?'

'I'm fed up with all this Nantucket grey,' Nan says. 'I wanted some colour, and the girls wanted a project. We think it looks great.'

'Doesn't it looks great, Daddy?' echoes Lizzie, suddenly catching sight of her mother as she opens the car door. 'Mommy!' she squeals, and she and Stella go running towards the car.

'Guess who's here!' Bee finishes squeezing the girls, covering them with kisses, and turns to her father. 'It's Poppa!' But Evan is now looking deathly ill, immobile, as white as a ghost.

'Oh my God!' Bee whispers as her heart skips a beat. 'I think he's having a heart attack. Daniel, do something. Help!'

Daniel and Nan rush over to the car, and Nan is starting to open the door, when she sees Evan's face.

'Oh my Lord,' she whispers, and she passes out cold, sinking into Daniel's arms.

Chapter Twenty-four

It is almost as if Evan, Everett, whatever it is he is actually called, has spent his entire life waiting for this moment, his entire life knowing that it would come full circle, that he would not end his days without somehow seeing Nan again, making amends, acknowledging his mistakes and his wrongs, and trying to right them again.

He just never thought it would happen like this.

When Bee first told him about Nantucket, that she and Daniel were going, first on a weekend they had won, and then for most of the summer, Evan had felt his heart almost stop, and he had known then that the time was almost upon him.

He had never figured out how he would make his way back to Nantucket, but had turned it over to God, had accepted that somehow it would happen. And he had thought he had prepared himself, thought he had known what to say.

It turns out he was entirely wrong.

*

All those years ago, he had lost everything. All he could think about, from the minute he awoke to the minute he went to bed, was how to get out of the mess he was in.

First, there were the small poker games on the island, then the large games in New York, where the stakes became so high he was throwing in things he didn't have – a Hinckley yacht that belonged to a friend but was moored by the house, giving the false impression it belonged to the Powells, large sums of non-existent money, jewels that Everett couldn't find when it came time to pay, Nan having wisely hidden them, more to protect them from the scores of strangers constantly passing through the house, never thinking the greatest threat would be her husband.

He would wake with a vice of panic around his heart, have breakfast with his son, Michael, and feel the vice grow ever tighter as the bills came in, people needing to be paid, then phone calls from the bank managers requesting he call them back urgently.

All he needed, he kept telling himself, was one big win. He had won before, it was surely only a matter of time before he would win again. He would turn it around. He had to. What other choice did he have?

Then came that final game, the game when he had been winning, when his luck had finally turned around. The buzz, the surge of adrenaline, and the final hand when he looked down and had a full hand, the best hand he'd had in months, the kind of hand that didn't come along too often, at least not in his lifetime, and he knew he'd won, knew this was the moment he'd been waiting for.

It was only him and James Callaghan left in the game, and Callaghan was known for his bluffs. Everett knew he would win, and he silently pushed everything into the centre of the table, the chips, the notes, everything that he had, and much that he did not, and he showed his hand triumphantly as the rest of the men in that quiet room held their breath. He smiled as he sat back in relief, preparing to gather his things, to start afresh with his family, to stop gambling and never put them in this precarious position again.

Callaghan leaned forward, and Everett stared into his eyes, waiting for him to throw his cards down, but he turned them over, expressionless, and still, to this day, when he thinks about it, it feels as if he were watching it happen as if in a dream.

Ten, Jack, Queen, King and Ace of Hearts. A Royal Flush. The world stopped and Everett knew that his life was over. He got up, still in a dream, and went back home, completely numb.

The idea came to him that night, after he'd kissed Michael, who had grunted and stirred gently in his sleep, after he'd sat for hours in the window seat looking at the harbour, making his way through a bottle of single malt.

He had gazed at Nan, sleeping soundly, before he left. Kissed his fingers and held them to her lips, then padded out of the house, under cover of darkness, careful not to let anyone see him as he made his way to the harbour, folding up some clothes and his father's watch, leaving them on the beach as he went.

Nan would be okay, that much he knew. She was the strongest woman he had ever met, and as hard as it was for him to leave the woman he loved, she would claw her way out of the mess he had got them into, would get over his loss, would continue to have a full and fulfilling life.

And Michael? Michael who adored his father, who begged to come along wherever his father was going? It was heartbreaking to leave him, but better to leave, better for Michael to think his father had died than to know what a failure he was. Everett hoped Nan would never tell him, never reveal the trouble he had left them in.

There wasn't another way, he thought, hunched up in the corner of the old ferry, coat collar pulled up high, hat pulled down low, not looking at the few people on the boat that early in the morning, careful not to draw any attention to himself.

He got to Hyannisport, and hitched a ride into New England, ending up in New Haven. It was a big enough city for him to remain anonymous, and far away enough from New York to ensure he wouldn't bump into anyone he knew, anyone who could dispute his suicide, for he knew that's how it would appear, knew it was the only answer, the only thing that would make any sense, particularly after Nan found out the full extent of their debt.

In many ways he wished he *had* been brave enough for suicide. He had thought about it, God knows he had thought about it, and as he gently placed the pile of clothes on the beach in the black of night he had wondered how hard it would actually be to set foot into the icy waters, to let the waves carry him away.

He couldn't do it, and New Haven turned out to be the right place for him to reinvent himself. Here he was no longer Everett Powell, scion of one of the East Coast's great families, but Evan Palliser, from Cape Cod, a divorced man who had moved to New Haven to start afresh.

Unlike Everett, who had been brought up in the lap of luxury and had never had to work, Evan was going to be different. Evan was going to stand on his own two feet, find a job, build some semblance of a life, learn to live with the guilt that followed him around every second of every day.

First, he had to conquer his demons. He went to the only place he could think of, a place he hadn't visited in years, a place he thought had no meaning in his life.

He went to church.

There, for the first time in his life, Evan fell to his knees and prayed for forgiveness. He knelt until his knees were sore, his bones creaky and painful, and he asked to be shown the way. As he knelt there, with only a couple of dollars in his pocket, no place to sleep, nowhere to go, he felt a peace settle over him, and he realized that if he were ever to believe that someone like him would have a spiritual awakening, if indeed he even believed in the possibility of a spiritual awakening, it was highly probable that he had just experienced one.

The reverend walked in at five, found Evan still kneeling, saw the suffering in his eyes, and brought him into the back to make him coffee. Evan confessed he needed a job, a place to stay. By the end of the night he had been set up with a bed in the home of the McCoughlin family, and a job working in the family business, making steel locks.

He didn't speak much in the beginning. He worked hard, kept his head down, kept his secrets to himself. The McCoughlin family were impressed, particularly Donald McCoughlin, the son of Scottish immigrants who had built the business from nothing; he saw that Evan had a bearing, a class that would serve them well.

He began selling the locks, swiftly rising to become head of the sales force, buying a small and rather ordinary house on the fringes of an up-and-coming neighbourhood, doing it up on evenings and weekends, taking books out of the library to learn how to carve trim, how to lay a wood floor, how to install window frames.

He would go to sleep at night and dream of his family, dream of going back, finding them again, making it right; but news of the Powell tragedy had reached them in New Haven, and he knew he had to let sleeping dogs lie, knew that to do otherwise would perhaps cause them all more pain. He had caused enough.

The poker games still called him, but he relied on God to get him through, and he found that as long as he went to church, stayed industrious, kept himself busy, the callings were fewer and fewer.

He saved his money, and when his house was done he didn't sell it, as so many might have, he kept it and rented it, and bought another, and soon another, and another.

Evan first saw Margaret at the McCoughlins' house, but only got to know her properly at a dance. He hadn't wanted to go; he continued to feel shame, and guilt at having fun, at doing anything other than work and paying his penance for his previous life, but this was a company dance and Mr McCoughlin had demanded he be there.

Margaret was Mr McCoughlin's daughter, and when he saw her at the dance it was the first time, since Nan, that he had looked at a woman with interest, thought of anyone other than his wife.

They chatted, shared one dance, and when he left she smiled at him and told him he ought to socialize more, ought to join her and her friends one night, for she had been watching him, had wondered how he could be such a recluse at such a young age, particularly when he clearly had so much to offer.

They were married two years later, Evan knowing he was committing bigamy, but telling himself it was okay because he was no longer Everett Powell. Marrying as Evan Palliser seemed somehow more acceptable. Margaret was desperate to get married, and it was true that he loved her; and he saw a chance, as selfish as it sounded, of happiness again.

Bee was born nine months after their wedding day, and from the moment the doctor stepped outside the delivery room to tell him he had a baby girl, Evan fell in love.

He had loved Michael, but things had been different then. He had been a terrible father to Michael, too consumed with gambling to pay him any real attention, constantly planning his next game, a new strategy, his next win.

Second time around he could be the father he'd never been, the father he knew he *could* be. From the beginning Bee was a daddy's girl, the apple of his eye, the daughter who could do no wrong.

Bee didn't need to know secrets, didn't ask questions about his past, how he grew up, where – questions he had learned to evade, dismiss, waving his hand as if they weren't important and swiftly changing the subject, trying to ignore the growing pain in his wife's eyes.

There were still many occasions when Evan woke up in the middle of the night, got out of bed and tiptoed down to the kitchen in their grand 1830s colonial – the nicest one in town, for Mr McCoughlin had become ill and Evan, said to have the golden touch, had taken over the company, with grand plans for expanding it – and drank tumblers full of whisky, shame building as he thought of Nan, thought of Michael, thought of what he had left behind.

He knew, by that time, that gambling was, for him, an addiction, a drug in the same way that alcohol was to an alcoholic, and he knew that he could never attend even one poker game, make one bet, or he would be right back at the beginning, living in the fog he had finally cleared.

For his life with Nan, with Michael, had been a fog, his clarity clouded by his constant need to gamble, and now, although he loved Margaret, there was always a piece of him he couldn't give to her, a piece of his heart that belonged to Nan, and a regret for the life he could have had if he hadn't messed it up so badly.

In the beginning Margaret found it fascinating that he was a mystery, that he wouldn't talk about his past. He would tell her about his life, but only talking about a life that started once he turned up, seemingly out of nowhere, in town.

Secrets take their toll. Evan wasn't surprised when Margaret left him; he found that he had subconsciously been waiting for it for years, part of the penance he knew he would, at some point, have to do.

He has been single since then, has attempted relationships, but they have always been half-hearted, and the memories of Nan, of what he left behind, have only grown stronger over the years.

Still, he didn't think he could go back, not until Bee brought up the subject of Nantucket, out of the blue. Then he knew it was finally time.

Evan was incredulous, stunned, and scared, when Daniel drove the car up the old driveway of Windermere, and he turned to Daniel, about to ask whether this was some sort of sick joke – how had he known? – when he looked up and there was Nan. As beautiful as when he last saw her.

He turned white, and watched the expression in Nan's eyes change from a friendly greeting to a slow recognition and pure and absolute shock.

As if she had seen a ghost, she sank slowly down, and Evan sat shaking, unable to move.

*

Nan opens her eyes and finds herself on a sofa in the living room, Daniel and Daff bending over her, looking concerned.

'Here –' Daff hands her a glass of brandy – 'have a few sips of this.'

'I . . .' Nan is confused, and for just a few seconds she looks far older than her years. 'I thought I saw a ghost. I thought I saw Everett.'

Daff and Daniel exchange a glance, then the door opens and Bee stands there, her father just behind her. Bee's face is white as she gestures for them to come out.

'Where are you going?' Nan calls.

'We'll just be a second,' Daniel says gently. 'Don't worry.'

He walks out and looks first at Bee, then at Evan.

'What the hell is going on?'

'I can't talk,' Bee says finally, her voice a dull monotone. 'I can't believe what I've just been told.' She refuses to look at her father before turning and walking outside, sitting down quickly in one of the Adirondack chairs on the porch.

'What is it?' Daniel looks at Evan, and Evan starts to tell his story.

*

Daniel returns to the living room to find Nan now sitting up, resting her head against the cushions on the sofa.

'So strange,' Nan murmurs. 'I had a dream about Everett just last night, so vivid I didn't know what it meant, and then I thought I just saw him. What do you think it means? And who was that man? Or did I dream that too?'

'Nan, I wish Michael were here because I shouldn't be the one to have to tell you this. I don't, in fact, even know how to tell you this, but ... you didn't imagine it.'

'What do you mean, I didn't imagine it?'

'I mean, Bee just arrived with her ... her father.' He speaks haltingly, not knowing how on earth to tell her. 'His name is Evan Palliser. But we've all just found out that wasn't the name he was born with ...'

'It is Everett, isn't it?' Nan looks into his eyes, whispering as the tears well up and Daniel nods.

'Where is he?'

'He's in the hallway. He wants to see you.'

Nan struggles to sit up, to compose herself, then nods, putting her shaking hands between her legs to still them.

Everett walks in, his eyes fixed on Nan, not needing to look at anything else in this room for it is all exactly the same. The smell is the same: beeswax and lavender, honeysuckle from the trellis outside, the musty fusty smell of the heavy antique crewel curtains framing the draughty windows.

It smells like home. A home he has thought about for so many years, thought he would never see again. Being here, smelling the familiarity, is shocking to him, overwhelming his senses in a way he could never have anticipated.

He knows the exact pattern of the needlepoint on the Chippendale chairs that his mother sewed when his father was away at war. He knows which leg of which table snapped off when he and his cousins were tearing through the room as children, and had to be glued back on by a furniture restorer they found on the Cape.

He knows each painting on the wall, each print, each dent and mark, but he is not looking at any of these things as he approaches the sofa.

He is looking at Nan.

'My God,' he says, sinking down without taking his eyes off her. 'You're still just as beautiful.'

Nan looks him steadily in the eye, then slaps him around the face, as hard as she possibly can.

'Do you have any idea,' she says, her voice cold, icy, imperious, 'what I have been through? Do you have any idea of the struggles I have had? The pain I went through, raising our son as a single mother, wondering what I did to cause you to commit suicide, the guilt I have carried my entire life?'

'I can only imagine,' Everett says, shame casting his eyes to the floor.

'No. No, I don't think you can. I don't think you can imagine how I went to bed in tears every night for years, wondering how I could have been so awful, what I could have done differently, how I must have been a horrible wife, a terrible person to have made you commit suicide. And while I've been struggling, look at you. You've presumably had a wonderful life, just sailed away, forgetting about us, letting us live this terrible lie all these years . . .' And Nan bursts into tears.

'Mom?' Michael bursts into the room and runs towards his mother. 'Mom? What's going on?'

He turns, sees Everett, and stops, his blood running cold.

'Oh Christ,' he whispers. 'Dad?'

Chapter Twenty-five

Under different circumstances, this place would be beautiful, although even under better circumstances Jordana isn't quite sure why she would ever come here when the Hamptons is so much closer for her, not to mention so much trendier.

Jordana loves the Hamptons. Loves stocking up on her Calypso tops and Miss Trish sandals, her armfuls of diamond bangles – because you never know who you'll bump into having dinner at Nick & Toni's, and you always have to look your best, just in case.

She loves that she could be sitting next to Jerry Seinfeld on one side and Martha Stewart on the other. She loves that every night is filled with different parties. It's all about seeing and being seen, dressing up, rubbing shoulders with the great and the good.

Nantucket is beautiful, no question about it, but, Jordana thinks as she looks slightly disdainfully around the pool area, where are all the gorgeous models? Where are the breast implants? Where are the diamonds, for God's sake?

This is not a world Jordana understands, and now that there doesn't seem to be any reason to stay, she can't wait to get out of here.

But where to? Jackson is at home, waiting, terrified

this will be permanent, wondering what he's done wrong, vowing to do things differently, to do anything she wants just for them to be together again.

For the first time, Jordana has to consider her future. She had convinced herself that she and Michael were destined to be together, that when he saw her again, found out she was having their child, he would do the right thing, would come back to her and they would build a life together, just as they had talked about during those heady early days of the affair.

She has spent hours lying in bed at night, planning how she and Michael will live, where they will live. Somewhere not too remote, close enough to the city for them to be able to get in when they need to, somewhere where they could open a small jewellery store, a place with a wealthy enough clientele who would come to them and buy, but simple enough for Michael to be happy.

Pound Ridge, perhaps. Or Katonah. Maybe Nyack. She had even gone to the real estate sites and looked at the kind of houses she imagined them living in. Not like the vast Great Neck mansion she and Jackson lived in – marble floors and sweeping staircases – but something that Michael had always dreamed of, an old farmhouse with wide-planked floors and cosy, low ceilings, fireplaces in every room, rolling fields behind the house. It had never been her dream before Michael, but she was willing to edit her dreams for him, willing to become the person she thought he wanted her to be.

It never occurred to her that it wouldn't happen. Now what is she to do? Go back to Jackson? Allow him to think the baby is his, even though technically it's impossible? God knows how she would get around that. Should she confess the affair, promise to never stray again?

She doesn't want to go back to Jackson. She wants to be with Michael, but if she can't be with Michael, can she really do this on her own, is this really something she wants?

A baby. Not an accessory. Not a puppy like her adorable little Maltese terrier, but a baby who couldn't be left at home alone when she went shopping, nor in the car, looking pleadingly out of the window as she sat in restaurants for lunch with her girlfriends. A *baby*.

Oh God. What is she going to do?

Jordana sits down on the bed and sighs deeply, rubbing her stomach unconsciously. She won't have an abortion, though. She can't. This is a child she made with Michael, a man she loves, and if she can't have him, she can have his child. It's the next best thing, and maybe once the child is here, maybe then he'll change his mind, maybe then he'll realize what they could have together.

She's going to have this baby. It's the only thing she's sure of right now.

She gets up to go to the bathroom, blinking twice as she sits down and stares, uncomprehendingly, at the blood.

And she bursts into tears.

*

The initial euphoria of being with her mom has worn off very quickly. Yes it's beautiful here, yes this house is kind of cool, but it smells old and Jess isn't sure she likes old, isn't sure she'd actually want to sit down on one of those threadbare velvet chairs in the living room, yes there's the beach, but none of her friends are here . . .

Yesterday was good. Her mom was so thrilled to see her, which was a bit of a surprise, and she didn't really say anything about the shoplifting, just told her that when she was ready to talk about it she would listen and wouldn't judge, and then she took her shopping which was really nice, especially when Jess was expecting a lecture.

Jess knows it was probably guilt, but look what she got out of it! A bunch of T-shirts, a baseball cap, a sweatshirt, a bathing suit and a ton of shells and note-books and fun stuff at the Hub. All she had to do was pick something up and say, 'Oh isn't this *so* cute,' and her mom would buy it for her. With hindsight, Jess now realizes that was probably to stop her taking it for herself.

They went for ice cream and walked around the little shops by the marina, and in the evening they had dinner at home with the other tenants, although not with Nan, who had excused herself and gone to bed early.

Jess is fascinated by Nan. She's never seen anyone like her before. She is old but she doesn't *seem* old, and she is nothing like Jessica's grandmothers, who wear twinsets or tracksuits, not flowing silk shawls in bright jewel colours and beaded satin slippers, just to hang out at home.

Her mom says Nan is wonderful, but she wasn't wonderful yesterday. Mom says she's had a big shock and she just needs some time to adjust, so hopefully she'll be back to herself soon.

Meanwhile, what's Jess supposed to do with herself for the next few weeks? There are only so many times you can listen to the playlists on your iPod without getting bored, and even though it's really, really nice to be with Mom, Jess doesn't want to hang out with her, and now her mom says she's taking the rest of the summer off and they're staying here. Jess wants to hang out with people her own age, and no one here is under the age of about forty.

Maybe this wasn't such a good idea after all.

*

Nan watches Jess from her bedroom window, sitting on the sand, hugging her knees, playing with the sand, gathering it up in her hand and letting it sift slowly through her fingers. Nan shivers, and puts on a robe from the bathroom, slips her feet into flip-flops and makes her way slowly down the stairs.

She isn't ready to talk to anyone in the house yet, knows they are all being careful with her, concerned; they all want to know how she is, how both of them are. Both Nan and Michael.

Poor Michael. To have a father again after all these years, to have learned that his life too has been a lie. It is perhaps worse for Michael, she realizes, because he is so sensitive.

He had looked at Everett after he had attempted to explain, interrupting him with a voice that was cold, colder than she had ever heard it, as he said, 'As far as I'm concerned you're not my father. I can't stop my mother from talking to you but I don't want anything to do with you.'

Everett reached out a hand to stop Michael walking out of the room.

'Please, Michael,' he said, his voice choked up. 'Please let me explain.'

Michael did stop then. He looked at Everett closely, barely able to contain his fury.

'Explain? You want to explain? Sure, I'd love to hear. I'd love to hear how you explain it to a six-year-old boy who is crying himself to sleep every night because he misses his dad *so* much. I'd love to hear you explain to him that it wasn't, as he always thought, his fault. That six-year-old grew up believing that his dad wouldn't have left them and killed himself if he'd behaved better, or hadn't been naughty, had listened more. Can you explain what to do with the pain and guilt and fear that little boy grew up with? Can you?' Michael stares at Everett, now sobbing openly, before dropping his gaze. 'No. I didn't think so.'

'I'm so sorry,' Everett whispered. 'I was sick. I didn't know what I was doing. And I missed you so much. I've spent years missing you, thinking about you, wondering what you were doing, how you turned out.'

'Well, now you know,' Michael said, turning and walking out of the room, making his way unsteadily up the stairs to his room, where it was his turn to cry.

Nan tried to talk to Michael about it later, but what could she say? She was still reeling herself.

In the middle of the night, she sat up, bolt upright in bed, a terrible thought having just woken her.

Did he want the house? Is that why he came back? Was she finally going to lose the house because of this? Of *course*. Why else would he come back after all this time?

She hadn't gone back to sleep after that. She sat up and worried about what she should do, how she could keep the house, or, at worst, sell it and keep the money herself. She didn't owe Everett a penny, and if there was a way to make sure he got nothing, she would find it.

Now, as the sun comes up, she notices Jess on the beach and is drawn to her. There is something about this child's unhappiness and confusion that seems to mirror her own right now, and she steps outside, trying not to think that she is very close to losing all that she loves.

*

'Hey!' Daff walks into the kitchen and is startled to find Michael there. It has felt as though he has been avoiding her these last twenty-four hours, and she is shocked at the sharp jolt of pain she felt upon realizing that this may be the case.

Pleasure and pain. There is the pleasure of having Jess back, of being able to spend time with her, with nowhere else to be, nothing else to do but be fully present for her daughter.

Not that Jess has opened up to her, not yet, but Daff is hopeful, and grateful that she wants to be here, grateful that it has happened so quickly and so relatively painlessly.

Focusing on Jess has stopped her focusing on Michael, on the pain he so obviously feels, on his withdrawing from everyone in the house, taking off into town and not coming home until late at night when he knew everyone would be asleep.

How quickly these people have become her family, she realizes. Living together perhaps it was inevitable, but she had no idea this would happen when she first phoned about the rental. She imagined Windermere as a boarding house in the truest sense of the word, a place where people had rooms but got on with their lives on their own during waking hours.

Never did she dream she would feel, from almost the moment she set foot here, as if she had come home. Never did she dream she would care about the other people in this house quite as much as she does, feel as comfortable with them as she does.

Michael looks up and gives her a small smile. 'Hey. I was hoping you'd be up soon.'

'Oh? Do you want some tea?'

'No. I have coffee. Thanks. I thought perhaps you'd like to go for a walk. I . . . I know I've been a bit distant and I wanted to explain.'

'Don't worry.' Daff's tone is light, careful not to convey how she really feels. 'I know you're going through a lot. You don't owe me an explanation at all. It's fine.' She busies herself filling the kettle with water, so Michael can't see her eyes, how she really feels.

'Please, Daff.' He walks up behind her and lays a gentle hand on her shoulder, and when she turns he puts his arms around her and hugs her. 'I'm sorry,' he whispers, and when they pull apart he looks at her with a raised eyebrow.

'A walk?'

'Okay.' She smiles. 'But let me find Jess.'

'She's fine,' he says. 'She's with my mom. They're working in the garden.'

'What?' Daff is stunned. 'Jess? Working? That's not my daughter. My daughter sleeps until noon and doesn't work or help out unless there's a bribe attached.'

'Well, perhaps aliens came down and swapped her during the night, but she's out there. Look.' Michael brings Daff to the window and she looks out in amazement to see, in the distance, Nan chatting away to Jess and showing her how to stake the now-flopping cucumbers, Nan stepping back as Jess bangs the stake in and clips the wire, looking to Nan for approval.

'Oh my God,' Daff says. 'I think your mother may be a witch.'

'There are those in town who've been saying that for years.'

'No, but seriously, my daughter's a teenager. She hates everything and everyone, but she actually looks – I can't believe I'm going to say this – but she actually looks like she's enjoying herself.'

'She probably is.' Michael grins. 'Remember when we were kids and we got to do chores or help out, or have jobs like waiting tables or working at gas stations? Remember the sense of achievement we got? Nowadays all the kids seem to work as interns for friends of their parents, and it's not real work, not like the work we did. She feels useful. It's probably a great feeling, and a new one for her.'

Daff tears her eyes away from Jess to look at Michael in amazement. 'Thank you,' she says. 'You're right. You're absolutely right. She feels *useful*. We don't give her anything to do; it would never occur to me to have her do gardening like I used to do. I always hated it and I thought I was doing her a favour, not having her do it and paying the landscapers to handle it, but you're right.' Daff sighs. 'That's probably what all the stealing was about. She needs something else in her life. She needs to feel useful.'

'She certainly doesn't look unhappy now.' They both look over to see Jess smiling shyly as Nan claps her hands in delight. 'I'd say she looks pretty great.'

'Thank you.' Daff's eyes fill with tears. 'She is. And

thank you for seeing that, and for saying it.' She blinks away the tears and sighs. 'That's enough about me. I wanted to find out how you are. I've been so worried about you.'

'It's all a bit of a nightmare.' Michael frowns. 'Jordana, the woman who turned up, is, well, you know who she is. And it seems she's . . .' He swallows.

'Pregnant,' Daff says softly.

'Yes. How did you know?'

'I didn't. It seemed an obvious thing she would come all this way to tell you.'

'It never occurred to me. And now I don't know what to do.'

'Will you go back to her, do you think? Try again?'

Michael sighs and shakes his head, and Daff can't help but feel relief. 'I can't,' he says. 'It would be entirely the wrong thing to do. I'm too old to live a lie.'

'Oh Michael,' she says. 'I'm so sorry.'

'I know. So am I.'

'It's definitely yours?' Daff thinks of the high heels, the brassy hair, the big diamonds. She wonders if Michael has truly been her only conquest of late.

'I think so. I'm pretty sure. I've known Jordana a long time and I don't think she's a liar. Although,' he snorts in mock laughter, 'I would also have said she wasn't the type to have an affair.'

'That's what I would have said about you.' Daff smiles wryly.

'Me too. It was a case of bad judgement. I'm still not quite sure what came over me.'

'I have to say –' Daff is careful – 'she's not quite who I would see you with.'

Michael starts to laugh. 'Who *would* you see me with?'

Someone like me, she thinks. But doesn't say it.

'I don't know.' She shrugs, embarrassed. 'Someone more down to earth, I think. Someone more natural.'

'A single mother, perhaps?' Michael grins, and Daff blushes and moves to the sink to wash up, stay busy.

'Then there's the small matter of my father turning up when he is supposed to be a bundle of bones at the bottom of the ocean.'

'Ah yes.' Daff turns to look at him. 'I was wondering when you were going to mention that.'

'It didn't seem important.' He shrugs, and they both laugh.

'I'm waiting for the next bomb to fall,' he continues. 'It feels as if everything in my life is not what I thought it was, everything has changed, and nothing will ever be the same. If everything I thought I believed, everything I trusted, was wrong, how can I ever trust again?'

Michael pauses, but Daff senses he has more to say and doesn't interrupt.

'Remember 9/11?' he says. 'After the planes hit the towers we heard the news about the Pentagon, then the plane in Pennsylvania?' Daff nods. 'We were all waiting for the next thing, waiting for the world to come to an end. That's how this feels. It feels as if my world has come to an end. Everything that was safe and secure

340

and real for me, is not. How do I trust?' He looks pleadingly at Daff. 'How can I trust in anyone again?'

You can trust me. The words are on the tip of Daff's tongue, but she doesn't say them, just stands there gazing at him as he sighs and runs his fingers through his hair. *You are a beautiful man.*

She wants to say: You will find your way through this, you will find a way forward because you are all good. You are goodness and kindness and perhaps the best man I have ever met. You can trust me because I trust you. Because even though I barely know you I would place my life in your hands. I know you would look after it.

'Can we go?'

'What?' Daff shakes her head, breaking her reverie. 'Go where?'

'For that walk.'

She laughs. 'Yes, I'll just get my shoes.'

They walk for hours. Along the pretty roads of Sconset, alongside the beach, neither of them with any time constraints, they are happy to just walk and talk, lapsing into occasional companionable silence.

'How do you feel about being a father?' Daff asks as they reach a pretty cove.

'I don't know.' Michael winces at the thought. 'I love kids, but they've always been other people's kids. I've never felt ready for my own.'

'I'm not sure any of us are ever ready for kids.' She laughs. 'They always seem to take you by surprise.

You'll be a great father,' she adds. 'If you choose to be involved.'

'Of course I'll be involved. Oh God. That's the next thing. Talking to Jordana and telling her just how involved I plan to be. I'm not going to just walk away from my child. I'd never do that.'

'I know,' Daff says.

'Shall we stop for a bit?' Michael points to another little cove ahead, smaller, hidden in the dunes.

'Sure.'

Suddenly it's awkward. The two of them are sitting on the sand, knowing what's coming, not knowing how to get there, unsure whether this is the right thing, or whether this is just another huge complication in an altogether-too-complicated life.

There doesn't seem to be a choice any more for either of them, and as Michael leans over to kiss Daff, he realizes that she is the only safe place for him right now. How could he possibly walk away from the only thing in his life that is good?

'Now I know why they always say sex on the beach is overrated.' Daff furiously shakes the sand out of her hair.

'Oh thanks!' Michael says.

'I didn't mean *that*.' She laughs, pulling on her shorts and allowing herself to be wrapped in his arms and kissed. 'Not that,' she murmurs, looking at him and smiling, unable to believe this has happened with someone so wonderful. 'That was lovely.'

'Was that your first time since your husband?'

'Ex-husband.' Daff smiles shyly. 'Yes.'

'Was it okay?' he asks nervously.

'Okay? It was better than okay. It was marvellous! Like riding a bike,' she says, laughing. 'Only better.'

Truly it was marvellous. Better than marvellous. Blissful.

Who would ever love me, Daff remembers thinking during those early days when she and Richard first separated. My breasts are saggy from childbirth, I have stretch marks on my stomach, legs I forget to shave for months at a time. The last person to fall in love with me did so when I was young, firm, gorgeous. When I was bathing-suit-ready every morning of my life, just by the sheer act of falling out of bed. Who would love me now?

She had thought that when she did come to have sex with anyone again, it would be awkward as hell, would have to be done with the lights out.

Yet there they were, on the beach, and it didn't feel awkward, it felt like the most natural thing she had ever done. And she didn't feel ashamed of her lines, or her veins, or her sag. She felt beautiful.

Lying in his arms afterwards, as they continued to chat softly, the thought occurred to her that this is intimacy. This isn't what she and Richard had. Ever. They never lay in one another's arms after the fact, but rolled over after a perfunctory kiss goodnight and went to sleep. Or, in the beginning, rolled over to get out of bed and get dressed. This feels like something she has been waiting for her entire life.

This feels utterly new and utterly familiar at the same time. It feels right . . . like coming home.

Chapter Twenty-six

'I'll take the girls to the beach.' Daniel holds his hands out for Lizzie and Stella as Bee nods gratefully, sinking down on the chair next to Michael, both of them smiling at each other before looking out to sea, letting the silence envelop them for a few minutes before Bee starts to speak.

'I always wanted a brother when I was growing up,' she murmurs. 'I had a best friend at school, Sophie, who had three older brothers. Going to her house was so exciting. There was constant noise and activity and friends over, whereas my house always felt like a museum.'

'You should have been here.' Michael laughs. 'I'm an only child too ... or at least I thought I was ... until now. But this house was always filled with people. I used to long for a little peace and quiet.'

'This is just so weird.' Bee shakes her head. 'I can't believe that my dad had this whole other life before us, that he abandoned you all. It seems so out of character.'

'I barely remember him,' Michael says. 'I mean, I know all the stories and I remember snapshots, but I was six when he ... left. It becomes harder and harder to distinguish memory from the stories you hear or the photographs you see.'

'You look like him,' Bee says, turning and gazing at Michael. 'It wouldn't have occurred to me before, but I wasn't looking for it. Now, of course, I can see how much you look like he must have done when he was younger.'

'So what did he tell you about his old life? I still don't understand how he could have just turned up out of nowhere with no friends, no family, and have no one question it.'

'Because I think we accept people at face value. My mom always said he fitted into the community, and they all thought he'd been through a bad divorce with no children, was making a fresh start somewhere else. I guess, as well, in those days people weren't as open, didn't feel entitled to know everything about a person, and of course how could you have found out, back then?'

'What was he like?'

'As a father or as a man?'

'Both.' Michael looks at her.

'He was a wonderful father,' she says. 'I don't want to hurt you, I can't even imagine the pain of growing up without a father, but maybe he was trying to do for me what he couldn't do for you, because he was always there for me. He was fun. He'd take me places and always talk to me. Talk and talk and talk. He would explain everything, so going out with him, especially when I was little, was such an adventure.' She sighs. 'I used to feel so proud.'

Michael lays his head on his arms to listen.

346

'When I went away to school, Dad was always the one I wanted to talk to. He always seemed to have such wisdom. We disagreed on a lot of things, though. He and Mom are both religious and I don't really do anything. But he would always pause and think things through before giving me advice. His advice was almost always good.'

'How old were you when he divorced your mom?'

'It was more like she divorced him. I was eighteen. She always used to say she was tired of the secrets. I never understood what she was talking about, although now of course,' she says with a snort, 'it all makes perfect sense. He was closed with her, at least that's what she always said, but I never felt it. Never felt him be anything other than warm and loving and open with me. What about you?' She turns her head to look at Michael. 'What do you remember?'

'Not much. I remember loving being with him. When he was here, all I wanted to do was help him do whatever he was doing. I remember hero-worshipping him, even though a lot of the time he wasn't around. When he was, he seemed to be lost in thought, concentrating on something else. I remember him being irritated a lot of the time.'

'Irritated? My dad? Wow.' Bee shakes her head. 'I don't think I've ever even seen him lose his temper.'

'I didn't know this until I was much older, but he left us in horrible debt. Mom had to sell off all the houses on this property and our home in New York. This was just a summer house but we had to move here because

347

it was the only place we had left. He used to gamble. He gambled away everything, plus –' he laughs mirthlessly – 'a ton of stuff we didn't have. For months after he ... disappeared, people would turn up at the front door demanding money.'

'God, what did your mom do?'

'She'd usually invite them in, pour them a stiff drink then pour out her story. They'd usually stay for dinner and end up friends. Seriously.' Michael laughs. 'A few of the more frightening heavies came to our Christmas parties for years afterwards.'

'I'm so sorry,' Bee says, tears in her eyes. 'I don't know what to say. I'm just so sorry that you thought your dad was dead, and I got him instead.'

'I'm sorry too,' Michael says. 'I grew up with such a loss, and now ... Well. Now I don't know what to feel, other than completely betrayed.'

'He says he didn't think he had a choice back then,' Bee says quietly. 'He's in so much pain. He wants to make it up to you, to you and your mom, but he doesn't know how if you won't let him in.'

'I can't. Not yet.' Michael exhales. 'I'm just not ready.'

'Could you at least think about it?'

'Yes. I could do that. I could think about it.'

'Please do,' Bee says. 'Instead of looking at this as a betrayal, could you maybe look at it as a blessing? That you have your father back after all these years, you have a chance to learn where you came from, before it's too late.'

'It's not as easy as that.' Michael shakes his head sadly. 'I'll try. Honestly. Hey ...'

'What?'

'Put your hand out.'

Bee puts her hand out and they both laugh.

'Look at that,' she says with delight.

'We have the same hands.'

'Even the way our little fingers curve slightly. How weird.' And the two of them sit there gazing at one another's hands before Bee starts to speak.

'I know you can't see this as a blessing,' she says, 'not yet, and I'm struggling with it too, but it is kind of a blessing, to have found something you always wanted, particularly at a time when everything in your life is horrible, when everything you thought was precious and treasured and safe seems to be falling apart.'

Michael turns to look at her. 'You're talking about Daniel and the divorce.'

'Yes. And the fact that he's gay, so my entire marriage, from the very beginning, was a lie. I've been feeling like there is no light at the end of the tunnel, like there will never be a light at the end of the tunnel. Until now.' Bee pauses and looks at Michael. 'I don't want to get soppy or sentimental, but I think finding a big brother may be a truly wonderful thing in my life.'

Michael reaches over and takes her hand, squeezes it gently. 'Thank you,' he says. 'My life's been pretty awful recently too. Thank you for showing me there's another way to look at this.'

'There's always another way,' Bee says softly. 'There's

a reason we came to Nantucket and rented the house, a reason Dad came back here and found you.'

'I believe the same thing,' Michael says with a small laugh. 'Everything does, indeed, happen for a reason.'

He thinks of Jordana, of his child growing inside her.

'Sometimes it's just hard to figure out what the reason is.'

*

'I'm calling a family meeting,' Nan says. 'I've been worrying myself sick. I've suddenly realized that I'm trying to do everything myself, make all the decisions myself, and I can't do it all alone. I need my family around me.'

Daniel and Daff exchange a look.

'Um, I've grown terribly fond of you,' Daff ventures. 'I'm just not sure I qualify as family.'

'You do now,' Nan says. 'As far as I'm concerned the people I love are my family, and I'm afraid that now counts you. And I'm still getting to know young Jessica but I'm pretty certain you're family too.'

Jess blushes but can't hide the beam of joy at being included.

'Michael, my darling, I don't want to say anything that might upset you. For years I tried to hide the truth about your father, but the time has come for all of you to know the truth . . .'

'He gambled everything away and you were forced to sell the cottages and then the apartment in New York?'

'Oh.' Nan stops. 'I thought you didn't know.'

'Of course I knew. You told me a million times.'

'I did? I always thought I was protecting you.'

'You did when I was younger. Then you'd just tell everyone who came to the house, and I'd sit on the stairs and listen.'

She sighs. 'That's all beside the point, rather. The point is I think he's come back because he wants Windermere. I can't think of any other reason why he would show up here, out of the blue. He did a terrible thing, all those years ago. As far as I'm concerned the sort of man who can fake a suicide, abandoning his wife and child without a second glance, is the sort of man who can steal a house that he believes is rightfully his.'

'Surely the house is in your name, though?' Michael says.

'Well, no. I never bothered changing it,' Nan says. 'I thought it was a way of honouring Everett's memory, to keep the house in his name. It felt like a way of keeping him alive somehow, although when I found out the nature of the debt he'd left us in I was furious. I just never got round to doing it.'

'Oh Jesus.' Michael whistles. 'He could. He could claim it.'

'No!' Daff says. 'Are you sure? I think any judge in the country would have a hard time awarding him the house after he's been presumed dead for over thirty-five years. I honestly don't think you have anything to worry about, even if he were to go after you. He's here because he had a fall, because he's Daniel's ex-father-in-law.'

'She's right,' Daniel says. 'He had no idea I was staying in his house. I agree that this is all coincidence.'

'There's no such thing as coincidence,' Nan says wearily, convinced she is right. 'Jessica? What do you think?'

'Me?' Jess, slouched in the sofa, sits forward, unused to being asked her opinion.

'Yes. Do you think he's come to take the house away or do you think it's innocent?'

'Well. This kind of reminds me of a show I once saw on TV. The husband came back, except he hadn't pretended to be dead or anything, but he came back pretending he wanted to get back together and he missed his family, but he murdered his wife and tried to steal everything.'

'Jess!' Daff is mortified.

'What?'

'Oh don't worry.' Nan bursts out laughing. 'I doubt very much Everett's come back to murder me.'

'What channel were you watching?'

'Lifetime,' Jess says, and Michael grins.

'Sounds like a Lifetime special.'

'I do think he's come back to reclaim the house,' Nan continues smoothly, 'and the only thing I can think of to do is sell the house and hide the money. I never thought I'd sell my house, but I'd rather sell it than let Everett get his hands on it, or a penny of the money that results from the sale.'

'How do you hide money?' Michael smiles at her benevolently. 'You can't hide it any more, Mom. The

IRS knows everything. You can't slip it into offshore accounts or pass it over to a bank in Switzerland. You have to declare everything now. Everything.'

'I know,' Nan says with a smile. 'So here's what I'm thinking. We sell it partly for cash – enough for me to live the rest of my days out quite happily, and we can always store cash in a safe deposit box on the island – and the rest of the money can be put in trust for you, my darling. That way, Everett won't be able to get his hands on it.'

'I'm not sure whether you can actually do that,' Daff says cautiously. 'But –' and she has to look away as she says this next bit – 'I know that Mark Stephenson is desperate to buy this house.' There. It's out there. She put his name forward and it wasn't so bad. It wasn't as if she had to talk Nan into selling Windermere: Nan is going to sell it anyway. Now she's just made sure that Mark Stephenson has a shot, that her own future is protected.

A six-figure number. She should feel good about this. Hell, she should feel great. She doesn't. She feels shifty and guilty, and suddenly she wants to be out of this room.

'Mark Stephenson! The perfect man!' Nan says. 'I'm going to give him a call right now.'

'Mom?' Michael stands up. 'Are you sure about this?'

Nan's eyes sadden. 'Oh Michael, even though I love this house more than anything, at the end of the day it's only a house. It's more important I have the people I love around me. I fully intend to buy a little house on the beach somewhere, a tiny cosy cottage that I will make just as much of a home as Windermere has been. A place to start afresh. A place that doesn't hold the memories.'

'Okay.' Michael steps back as Nan walks into the kitchen, and Daniel and Jess move silently out of the room.

'Wow,' he says, turning to Daff. 'It would never have occurred to me that he's come back for the house. Do you really think that it's possible he would end up with it?'

'I don't know,' Daff says, unable to quite look him in the eye. 'But I very much doubt it. Either way, though, it's probably better to be safe than sorry.'

'Are you okay?' Michael says.

'Fine. Why?'

'You suddenly seem a little odd,' he says. 'Distracted.'

'I'm fine.' She forces herself to smile and look at him. 'I guess I am a bit distracted. I got a call this morning about a client looking for a house back home, and I'm just trying to think of the inventory I can show them when I get back.'

'Of course! I always forget you work in real estate. You need to help Mom do this. You're the perfect person to hold her hand and make sure that Mark Stephenson doesn't take advantage of her.'

'Sure,' Daff says, wishing he hadn't said that.

'Mark Stephenson?'

'Speaking.'

'It's Nan Powell here.'

'Mrs Powell!' His voice is loud and cheerful on the phone. 'What a glorious surprise.'

'I've told you before,' Nan says. 'Please call me Nan. And it may turn out to be an even better surprise. I have a business proposition I want to discuss with you. I was hoping we could get together sometime.'

'Now that's exactly the kind of phone call I enjoy receiving,' Mark Stephenson says. 'How about I come over this afternoon?'

'Why don't we say five? Cocktail hour. I'll make Martinis.'

'Now how do you know that's my favourite drink?'

Nan laughs. 'I'll see you at five, Mark.'

*

Daniel is not used to picking up the phone and asking someone out for dinner. He was never particularly good at it, hence his tendency to stay in long relationships. However, he is single again and at some point he is going to have to get out there, to actually live his life as a single gay man. He knows that the hardest part will be the beginning; once he starts, it will be plain sailing.

Matt is clever, and helpful, and good to be around. He's also handsome, funny and cute. He seems a little like Daniel's guardian angel, and the very least Daniel can do to repay him for his kindness is take him out for dinner. Somewhere nice. Somewhere special. Somewhere Daniel can truly thank him.

'I was wondering about the Pearl,' he says, after Matt has picked up the phone and they have exchanged the requisite niceties. 'I thought perhaps you'd like to have dinner there.'

'Is this a date?' Matt smiles down the phone.

'No! I mean, yes. I don't know . . . is it?'

'I'm kidding,' Matt says. 'You sound so awkward. It's adorable. Yes, I'd love to have dinner with you and the Pearl is just fabulous. When were you thinking?'

'When are you available?'

'If I said tonight would you think I was easy?'

Daniel laughs. 'Tonight would be great. The girls are with Bee. Everything's gone slightly crazy here.'

'I've heard,' Matt says. 'Is it really true that Nan's husband, presumed dead, has suddenly reappeared to claim the house?'

'Oh my God.' Daniel's eyes widen. 'Where did you hear that?'

'You can't keep anything a secret on this island,' Matt says. 'So it *is* true. I hope you have good stories for me tonight.'

'I can't say anything.' For as much as Daniel is tempted to gossip, his loyalty lies with Nan. 'Shall we meet there?'

'Absolutely not. If this is a date you can come and pick me up.'

Daniel laughs again. 'Okay, I'll pick you up at eight.'

*

'Nice to see you again.' Mark Stephenson winks surreptitiously at Daff as he shakes her hand, and she shivers, knowing how awful it would be if Michael found out, how wrong it feels to be taking a kickback.

'The house looks wonderful,' he says to Nan. 'It looks like you've spruced it up hugely since I was last here.'

'A little.' Nan laughs, handing him a Martini, straight up, with olives. 'I had to get it ready for the tenants. You still love it, then?'

'I do.' Mark leans forward on his chair, the excitement in his eyes clearly visible. 'As I told you before, Nan, I've always wanted this house.'

'I've loved it here,' Nan says. 'But I think the time has come for me to move on. I'm not entirely convinced – not yet – however I'm curious as to what you think the house might be worth if, say, I were to sell.'

'Well, it would depend on a number of factors.' Mark Stephenson stalls for time, wanting to delay having to give an actual number for as long as possible. 'How many acres do you have here? Seven?'

'Nine point two,' Nan says firmly.

'Right. That's good. Ocean views, direct beach access. I'm interested in it for me, as my family home, but I'd still need to put a fair amount of money into it. I noticed there are a number of missing shingles and the windows will all need replacing. With these old houses once you start renovating they usually turn into a money pit, so I'd say it would probably need around a million put into it.'

'A million dollars?' Nan gasps.

'Absolutely. That's the starting price.' He nods sincerely. 'Most people would just knock it down and start again, it's probably cheaper in the long run, but I love these old houses and I've always wanted to live in something like this.'

'You really wouldn't knock it down?' Michael is dubious as Mark Stephenson shakes his head. 'Surely you'd get far more money if you sub-divided it and developed, say, three or four houses here.'

'Most other builders would do that, you're absolutely right. I see this as a home, a home that's held wonderful memories, and you can't build that. I could see my children growing up here, climbing up the ladder to the widow's walk, running down to the water.' He is looking at Nan as he talks, trying to convince her, and doesn't see Michael look at Daff and suppress a grin.

'So what do you think it would fetch?'

'Difficult to say,' Mark says. 'I would think anywhere between three and four.'

'Three and four million dollars?' Nan says incredulously.

'I know. Property has gone up tremendously on the island.'

'Is that all?' she says imperiously. 'Tell me, Mr Stephenson —' he has gone back to Mr Stephenson, which, in this case, is not a good sign – 'how is it that the Clearys' house, on five acres, which was torn down to make way for two giant houses, each of which, incidentally, is on the market for around five million, sold for six point seven? And the Harbinger house, on ten acres, with no ocean view, sold for eight?'

'Ah ...' He stalls. 'I'm not completely familiar with those houses. I'd have to look into them more. That's the problem with pricing,' he says unhappily, dismayed that Nan has done her research. 'I didn't want to give you a figure because I haven't had a chance to go through the comps.'

'Well, I suggest you do,' Nan says cheerfully, holding up her glass. 'Cheers.'

'So what did you think?' Michael watches as Mark Stephenson's Land Cruiser takes off down the drive-way, spraying gravel.

'What do I think?' Nan says slowly. 'I think he'll be knocking Windermere down faster than I can say Sconset, that's what I think. And he'll put up four huge houses, sell each one for five or six million dollars, minimum.' She turns to see Jessica staring at her with her mouth open. 'Darling, close your mouth. You look like you're catching flies. I showed him, though, didn't I?' She grins delightedly. 'I'm not quite as dumb as I look.'

Chapter Twenty-seven

Now when Michael's mobile phone rings and he sees Jordana's number, he has to answer. With a sinking heart he realizes, as he presses the green button, that he will have to answer every time she calls for the rest of his life.

He can't divert the call when she is the mother of his child, can't pretend she doesn't exist in the hope she'll go away. Every time she calls, for the rest of his life, he will have to answer because it may be something important. He never realized until this moment just how much of an impact that will have.

'Michael, it's Jordana.'

'Hi.' An awkward pause. 'How are you?'

'I'm okay,' she says. 'I'm leaving today. I thought you ought to know.'

Michael feels the panic rising. 'Where are you going? How can I get hold of you? There's still so much left to talk about.'

There is a pause, then: 'Not any more.' The bitterness in her voice is palpable. 'You'll be happy to hear I am no longer pregnant.'

'What?' Michael gasps, unsure he has heard correctly.

'I miscarried yesterday,' she lies, although part of her has convinced herself that it is true, that her period was unusually heavy, therefore it must be true, could not possibly be a late period due to something as prosaic as stress.

'So,' she continues, 'you're off the hook.'

'Are you serious?'

'Yes, I'm serious.' She spits out the words. 'I take it you'll be out celebrating.'

'No ... I'm sorry. I didn't expect this to happen. Why didn't you call me? Are you ... okay?'

'Not really. I feel awful. And I'm calling you now, aren't I? I'll be fine.' She knows she will be, for as much as she tried to convince herself she wanted this baby, that this was a child conceived out of love, she can finally admit that the low-grade anxiety she has been carrying with her the last week or so has disappeared.

'Jordana ... I'm so sorry. I'm sorry you had to go through that on your own.' Mixed in with the relief, Michael feels a sadness, realizes suddenly how lost Jordana is.

Not because of him, not because of Jackson, but because of who she is, because she is a woman searching for happiness. Michael sees quite clearly that until she can look within herself, until she can find peace inside, she will never find the answers she is looking for.

But the relief ... oh Lord, the relief is huge. After he says goodbye, he turns to Daff, his eyes dancing in a way she hasn't seen since Jordana turned up on the doorstep.

'Good news?'

'I can't believe it,' Michael says, pulling out a chair and sitting at the kitchen table. 'It was Jordana. She's not pregnant.' And as the relief overwhelms him, he bursts into tears.

*

'This is my favourite restaurant,' Matt confides, as he and Daniel walk through the door of Water Street.

'I'm glad.' Daniel smiles. 'When we couldn't get into the Pearl I chose this one because the food's organic, and home-grown. That seemed to be right up your street.'

'That's exactly up my street. I couldn't have chosen anywhere more perfect myself. Thank you for doing this, it's a real treat.' He smiles at Daniel, who feels his heart flutter ever so slightly, in a way it hasn't done in a very long time.

'So give me some dish.' Matt leans forward, lowering his voice. 'What's going on with the house?'

'All I can say is that what you heard may be true.'

'I've a reason for asking, though. Do you remember Stephen and Keith from the dinner party at my house?'

'Sure.'

'Well, Stephen is seriously wealthy, and he did say the Powell house is the one he's always wanted. I know that if Nan's truly considering selling, he would definitely want to buy.'

'Could he afford it?' Daniel looks doubtful. 'I don't want to be rude, but the prices here are extraordinary. I think the house is worth millions.'

'That's not rude.' Matt laughs. 'It's true. He can afford it, though. I know he'd be devastated if the house sold to someone else. If the rumours are true, would you at least tell Nan there's someone interested in buying it who really would do it justice, because he wouldn't tear it down, he really would renovate it and do it beautifully.'

'I'll tell her,' Daniel says, pausing before asking, 'Do you know anything about a guy on the island called Mark Stephenson?'

'The builder?' Daniel nods. 'Nasty piece of work, I've heard, although I don't know him personally. I've always believed in judging people as you find them, not by what you hear. Is he the one trying to buy it?'

'Maybe.' Daniel shifts uncomfortably.

'Makes sense,' Matt says. 'Just make sure Nan knows he may not be what he seems.'

'Thanks,' Daniel says. 'Forewarned is definitely forearmed.'

'It is in this case.' He sits back in his chair. 'So, how much longer are you on the island?'

'Another two weeks,' Daniel says. 'I can't believe how quickly it's gone.'

'Neither can I.' There is disappointment in Matt's eyes. 'I can't believe how much ground there is to cover in such a short space of time.'

'Ground to cover?'

'You know, the getting to know you bit. We've just met and boom, you're disappearing before we even know anything about one another.'

'What do you want to know?' Daniel smiles. He likes how direct Matt is, likes that there's no pretence. The longer he looks at him across the table, the cuter he's becoming. He likes that Matt has intelligent eyes that crease deeply when he smiles. He likes that his forearms are strong, suntanned, with light golden hair bleached by the sun. He likes that Matt is interesting and, seemingly, interested in him.

He likes that not only is he attracted to Matt, but that he's allowed to be attracted to Matt. He doesn't have to feel guilty, as if there's something wrong with him. He doesn't have to go home and mentally beat himself up for not being like every other husband in town.

Matt smiles. 'Tell me what your perfect date would be,' he says. 'Then let's see if we can make it happen.'

Their passion is intense, the excitement so strong, Daniel can hardly breathe, until Matt pushes him away.

'What's the matter?' Daniel gasps, for they have only just sat down on Matt's sofa, only just begun kissing.

Matt sighs. 'Oh God.' He buries his head in his hands.

'What is it?'

'I don't know how to tell you this,' Matt says slowly.

'*What?*' Daniel looks at him, a twinkle in his eye. 'You're *straight.*'

Matt bursts out laughing.

'Hardly. But I've been out for years, forever. I've had more casual encounters than you've probably had hot dinners, and I shouldn't be doing this. I knew this

would happen. Jesus, I *wanted* it to happen, but now ...'
His eyes soften as he raises them to meet Daniel's.
'Now I can't. This isn't what I want any more. No,
that's not true.' He shakes his head with a small smile.
'I do want this, but I can't do flings any more. I can't
do this.'

'Who says this is a fling?' Daniel says, confused.

'I do,' Matt says sadly. 'I do, only because I've known
too many men who have been in your situation. We're
in very different places. I'm ready to settle down, to find
my life partner, to grow roses around the door and
settle in with my slippers, my dog and my man –'

'I want that too ...' Daniel interrupts, but Matt
shakes his head.

'You might, but you're not ready for that, not yet.
You need to experiment, have fun, get it all out of your
system before you're ready to settle down. There is
nothing I'd like more right now than to sleep with you,
but I'd get too involved, and I'd be the one who would
end up getting hurt. Not to mention,' he adds sadly,
'you're leaving in two weeks' time.'

'I wouldn't hurt you,' Daniel says, looking Matt
straight in the eye. 'If anyone's likely to get hurt, it
would be me.'

'No,' Matt says. 'I think you're wonderful. I think
you're exactly the kind of man I've been waiting for,
but it isn't the right time for us. You need to play the
field, and then perhaps we can see how it goes, if, of
course, you ever come back to Nantucket.'

'You could come to Connecticut,' Daniel offers.

'I could,' Matt says. 'And maybe I will.'

'Oh God,' Daniel groans. 'I was really looking forward to seeing you without clothes on.'

Matt laughs out loud. 'I'm sure you will, just not tonight.' His face turns serious. 'Know this, Daniel. I'm saying no not because I don't like you, but because I like you too much. I hope during the rest of the time you're on the island we see each other, get to know each other better, maybe see whether it's worth staying in touch, because God knows, people come and go here, never to be heard from again.'

'You'll be hearing from me,' Daniel says. 'Without question. Thank you, Matt. I've never met anyone so honest, so straightforward. I couldn't have done any of this without you.'

'Yes, you could,' Matt says. 'It's just easier when you have support. Come on,' he says, shaking his head. 'You'd better go before I change my mind.'

'You sure?' Daniel raises a flirtatious eyebrow at him, the first time in his life, perhaps, that he has done anything in a flirtatious, suggestive way.

'No.' Matt laughs. 'But I think it's the right thing. Don't forget to warn Nan about Mark Stephenson, and ask her if it's okay for Stephen to call her.'

*

Mark Stephenson turns down Nan's offer of a Martini. This time it's all business, no pretending this is a social call, no more pretending he is a nice guy who is simply doing Nan a favour out of the kindness of his heart.

He had thought that Nan was the last of a dying breed, which in many ways she is, but in thinking that she was isolated enough in her house on the bluff to not realize the true value of property on the island of Nantucket in 2007, he was very much mistaken.

Mistaken too in thinking Nan would believe he wanted the house for his family, would somehow be more amenable if she thought he wouldn't knock it down.

Of course he's going to knock it down. He hasn't slept these last few nights, thinking of the money he could make from the Powell property. He could get four, even five houses there. Huge shingle houses, all the amenities, sell them for a cool six or seven million each, still making an enormous profit even after the building costs, which are now as inflated as everything else.

He would build what all the new money wants these days. Their interpretation of a beach cottage, but for millionaires. Gunite pools, high-speed covers to keep their small children safe, kitchens that are equipped with everything, even though it is rare for the wives to actually cook.

His men are already lined up to tear down the house, he's made preliminary calls to the architect he works with, letting him know, confidentially, that there's a huge project in the works in Sconset, on the bluff, that he should start thinking about dividing a property of approximately nine acres into building lots.

It didn't take the architect long to figure out which

house he was referring to, even though, naturally, no names were mentioned.

He will have to pay market price to Nan, this much he now realizes, but this project could make him a very rich man. This project could put him up there with the highest-ranking builders on the island, ensure he would never have to worry about money again.

'I've done the numbers,' he says, sitting down on the sofa next to Nan, and pulling out a sheaf of papers. 'You're right about the other properties and what they've sold for. I've pulled all the properties in Sconset that have sold during the past year, and I'm happy to go through them with you, talk to you about the prices and whether they were fair, why they got what they got.'

An hour later, Nan puts down her second Martini and looks at Mark Stephenson.

'Mr Stephenson,' she says and smiles. 'Thank you. This is all fascinating, but I'm sure you have a number in mind. I . . . we . . .' she looks at Michael and Daff, 'would very much like to hear what it is, and this is assuming, as I think we all know, you will be tearing down Windermere and putting up a number of properties.'

He doesn't bother disputing it, merely takes a deep breath. 'Well, I think, based on the comps, the Harbinger house is the closest one. You pointed out the other day that it has no ocean views, and obviously this one does, but it's also on more acreage.'

'Point eight more,' Nan says dismissively. 'I'd hardly say that counts.'

'It does, though,' Mark Stephenson attempts feebly. 'On an island, every square inch counts. But, as you know, the Harbinger house sold for eight, and taking the ocean view here into account, I'd like to make an offer of eight point five.'

There is a silence. Daff and Michael both watch Nan's face closely to try to gauge her reaction, but there doesn't seem to be one. She gets up, pours herself another Martini and turns to face Mark Stephenson, suddenly seeming to grow in both stature and imperiousness as she holds herself straight and looks him in the eye.

'Mr Stephenson,' she says with a gracious smile. 'You appeared to have taken me for a fool the other day. Now you are insulting me by doing it again.'

Mark Stephenson colours slightly, then throws his hands up and sighs. 'Mrs Powell, I apologize. What do you want for the house? What's your price?'

'Ten million,' Nan says coolly, as if she were saying ten dollars. 'Two million in cash.'

'Ten million?' He is not happy.

'Ten million,' she says again. 'I have done my research too, Mr Stephenson, and I think ten million is fair market value for properties that I imagine you'll be selling for many, many millions.'

'Not *that* many millions,' he says. 'I need to think about it. Let me go away and do the numbers. I'll get back to you later today. I just don't know ...' He shakes his head and huffs. 'I don't know if I can make the numbers work.'

'I'll show you out,' Daff says. She can't do it, she realizes. She can't take any money from him, couldn't live with herself if she did, couldn't rest easy in her relationship with Michael, knowing that she had kept a secret from him.

For already, this early on, she knows this is something special she has with him, knows this is not something that will end this summer. There is an honesty about their relationship that is new to Daff, who knows she has found something more than just a summer fling.

Late at night, when the house is sleeping, Michael has been sneaking into Daff's room, sometimes waking her up by stroking her hair, or slipping underneath the covers and tucking in tightly behind her.

She hadn't realized, until now, how much she has missed being with someone. It isn't even the sex, the physical act, but the intimacy, the cuddling, the lying in bed for hours afterwards and talking.

She misses it more precisely because she never had it with Richard. This was what she always imagined her marriage would be like, when she was a young girl trying to picture her knight in shining armour, what he would be like, what their relationship would be.

She imagined someone who adored her, just as she adored him. Who went to sleep holding her in his arms, who lay in bed softly talking about anything and everything.

When she didn't get that with Richard, Richard who rolled off her with a quick peck before turning over and falling immediately asleep, she forgot about the dreams she once had, tried to pretend that what she had was enough.

Just last night, lying in bed with Michael, she remembered the pain of her divorce. The pain of discovering Richard was in love with another woman, the sheer hardship of being on her own, having to deal with everything on her own after years of Richard taking care of things.

She thought, then, there would never be a time when she would be, could be, happy again, or at peace. Indeed, she wasn't sure what peace was, other than something she had thought she'd had – mistakenly she now knows – for a short time at the beginning of her marriage.

Late at night, in Michael's arms, she now knows this is peace. Michael calms her down, makes her feel safe and secure, completely *home* in a way that is entirely new. Now she understands why the divorce happened, why she had to go through the pain to finally reach the pleasure.

There is no way she's going to screw this up by starting the relationship with a secret, and she walks Mark Stephenson to the door, about to tell him she cannot take the money.

'Our deal's off,' Mark Stephenson says, bitterly, his voice lowered as they cross the hallway.

'What?' She was going to say the same thing, and is shocked he has said it first.

'I'm not giving you any percentage of this deal,' he

says. 'I'm sorry if you're disappointed, but the point was you would get her to sell it to me for a fair price. Ten million's a fortune. It's what she'd get on the open market, not what I expected to pay in a private deal off-market, particularly one that was being brokered by you on the quiet.'

'That's completely unethical,' Daff says, not because she has changed her mind, but because she can't believe how this charming, self-effacing man has suddenly turned into the devil.

'That's business, I'm afraid,' he says, walking out, climbing into his car and pulling the car door shut.

In the study, standing against the wall, is Michael, the colour gone from his face. He, too, has discovered something with Daff he never thought he'd find. Comfort, ease and serenity. It is unlike any relationship he has ever had, and the more he sees her, the more he wants to see her.

But what he has just heard is sickening. He thought he knew her, thought she was a good person, but it seems that, yet again, he has made a horrible error of judgement.

He turns and walks back to the living room, his feet and his heart both heavy with disappointment, and sadness.

Chapter Twenty-eight

Bee has been quiet since finding out her father's secret, and it is breaking Everett's heart, on so many levels, to have added to Bee's already heavy burden.

He had always carried this naive hope that when he was able to return to Nantucket, to see Nan again and apologize for everything, she would welcome him back, understand that he did it because he was a desperate man, a different man from the one standing before her today. Although he knew forgiveness might be hard, he had no doubt that forgiveness would come.

He never thought about what it would do to Bee. His beloved Bee. Throughout her entire life he has tried to protect Bee from harm, but now he has seen her being hurt by one blow after another. First there was the separation, then she found out her husband is gay – not that that was any surprise to Everett, who suspected it the first time he met Daniel – and now she has found out her own father told a most terrible lie, one that he tried to bury as he built his new life.

Bee has avoided him since finding out. Of course she has been around, has tended to him, fed him, helped him dress, let him play with the girls, but she hasn't been able to look at him, hasn't engaged with him. When he has tried to talk to her, she has shaken her head, said she isn't ready, disappearing into her bedroom for hours at a time, the only sound her tapping on the computer.

Today he takes Lizzie and Stella down to the children's beach. They play on the playground for two hours, Everett pushing the girls on the swings for far longer than either their mother or father would, buying them sandwiches, ice creams, giving them his undivided attention, which they lap up like kittens.

Over to the whaling museum for crafts – today they make scrimshaws out of large, oval bars of white soap – then finally back home when Everett can put it off no longer, for the girls are tired and want their mother.

He walks in to find Bee in the kitchen, and for the first time in what feels like weeks, is in fact days, Bee looks directly at him.

'I'm sorry, Daddy,' she says. He puts his arms out, and Bee walks over, allowing herself to be hugged.

'I'm sorry,' she whispers. 'It was just such a big shock. I needed time to adjust, to think about everything, to take it all in.'

'I'm sorry too,' he says. 'I'm sorry for lying to you, for not telling you the truth, and I'm sorry that this was the way you found out.'

Bee sighs. 'This feels like a dream, or a movie. Like something that happens to other people, not to me. Not to us.'

Everett says nothing, just looks at his hands.

'I have a brother!' Bee says. 'Well, half-brother. Remember how I always begged you and Mom to have another baby because I wanted brothers and sisters?'

Everett smiles at the memory of Bee, golden curls and big eyes, chubby cheeks, as she climbed on his lap and asked him if there was a baby in his tummy because she had asked Santa for a baby and she thought maybe he was cooking one for her.

'I can't believe I have a brother,' Bee says, almost to herself.

Lizzie and Stella are chasing one another round the kitchen island. 'Girls, how would you like to watch a movie?' Bee asks them. 'I have *The Wizard of Oz*.'

'Yay!' The girls cheer as Bee takes them into the other room and settles them in front of the television to enable her to talk to her father in peace.

'I've been thinking so much,' Bee says to Everett, once the girls are absorbed. 'I know this might be … unexpected, but I think we should stay here a while.'

'Nantucket?' Everett is shocked.

Bee nods. 'There are a number of reasons. I … to be honest I can't bear the thought of going back home and being the subject of gossip. Everyone will find out about Daniel, and I can't bear it, I just can't bear the thought of going home.'

'You can't run away forever,' Everett says wryly.

'You would know,' Bee says softly. 'Maybe it is running away a little, but I feel at peace here, at home in a way I never did in Westport. I've even started writing.'

'Oh Bee!' Everett's face lights up. 'You were always such a wonderful writer. I could never understand why you gave it up when you got married.'

'I didn't feel I had stories to tell,' Bee says. 'Now, I guess one of the hidden benefits of all this turmoil is that I've suddenly found I have so much to say.'

'Do you mind me asking what you are writing?'

'A memoir,' Bee says carefully. 'I started off just journaling, writing about what I've been going through with Daniel, then since the other night, when I found out about you, I haven't been able to stop.'

'I'm delighted,' Everett says quietly, tears welling in his eyes. 'You always had a passion, and a talent, for writing. I'm thrilled you've found your passion again.'

'So am I. I had forgotten how much it meant to me, how cathartic I found it. I've been writing about my marriage, meeting Daniel, those early days. The more I remember, the more I can't believe I didn't know.'

'You didn't see the signs,' Everett says. 'I can understand that. Don't punish yourself for that.'

'But I did see them. Of course I saw them. They were as clear as day.' Bee sighs. 'I just chose to ignore them; I pretended that if I didn't think about them, didn't acknowledge them in some way, they would simply disappear.'

'I think that's called burying your head in the sand,' Everett says and smiles. 'I'm something of an expert on that, so we know where you get it from.'

'Then there's you,' Bee says. 'And Nan. Michael. I feel excited about writing again, about finding out about this family, and about you, who you really are.

I feel . . .' She pauses. 'I feel alive again. I feel like I've been underwater for such a long time, and suddenly I feel alive, excited . . .' She trails off.

'So you want to stay to write?'

'Yes. To write, and to be by the sea, and to get to know who you are, who you *really* are, and where you come from. I think you should stay here with us too.'

'It's an interesting proposition,' Everett says. 'But I'm not wanted here. Both Nan and Michael –' he chokes slightly saying his name – 'made that quite clear the other day.'

'They have just found out,' Bee says, laying her hand on his arm. 'Their reaction was entirely natural. Give them space, give them a little time to adjust, and they will want you here, I'm sure of it.'

He nods. 'Thank you, Beezy. I do know what you mean about feeling at peace here. I have dreamed of Nantucket for years, but even in my dreams I had forgotten quite how magical it is to be here. I also feel a sense of peace, now that I'm home.'

'This is your home, isn't it?' Bee says. 'I mean, your real home.'

'It is. Generations of Powells have lived on this island, have had a hand in most of the building or renovation of what you see here today.'

'Will you tell me about my family?' Bee has tears in her eyes. 'My grandparents. Do I have aunts and uncles? Who are we? Where do I really come from?'

'I've been waiting to tell you all your life,' he says, suddenly realizing that it is true. He thought he could lose his identity, reinvent himself all those years ago, but he could never lose who he really is.

For the first time in years, no longer living a lie, he feels like he can breathe.

*

'Where's Jess?' Daniel startles Daff, deep in thought as she paints a delicate watercolour of the house.

'She's gone into town with Nan,' Daff says. 'I think they both had a craving for ice cream.'

Daniel shakes his head and grins. 'What an unlikely friendship. Who would have thought a teenager would feel comfortable with Nan?'

'I think in theory it's unlikely, but I get it,' Daff says. 'I remember being a teenager. I hated my parents, but loved other adults who treated me as an equal, who stopped to listen to me, who valued what I had to say.'

'Nan definitely treats her like an equal. I think she has no idea Jess is only thirteen. By the way, what would you think about Jess doing some babysitting for us?'

Daff cocks her head.

'Bee just phoned me. She wants to go out with her dad this afternoon – I think he's going to show her around the island, tell her about his family. She wanted me to have the girls but I have an arrangement.'

'With the lovely Matt?'

'We're just friends,' Daniel says quickly.

'I'm sorry. It's none of my business.' Daff looks away

then looks back at Daniel with a grin. 'But he is lovely, and there's nothing wrong with being just friends.'

'Unless one of you wants more.'

'Which one? You?'

Daniel looks sheepish.

'So what's the problem? It seems like he adores you.'

'He wants a relationship and he doesn't think I'm ready.'

'Are you?'

'I don't know. He thinks I'm too new to this, that I need to play the field before I settle down, and if he gets involved he's going to get hurt.'

Daff nods thoughtfully then shrugs. 'It doesn't sound unreasonable.'

'I know.' Daniel sniffs. 'It's just damned hard, and it gets harder every time I see him.'

'Because you just want to jump his bones?' Daff laughs.

'Jump his bones?' Daniel barks with laughter. 'Well, yes. I guess.'

'So . . . babysitting. Jess should be back in about half an hour. I think that's a wonderful idea. She adores Lizzie and Stella, and she's responsible. That could be just what the doctor ordered this summer.'

'That's what I thought. Do you want to phone Bee and talk to her about it?'

'I will. Just as soon as Jess gets back and I talk to her.'

*   *   *

'Real babysitting?' Jess is dubious. 'For *money*?'

'Of course,' Daff says. 'Nobody's asking you to work for nothing.'

'The girls already adore you,' Daniel says encouragingly. 'Lizzie asked me yesterday if you could be their new big sister.'

Jess's eyes sparkle with delight.

'I spoke to Bee,' Daniel said, 'and she said she was thinking, if you were interested, of offering you a job, Monday to Friday, every afternoon for four hours.'

Jess almost squeals with excitement as Daniel turns to Daff to explain, 'Bee's writing again, and although her dad wants to look after the girls while she's working, she thinks it's too much for him, given his health.' He turns back to Jess.

'Bee will be in the house, so it's really just playing with the girls. Taking them to the beach or the lake, looking after them while she works. She's thinking of five dollars an hour.'

Jess does a quick mental calculation. 'A hundred dollars a week?' She gasps. 'Are you serious?'

'Absolutely,' Daniel says.

'Oh my God!' Jess starts to jump around, grabbing her mother in excitement. 'That's so much money! I never had a proper job before!'

'Is that a yes?' Daniel is unsure.

'Yes! Yes! Yes!' Jess says. 'When can I start?'

Daff laughs along with her, loving seeing her daughter in such a good mood. It is like having the old

Jess back, the real Jess; and babysitting is a wonderful idea – she wishes she had thought of it herself.

She turns as she hears the crunch of gravel outside, and sees Michael walking across the driveway to the car. She wants to run out and talk to him, but he has been so distant these past couple of days that she now feels awkward about seeing him. She knows that something must have happened, something has changed.

Last night she sidled up to him in the kitchen, and asked him, in a low voice so no one else could hear, whether he was coming to her room later.

'I'm not feeling so good,' he had replied, barely able to meet her eyes. 'Not tonight, I think.' He had quickly looked away, moved off, busied himself somewhere else, while all the disappointments of her youth, those teenage let-downs, the number of times she had had her heart broken, came flooding back as she stood there trying to understand what could possibly have changed.

*

It has been an extraordinary afternoon for Bee. She had driven her father into town, stopping along the way as he pointed out sights, showed her where he used to play as a child, told her stories he hadn't thought about for years.

They went to the museum, where he showed Bee her ancestors and a painting of her grandmother Lydia, who looked exactly like Bee. He told her everything he could remember about his childhood. He barely took a breath, there seemed to be so much to say. The more he talked, the more memories came flooding back, Bee eagerly drinking them in, asking for more.

The cranberry flats, the Sankaty lighthouse, his school, their church.

Everett was wearing a baseball cap and sunglasses. He saw a number of people he hadn't seen for almost forty years, but he knew them, and he also knew there was a very good chance of them dropping down dead from a heart attack were he to remove his hat and glasses, allow them to see his true identity.

But he wanted to. Oh how he wanted to. Arthur Worth. Goodness, how old he has got, his hair now entirely white, his face leathery from the sun, the same twinkling blue eyes. Sally McLean. Remember how beautiful she had been? They had played together in kindergarten, he had loved her from afar throughout elementary school. Now she is large and dowdy, barely recognizable were it not for her wonderful voice which, judging from the brief conversation he overheard her having in a store, hasn't changed at all.

'You didn't have a crush on her!' Bee said in delight as they left the store. 'No!'

'I did,' he confessed. 'She was my first love, and she was a tiny slip of a thing, so beautiful. Long, silvery blonde hair and big green eyes. We all loved her, every last one of us.'

'Don't you want to talk to her?' Bee asked.

'I do,' he said. 'I want to talk to all of them. Arthur Worth was my best friend for years. We were room-mates at school. He taught me how to fish. I have spent my life missing him, but I need to be re-introduced slowly, if at all. I suspect people will find out, eventually, however hard we try to keep it a secret, for Nantucket is not known for being good at secrets. I imagine most will have a similar reaction to Nan. They will hate me for it and they will be furious.'

'Even people who loved you?'

'Nan loved me once upon a time,' he said slowly. 'It doesn't seem to mean anything now.'

They get home and the girls are in heaven. Jess has played with them, given them piggyback rides for hours, has even fed them.

'I'm sorry,' she says. 'I can't cook so I gave them peanut butter and jelly sandwiches for dinner.'

'That's okay.' Bee smiles. 'It's entirely my fault. I had no idea we'd be gone for such a long time. How was it? Were they good?'

'They were amazing.' Jess beams.

'Girls? Do you want Jess to come back tomorrow?'

'Yes! Yes! Yes!' they chorus, dancing around Jess and flinging their arms around her legs as she giggles. 'We love Jess!'

'Dad, will you stay here while I drive Jess home?'

'Of course,' he says with a smile, and Bee and Jess head out to the car.

*

Michael sits at the bar in the Tap Room, nursing a beer and watching the television numbly. He knows he ought to say something to Daff, tell her what he heard, tell her that he knows she and Mark Stephenson are somehow working together and she is getting a cut of this deal. He just doesn't know how to.

What kind of person would do that? How could he have got it quite so wrong again? He thought his days of choosing women who were bad for him were over. He was just beginning to congratulate himself on having found someone so real, so normal, so honest and calm, before he heard that furious, whispered conversation.

If someone is dishonest, withholding from the beginning, what hope is there for an honest relationship, and what can a relationship be if it doesn't start with trust?

He shivers at the thought of what he has revealed these last few nights, lying in bed with Daff into the early hours, telling her all the things he hadn't thought to tell anyone for years, his feelings about his father, now he's discovered he's alive.

He can't keep running away, this much he knows. He tried to run away from Jordana and look what happened. At some point he'll have to deal with this. He knows she's watching him, a look of sadness and confusion on her face because she feels him withdrawing, and she doesn't know he knows.

He'll deal with it soon.

Just as soon as he can.

*

Bee loves the mornings when she wakes up first. Most mornings she is woken up by footsteps pounding down the hall, and a yell of 'Mom! Mom! She's being mean to me, Mom!' Not what Bee needs to hear first thing in the morning. Unsurprising that she has a tendency to start her day off on the wrong foot.

Those days when she wakes up first, to peace and quiet, and can pad down to the kitchen and make herself a fresh cup of coffee, set the table for breakfast, sip her coffee as she reads over what she's written the night before, that is perfection, the perfect way to start the day.

She was up late last night, scribbling notes about what her dad told her, not wanting to forget a thing, and she sits down at the table this morning, rereading, making sure she hadn't forgotten anything.

The girls come in, and she gives them bowls of Rice Krispies, cracking four eggs in a pan as she sends Lizzie to go and get Poppa.

'He's sleeping,' Lizzie says, coming back to the kitchen.

'Okay, darling. There's one extra egg, then.' The girls fight over who gets the extra egg.

'He must be tired,' she says to the girls as they clear the table. 'Poppa never sleeps in like this. I'll go and wake him up.' And she goes to his room.

'Dad?' she says quietly. 'Time to get up. Coffee's ready and you missed breakfast. Dad? Dad?'

She walks over to the bed and starts to shake as

she looks down at the inert figure lying there, his eyes closed, his last breath having left his body some hours before, in the middle of the night.

'Dad?' Bee starts to cry. 'Dad? Daaaaaaaaaad!'

Chapter Twenty-nine

Daniel puts the phone down, stands still for a few seconds, then takes a deep breath, knowing he has to be the one to tell Nan.

He looks through the window and sees her, bent over in the vegetable garden, pulling weeds out and placing them in a plastic bag next to a trug filled with peas. Jess is sitting on the grass next to her, laughing as she chatters away, shelling the peas into a large bowl from the kitchen which is balanced precariously on top of her crossed legs.

Daniel walks out through the back door and trudges wearily over to the garden, filled with sadness at the loss of a man he has always liked enormously, a man who has been, in many ways, more of a father to him than his own.

He hates being the bearer of bad news, but he would have to either tell Michael, who would tell Nan, or tell Nan himself. Telling her himself feels cleaner, somehow, easier this way.

'You look ghastly.' Nan looks over the fence at Daniel with a smile. 'Nothing can be that bad, my darling.'

'Nan, can we go somewhere and talk?'

Nan's face turns pale. 'Why? What is it?'

'I . . . I need to talk to you.'

'What is it? Who's been hurt? Is it Michael?' Her voice rises in panic.

'No.'

'Tell me, Daniel.' She pulls herself up straight, steeling herself.

'It's Evan . . . Everett,' he says. 'He had a massive heart attack last night. The ambulance came quickly but there was nothing they could do.' His face is a mask of sympathy; he doesn't know how to break this sort of news, nor how Nan will take it.

Nan nods slowly. 'So this time he is truly dead?' she asks, her voice devoid of all emotion.

'Yes.' Daniel nods. 'This time he is dead.'

Nan bends down and lays her clippers neatly next to the trug, straightening up and placing a soft hand on Jess's head, almost as if to steady herself, yet there is no expression on her face, no sign of any sadness at all.

'I'm going inside,' she says softly. 'Thank you for telling me.'

'Nan, are you okay? Shall I come with you?' Jess has jumped to her feet.

'No, child.' Nan looks at her. 'I shall be fine. It just wasn't what I expected to hear.'

'I'm so sorry, Daniel,' Jess says awkwardly, not knowing what else to say. 'How's Bee?' she asks, once Nan has disappeared into the house, the pair of them watching her go. 'And the girls?'

'The girls don't really understand,' Daniel says. 'Bee's a mess. I'm going over there now. Maybe you could come and watch the girls, or give Bee a hand, just make sure they're all okay.' He doesn't think that Jess is only thirteen, too young to be given this sort of responsibility, and Jess is eager to help.

'Of course.' Jess jumps up and carries the bowl into the kitchen, scampering up the stairs to find her flip-flops, which are somewhere under an enormous pile of clothing in her room.

'Did you tell your mom we were going?' Daniel asks when she comes back down the stairs, taking them two at a time.

'No. I don't know where she is,' Jess says.

'She's on the back porch,' he says. 'Reading.'

Jess runs out through the living-room doors and startles her mother. 'Bye, Mom.' She bends down and kisses her mother. 'I have to go and look after the girls. We just heard that Bee's dad, Nan's old husband, died last night, and Daniel and I are going over there to see them. Love you,' she calls, disappearing round the side of the house, leaving Daff open-mouthed in shock.

Not because of the news, not because of Everett, but because her daughter spontaneously kissed her, and told her she loves her. Something she hasn't done for *years*.

She sits for an hour, replaying it over and over again in her mind, a tear of gratitude rolling slowly down the side of her face before she gets up to wander inside.

*

Daff knocks on Nan's door, waiting a few seconds before knocking again.

'Yes?' Nan's voice is soft.

'Nan? It's Daff. I've brought you a cup of tea.'

'Come in, sweet girl.' Daff pushes open the door to see Nan sitting on the window seat and looking out to the ocean.

'I heard the news.' Daff places the cup and saucer down on a low mahogany table. 'I'm so sorry.'

Nan turns her head to look at her. 'Isn't it odd, that we are always sorry when someone dies, but with Everett I don't know how to feel. I don't feel sorry. I feel that I got all my sorries out all those years ago when I thought he was dead. I feel ... I don't know. Empty perhaps. Relieved. Oh dear, I don't suppose I'm meant to say that, and poor Bee, she must be in so much pain to have lost her father. I feel as if there has been this huge upset in my life, and I was steeling myself for more, for more pain, yet another tumultuous event, but now, finally, I feel a sort of calm.'

'I can understand that.' Daff sits down gently on the seat next to Nan.

'I loved him so much,' Nan muses. 'For so long. As the years went by I built him up into a superman, a demi-god, pouring all my love into his house, into the memories that Windermere held, turning our marriage into something so perfect that of course I would never marry again, never do anything to defile what I convinced myself was the greatest love of all time.' She pauses, looking out of the window again before turning back to Daff.

'To discover the lie, the betrayal, to see Everett again as an old man ... to see him weak and ill, and, more, to know that he didn't have the courage to face up to his defects, that he chose running away from us rather than finding a way for us all to work through it together ...' Nan shakes her head and sighs. 'I don't feel sad that he is dead. I feel grateful.'

'Grateful?' Daff furrows her brow. 'I don't understand.'

'I am grateful that I got to see him again. Grateful that I saw him as human, and flawed, and weak. Grateful that I no longer have to live my life missing a perfect man, a perfect marriage, staying in this house because of all the perfect memories it holds.'

Daff frowns. 'But, Nan, you love this house.'

'I do. I have always loved this house. The difference is I don't *need* to stay here any more. By holding on to Windermere, I was holding on to a memory of a marriage, a memory of a man who only really existed in my imagination. Seeing Everett again means I can let it go.'

'You *want* to move?'

Nan shrugs. 'The house is too old and too big for me. Even if I had the money to make it beautiful, I can't look after it, not even with Sarah's help.'

'What about Michael?'

'Michael needs an old rambling house even less than

I do,' Nan says. 'It's time to say goodbye. I wasn't sure when I saw Mark Stephenson, but I'm sure now. Tell me honestly –' she leans towards Daff and takes her hand – 'could you see you and Michael living in this house?'

Daff blushes and looks away. 'I . . . I'm not sure . . .'

'Come on, Daff.' Nan smiles. 'I know what's going on with you two. I'm delighted. I couldn't be happier. I haven't seen Michael this at ease with anyone ever, and there is a light in your eyes now that was missing when you arrived. I think the two of you are perfect together, and I, for one, certainly see a long and happy future –' Nan stops short, seeing Daff's eyes fill with tears. 'What is it?'

'Oh Nan,' she says. 'It has been so lovely but something has happened. I don't know why, but Michael isn't talking to me, he can barely look at me. It hurts so much. Oh Lord,' she says and begins to sob, 'I had forgotten quite how much this hurts.'

'You love him,' Nan says simply, and Daff looks up with shock, not having thought about love, not thinking that love would find her, here, in Nantucket, so unexpectedly. She nods slowly as Nan smiles.

'Then go to him and talk,' she says. 'And for heaven's sake find out what the matter is. You know as well as I do, my dear, that the key to a good relationship is knowing how to communicate. Everybody argues, everyone has misunderstandings, but you have to know how to get through them, not to let resentment build up until you can't find your way back to one another.

Perhaps,' she muses, 'perhaps things might have been different if Everett had known how to communicate with me.'

'Thank you, Nan.' Daff leans down and kisses her. 'You're a wise woman.'

'You will be fine.' She pats Daff's hand. 'Go to him and tell him how you feel.'

*

Daff walks off as a rusty old jeep pulls into the driveway, and Nan walks over, unable to conceal her delight.

'Sarah!' Nan opens her arms as Sarah, grinning, climbs out of the car and runs over to give Nan a huge hug, noticing how frail she seems.

'Nan!' she scolds. 'You're so thin. You haven't been looking after yourself.'

Nan laughs. 'Oh I have, and I've been busy looking after everyone else. I missed you.'

She pulls back and suddenly holds Sarah at arm's length, looking her slowly up and down with a knowing gleam in her eye. 'Never mind me being thin,' she says, a smile spreading on her face. 'Is there something you want to tell me?'

Sarah's mouth drops open in disbelief. 'How do you know?' she sputters. 'How can you possibly tell? I'm only six weeks!'

Nan raises an eyebrow. 'You know some people say I'm a witch.' Nan winks at her before kissing Sarah on the forehead and taking her hand. 'What lovely news. A baby. I can't think of anything nicer.'

'I know, it's so exciting.' Sarah grins. 'But we're not supposed to be telling anyone until twelve weeks.'

'Don't worry. Your secret's safe with me.'

'Where is everyone?' Sarah asks. 'How's Michael? And the tenants? Any romances I ought to know about?'

Nan laughs. 'Oh my goodness, Sarah. I don't even know where to start. Let's go inside and make some tea.'

*

The cars and bicycles are all there, other than the truck Daniel has taken to Bee's, so Michael can't be far.

Daff finds him, eventually, down at the beach, bobbing in the whaler that he is painstakingly oiling. He doesn't see Daff as she strips her shorts off, quickly and quietly, wading into the water in her bathing suit without a sound, swimming noiselessly out to the boat.

Michael looks up to see Daff swimming, her hair slicked back, seal-like as she glides towards the boat. He feels an instant mix of desire, warmth, pain, confusion. He can't avoid her here, so he puts the oil and rag down, extending a hand to help her onto the boat, silently handing her a towel to dry herself off.

'I'm sorry,' Daff blurts out, breathless both from nerves and from the swim. 'Whatever it is I've done, I'm sorry. I would never do anything to hurt you, not intentionally, but clearly I have. I want you to know that whatever I have to do to make it better, I will do.'

'It's not what you've done to me,' Michael says quietly, not looking at her. 'It's what you've done to my mother.'

'What are you talking about?'

Michael finally looks up and meets her eyes. 'I heard you,' he says. 'I heard you and Mark Stephenson. I heard about the dirty little deal you have with him, the fact that you'll get money from persuading my mother to sell him the house, except –' he laughs bitterly – 'I also heard the part about him reneging because you didn't fulfil your part of the bargain by getting him the house cheap.'

'Oh Michael.' Daff hangs her head in shame. 'I am so, so sorry you heard that. Listen to me.' She stands in front of him and takes his hands. 'Mark Stephenson offered me a percentage the night of that party. I never said yes to it, although for a while, I'll admit, I was tempted. I kept thinking I wouldn't have to worry about child support running out, I wouldn't have to lie awake every night worrying about money, about putting Jess through college. Then I realized I couldn't do it.'

'It didn't sound like that from what I overheard,' Michael says.

'I know. Because I was about to tell Mark Stephenson I didn't want his money, didn't want anything to do with it because it all felt too dirty, and because I didn't want to lie to you, or Nan, or start this relationship with a betrayal. Before I had the opportunity to tell him I didn't want the money, he said he wasn't paying me anyway, and I was so stunned by how unethical he was, I couldn't even speak.'

There is a long silence as Michael digests what she is saying.

'Do you swear you weren't going to take the money?'

'I swear to you,' Daff says. 'I couldn't do it, and I wouldn't do it. And . . .' She takes a deep breath. 'This means too much to me for me to fuck it up. I never ever expected to find this, but you're the best man I've ever met. There's no way I'd do something that stupid.'

Another silence. Daff looks away. When she looks back it is to see Michael grin. 'You thought about it, though.'

'Yes.' Daff feels a pang of relief. She knows from his grin it will be okay. 'I did.'

'I suppose I can forgive you.' He slides the strap of her bathing suit off her shoulder as he puts his arms around her and pulls her close, burying his nose in her neck, inhaling deeply, loving the feel of her, the smell of her, the taste of her. 'You're only human after all.'

As the pair of them sink to the deck of the boat, the water laps gently around them and the seagulls cry overhead.

*

'I love this house.' Stephen pauses at the bay window in Nan's room and looks out at the water, turning to smile at Nan. 'I have spent years sailing past and looking at it from the outside. It's just as beautiful on the inside.'

'Thank you,' Nan says. 'It has been a warm and happy home for us for many years.'

'I've heard about the parties that used to be held here,' Stephen says as he turns back to gaze at the lawn. 'What a shame people don't throw parties like that any more.'

'Well,' she says, 'perhaps if you buy Windermere you can hold those parties again.'

Keith's eyes light up. 'Oh we do love a good party.' He moves next to his partner to admire the view.

'We do too.' Nan muses, 'I do think when we leave we ought to go out with a bang, don't you think? A party on the lawn? A band? A wonderful supper?'

'Oh God.' Keith shivers with delight. 'Even the word "supper" makes me think of Cary Grant and Grace Kelly. This is the perfect house for a party like that . . . we could do white tie, or a black and white ball like Truman Capote! Oh Nan! Oh Stephen! Think of the parties we could throw!'

Nan laughs delightedly and turns her head slightly to whisper to Daniel, 'Thank you for bringing them here. I can't think of anyone I'd rather see living here.'

'Do you mean that?' Daniel whispers back as he looks across the room and catches Matt's eye.

'I do,' she says. 'I love Stephen's portfolio. I love that he brought it along, to show me that he really does want to restore Windermere. And Keith is a gas! I think they're the perfect people to inject new life into the old girl.'

*   *   *

'They're so much better than that Mark Stephenson,' Nan says to Michael and Daff when they are back downstairs and Daniel and Matt are walking Stephen and Keith round the garden. 'What a dreadful man he was.'

'You did know, then?' Daff is amazed. 'I was worried you were taken in by him.'

'Not for a second. I knew he'd tear down this house immediately, and frankly I expected it. I mind that far less than him lying about it, trying to tell me that he wanted to raise his family here because he thought I'd sell it to him for less.'

'Have you told him you won't sell it to him?' Michael is worried.

'No, darling, of course not. I wanted Stephen and Keith to see the house properly first, and let's just wait for them to make an offer. I must say I'm still keen to do a private deal – those realtor fees are extortionate – sorry, Daff.'

Daff shrugs and looks away, catching Michael's eye as she does so, the pair of them exchanging a small smile.

'We love it,' Keith says, his eyes filling up as he wipes a tear away. 'I think we'd be incredibly happy here, and Stephen already has wonderful ideas for restoring her.'

Nan smiles. 'How funny, I have always thought of Windermere as a her, too. The grand old lady on the bluff.'

'Rather like you,' Keith says, 'if you don't mind me saying so.'

'Not at all. Far better grand than mad,' she says with a wink.

'I love her!' Keith mouths silently to Matt, who mouths back, 'Told you!'

'Perhaps you and I could go somewhere quiet and talk business?' Stephen says softly.

'Of course.' Nan stands up and allows herself to be escorted out of the room. 'Let's go into the study.'

'Five million?' Michael looks confused. 'But you wanted ten from Mark Stephenson. That sounds like far less than the house is worth.'

'But he wants less than half the land!' Nan says. 'He wants the house, and three acres. Says the rest is too unmanageable for him. We could build another house, right here! It couldn't be more perfect!'

'Wow!' Daff starts to smile as she turns to Michael. 'That really does sound perfect.'

'We could even build two houses,' Nan says, her excitement barely contained. 'One for me, and one for you two – well, three, including Jess.'

Daff blushes. 'Us two? No . . . we're . . .' She looks at Michael, embarrassed, for she would never dare think that far into the future, would never dare say something that would expose her that much, make her that vulnerable.

Michael takes her hand and grins at Nan. 'What a splendid idea,' he says, and Daff feels stars of joy explode inside her.

'Now the question is,' Nan says, with a small devilish

frown, 'how do we tell Mr Stephenson that the house is not his after all?'

'Oh let me!' Daff says. 'Please let me! I'll enjoy every second of it.'

*

Michael sits in the waiting room, flicking through a boating magazine as Daff goes into Mark Stephenson's office, where the walls are so thin Michael can hear every word.

'I thought it only fair to come here in person,' Daff says quietly, 'to inform you that Mrs Powell has had an offer on the house that she has decided to accept.'

There is a silence, then an explosion. 'What?'

Daff starts to repeat herself until Mark Stephenson interrupts.

'I heard you! What do you mean, she's had another offer? What the hell are you playing at? You can't just accept another offer without coming back to me first!'

'Do we have anything in writing?' Daff plays dumb.

'No we damned well don't, but we had an agreement.'

'We did? I thought our agreement was off.'

'No, it's not off!' Mark Stephenson yells. 'Get me that house, and of course I'll pay you! What's the offer for? How much do I need to pay?'

'I'm sorry,' Daff coos. 'I'm afraid the deal is now off the table. I only came here as a courtesy, not as a negotiating tactic.'

His voice turns menacing. 'You listen here. There's

no such thing as fucking courtesy in this kind of deal. You tell me right now how much I need to pay, or I swear to you . . .'

'You'll swear to her what?' Michael appears in the doorway, just as Daff is starting to worry.

'Oh!' Mark Stephenson's expression changes instantly, affecting a charm he quite clearly doesn't have. 'Michael.' He extends a hand which Michael ignores. 'I had no idea you were here.'

'Clearly,' Michael says wryly.

'I was just making the point that this is no way to do business,' Mark Stephenson says. 'I understand that your mother has an offer on the table, and I'd like to come up with a competitive offer. Whatever it is, I'll top it by . . . half a million.'

Michael shakes his head. 'No. I don't think so.'

'Well, how much is the offer? I can go up if I have to.'

'No,' Michael says firmly. 'I don't think you understand. Some things, and some people, cannot be bought. My mother is one of them. Come on, Daff, we're done here.'

Taking her arm, he leads her out of the room.

Summer 2008

Bee wakes up, as she does every day, just before 5.30 a.m. In the old days, living in Westport, married to Daniel, waking up was always a struggle for her — she'd lie in bed trying to sleep her life away, until one of the girls woke her up, and bleary-eyed she would be forced to get up, stumble downstairs and blindly reach for the coffee as she made breakfast for the girls.

Now it is an effort to sleep past five. She awakens every morning filled with energy, jumping out of bed, padding across the floor, stepping onto the deck outside her bedroom to watch the early morning sun, listen to the crickets, the soft silence, and gaze at the boats bobbing lazily on the water in the distance.

She runs downstairs, pours herself some coffee and sits outside on the doorstep, sipping slowly as Albert, a stray kitten that seems to have adopted them, winds himself around her ankles, mewing for breakfast, before jumping on her lap and purring contentedly as she absent-mindedly rubs him under the chin.

Every morning, as she sits here, she is filled with bursts of joy, a happiness she didn't know she would ever find, for she always looked for it in the wrong places.

For years she thought a man would bring her

405

happiness. When she married Daniel, she expected to finally find it, but it is only now, now that she is truly on her own, with her girls, doing work she adores, that she knows what happiness is.

She and the girls are still in the house on Quidnet, but it has been a year since they moved in, a year of testing the waters, finding out whether Nantucket is a place they could live, rather than just stay until they find their footing again.

A year later, Bee knows Nantucket is home.

When her dad died, it was a huge scandal. There had already been gossip about Everett Powell returning but a tenacious journalist had followed it up and got the story, and for a few weeks Bee had the unpleasant experience of being at the centre of a news story that felt like it had no end.

The *New York Post* got hold of it, running the story for days, photographers and journalists camped outside her house to get pictures of her and the girls. The local papers all tried to woo her into talking, as a new-found member of island royalty, but she didn't speak.

Eventually they all left her alone, moved on to the next story, and other than a few stares when she went to do her shopping, she was able to live her life. In some ways, she was relieved the story came out. Arthur Worth wrote to her, and she went to his house, staying for hours to listen to stories about her father as a young man, putting together the pieces of the puzzle that made up her father's life.

There have been others. Many others. People who had known her father, who had loved him, who were shocked by the story but eager to get to know Bee, help her put her history together, find out who she really is.

Now she is writing a book. Part memoir, part biography, she is writing about her life: growing up thinking her family was perfect, marrying a man with whom she thought she could mirror her parents' marriage, then discovering everything she thought was true and real was in fact a sham.

She is writing about the Powell family. How they reached the island, how they came to be such an important part of Nantucket's history. And she is writing about her father. His life, his marriage to Nan, the trouble that led to him faking a suicide; how life came full circle, finally bringing him home.

She misses him still, but writing this book has brought him to life again. She feels him around her, supporting her, loving her, gently encouraging her and leading her to people and places she is convinced she would not have found had he not been somewhere, watching over her.

After a few minutes of feeling the early morning sun wash over her, Bee takes her coffee to her computer in her bedroom, and opens her notebook, reviewing what she wrote yesterday, what she has to write today.

She still doesn't think of herself as a writer, yet over the past year she has had three short stories published, one in the back of the *New York Times* magazine. Just a few weeks ago she sent a synopsis of her book and three sample chapters to one of the big New York agents, fully expecting never to hear from them.

Three days later the agent called her, said she loved it, could they meet.

Now she has an agent, and as soon as the book is finished they are sending it out to the publishing houses. Bee still can't quite believe it. She celebrated with the girls when she found out: champagne for Bee, sparkling apple cider for the girls, as they danced around the deck, cheering.

Today will be a difficult day to write. Some days it comes so easily, like writing on auto-pilot, the words flowing from her fingers, her mind so calm it is as if the book is writing itself. Other days it is like squeezing blood from a stone.

Bee has learned the secret – the magic tool that separates the true writers from the people who merely dream of being writers, who have a wonderful idea but never get started, or get started but never finish. She has learned the secret of discipline, of ploughing through even when it feels like she has nothing to say; of writing even though she doesn't know what to write; of writing even when there are days, like today, when she is fighting the excitement of the party tonight – the farewell bash at Windermere, for Nan is moving out of the house next week.

Bee has come to love Nan, to think of her as a second mother. She has taken to dropping in to Windermere almost daily, often with the girls, who now, unsur-prisingly, call Nan 'Nanna', since Nan is more of a grandmother to them than Bee's own mother.

Bee had never quite understood what family meant. She had always ached for a large family, had grown up feeling she was missing something. What she has come to understand since her father passed away is that the people with whom you surround yourself, the people you love, become your family. Whether there are blood ties or not.

Nan is now her family. And Michael, who she thinks of as her brother, and Daff, and Jess. These people, who she didn't know a year ago, are now part of the fabric of her life, have helped her settle down on this island that is already more of a home than anywhere else she has ever lived.

There is more to it. For the first time in her life, Bee is comfortable in her skin. No longer buttoned up, playing the part of the successful suburban housewife in her pink and green capri pants, her sparkly gold and diamond jewellery, her hair perfectly blown out twice a week at Peter Coppola, lunching with girlfriends at V or Zest, or swinging into school in her Lexus wagon to collect the girls.

Now her hair is long and curly, with natural golden highlights from the sun. Her skin is bronzed, her face make-up free. She lives in shorts, T-shirts and flip-flops, and dresses up only for very rare occasions, and when she does so she pulls on something she already owns, instead of doing what she used do: buying something new at Mitchells, for you didn't want to be seen out wearing the same thing twice in a row.

Bee does yoga four times a week, joining a small group of women on the beach early in the morning, women who are slowly becoming friends. She takes her girls to school every day, and bakes cookies with them in the afternoon, plays with them on the beach, brings them with her as she looks at houses to buy.

The time has come for her to buy a house. This house on Quidnet, while beautiful, is not hers, and she and the girls need to build life anew, in a place that is home. She wasn't going to buy anywhere until she was absolutely sure, but these past couple of months she has started to look at houses, knowing that Nantucket is where she wants to raise her children, where she wants to spend the rest of her days.

The house in Westport has been sold, the furniture divided, although Daniel didn't want much. Her share of the furniture sat in storage for a while, Bee eventually selling it all, wanting to start all over again, wanting a true beach house, in blues and whites, fresh and beachy, to signify the new beginning.

Last week she saw a cottage that was so perfect, she almost burst into tears walking through it. A bright hallway led into a small office, and beyond a large archway you came into a huge open kitchen and family room that had three walls of windows overlooking the bay, sunlight streaming through, creating dappled patterns on the floor, a fan spinning lazily from the vaulted ceiling.

Upstairs were three bedrooms: the master suite at the back, with a wide bay window opening onto a deck, a bay window that would be the perfect place for her desk and her computer, and the girls' bedrooms at the front, sharing a Jack and Jill bathroom.

The girls had scampered up the stairs with excitement. 'Mommy! I love it!' Lizzie had cried, running into the bedroom she immediately claimed would be hers.

Outside was a beautiful garden. High, clipped, privet hedges separated a small swimming pool from a cutting garden; there was a stone terrace covered with a pergola, honeysuckle and clematis tumbling over the top. Bee instantly saw herself at a small glass table under the pergola, glass of wine in hand, having dinner with the girls.

She didn't want to show the realtor how much she loved it, but she couldn't wipe the smile off her face. This was, she knew instantly, home. This was what she had been waiting for.

She had checked the details. It was a fortune, but then everything on the island was a fortune, and thanks to her father she wouldn't have to worry about money again.

Her father had been, it seems, a very wealthy man. Since conquering his gambling addiction in his former life, he had learned to be clever with his money, had grown the family business into something huge, and had invested his own money in the right deals.

When he died, he had left Bee a third of his money.

The rest was split evenly. Between Michael and Nan.

*

Nan pushes the boxes out of the way and grabs the phone.

'Hello? ... Why, Mr Moseley! Again! What a lovely surprise, but I do hope you're ringing to tell me you're coming to our little get-together tonight ... No? ... Oh I am sorry.' A pause and Nan catches Sarah's eye and grins at her. 'Why, that's so sweet of you to think of me, Mr Moseley, but I'm afraid my money is busy working elsewhere ... Absolutely you can call me again ... Yes ... No ... No. We'll miss you too. Cheerio!'

Nan makes a face as she puts the phone down. 'I always thought that Mr Moseley was terribly nice, but I do wish he wouldn't keep asking me to give him money to invest.'

'You'd think after what happened last year he'd be too embarrassed,' Sarah says.

'He's a financial advisor. I think he was born without the embarrassment gene,' Nan says with a chuckle. 'Sarah, let's leave the packing for now. There's still so much to do for the party.'

'There really isn't.' Sarah smiles. 'Stephen and Keith have sent over their party planners and the caterers are setting up in the garage. Keith's outside with a walkie-talkie telling people where to hang the lanterns. I honestly don't know how we could help.'

'Isn't this so much fun!' Nan claps her hands

412

together. 'Finally throwing a party like the ones we used to!'

'And, more to the point, throwing it with the new owners.' Sarah laughs. 'I love that they're insisting on paying for other people to do all the work.'

'I'm going to take a rest upstairs before I start getting ready,' Nan says. 'I can finish packing my clothes up while I'm at it.'

Nan walks up the stairs slowly, running her hands over the mahogany banisters, feeling every nick and groove, thinking about all the years she has spent in this house, loving it, thinking she would never leave.

And yet, now that the time has come, it feels easy. More than easy, it feels right. Not that she was forced to sell it. The day before going to contract with Stephen and Keith she discovered she was a beneficiary of Everett's will.

He had finally done the right thing.

He left her more than enough money to do the repairs at Windermere and live out the rest of her days here, but once she had made up her mind she knew there was no going back.

Now she truly is a wealthy woman, and most of Everett's money has been put in a foundation that will fulfil the work the Powell family started on the island, making Powell once again a great Nantucket name.

There was some put aside for investment purposes, hence the repeated calls from Andrew Moseley, but

Nan no longer wants to put her money into stocks and shares, things she doesn't understand. Instead she has bought a couple of rental houses, knowing that with the prices on the island going up as they do it is a far safer bet than risking anything on the stock market.

The money from the sale of the house has gone into building a cottage on the other two-thirds of the land, half of which she is keeping, and half of which she has deeded to the town, to preserve as conservation land and a bird sanctuary, in perpetuity.

The phone rings again as she walks into her bedroom, and this time she is genuinely delighted when she picks up.

'Daniel! How I've missed you! Are you back? Are you on the island? More importantly, are you ready for tonight?'

'I wouldn't miss it for the world,' Daniel says with a smile. 'I'm on my way to Michael and Daff's. I can't wait to see you.'

*

Michael walks up behind Daff, who is standing in the kitchen washing up the leftover breakfast things in the sink, puts his arms around her and kisses her shoulder. She smiles, looking at their reflection in the window, and turns, careful to keep her soapy hands off his clothes, letting herself be drawn into a long hug and kiss.

She watches him as he moves around the room, his long, muscled legs striding confidently through the little kitchen, and she can't help but smile as she thinks how happy she is, how she didn't know she deserved a relationship like this, didn't know what love was until a year ago.

Nor did she dream she could be so happy, so settled, in so short a time. She moved up here permanently two months ago, bringing Jess with her. Richard and Carrie agreed that for now Nantucket seemed to suit Jess, and Carrie was pregnant, Richard busy focusing on his new family. Jess would be going back to them for the holidays.

Although Daff didn't ever want anything to come between the relationship Jess had with her father, she also knew Jess could be happy, *happier*, on Nantucket. The beach life suited her, the simple life; she adored Nan, and was still helping Bee babysit the girls some afternoons and weekends.

Jess was busy, and happy, feeling both needed and wanted. She had found, in short, her place in the world, a firm footing on this island, which she had never felt before.

When Michael first found out he was a beneficiary, he and Daff bought a pretty house that came with some run-down cottages, run as bed and breakfasts, just outside town. Together they have renovated them, spending weeks and weeks in overalls, directing plumbers, electricians, attempting much of the work themselves.

Outside, a profusion of blue hydrangeas sprout in front of a low white picket fence, an old brick path taking you to the front door of the house, winding paths off to the sides, leading to the cottages.

Roses climb haphazardly over arbours, hidden archways cut into high privet hedges surround secret gardens. There is an air of magic that seduces everyone who comes over.

Windermere Cottages are now finished, ready to throw open the doors to welcome the summer guests.

'I love it!' Daniel exclaims, dropping his bags in the middle of Honeysuckle Cottage, the one they had picked out for Daniel this summer. Modern without being minimalist, the cottage is decorated in shades of sand, white and blue, with scrubbed pine floors, white-washed reclaimed barn siding on the walls, sisal rugs strewn on the floors. The curtains are chocolate-brown linen panels, edged with white, the sofa and armchair in the living room slip-covered in white denim, patterned pillows scattered neatly at the back.

It is the personal touches that make it so special. Whelk shells they have found together on the beach, now varnished and left on a white painted table. Pretty beach scenes Daff has painted, which are for sale, and books everywhere – fiction, non-fiction, books about the island – and on the wall above the sofa in each cottage, a large antique map of Nantucket.

'God, it's good to see you.' Daff winds her arm around Daniel's waist and beams up at him. 'It feels like *years*.'

'It's only been six weeks!' Daniel says. 'Remember?

I was up in April to see the girls, except you wouldn't let me see the cottages until they were finished. Do you swear I'm the first guest?'

'Absolutely.' Daff laughs. 'First and hopefully not the last. So . . . what are your plans this summer?'

Daniel looks at her suspiciously. 'What do you mean?'

'Nothing.' Daff tries to look innocent. 'I just meant . . . any news from Matt?'

Daniel looks away. 'As a matter of fact we're meeting for a drink before the party.'

'Good.' Daff nods. 'You know he cleaned up all the landscaping here? We had no idea there was such a beautiful garden hidden underneath. He did an amazing job.'

'I did know that,' Daniel says. 'I speak to him almost every day.'

It's true. While Daniel has been back in Westport this past year, he has flown to Nantucket every month or so to see the girls, or they have come to him, and during that time he and Matt have formed a close friendship.

A true friendship, one that is built on history, rather than merely an instant attraction they felt for one another when they met.

They have had dinner every time Daniel has been on Nantucket, but have really got to know one another first through emails, then, later on, when emails didn't feel like enough, through phone calls, which soon

417

became a daily occurrence, some of them going on half the night.

Neither has broached the subject of a relationship, and Daniel has been honest with Matt about the flings he has had over the past year. Matt has listened, given advice, never once shown anything other than support for Daniel's journey, although Daniel couldn't help feeling a twinge of jealousy when Matt revealed a fling of his own.

Daniel is ready. Ready for the next step. His rental in Westport has just ended, his stuff is in storage while he decides where to go next. He isn't entirely sure. He saw a small house in Cornwall, Connecticut, that he loved, and there's always New York City, and now, of course, Nantucket.

But wherever he is, he's ready for Matt to be there with him.

*

Windermere is excited, you can feel it as you crunch up the gravel driveway, lined tonight with torches blazing in the warm night air.

People have dressed for tonight, long chiffon dresses being held up so as not to get dirty on the gravel, and people are chattering away, squinting through the darkness as they make their way up to the house to wish Nan well on her way, to welcome the new owners, trying to see who else is here.

And in the living room, about to go outside to greet the first of her guests, is Nan, glorious in a floor-length turquoise gown, her eyes sparkling with the excitement of seeing Windermere come to life, and come to life with such style, the night before she moves out.

There is no furniture left inside the house. The rooms are empty, the memories still intact. This evening, before she got ready, Nan moved around the house, whispering her goodbyes, thinking of the memories this house contains, thinking first of all the wonderful years she spent here, then about all those years she felt were sad. But, finally, she realizes it wasn't the house that was sad. It was her.

She doesn't have to be sad any more.

Michael opens the champagne as the others cheer, then he peers out of the window.

'Mom!' he urges. 'The guests are starting to arrive.'

'Don't worry, darling,' Nan says, taking a glass. 'Stephen and Keith are there to greet them. We'll be out in just a second.'

'May I make a toast?' Daniel asks when the champagne has been handed round, the small group standing in a circle.

'Of course.' Nan smiles, and Daniel raises his glass then looks slowly at Nan, Michael, Daff and then Matt, standing slightly apart until Daniel beckons him closer, into the inner circle.

'To Windermere,' he says firmly. 'May she be as happy, happier, with her new family.'

'To Windermere,' they all echo.

'Wait!' Michael stops them as they're about to

take a sip. 'One more. To new beginnings –' he raises his glass, looks over at Daff with love in his eyes – 'and happy endings.'

With a cheer they step forward to hug one another, before moving outside to begin the night.

Acknowledgements

My thanks and love to my usual 'superteam': Louise
Moore, Tom Weldon, Anthony Goff, Deborah
Schneider, Clare Ferraro, Carolyn Coleburn, Nancy
Sheppard, Natalie Higgins, Liz Jones, Louise Braver-
man, Clare Parkinson, Harvey Tanton, Elise Klein.

To the people who helped, knowingly or otherwise, during the research and writing of this book:
Walter and Gina Beinecke, Maxine Bleiweis and all at
the Westport library, Chloe Chigas, Dia Wasley and
their families for welcoming us so graciously into their
wonderful home, Keirsten Dodge, Karen and Franklin
Exkorn, Laraine and Alan Fischer, Shirley and Bob Siff,
Maximiliana Warburg.

To my friends and family who carry me through:
Harry, Tabs, Nate and Jasper, the Greens, the War-
burgs, Dina, Nicole, Heidi and Deborah.

Thank you.